USED

(Unlovable, #1)

LYNETTA HALAT

This is a work of fiction. Names, characters, places, brands, media, and incidents are either the product of the author's imagination or are used fictitiously. The author acknowledges the trademarked status and trade- mark owners of various products referenced in this work of fiction, which have been used without permission. The publication/use of these trade- marks is not authorized, associated with, or sponsored by the trademark owners.

Copyright ©2014 by Lynetta Halat
Edited by Tracey Buckalew
Proofread by Lea Burns
Cover design by © Sommer Stein of Perfect Pear Creative Covers
Photography by © Toski Covey Photography-Custom Design

All rights reserved. All rights reserved. Without limiting the rights under copyright reserved above, no part of this publication may be reproduced, stored in or introduced into a retrieval system, or transmitted, in any form, or by any means (electronic, mechanical, photocopying, recording, or otherwise) without the prior written permission of the above copyright owner of this book.

Printed in the United States of America
First Edition: January 2014
Library of Congress Cataloging-in-Publication Data

Halat, Lynetta. Used / Lynetta Halat. – 1st edition
    ISBN-13: 978-1495317040
    ISBN-10: 1495317048

Used—Fiction. 2. Fiction—Romance 3. Fiction—Contemporary Romance:

Dedication

For the flawed, the broken, the dreamers, the unique. And for those who don't find us unlovable.

.

Used Playlist

If you're anything like me, you love music with your books. I hope you enjoy these beautiful songs that embody so much of this book. You can listen to the playlist on **Used on Spotify** for free.

Slut Like You – P!nk
Big Jet Plane – Angus & Julia Stone
Wherever You Will Go – The Calling
I Don't Wanna Be Your Friend – Scotty McCreery
I Will Possess Your Heart – Death Cab for Cutie
Song For Zula – Phosphorescent
Kerosene – Miranda Lambert
Hang Me Up To Dry – Cold War Kids
Fastest Girl in Town – Miranda Lambert
Real Good Man – Tim McGraw
Angels – The xx
Come a Little Closer – Dierks Bentley
Gods & Monsters – Lana Del Rey
Use Somebody – Boyce Avenue
Body Electric – Lana Del Rey
Falling – The Civil Wars
Come Over – Kenny Chesney
Somewhere With You – Kenny Chesney
Wonderful Tonight – Eric Clapton
Alive – P.O.D.
Gives You Hell – The All-American Rejects
If I Loved You – Delta Rae
Toxic-Live Acoustic – VersaEmerge
Lazy Eye – Silversun Pickups
I Don't Want This Night to End – Luke Bryan
I Touch Myself – Divinyls
Highway Don't Care – Tim McGraw, Taylor Swift
The Cowboy in Me – Tim McGraw
Comin' Home – City and Colour
Jealous Again – The Black Crowes
Brick – Ben Folds Five
Only Prettier – Miranda Lambert
You and Tequila – Kenny Chesney, Grace Potter
Possession – Sarah McLachlan

Wake Me Up When September Ends – Green Day
Down – Jason Walker
Try – P!nk
arms – Christina Perri
What Hurts the Most – Rascal Flatts
Prize Fighter – The Killers
Help I'm Alive – Metric
The Great Escape – P!nk
In the End – Linkin Park
Control – Puddle of Mudd
Fix You – Coldplay

Prologue

I LOST MY virginity on the floor of my sister's bedroom. I was sixteen years old.

It wasn't pretty. It wasn't good. It wasn't in the slightest bit romantic.

But what it was, was done. Finally done ... and on my terms. For years, various so-called men had been trying to take it, the most treasured prize in a most dangerous game because of what I had deemed as a curse upon all of womanhood—possessing innate innocence. An innocence that many were determined to rip away and own for themselves.

Determined to be in control, I was more than happy to hand it over to someone I trusted—my best friend. After that, I knew he'd never be anything more, but at least he wasn't taking it from me. At least I could tolerate to be around him, and at least he didn't make my skin crawl. He understood what I needed, let me set our terms—friendship and sex. Nothing more, nothing less.

What I didn't bargain for was what I felt when it was all said and done ... absolutely nothing. In many ways, feeling nothing was more excruciating than feeling everything. Even worse, with all my calculating and planning, I failed to consider how my act of desperation and defiance would shape him.

Chapter One

Denver

"SHE'S, AT BEST, a fuck buddy. However, I prefer the term 'whore.' Fuck buddy is far too nice a term for the likes of her," a catty voice cracks from behind me.

I take a deep breath and look up at the ceiling, saying a little prayer that maybe the venomous voice isn't referring to me. I thought I left all that behind in Anaconda. We'd been here for all of three days, so it's highly probable they're not talking about me, right? Looking back down, I continue pouring Jack in my Solo cup, surpassing the line that is recommended for liquor.

"Yeah, so apparently, she's got some serious issues and doesn't 'do' relationships. So, she puts out for her guy friends whose girls are too good to give it up. That's her idea of a relationship."

"Really? That's kinda gross," I hear the other girl mutter.

Sonofabitch! I groan. Yep, they're talking about me. I splash a little bit of Coke in my cup and stick my finger in to stir it around a little. Tears spring to my eyes, and I berate myself for still having feelings and giving a shit what people think about me. Years of dealing with this crap should have made me immune, but I really hoped college would be different. And how the hell do they even know about that shit? Strengthening my spine, I turn and give them a beguiling smile, which causes them both to blanch. *Yeah, bitches, you've no idea who you're dealing with.*

"Ladies," I say with a quirked eyebrow. Removing my finger from the drink, I place it in my mouth and suck off the excess. With a pop, I release it. "I see my reputation precedes me. Well, let me just reassure you that I'm *very* good at what I do. When you won't give it up for your guy, he'll be looking me up, and I'll be more than happy to take care of him. No questions. No strings. Just lots of meaningless ... hot ... sex." I peer around them with a searching look. "Are they here? Your boyfriends?" I look back at them innocently. I almost snort at their mutual expressions of surprise and disdain. "Or," I continue, "are the sticks up your asses enough so that you don't need a man?" Both of their mouths drop on that line. *Yep, gets 'em every time.* "Oh, no judgment here," I vow. "I *totally* get not wanting to be tied down to any one Dick ... or Tom ... or Harry."

I skirt around them and mutter, "Later," as I search out the only friend I'd made—my roommate, Maggie. I sure as hell hope she hadn't already heard the rumors and now wanted nothing more to do with me. Hopefully I could explain, and we could continue with our new friendship.

Spotting her red hair from across the room, I make a beeline for her. I'm not much on girlfriends, but I'd like to have at least one. And I certainly don't want my roommate to become my enemy. I smile her way, but she's not paying me one bit of attention. I follow her gaze to one of the newly-arrived cowboys. *Holy shit!* He is hot. Shaggy, blondish brown hair, blue eyes, and cut. Even that is obvious with his button-up checkered shirt and Wranglers. *Check the boots.* Yep, nice boots. Worn, but cared for, expensive, a nice, manly brown. I glance back up at his face and get a decent vibe from him. Shy smile, but it reaches his eyes. Holds his drink casually, like he's relaxed. *He'd do.*

Looking back to get a read on Maggie, I see lust at first sight written all over my roommate's face. Her admiring eyes haven't strayed, and she's sporting a giant smile. I laugh a little at her obviousness. She's a sweet girl.

On move-in day here at Montana State University, I was nervous, and I don't do nervous, but I didn't want to end up with a stick-in-the-mud or a raging bitch. I wanted someone right in the middle—laid back and easy going. Someone I could easily talk to and who wouldn't be judgmental 'cause, let's face it, I'm different. And I can be difficult. I also needed someone who had a damn backbone. But at the same time, she couldn't be like me. Anyone like me, and we'd probably kill each other.

My eyes about bugged out of my head when Maggie strolled in wearing her all-pink ensemble, promptly dropping her pink luggage and making it look like someone had puked Pepto Bismol all over our room. When she hugged me fiercely, I was thrilled. I made a snap judgment—black and pink would complement each other perfectly. She squeezed and jostled me while her parents stood a step behind, beaming at her. Yep, she was perfect.

"Denver, I'm so happy to meet you. We're gonna be best of friends, I just know it," she squealed in my ear.

I cleared my throat because I didn't want her to hear the desperation in my voice. "Maggie, it's awesome to meet you. Is everyone from Shelby as sweet as you?" I asked.

She pulled back and slapped me on the arms. "Oh, yeah, honey. It's those sugar beets we produce, don't you know?"

I grinned as I assessed her. At the outset, we looked nothing alike. I was all wavy, dirty blonde to her curly strawberry red. Her eyes were as big and as round as mine, but where mine are a honey-gold, hers are electric green. She was curvy like me but just a hair shorter. My boobs were slightly bigger than hers, but when she stepped back and spun toward her parents, I noticed that her ass definitely rivaled mine. We could probably trade clothes if she owned anything that wasn't pink.

"So Denver Dempsey, meet my parents, Mr. and Mrs. Myers," she said, gesturing for me to shake hands with them.

"Hi, nice to meet you both." They looked like an ad for the perfect parents—all smiles and beaming brightly at their pride and joy. My heart twisted a little.

"Oh, Denver, we already know so much about you," her mother said. I froze. Surely not. "Highest paid high school barrel racer. All county, all state, a national star. Primed to go pro but was smart enough to say no and go to school. Honey, that's fantastic. Congratulations on all your hard work paying off." I breathed a sigh a relief that she hadn't been commenting on my activities outside of the arena. My notoriety forced me to forget my fame sometimes.

"Yes, ma'am," I agreed. "You're nothing without an education. I could get hurt tomorrow and not be able to compete. Seemed like the best idea to have something to fall back on."

"I like her," her otherwise quiet father added. "Good head on her shoulders. Seems bright. Maggie, you girls stick together. I know you're both eighteen and got all kinds of freedom. The boys'll be circling their wagons. You two don't lose sight of each other, ya hear?"

"Yes, sir," we replied. We looked at each other and grinned because we said it at the same time. My grin was wider, though, because I couldn't remember the last time I had parental approval. It was ... nice.

I am pulled from the memory when I reach Maggie, and I bump her elbow with my free one. "What's up, girl?"

"Oh, nothing," she says with a blush.

"Umm, hmm. I just spotted this *really* cute cowboy."

"You did?" she asks, smiling.

"I did. He's at about 2:00. Shaggy, sandy brown hair." I glance over at her and see her smile has fallen.

"Yeah, I see him too."

"I know you do, crazy. I was watching you ogle him from across the room," I joke.

She throws her hand over her heart. "Denver, that was just plain mean. I thought I was gonna have to fight you for him."

I laugh. "No way. He's all yours. I had to mess with you though." He's a little too pretty for my taste. Kind of makes me think of Greer. Greer is beautiful, but his beauty is unique. His inner beauty shines through and far surpasses what's on the outside. And as much as I know I need to do this on my own, I still miss him. I nod at him. "He's good lookin' all right. Gives off good vibes too."

"I thought so too. He watches who he's talking to and doesn't check out every*thing* that walks by."

"So, you gonna go talk to him?"

"Ugh! I don't know. I tend to freeze up and look like an idiot around boys. And he looks older. More experienced. What if he sees right through my naïve self?" she says with a groan.

"Never know until you try. Have you had a boyfriend before?"

"Uh, no. Momma and Daddy weren't too keen on me dating. And, to be honest, high school boys were so immature I never pushed it."

She was right about that. "Hmm ... I've never had a boyfriend either."

"What?" she asks shocked. "I mean, you seem experienced. Uh, not like that ... I mean—"

"It's OK," I interrupt to help extract her foot from her mouth. "And I am kind of experienced. Speaking of which, will you do me a favor?" She nods, her eyes even bigger. "If you hear any rumors about me tonight, will you give me the benefit of the doubt? Don't judge until we can talk?"

"Of course, Denver," she readily agrees.

"Thanks," I say with a relieved sigh. I look back to

the object of her lust and notice *him*. Wow. He's a big deal so, of course, I knew I'd see him soon. I was hoping for some more time to get intel on him before I actually introduced myself. But here he is in all his badass glory, and I'm dying to meet him.

In every possible way, he is a contradiction to his sport and his country roots. Regardless, he is the best at what he does. Buzz cut, tattooed, tall (for a bull rider), and built like a Mack truck. Most bull riders are shorter, leaner, longer hair. Not him—he took convention and gave it a big FU, and I ate that up. He was right up my twisted alley. I already decided that we were kindred spirits and would be good friends, especially seeing as I had wanted to be him at some point. Well, not him exactly. I wanted to be a bull rider. My momma and daddy never laughed harder in their lives. At five, I was crushed. In my young eyes, bull riders were the coolest and the baddest. And I'd always wanted that.

My heart longed to ride the untamable, pissed off beast. To show him, and the world, that no matter how much shit they gave me, I could hold on for as long as I needed to bring it home. That, no matter what, I would live my life on my own terms. Too bad I didn't have the right parts so I could never do more than ride sheep. I had to settle for the coolest thing for my gender—barrel racing. I worked hard at being the best barrel racer around, which is badass in its own right, and I even managed to put my own stamp on the sport.

Shaking my head, I focus on *him* again. He's talking to Maggie's guy. They seem real friendly, so Maggie was right, her guy must be older. My rodeo god's a senior and getting ready to go pro. He's got his arms folded so that his faded blue jean shirt is pulling tight against his muscles. His sleeves are rolled up, putting his tattoos on display. It's untucked, but not so long that I'm missing out on that spectacularly tight ass accentuated by his Wranglers. They're a shade or two darker than his shirt. He's finished it off with probably the sexiest boots I have ever laid eyes on. Dress black Laredos with silver accents and Concho boot chains. I'm practically salivating.

"Come on," I tell Maggie, taking a long pull from my liquid courage. "Let's go meet them."

"Them?"

Garth Brooks's "Friends in Low Places" kicks on and promptly gets turned up, so I lean in. "Yeah, I want to meet his friend. In the blue? With the buzz cut? See him?"

"Oh, yeah," she murmurs with a chuckle. "I see him all right. You'll be knocking on trouble's front freakin' door if you're interested in him, Denver."

I give her a little laugh. "I can handle myself," I assure her.

She takes a deep breath and nods. "OK."

We cross the small space to meet him and his mystery friend. There's a third guy standing with them as well. I clear my throat a little when we're closer. My hands are suddenly clammy, and my heart is racing. Oh shit! I'm so anxious, and it's not that he's a badass, that he's probably a heartbreaker, or that he's sexy as all hell. He's a rodeo god, and suddenly, I feel unworthy. Me—the best of the best. Too late now, my boobs have gotten the third guy's attention, and Mr. Rodeo God himself glances back at us.

"Well, what've we got here?" the guy asks my breasts.

Rolling my eyes, I answer, "Well," I point at my chest, "these here are called breasts. But ... I'm Denver," I joke, as I scrunch down to try to make eye contact with him. The gawker isn't fazed when I address his obvious rudeness, but the rest of us share a laugh. Having grown up around rough and ready cowboys and ranch hands, not much bothered me, but I couldn't resist giving them shit for their crude ways. I reach around and pull Maggie next to me with a laugh. "And this is Maggie."

"Denver ..." my rodeo god prompts.

"Denver Dempsey," I state before throwing out, "Maggie Myers," even though he didn't ask.

The guy still eyeballing my tits moans, "Double D," and shifts his eyes to Maggie's, "and Mmm Mmm. Got it."

Again, my eyes seek divine intervention. If I had a dollar every time someone called me that, I'd be able to adorn these bad girls in a brand-spanking-new Victoria Secret every single day for the rest of my life. I look over to Maggie and see her blushing profusely.

"Denver Dempsey," my rodeo god says, thrilling me with the use of my full name. "I figured as much but didn't want to assume. I've been looking forward to meeting you."

That throws me for a loop. "Me?" I can hear the surprise in my voice.

"Yeah, you. You're already a legend. Glad to have you on our team," he says with a wide, white grin.

"And here I've been excited to meet John Ransom,"

I'm barely able to return. *He's excited about me?* The best bull rider in his class? That's crazy.

"Just Ransom. So how's it feel to be the number one barrel racer?"

He knows I'm number one? What alternate universe have I woken up in? Again, this is crazy. *Play it cool.* "Feels pretty damn good. But you would know how it feels to be number one, wouldn't you?"

He lifts his chin, and a bashful grin lights up his features. I find this not a little surprising and most definitely intriguing. "I guess I would," he agrees. "Pretty damn good seems fitting."

I hear a throat being cleared and realize that we're being rude. "Umm ... Ransom, if you're done fangirling, we'd like to meet your new friends," the pervy one jokes.

Ransom gives a sly smile and leans back on the heels of his boots. "Shit! Sorry about that." He gestures to Maggie's guy. "This is Pete Ford. And this dumbass here is my cousin, Austin. Same last name."

"Hi, Pete." I nod my head at him. "Hi, Austin Same Last Name," I say with a light laugh.

"Don't start that," he complains, pouting.

"What?" I taunt. "You gave me and my friend here ridiculous nicknames."

He throws his hands up in mock surrender. "OK, OK. I'll behave," he says with a crooked grin.

I raise my brows. "Yeah, I bet."

Ransom pops Austin in the back of the head. "Be good, numnuts." Austin would be cute, with his short brown hair and bright, brown eyes, if he weren't annoying, which happens to be his main attribute at the moment.

"So what's your event, Maggie?" Ransom asks.

"Pole Bending," she replies seriously.

Austin pinches his lips together in effort to keep from laughing, but I can't contain mine. You'd think it wouldn't be funny after years of hearing it, but it just sounds so dirty.

"Thanks, y'all," Maggie mutters and rolls her eyes. "You try weaving your horse in and out of those poles at a breakneck speed without hitting them or falling off, and then we'll talk." I want to pat her on the back for not taking our shit.

"Hey, I've seen you ride," Pete interjects quietly.

"Really?"

"Yeah, you ride a strawberry roan, don't you?" She nods. "I saw you in Oklahoma last year."

"You did?" How fitting that my strawberry friend rides a strawberry and cream-colored horse.

"Yeah, your horse is beautiful. I had one growing up. I've got a silver dapple now."

"Oh, those are pretty too."

With each phrase uttered, they subconsciously moved toward one another until now, they were moving off together. It is the cutest thing I've ever seen. After a few seconds, Maggie looks back at me with a beaming smile. I can't help my answering grin.

I turn back to find that Ransom and I are alone now too, and his piercing gaze makes me swallow hard. "Looks like Pete and Maggie hit it right off," he says with a chin lift toward the enraptured couple.

"Looks like," I agree.

"So what's your story, Denver Dempsey?"

Now that we are alone, I can take the few seconds I need to really focus on him in all his perfectly imperfect beauty. The eyes draw me in first, pale, almost-translucent greens that remind me of sea-foam, huge and surrounded by long, lush eyelashes. As I take in the rest of his face, I notice the scars slashing through each eyebrow. The outer tip of one is interrupted with a clean line while the arch of the other has a jagged break. He has a darker complexion, from the sun I'm sure, with a few freckles dusting his obviously broken and healed nose. From the looks of it, he's suffered more than one break. I'm sure it's from butting heads with some particularly nasty bulls, which is probably how he got the crescent-shaped scar that adorns his chin as well.

Ransom catches me off guard by leaning in and whispering, "So, do I measure up?"

I give a mischievous laugh for having gotten caught. I guess my strategy was off—should've checked him out while everyone else was there to distract him. "You caught me. I'm sorry. Your eyes had me mesmerized," I hear myself confess.

His eyes flare a little, taken aback by my honesty. "Do you always say what you're thinking?"

I really hadn't meant to say that aloud. Brain, but no filter. "Pretty much," I admit with a shrug.

"Yeah, me too," he says with a frown. "How old are you?"

"Eighteen. Why?"

"You seem older."

"I get that a lot," I admit with a laugh.

He narrows those gorgeous eyes at me. "So why MSU? You had the best of the best courting you. Not that MSU isn't great, but you could've gone anywhere."

He throws me with his swift change in subject. What's strange is that he seems to know a whole lot about me. "I'm a Montana girl," I tell him with a grin. "There was no other choice for me."

"Lucky me."

I finally remember I have props and take a sip of my drink, giving me a second to ponder what he could mean by that. But I have to know for sure. "How's that?" I ask, hoping he means what I think he means.

Ransom leans in, his breath stirring the hair that falls by my ear. "If you weren't a Montana girl, I would've had to figure out another way to meet you," he says softly. I pull back a little to see if his eyes mirror his words. They do.

A look of horror briefly crosses my face as I'm shoved from behind, and I'm suddenly colliding into him and watching a little of my drink slosh out onto his shirt. He catches me by both my arms and steadies me against him, since whoever has bumped into me is still leaning into me.

"You all right?"

I pat his chest like my hand will dry the liquid. My light pat turns to more a rub, and the heat from his chest seems to transfer itself to my cheeks. His chest feels incredible—strong and warm. I roll my eyes at myself for behaving like such a girl. "Yeah, I've spilled my drink on you though."

I hear light laugher behind me. "Alcohol abuse!" I recognize Austin's voice and hear a low hum from whomever is pressed into me. I turn my head and watch with disgust as Austin attacks this girl who's keeping me pinned against Ransom. She's using me as her support beam, and practically orgasming from his kisses.

I glance back to see Ransom watching my face closely. His eyes don't leave mine, but he barks out, "Austin, get the hell off us. Go find a dark corner somewhere and do that shit."

After a few seconds, I hear Austin come up for air and shout, "Yes, boss!"

Laughing, I right myself again and feel cold as I lose contact with him. "Your cousin's something else," I say, trying to distract myself.

Mirth dances in those eyes, reminding me of the sun playing on the waves. "That he is. He's harmless enough," he says with a shrug.

I turn and watch them walk away, and once they leave my line of vision, my eyes catch on a beautiful, familiar face smirking at me from across the room. I can't help the huge grin that pops up on mine. Happy tears spring to my eyes. What is he doing here? I shake my head and turn back to tell Ransom I'll be back. He has a hard look marring his features, and I'm stunned, especially when I realize who his gaze is trained on.

"Ransom? You OK?"

"Yeah, who's that?" he asks with a nod toward Greer.

I look back again and roll my eyes when I realize he's being entertained by the two bitches who were trying to start shit with me earlier. "That's my best friend from back home, Greer Tanner."

"Just a friend, huh?" he murmurs. "Does he know that?"

I swallow nervously. That was part of the reason I

broke things off. I shake my head. "Yeah. But I don't know what he's doing here."

"He's our team member. That's what."

Swiftly, my head flies around to see if he's messing with me. "What? No. Greer's going to Wyoming."

"Nope, he's just signed on as a our newest calf roper."

Chapter Two

Then

HOLDING TIGHT TO Liberty's mane, I wrap my legs around her and make the jump over the stream that separates Greer's property from mine. It's our first ride of the summer after finishing our sophomore year, and I can't wait to see him. I urge my horse into a light canter as I wind my way through the trees and brush. When I realize I'm grinning ear to ear, I correct my earlier thoughts. It's not Greer I'm thrilled to see. It's his brother, Lawson. I've had a crush on Lawson for as long as I can remember, but he's never noticed me as anything except his annoying little bother's best friend. Yesterday, I had my chance to change that.

I'd gotten in trouble for drawing inappropriate pictures during English class. I mean, it was the last day of school, and she had popped in a movie. Who cared? Apparently Mrs. Black, because she held me after class to chastise me about being too bright not to do better in school. I'd reminded her barely-redheaded self that I'd had an A in her class all year. She'd insisted that, if I focused a little more, it could have been an A plus. And now that I was a junior and headed for Advanced Placement English, I seriously needed to increase my dedication to my GPA. "Woman, please, I have a 4.0." When she narrowed her beady little eyes, I rolled mine. She berated me a little longer for being impertinent on top of being lazy. Even though she was boring me into a coma with her monotone lecture, my eyes wandered to the clock. She chewed me out a little more for being impatient. Finally, I cut her nasally voice off and asked her if she would bring me home if I missed my bus. She screeched at me for not telling her I didn't drive.

Darting out of the building, I saw the last of the busses pulling away, and I cringed. I did not want to call my mother. I'd never hear the end of it. Glancing toward student parking, I saw a couple of people I knew and took off toward them in hopes of bumming a ride. When I hit the parking lot, a big dually pickup pulled out, and I saw him. Lawson Tanner was leaning against his truck talking to some senior. With straight, dark brown hair and big chocolate brown eyes, he's the polar opposite of Greer. And while not beautiful like Greer, he is still good-looking in his own way. My already pounding heart sped up even more.

I took a deep breath, licked my lips, and headed toward him. He didn't notice me until I was standing right in front of him. I tripped over my words and told him my dilemma, asking for a ride home in the process. He looked at the hot little piece talking to him, told her he had to bring his little brother's friend home, and he would call her later. When she leaned in and made him promise in a whiny tone, I threw up in my mouth a little bit. Desperation exuded from her in waves. I was a little nervous, but I hoped I never put that vibe off.

It was less than thrilling, I will admit. He barely spoke to me on the way to my house while I did nothing more than stare at him like I was a lost puppy. Then he dropped me off with a small smile and a wave, and that was it. And again, I missed my opportunity with him.

Today, I am taking no prisoners. I dressed in my tightest blue jeans and my red button-up with the top three buttons undone. I let my hair down from its usual French braid, and I wore my favorite red boots. All that and, so he would see that I'm grown up now, I even blushed my cheeks, sported some mascara, and applied some lip-gloss. Being the daughter of a whore did come in handy at times.

I snap out of my reverie when I emerge from the line of trees that runs along the Tanners' long, winding driveway. As I do, I see his truck headed my way. He doesn't even slow down, just gives me another little smile and a wave. Dang it! I slip my cell phone out of my pocket and call Greer.

"What's up, chicken butt?" he says, knowing I hate it.

"Nothing much, dingleberry. I'm on your driveway. Wanna ride?"

"Hell, yeah. Be right out."

"'K."

I hang up and make my way up the rest of his long driveway. Rounding the house, I urge Liberty toward the barn to wait for him. I'd go in, but his mother hates me. And I really don't want her to dampen my otherwise good mood.

As soon as I spy the back porch, I get an eyeful of a

naturally tanned, shirtless Greer. He's got his back to me, but I can hear him cooing to his black lab. My mouth splits into a grin when I hear him say to her, "Who loves ya, baby?" because I know what's coming. Frisco growls a gurgling response that sounds just like, "You love me," spins herself around, and jumps up for a kiss. He rewards her by scratching her behind the ears and cooing some more. She is, by far, one of the most intelligent animals I have ever seen. Her trainer's not too shabby either.

I hear him give her a couple more commands, to which she readily complies. He always finishes with his favorite trick that he taught her. When he asks, "Who's my pretty girl?" She bows, lies down, and covers her eyes. "She's so bashful too," Greer praises before giving a deep, heartfelt chuckle that resonates deep inside of me.

And it's the strangest thing. His chuckle knocks around inside me until something stirs, warming and wrapping me as tight as a bud on the new rose. I take in his strong, lean back muscles as he bends over and rubs Frisco back and forth on her stomach before righting himself again and turning toward me. My mouth's gone dry, and I'm puzzled as the stirring and warming blooms into a fierce pulling.

I give my head a little shake as I try to discern what's going on with me. I can't even count the number of times I've seen him without his shirt on. Hell, I can't count the number of times he's seen me without my shirt on. But it's the craziest thing—like I'm seeing him for the first time.

When he spots me, he flashes me a devastating

smile. It starts as one I've seen him give countless other girls except, when he gives it to me, it widens, reaches his eyes, and makes him look even more handsome. I can't help but return it for a second before it falters and crumbles. Wait! Wasn't I just lusting after one brother? And now I'm lusting after the other?

Reaching over, he snags his hat and shoves it in the back of his waistband. He grabs his t-shirt that's hanging from his belt loop and starts to make his way down the stairs while pulling his shirt over his head. Mesmerized, I can only stare as each of his glorious muscles move in time with each step and each pull. Has he always had those abs? I mean, I know he's had abs. But *those* defined abs that I just got an eyeful of?

Why the hell am I looking at Greer like this? What is wrong with me? And then it hits me with such force that I almost lose my balance and tumble off my horse.

I am my mother's daughter.

I am fickle and needy.

I have the hots for one brother and am considering the other as well. I can see history repeating itself before my very eyes, except I'm the whore. God, I feel sick. I glance down at my reins and debate on whether I should stay and ride with Greer or go home and ponder this and the many consequences that come with being a first-class whore.

I jump as Greer's hand grazes my thigh. "Sorry, chicken. Didn't mean to scare you. You OK?"

I shake my head as tears fill my eyes rapidly. I've just made a startling realization about myself, and it's scared the hell out of me. How many nights have I lain awake praying that I would never be like her? "Greer," my voice cracks, and I clear my throat. "I think I should go home. I'm not feeling up to a ride."

He rubs my leg reassuringly, which only fuels my sudden impure and inappropriate thoughts, since his touch sends tingles throughout my body. We've been best friends since before we were born for God's sake. "Hey now. What's going on? You were fine a second ago."

"I, uh, I don't know. I'm fine. I think. I just—"

My sentence is cut off as I'm grabbed around the waist, jerked off my horse, and slammed into his chest. I breathe deeply to try to get my bearings. When I do, my world tilts further. His scent is comforting, but not in the way that makes me want to curl up and play board games with him, like usual. It's the kind of sensation that makes me want me to reach up and kiss him, softly and tenderly and whole-heartedly. I shake my head again, trying in vain to clear my stupor.

Greer's hand fits around the back of my head, and he runs his hand over my hair. "You sure look extra pretty today," he coos. "Too pretty to be this upset. Is it Blake?"

I snort. Blake, my latest stepfather in a long line of stepfathers, is closer to my age than my mother's and has been making disgusting comments about me and trying to get in my pants. Slamming a shovel down on his foot hadn't helped matters. It seemed to serve only to intrigue him further. *Nauseating.* "Umm—"

"It is!" Grabbing my arms, he pushes me back and pierces me with his blue-eyed gaze. They suddenly remind me of the Bunsen burner in chemistry class, a steady and bright heat. "Did that bastard touch you?"

He's going to pester me until I tell. That's Greer. He's a dog with a bone, and a fixer to boot. How am I going to get out of this? "No, no. He's laid off mostly. I, uh, I'd like to go for our ride now. I think it's passing, whatever it was. I think I'm good." He pulls me back to him and gives me a quick hug before stepping away. I lose my balance when he releases me, but he steadies me and laughs. He's not used to me being a klutz.

His brow furrows, his eyes assessing. "You sure you're OK?"

"Yeah, I'm fine."

Turning back to Liberty and pushing her reins aside, I grab a handful of mane and take a step back, swinging myself up onto her bare back.

"Holy shit," he murmurs. "That's hot."

"What?" I gasp, as I peer down at him. Did he just say I am hot? Are his thoughts in line with mine? He had never been inappropriate or gotten out of line with me.

"Umm … nothing. I'll be back." Running his hand through his hair, he snatches the cap he shoved in his waistband and pulls it low over his brow. He gives me a wink before turning and dashing back to the porch to get something from a waiting Ms. Juanita. I chuckle as he kisses her on the cheek and takes off toward the barn. She's practically his second mother. She shakes her head at his retreating figure and gives me a big smile and a wave.

WE'VE BEEN RIDING for an hour or so. It's been a quiet ride, and I've felt Greer's eyes on me a number of times, but he doesn't speak, and neither do I. We're caught up in our own musings, I suppose. I can't help but wonder what's got him all introspective. Usually he talks my head off. I always joke that he's the girl in our relationship. The funny thing is I wouldn't change a thing about him.

The memory of him with our dying cow pulls me back into my head.

"I don't understand. Why would you shoot your own animal?" A sniffling Greer asked.

For the fifth time at least, I told him, "'Cause, Greer, if we don't, she has to suffer. Be in pain until she dies. And she's as good as dead anyway."

He sucked it up, breathed deep, and sat up straight. "You sound like your daddy."

"Well, 'cause that's what he told me. You trust my daddy, don't cha?"

"I guess."

I looked out over the wide-open field and thought about all the life I'd seen come and go over the years. Daddy told me once ranching ain't for the faint of heart. He had that right. I still hated loss though. And I felt his loss the hardest. I mean, he didn't die. But he may as well have. No spirit. That's what we'd say if he were a horse. He's got no spirit, no mettle. He had it before. Before what? I don't know exactly. I just know it had something to do with my momma. It'd been a few years since he left, and he still hadn't bounced back.

"Would you feel better if we slept out here with her? We're not gonna ... do it till morning. If she even makes it through the night."

"Yeah, can we?"

"Yeah, I'll go up and get some supplies. You OK

here by yourself?"

He stiffened and sat up even taller. "I'm not a little girl, Denver."

"You're sure acting like one," I joked.

"You should try it sometime."

"Ouch! That hurt, golden boy."

"Whatever, chicken butt."

He may be mad at me a little, but at least he was focused on something else for a minute.

So all those years of being as close as brother and sister, and I suddenly feel drawn to him in another way? It seems unreal, but it is what it is. I had a distinct physical pull to him when I saw him this morning, and parts of me I didn't even know could feel—felt. And, now that I really think about it, I know it's life-changing and real because I've never felt any of that for his brother. Maybe I've always been destined to fall for Greer, and God had kept me from feeling it all at once because we were too young for that kind of friendship. I've always loved his personality, his tenderness, his protectiveness, but his easy way and ability to put up with me were probably his most endearing traits.

And so in tune … we've *always been so in tune*. Our moms, back when they didn't hate each other, used to joke that we were twins separated by a womb. Our favorite colors were the same, we liked to do the same things, and our dreams were the same. Our personalities? Not so much. He was Yang to my Yin, and we've always complemented each other perfectly.

Do I still feel my crush for his brother? I'd be lying to myself if I said no. I still feel tiny butterflies when I think of him. But the pull toward Greer is much more direct and tangible. I think what I feel for his brother is a childhood crush made up of adoration and hero worship. This with Greer feels more natural yet more ... I don't know, *just more.*

Surely that makes me different from my mother. I'm not jumping from one brother to another. Am I?

"Wanna head up the side of the mountain to the creek? Get some water? Take a break?" Greer asks, pulling me from my internal struggle.

"Yeah, OK."

Greer kicks his black swiftly as he laughs and looks back at me, egging me on.

I can't help the laugh that escapes me as I spur Liberty into action. The jerk knows I'm riding bareback and that she's worked up a little sweat. He also knows that neither Liberty nor I like to finish second. I tighten my grip on her with both my hands and my legs and gallop past Greer and Shadow. Looking back, I laugh at his furious expression. I'm in the lead and going really fast, but as I approach the trail that cuts through the trees and leads to the creek, I slow my horse down.

Suddenly, Greer darts past me with a maniacal laugh and jolts Liberty into action. As she bounds forward, I lose my balance, sliding around on her for a second before tumbling off. I manage to right myself into somewhat of a standing position, but then Liberty's gone from beside me, and I land in a heap on the side of the trail. In mud, of course. I groan and sit up, cussing Greer and Liberty under my breath. I hear Greer calling for me since I've rolled to the side of the trail in the tall grass, and he can't see me. Liberty snorts and ambles back in my direction, snatching patches of grass along the way.

"I'm over here, jerk!" I call out, as I stand up. My bottom stings, and I rub it gingerly, gauging the tenderness. Looking over my shoulder, I see thick, black mud smeared over my shirt. I can feel clumps of it in my hair too. Ugh!

Greer swings off of his horse. "Permission to approach?" he asks with a laugh.

"Only if you want to be walking funny for a week," I grunt.

"Oh, don't be mad because I finally beat you at your own game, Denver."

Outraged, I gasp and spin around. "You knew she'd jump like that when you rushed past us, and you knew that I was riding bareback. I'm covered in mud, and now my butt hurts," I gripe, pouting.

Crossing his arms over his puffed-out chest, he eyes me, and I catch the sparkle of laughter dancing there. "More like your pride hurts. You've always been a sore loser. Want me to rub it?"

Tilting my head, I ask innocently, "What, my pride?"

His eyes darken a bit, and his smile becomes lethal as he slowly shakes his head. I bite my lip a little to keep from grinning. He's definitely flirting with me. I can't help but think he feels it too. Changing the subject, I ask him, "And what have I lost at anyway? I never lose." Gathering up Liberty's reins, I saunter through the grass toward him.

"I've beat you at horseshoes three times, pool twice, and Monopoly countless times." Walking our horses side by side, we continue on the path that will lead us to the creek. I wish it were warm enough to swim so I could get this mud off me.

"I just suck more at horseshoes than you do, and Monopoly doesn't count. I don't lose. I quit," I sneer.

"Same difference."

"Bullshit. I just can't sit still long enough to beat you. And one of those games of pool doesn't count either because you spiked my Dr. Pepper with extra Wild Turkey."

"Oh, shit!" He slaps his knees with his reins as he remembers. "That was so funny. You thought we had the same amount, and you wouldn't dare say a word. You didn't want me to out-drink you. God, your competitive nature really works in my favor sometimes," he teases, chuckling.

I can't help but laugh with him. I'm glad he's back. He was way too quiet. His incessant chatter sheds light in the dark corners of my mind, and I love that about him.

He continues to chat me up while we head up the mountain a little further, rubbing it in my face about the one geometry test he outscored me on as well.

When we reach the clearing that opens up alongside the creek, we walk our horses over to the water and let them get their fill before taking off the tack and letting them graze freely.

Spinning around from the horses, I head back toward the creek. I hear him jog up behind me, but I'm too focused on getting this mud off of me to pay him any attention. The mud is thick and heavy, forcing the material to cling to my back. Untucking my shirt, I start at the bottom snap and pull, shrugging it off in seconds and tossing it aside. Kneeling down in the grass, I flip my hair over and into the creek, scrubbing the ends vigorously until all the clumps dissipate. When I toss my hair back, the freezing cold water slaps my bare back and I screech. Giggling, I look over at Greer to find him paused mid-bend and mouth agape.

"What?" I ask breathily, his look causing me to be hyperaware of the fact that I'm not wearing a shirt. *Oh my God!* My nipples harden under his gaze. *Well, that's embarrassing.* I fight the urge to cross my arms over them. Dead giveaway!

He shakes his head at me. "You took your shirt off," he says, stating the obvious.

"Yeah, you've seen me in less." I shrug, pretending nonchalance. "This is just like my bikini." Except it's not. It's thin and lacy, and why have I never noticed whether or not it's see-through? "I used to run shirtless around you all the time." His eyes dive down to my breasts, back to my eyes, back to breasts. I roll my eyes and exhale loudly. "Just toss me your shirt."

He looks at me like I've spoken in a foreign language. "Huh?"

"Toss me your freaking shirt, Greer. It's your fault mine's covered in mud. You can go shirtless. I promise not to ogle your chest the way you are mine." The lie rolls so easily from my tongue.

He rights himself and pulls his shirt over his head by the neck in one fluid motion. Tossing it, he hits me right in the face with it before I can intercept it. I don't even have to inhale deeply for his scent to sink into me this time—it's woodsy and fiery with a trace of fabric softener, and it's divine. I'm being pulled taut again, deep inside. "Thanks," I mutter, quickly donning his shirt.

Bending down again, he scoops water into his cupped palm and sips. When he stands, he puts his hands on his hips and stares ahead, contemplative again. He takes his hat off and runs his hand through his golden blond curls. He looks nothing like the rest of his family. Behaves nothing like them either. They totally do not get his obsession with horses and cattle. Fortunately, he lives next to us and has been able to learn ranching and rodeo. His family had inherited all that land, but it is all for show. Greer's daddy is a powerful judge, his momma is what our smallish town would call a socialite, and his older brother wants to follow in his father's footsteps. Greer's goal is to someday run his own ranch—a calling that ran deep in his blood from earlier generations and couldn't be denied.

All of a sudden, I wonder what I ever saw in Lawson. His dreams are nothing like mine. I want to run a ranch and have babies. I want to train championship barrel racing horses, and I want a good, strong man to do that alongside me. Greer is perfect for me in every way. He's my best friend. Who better to spend my life with? It took a jolt for me to see all that so clearly. Hormones … go figure.

Standing up, I move toward him, not really sure what I'll say or do, but he spins and smiles at me, stopping me in my tracks. I'm caught in his gaze and unable to speak for a minute. He puts me out of my misery. "Hungry? Ms. Juanita made us sandwiches."

"Yeah," I breathe.

"C'mon." He motions to his tack. Grabbing his

bedroll, he unrolls it to expose our hidden lunch. Handing it to me, he turns to find some sunshine and spreads the blanket across the grass. I just watch as the sun dances across his golden hair and skin. I've always joked and called him "golden boy," and he hates it every time. But he really is golden ... fabulous roper, all-star in every sport he ever played, good grades, all the girls wanted to be with him, and all the guys wanted to be him. But he's also more than that. He's kind, generous, and compassionate. And he's *my* golden boy. I grin wide when I think of his nickname in those terms because he'd get a kick out of that. He sits down and stretches his legs out in front of him, patting the blanket at his side. I cradle the sandwiches to my chest and move to sit beside him.

We eat and chat a little about what we want to do with the summer. Mostly, it's comprised of working the ranch, training, practicing, and hanging out with each other. I finish before him, since he did most of the talking, and lie down on my back to soak in the sun. The woods is the only place I can be still, and I want to absorb it all. I get lost in the light playing on the leaves for a bit. Closing my eyes, the water streaming over the stones in the creek is a lullaby. The fish splash every now and then. Occasionally, the wind sifts through the leaves on the trees. This is my church, and these sounds conspire to create my hymn.

After a few minutes, Greer stretches out beside me and searches for my hand. Only his hand touches mine, but my whole being tingles. He threads his fingers through mine and runs his thumb over my palm. Something in me twists and splinters, shooting chills all through my body. My breath hitches in my throat because I can't breathe around the knot that has formed there.

"You feel it too," he says simply.

I close my eyes tighter, suddenly embarrassed by the fact that I'm not slick. "Yes," I admit in a whisper.

"Look at me, Denver."

Turning my head to the side, I open my eyes to find his blue-eyed gaze roaming over me. His eyes find mine, and we just take each other in. I want to say something, but I can't think of one darn thing that sounds intelligent or even ... sexy. Do I even want to be sexy for him? *Yes. Yes, I do.* I see stupid girls flirt with him all the time. I don't want to be *that* girl, but I do want him to see me as a girl and not just his friend. Ironic, since I've spent my whole life telling him *not* to treat me like a girl.

"I want to kiss you so bad ... but if I kiss you, it will change everything," he says in that gravelly voice.

"Change is good," I whisper.

Rolling to his side, his mouth is centimeters from mine. I can't make myself move although I'm aching with want. But I haven't been kissed—ever. And I haven't kissed anyone since that time on the monkey bars in seventh grade when I stuck my tongue in Brian Thomas's mouth on a bet. I shocked the shit out of him, and he didn't even kiss me back. When the bell rang, he jerked back and hit his head hard, sending him to the nurse for the rest of the afternoon. Not my finest moment.

"I don't want to lose my best friend," he tells me.

I bring up my other hand and run it over his jaw. "You're not going to lose me. No matter what. We'll still be friends."

"Relationships ruin friendships. We've seen enough of that."

I shiver with that truth. "True. But we're different. We've been together since before we were born. I can't live without you, so I won't hurt our friendship."

Bringing our entwined hands up, he kisses my knuckles. "Me either. We'll take it slow, all right?"

"All right, my golden boy," I whisper.

The effect of my words is instantaneous; the blue in his eyes intensifies to boiling. He leans in, his lips brushing mine softly. "Denver," he whispers against me. "I've always wanted to make you mine. Ever since I understood what that meant. I've never seen anyone but you." And even though his eyes burn with passion, I hear a little tremor in his voice. Now, him always putting off those girls makes a whole lot more sense.

"I thought we were taking it slow," I chastise, but I delight in knowing that he feels something more for me.

"I just want you to know that I don't take this lightly. You're the most important person in my universe. And I'll do anything to protect us."

His declaration unleashes a torrent of need in me, and I no longer want him to kiss me—I *need* him to kiss me. "Greer, will you shut up and kiss me, please?"

"Yes, ma'am," he says with a laugh, and bringing one of his hands up, he cradles my jaw and draws my lips to his. He shudders against me as my free hand skims down to rest at his waist, his jeans riding low on lean hips, I hook a finger in the belt loop and brush my thumb across his warm, bare skin. His lips are soft and explore mine as I match his movements. His indulgence ruins me—spoiled by his goodness. I try to savor how tender and sweet he is even though I am impatient for more, so when I feel his lips part, I follow suit quickly. His tongue sweeps in, seeking and teasing. An involuntary moan works its way out of me. I'm almost embarrassed by my eagerness, but when his moan echoes mine, I'm reassured and reignited.

He pulls back after a few more seconds and places a gentle kiss on my lips, then on my nose. "Denver ..." he breathes. My name packs a punch, and I feel it everywhere.

Keeping my eyes closed, I just nod and lick my lips, trying to savor every bit of him and his sweet words.

OUR SUMMER PROGRESSED like that—stolen moments, playful times, sweet ... and hot ... kisses. Until one day I woke up and realized I was falling in love. I've always loved Greer as my friend, but now my feelings had morphed into something that consumed me, making me crave him. I wondered if that was normal, or healthy, to feel that intensely about someone.

When we weren't together, which was pretty rare, we were texting or talking on the phone. I wrote him letters and gave them to him with a promise that he wouldn't read them in front of me. I babbled about my plans for my horses, for my future, and for us. He was so cute. He answered every sentiment with his own thoughts and ideas, feeding off of mine, yet growing them, until our ideas were bigger and better together.

A few weeks before our magical summer would

come to an end, my world was shattered. And I used the broken shards from the wreckage to carve up my life until it was virtually unrecognizable … but necessary. Although Greer never left my side, our relationship would never be the same. Never again would it be the pure and innocent thing that it once was. He did his best by me, but I knew deep down that I had forever tarnished my golden boy.

Chapter Three

Now

MAKING MY WAY across the room to him, that familiar pull is as tangible as a tightly held string being wound around its spool, but I am so confused as to why he didn't tell me he was coming here that it's hard for me to be excited to see him. I start to worry about the plans I have of making it on my own and changing my reputation and path. Of course, now I know that changing my reputation is going to be more difficult than I thought.

Even though he's got two girls fawning all over him, his eyes never leave mine. When I reach him, he says, "Girls, have y'all met my best friend, Denver?"

They turn to me, and the look of disgust that passes over their faces is almost comical. One of them sneers, "Yeah, we met her earlier. She's the one, huh?"

Greer exhales loudly and grabs me by the wrist. "Yeah, she's the one," he mutters quietly, as he whisks me from the room.

"Greer, what are you doing here? You're supposed to be in Wyoming."

He ushers me out the door and into the breezeway where our party has spilled out. Lacing his fingers through mine, he continues leading me until we round a corner onto an empty walkway outside of the campus apartment building. When we reach a quiet spot, he pulls me against him.

"I couldn't do it," he murmurs into my hair.

"Couldn't do what?"

Hugging me tighter, he says, "Leave you. I couldn't leave you."

I hug him back and kiss his cheek. "It wasn't forever."

"It felt that way."

"How long have you known you weren't going to Wyoming?"

"Since we said goodbye."

I slap him on the shoulder. "Greer, that was weeks ago."

"I know. I wanted to tell you, but there was never a good time with you being gone to your dad's and all. And then I thought you might like the surprise. Girls like surprises, right?"

I laugh and pull back to see amusement dancing in his eyes. "Usually. But I wish you'd have been honest. I was honest with you."

"About that ..."

"Yes?"

He takes a deep breath, and I see the resolve building in his eyes. "I want us to be together. What I said back there about you being the one—you are my one. *My* one and only. I want a fighting chance with you, Denver. You didn't give me one. You determined that we were ... what was the word you used ... *toxic*."

"Greer—" I start to protest and try to move from his embrace. He cuts me off and pulls me tighter.

"You've never given me a chance, chicken. You put me in that damn compartment, and that was it. You owe me better than that. I've always been there for you, and you know it. I don't deserve that." Determination rings in both his voice and his eyes.

I know he doesn't deserve that, but it's what I had to do for my sanity. He was all right with it until he wasn't anymore. I don't know how to answer him without hurting him, so I change the subject. "I hate when you call me chicken. And we're in college now, so do you think you could drop it?" I tilt my head and ask, "Why *do* you call me that? Just to get on my nerves?"

Laughing, he rubs his jaw for a minute. "Chicken butt is to get on your nerves. But not chicken." I raise my brows, prompting him to continue. "When I was little, I was obsessed with chickens. Loved 'em."

"I remember." His favorite thing had been to feed the chickens, but he didn't leave when his task was completed. He hung out and watched and laughed and carried on.

His look turns a little shy, but he continues." Yeah, well, I thought they were pretty, with all their colors and gracefulness and conversations."

I can't stifle the laughter that bubbles up. "Conversations?"

He drops his head back on the wall. "Yeah, conversations. You can't sit still long enough to notice, but they're actually really smart and beautiful and unique." I let out a deep breath. "You're *my* chicken."

I roll my eyes and shake my head at him. "That's sweet, Greer. But I'm still not crazy about it."

His eyes turn serious and capture mine. "And it's been my secret way of saying 'I love you' ever since we were eight years old."

My heart slams to a stop inside of my chest before slowly picking back up and regaining speed. I say nothing. Couldn't if I wanted to. He'd told me he loved me before, but not until we were sixteen—the knowledge that he has been telling me long before that is humbling.

He grabs my belt loops, pulling me even closer. "All I'm asking for is a chance, Denver. I know the commitment thing is hard for you. I'll be patient," he says with all seriousness.

Committing to him is not the issue. God, I'd give anything to be commitment-phobic. That would be a walk in the freaking park compared to my issues. I finally nod, and leaning in, I admit, "I get it. I do. But it's not a good idea to be with me, Greer. I just don't trust myself. You shouldn't trust me either."

"But I do. I know you better than anyone. Hell, I know you better than you know yourself sometimes, especially where this is concerned."

"I don't want to hurt you," I persist. It's always been about protecting him from me. Can't he see that?

"I've never known worse pain than when you left me and told me that what little we had was over. I'm hurting right now," he pleads, his voice desperate. "But I believe in us. Can't you try?"

I don't want to hurt him with my next statement by making him feel like he's old news, but I need him to understand where my head is. "I hoped college would be a fresh start for me."

His hands slide around my waist, holding me tight to him. "Maybe it's a fresh start for *us* too."

I should've known better. He always sees the positive. Who could say no to his hopefulness? I take in his earnest expression. His beautiful blue eyes shimmer with the moonlight and promise. "I'll think about it," I somewhat relent.

"I CAN'T BELIEVE you're not drunk," Maggie says as we enter our dorm room. I have to admit, college is pretty cool so far, seeing as we can party right on campus and not have far to go to crash. I'm pretty jealous that Greer had gotten the apartment deal too.

"I can hold my liquor pretty good. Except for tequila. I only drink that if I have no desire to feel or think or remember shit. Did you even have a drink?"

"No, not big on it."

"So ... Pete?"

She turns and sinks in a dreamy state onto her bed, letting out a loud sigh. "Pete Ford," she singsongs. "He drives a Chevy."

I laugh loudly. "Well, that confession is not the one I expected to hear from you since you two snuck off for a bit."

"I know," she squeals. "I just thought it was cute. He's so ... spectacular."

"Spectacular? Do tell." I crack the bathroom door open while I change quickly into my pajamas and brush my teeth.

"I don't know. He's just ... different. We talked about everything, like we were old friends. He was so nice to everyone who came up to him. He actually recounted the times he's seen me ride." She groans loudly, causing me to poke my head out of the bathroom. She looks mortified. "He saw my fall last March, Denver."

I grunt around my toothbrush and quickly spit into the sink. "And he still thinks you're cute? He's a keeper!" We watched the tapes while we were prepping. It was gruesome, and she still had the knot on her head to prove it.

"I know, right? And, what's better, he asked me on a date. Like an actual date! He didn't do that annoying thing that guys do nowadays. You know? That immature as hell thing they've got going on." Her voice drops and she mimics, "You wanna hang out sometime?" I burst out laughing as I try to rinse my mouth out. "Anyway, he's Ransom's best friend. They've been rodeoing together since they were real little."

"Really?" I can't keep the interest from my voice.

"Yeah, he said Ransom's a good guy. Tough, of course. Grew up real harsh, but is set on making something of himself."

"Hmm ... I didn't get to talk to him for long, but he seemed intense and interesting." When I went back to the party, the two bitches, whom I later learned had actual names, Becky and Amber, were chatting him up. Then I watched him leave with a different girl altogether.

I ended up shooting the bull with Greer and the other ropers before grabbing Maggie and calling it a night. "So you're interested in him?" she asks.

"I don't know. I mean, I think I'd like to be friends with him." I give myself a hard stare and question which type of friendship I'm looking for. Even if he wasn't the one I could have *that* kind of friendship with, I still want to be actual friends. "I've just always admired him and his dedication," I finally admit. "I'd like to get to know him better."

"Well, I'm thinking maybe I judged him too harshly based on his looks. Pete spoke very highly of him. Speaking of looks, who was the good-lookin' blond you were talking to?"

I blow out a deep breath and join her on her bed. "He's a long, complicated story. That's who."

"Well, I'm not going anywhere except to change." She bounces up and leaves the door open as I stretch out on her bed and contemplate where to start. She pokes her head back out after a few seconds and orders, "Talk."

Laughing, I launch into a quick recount of my growing up with Greer. How we lived and breathed every moment together because our mothers and fathers had been best friends before they had a huge falling out. Fortunately, we were older when that happened, so it didn't keep us apart. By the time I get to our brief attempt at something more than just friends, Maggie's stretched out beside me and listening intently.

"The next part is not so simple." Releasing another deep breath, I look her in the eyes and pray that she gets it without asking too many questions. "A couple of years ago, our relationship took a turn and we became … involved. A physical relationship, but nothing more … not *in* a relationship." I bite my lip and wait for it. I tried to explain it to one other person, and she never got it and actually stopped talking to me. She then promptly told the biggest male gossip in school about our arrangement. That grew and festered into what I had to deal with at the party tonight from Becky and Amber.

Maggie shifts and looks like she's thinking for a second before blurting out, "I don't understand."

That's what I was afraid of. I'm going to have to be blunt. "We used each other for sex, Maggie."

"Oh." She nods once.

"Yeah, look, that's the thing I wanted to talk to you about, and I hope that you don't hate me and join in on the let's-bash-the-hell-outta-Denver-club, but I have a reputation for having ..." I search for the softer term for it. She's too sweet. There's no way I can say fuck buddies. "Friends with benefits," I finally finish.

Her mouth makes the O shape before she finally breathes out, "Oh ..."

"You know," I tell her with a shrug, "it just works for me. I'm not tied down, and there are no expectations of them or me. We have a great friendship and then we ... have sex. And everyone is happy."

She narrows her eyes at me, assessing me. "You're really happy with that?"

I flip over on my stomach and put my head on my folded arms. "Yes and no. It's why I was shocked and a little disappointed to see Greer."

"What do you mean?"

"We were supposed to go our separate ways, but he followed me."

Her eyes widen. "Wow."

"I know," I say with a groan. "He's asked me to

give him a chance at an actual relationship. He's never asked anything of me. I don't know what to do."

"I think it's kind of romantic," she says with a sigh. "And he is your best friend. Who better to fall in love with? Do you love him?"

I suck the air between my teeth sharply. That's the crux of the problem. I do love Greer and at one time, I was falling *in* love with him, but I ruined that. And I don't know that I can ever get that feeling back. "I love him like a friend. I don't know if it can be more than that, though."

Maggie further narrows her eyes at me like she's bound and determined to get to the bottom of this. "Do you want it to be more?"

He did nothing to deserve my denying him, but things between us had been so strained because I had done some awful things. Now I wonder if I really was all right ending our relationship on that note. All those years, tainted with the ugly, unraveled threads I'd woven in. Our once-beautiful history cannot be denied, and if I let him back in, maybe we can capture that again with some work. And if I'm with Greer, that may be enough to keep from living up to my full slut potential. Even though it's probably not the smartest decision, I find myself whispering, "I think I might."

How we'd come to this crossroads in our relationship is a lot more complicated than I let on to Maggie, and it kills me how we were both jarred from our innocence with a series of soul-crushing events.

Chapter Four

Then

I HANG UP the reins and run my hands down the leather. We had a good ride. I smile when I think about Greer climbing on behind me and riding a little ways. His hands had never left my hips, and his lips had never left my neck. He's been so wonderful, but we've never really discussed where we're going with this. It has only been a month, but I hope our lack of labels is because he sees us like I do—undeniable and strong.

Our connection is so strong, and our being together seems like a "given" to me now. I can't imagine not being with him after what we've shared this summer. Still, it's like we've existed in a bubble, and I'm afraid it's about to land on a sharp piece of grass. Our summer's coming to an end all too quickly, and I wonder how things will be when we return to school. Will he tell everyone I'm his girl? Will I ride beside him in his new truck? Will he write my name on his notebooks, doodling little hearts around it? He certainly has doodled his name all over my heart.

Letting go of the reins, I spin around to head to the

house. The ridiculous grin falls from my face immediately.

"What are you doing in here?" I ask Blake. My mom's new husband cares absolutely nothing for our animals and has no right to be in here. Clearly, he's been standing there a while watching me.

"I could ask you the same question, little missy. You're supposed to be in bed." *Shit!* Greer and I had sneaked out for a midnight ride. My mother doesn't really give a shit; she might yell a little, but Greer's mother will flip the fuck out. I hope they didn't call her.

I narrow my eyes suspiciously. "How'd you know I wasn't?"

"I just went in to check on you," he says, as he closes the tack room door behind him. I swallow nervously. I can hear a slight slur to his words, and I know firsthand that he can't handle his liquor.

I strive to keep the panic from my voice. "You went into my room? It was locked. How'd you get in?"

"I picked the lock, missy. I was worried about you when you didn't answer the door."

My blood boils and calls for me to throw myself at him, clawing and scratching, but I maintain my calm façade. "I'd appreciate it if you didn't do that again. I'd also appreciate it very much if you stay out of my room and away from me. I don't trust you, Blake." As soon as I utter those words, my control snaps. "And, as soon as my mother wizens up, your sorry ass will be down the road just like the rest and her number seven will be a distant memory." I am seething by the time I finish my little speech. I'm hoping that my strength puts him off like it has the ones who have come before him. How many times have I had to fight off my mother's perverted husbands or their perverted friends and family? It's repulsive. I need to make him see that I'm too strong to be fucked with. That I'll shout the barn down and rip his head off if he messes with me. His free ride would effectively come to an end, and I'm praying that he won't risk it.

"Sorry ass, huh? How you figure?"

I point my finger at him, and I curse myself at the little tremor that courses through me. "Because I'm not stupid. I know what you want from me, and I'm not gonna let you take it. I'll die before I let you touch me, but I won't die before I fight you with every ounce of life that beats within me."

Blake throws his head back in laughter, surprising me. When he quiets down, he surprises me further when he says, "You have a mighty high opinion of yourself, little missy. I don't want nothin' from you. I just came to check on you. And don't lie to your mother again, or I'll be telling her all about your little midnight ride with Mr. Tanner." I open my mouth to tell him not to talk about Greer, but he raises his hand and keeps on going. "Did you lay down for him?"

"What? No!" I admit, caught off-guard. I can't believe I just told him that, but I didn't expect him to have the nerve to ask.

"You know what happens to little girls who put out for their little boyfriends, don't you?"

I just nod. I have no idea what he's talking about. I just want him to leave.

"Umm, hmm," he murmurs as his dark eyes roam over me. I fight the urge to shiver from the cold that sweeps over me. "Well, I'm going back to the house. You need to get yourself up there too. It's not safe for little girls to be out in the middle of the night. Boogey man and all," he warns with a stilted laugh. When he closes the door behind him, I collapse against the wall.

That was close. Too close. I told my mother he was making comments like that toward me, and she said she'd "talk to him." Well, obviously, he needed more than a talking to. Maybe I need to start sleeping with my 20-gauge. I imagine the look he'd give me if I pulled that on him, and it makes me grin. He really doesn't want to mess with me.

I wait a few more minutes so I don't have to see him as I head back into the house. As I turn to latch the door, I'm pushed into it, and a hand is over my mouth before I can scream.

I throw my hands behind me to swat at him, but he just pins one of them, and the other swings blindly, missing its target. "Shh," he breathes in my ear, "this can be fun or not. Depends on you. I'm gonna let your mouth go, and you're not gonna scream. Got it?" I nod frantically.

The second his hand slips away, I start screaming bloody murder and kicking at him. My boot connects with his shin a few times, and he cries out in pain.

"You're gonna fight me? Even better," he mumbles against me. A wave of nausea washes over me. Pulling my hands behind my back, he clasps them both in one of his strong hands and forces me to the ground face up, effectively pinning my hands behind me. I am trapped under him. There's no fucking way this is happening. With one hand, he starts undoing my jeans, but it's hard for him because I'm squirming so much. Pain shoots through my arms as I pull against him.

"Get. Off. Of. Me. I will kill you, you sick fucking bastard," I stress every single word.

I hear the crack before I see his hand move, and I whimper as my cheek explodes with pain from the backhanded blow. The sting radiates out from my cheekbone, and for a second, my brain focuses on that instead of how to get away. "You're not gonna do *shit*. You see, you've been wiggling this sweet ass in front of me for months now, and I'm done with that."

"I have not. I hate you. You're si—"

Crack.

Pain.

Warmth.

Blood.

"Oh, that's gonna leave a mark. Now, how are you gonna explain that to your momma?" he taunts.

I suck air between my teeth, willing myself not to cry, but I can't *not* cry. God, it hurts, and for the first time in my life, I feel completely helpless. Panicked whimpers erupt from my mouth as I glance around wildly, trying to figure a way out of this. The fight leaves my body like a retreating army, and he feels it too. He's finally gotten my jeans down to my knees, and all that's protecting me is the slight fabric of my panties. I hear him unzip, and my whimpers turn into pathetic sobs.

"Oh, yes. This will go much better for you that way, Denver. Much better," he murmurs as he moves his body over me. He looks down, focusing on freeing himself, and I realize I have an opportunity because he's somewhat moved off of my legs. I go slack in an effort to get him to relax even more, and it works. The second I feel some room between us, I bring my knee up hard, making contact with his groin. I don't stop, though, when he stills and cries out. I force my knee into his crotch again, and once more, until he crumples and falls off of me. I roll over to the side, crawling away from him. I push myself up on my knees and run the back of my arm over my face to clear the snot and the tears and the blood from my face.

"You little bitch," he breathes through clenched teeth.

"And don't you forget it!" I scream. "I'll kill you. I'll fucking kill you," I cry.

"Denver?" My head flies up when I hear the familiar voice. Oh, no. Oh my God.

"Greer," I choke out.

He looks confused and frozen. "What's going on?"

"He was going to …"

Greer whips around and stalks to the corner, grabbing a pitchfork.

"No, Greer," I cry, as he runs at a cowering Blake. He's standing over him before I can move.

"She's not going to kill you. I am," he says quietly. His quiet is deceiving because I can feel a cold, calm vehemence steeling his every word.

I shove to my feet, and pulling up my jeans, I stumble to him and throw my arms around him. "No, Greer, come on. Don't do anything you'll regret."

"Oh, I won't regret it."

"Please, Greer, he didn't hurt me. I'm OK. Let's go tell my momma." I cling to him and squeeze him tighter.

"I want to hurt him," Greer says. "I want to hurt him like he hurt you." He slices the air with the pitchfork, and both Blake and I cry out. He stops an inch from Blake's face. "Do you see this, you bastard?" Blake whimpers and nods. "This is the least of your worries. You ever come near her again, you'll never see me coming. Do you understand?"

"I'm sorry," Blake cries out. "I thought … I thought she wanted it."

"You thought no such thing. I heard her screaming. Did that sound like *want* to you?" he screams the question.

"No, no. I'm sorry, Denver."

"Don't speak to her, you scum. Come on, Denver. Let's go tell your momma."

Blake's sobs grow louder, and he whines, "No, Denver. I can't lose her."

"Don't you mean you can't lose her money? You should have thought of that before."

I unwrap my arms from around Greer and pull him backwards until he begins to walk with me out of the barn. He drops the pitchfork and sweeps me in his arms, hugging me tight. A shiver courses through him, and my body shivers in response. Pulling back, he places his hands on the side of my head. "Denver, I'm sorry. I'm sorry I wasn't here sooner."

"Oh, Greer, don't be sorry. I got away. It wasn't going to happen. I'd rather die."

"That's just not acceptable, chicken." He turns my face toward the light and lets out a muffled curse. Running his hands down my arms, he rubs up and down, and I realize it's because I'm trembling. "You're OK," he soothes. His eyes do a once-over. "Here, baby," he murmurs, as he zips and buttons my jeans. He's so gentle and treats me as though I'm shattered but not yet broken. I close my eyes tight, my mind whirling with "what if's." Number one on my list of worries—is my golden boy going to hold this against me like I asked for this or something? Isn't that what guys do? Take it out on the girl because he had no control over what's happened.

"Come on. Let's go see your mom." I just nod and follow him to the house.

It's quite the scene. My mom screams and cries and throws Blake out of the house. She hugs me and thanks Greer for coming back to the barn. He assures her that I'd gotten him off of me. He tells her I may not be so lucky next time, and that it's up to her to protect me and keep Blake away from me. She agrees and heads off to bed because she's "overwrought." And she should be exhausted. She put on an award-winning performance.

As I sit at the bar with an icepack on my tender cheek, Greer leans against the kitchen counter with his arms crossed, looking deceptively relaxed with one boot kicked out over the other. We just stare at each other for I don't know how long. My eyes get heavy as the weight of what has happened catches up with me. Pushing himself off the bar and unfolding his arms, he strides around to me and scoops me off my barstool.

"Greer," I protest.

"Hush now," he whispers. "I'm gonna tuck you in." He takes me to the bathroom and deposits me at the door. "Go in and clean up. I'll get you something to sleep in."

As I ease into the shower, it hits me again how close I actually came to being viciously brutalized, and I wonder for the millionth time why men, my *mother's* men, honed in on me like that. What made me such a target? I'm strong. Is that it? They want to break me, break my spirit? Is it that I'm a challenge to them? I'm pretty, but I'm not exceptional. I do have a great body though. Maybe that's it? If I understood why they came after me, I would do everything in my power to prevent it.

Everything about me should scream hands-off, yet I've always been a target. I am a champion barrel racer who's responsible for getting a one ton pickup from competition to competition while carrying two amazingly athletic horses that I've trained using my own capabilities and intuition, yet I've had to endure my mother's lover watching me and getting his rocks off. Fucking peeping Tom.

I've won bigger purses than some folks make in a month working a full-time job. I was offered almost a quarter million dollars for my horse based on everything she and I had accomplished together. When that didn't faze me, I was offered a ton of money to train other people's barrel racing horses. All that—on my own, yet I wasn't strong enough to repel the men that kept coming at me and after me.

I'm strong. I'm brave. I'm independent. But despite it all, I always attract scumbag men like a shit fly to manure. The *why* of that finally hits me and fucks with my equilibrium, and I have to throw my arms out to the walls of the shower to catch myself from falling. Another wave of nausea rushes over me.

You can try to disguise manure.

You can dress it up pretty.

You can put a son-of-a-bitching leash on it and parade it downtown on Memorial Day.

It. Is. Still. Stinking. Ass. Shit.

And, despite all my defense mechanisms—I am still my mother's daughter.

I don't cry anymore. I had to have shed all the tears my body was capable of making. And crying won't do me any good anyway. I've had a plan formulating since Blake showed his true colors. I am going to have to rely on my mother mostly for my plan to work, but if I can convince her not to move anymore men in before I could get graduated and move out, then maybe I stand a chance.

Maybe I can leave this house and come back grown-up so her men can't prey on me anymore. Maybe I can even break the whore trajectory that my mother has so lovingly set me on.

Convincing her to be alone is going to be a problem. She's never been alone. Usually she has a main man and a couple of spares. I don't see why she can't go off and get her fix and just not bring them around, though.

After I scrub myself clean, I step out of the shower and wrap myself in a towel. I look around for some clothes but don't see any. Opening the door, I glance down the hallway and think about making a dash for it, but notice a t-shirt and pajama bottoms folded nicely on the floor in front of the bathroom door. I step back in and get dressed quickly. After I towel dry my hair, I throw it up in a ponytail and head to my room.

There's still no sign of Greer. I guess he left. My heart sinks. I'd give anything to have him hold me tight and tell me everything is going to be all right. That I'm not destined to be the whore my mother is. That I don't invite this kind of attention.

I open the door to my room, slip in quickly, and close and lock it behind me. I turn and gasp when I make eye contact with my golden boy sitting at my desk. He's kicked off his boots and is sitting there with one leg crossed over the over. Arms crossed again.

"I want to stay. Will you let me?" he asks, a tremor in his voice.

I nod. We've slept together before, but that was usually by accident, having stayed up too late watching rodeo or talking or whatever while we were on the road.

"I can't imagine leaving you tonight. I just ... I need to know you're OK."

I walk to him, push him to sit back in the chair, and climb into his lap. I hold his face in my hands. "I'm gonna be fine, Greer. But I'm glad you showed when you did." My brow draws together. "Why did you come back?"

He grins at me. That *I've got a secret* grin that I adore. "What?" I ask. Despite the fucked-up morning, I can't help but mirror his grin.

"Nothing. You're tired. Come on," he says as he lifts me from his lap and helps me stand. Climbing into the bed, I turn the covers down on his side. He shakes his head at me and grabs my quilt from its folded place at the end of the bed. Pulling the covers back up, he unfolds the quilt and drapes it over his side.

I can't help the small grimace that pulls at my

mouth. My fears of being tainted hit me full force. "Don't want to be that close to me?" I whisper.

Greer blows out a deep breath and scratches his head. "I wish I could say I trust myself completely in this bed with you, but, uh, I don't."

Oh, thank goodness. I relax and admit, "I trust you, Greer. You're the only man I do trust."

"That means more to me than you'll ever know, Denver."

He pulls his t-shirt over his head and tosses it aside. I smile again, but my breath leaves in a whoosh as he pushes his jeans over his hips. I don't get to marvel at him for long. When he's down to his boxers, he climbs in bed. "You are so beautiful," I whisper.

"Isn't that supposed to be my line?" he asks with a light laugh.

"Guys can be beautiful," I tease.

"Oh yeah?"

"Yeah, and what that means to me is that you're gorgeous here." I pause and run my fingertips over his blond curls. "And here," I say, running them around his eyes. "And here," I breathe as I run them over his chest and down his stomach. Keeping my eyes glued to his, I lean in and whisper, "But most importantly," I place a light kiss over his heart, "here. What's in here makes you so beautiful." Looking up at him through my lashes, I watch his eyes close tight as if he's in pain.

I move my lips over his thundering heart, and my hand roams over his chest before he stills and kisses it. "I can't take anymore of that. I know my limits, baby."

An embarrassed heat sweeps across my cheeks. I didn't mean to get so carried away. I just wanted him to know how much he means to me and how wonderful I know he is. "I'm sorry."

"Don't be sorry." He rests his hand on my hip and pulls me to him, his warmth enveloping me even though there are barriers between us. I finally close my eyes, feeling the weight of today's events dragging me under.

"I came back to tell you that I love you." My eyes spring open, wide and staring. They meet his, and I see his love for me shining there, like always, but this time, it ignites a bright spark that sets fire to my soul. "I love you, Denver. And I couldn't wait another minute to tell you."

I open my mouth to speak, but instead of words, sobs erupt. What is wrong with me? He's just opened up his heart to me, and I'm crying. He pulls my head to his chest and runs a hand over my hair.

"Shh ... baby. You've had a traumatic night. Probably wasn't the best time to tell you that. I just wanted you to know that I loved you before all that, and I'll keep on loving you. What happened—it has no bearing on how I feel about you. Do you understand?"

I nod my head ... focus on breathing and on how strong Greer feels against me. Sleep finally pulls me under.

Chapter Five

Now

THE WIND THROUGH the open window whips around my low ponytail as I head toward the stables where my horses are boarded on the outskirts of town. My giddiness over not having seen Liberty and Indy causes my foot to press heavier on the pedal, and I'm there in record time. I can't believe I've gone four days without seeing them. There was just so much to get situated with school though. Grabbing my shades from the dash, I shove them on as those first bright rays of morning cut across the mountain. My arm falls back to the windowsill, and my hand taps out an impatient beat on the side of my truck that's completely discordant from the Miranda Lambert tune blasting from the speakers.

Pulling into the long, gravel driveway that leads back to the stables, I worry for the second time that I'd upset Maggie by telling her I preferred to drive out on my own today. I didn't want to be on anyone else's schedule when it came to spending time with my horses. She promised her feelings weren't hurt and that she'd catch a ride with Stephanie, another barrel racer who is just as sweet as she is. I found myself hoping again that she wasn't one of those passive-aggressive girls who told you what you wanted to hear and then held a grudge like nobody's business.

I see another truck by the barn when I pull in, and I'm surprised. It's barely even light out. My jaw drops right before I let out a squeal when I see what kind of truck it is. I admit it's a little ridiculous that I love my truck to an extreme that when I see one like her I squeal like a girl, but they're pretty rare nowadays, and the people who drive them are kind of kindred spirits.

Rolling up my window quickly, I climb out of my truck to get a better look. This one is black with some chrome, whereas mine is cherry red and white two-tone with a white roof, and she's definitely not out-done on her chrome. I look over his truck as I make my way toward the front, noticing that it needs some work, but overall, she's in good shape.

I take a peek at the interior. Yep, needs work. Quite a few rips and catches in the tweed bench seat, but it's clean. I start to move away, but my eyes catch on the coolest thing. *Oh my gosh, is that an eight-track player?* Intrigued, I cup my hand around my eyes and plaster my face against the glass as I try to see what kind of music he's got in the deck. Jethro Tull. *No freakin' way.* My dad would flip. Well, the dad of my childhood would anyway. Today's dad? Not so much. It was one of the things he passed on to me. My love for Classic Rock with an emphasis in Southern Rock was unparalleled. Until now, apparently. My eyes bulge from their sockets as I scan the artists in the holder resembling a small filing cabinet—Led Zeppelin, Marshall Tucker Band,

Allman Brothers. I just—

"Am I about to be the victim of grand theft auto?" I close my eyes behind the mirrored shades of my aviators as that voice washes over me. I only spoke to him for a few awkward moments last night, but I'd never forget it. It was deep and rich and a little smoky ... and the strangest image of charcoal just popped into my head. I knew this truck belonged to a guy—I just never would've guessed it was *that* guy.

I rein in my surprise and temper the look of adoration for his ride and his taste in music before I straighten to take him in. He's got his hands on his hips and is wearing a shit-eating grin. I glance up to see gorgeous, sea-green eyes looking at me from under a mud-colored cowboy hat that matches his t-shirt. It pulls tight over all those muscles that I'd only gotten a glimpse of last night. He is just too masculine for words. On second thought, There's a word for it. I think back to the werewolf romance I read last summer ... Alpha. My body hums in agreement.

He asked me a question. I think. Umm ... oh, yeah. "Nope, don't want your ride." I gesture at my truck indicating I was all set there. "But don't think I'm above lifting those eight-tracks from you," I joke.

"Oh, yeah. A fan of the classics?"

I nod my head, but mockingly chastise, "It looks like you might need to be schooled, though. I didn't see any Lynyrd Skynyrd, and everyone knows you can't have a classic rock collection without them."

Sauntering over to my side of the truck, he doesn't pause in his movement, forcing me to step aside unless I want him plowing over me. I step out of his way with a smirk that he immediately returns. He opens the door with a creak, reaches in without looking, and produces an eight-track. "What's this?" he asks with a gleam in his eye.

Glancing down, my grin widens before I bring my eyes back to his. He's just too cocky. I have to take him down a notch. "Creedence Clearwater Revival's *Bayou Country*," I answer through my smile, knowing full well he's holding Lynyrd Skynyrd's first album in his hand.

He looks down quickly to see if he's made a mistake, and I burst out laughing. "Ah, you're good, Denver." He shakes the eight-track at me. "You had me thinking my game was off." He laughs with me as he replaces Lynyrd Skynyd in its rightful slot. "What are you doing out here so early?" He closes his door and reaches around me to pull out a new horse blanket from the bed of his truck.

Placing my sunglasses on the top of my head, I look up at him. "I came to ride some and visit with my horses before practice. You?"

"Same."

"Bull riders don't need horses, Ransom," I joke.

"True, but I board my horse here so that I can ride whenever I want."

"Ah, I understand."

"I bet you do," he says with a nod. "So a 1971 F-100, huh?" he asks as he pats my truck.

"Yep, what year's yours?"

"Same."

"I figured. They look identical."

"Yours sure is souped up," he says with a whistle as he looks her over.

"Yeah, my dad fixed her up for me, and I drove her back here from Mississippi."

His eyes narrow with doubt. "By yourself?"

"Uh, yeah. Look, I'm gonna get my horses saddled up, all right?" Ransom nods and walks with me to the barn.

I breathe deeply when we hit the barn. The sweet smell of clover and manure and horse sweat may sound disgusting to some, but it sings home to me. Ransom ducks down one hall while I keep going straight. I click my tongue as I get closer to Liberty's and Indy's stalls. It doesn't take long for their heads to poke out when they recognize my voice. "Hey, pretty girls," I coo at them. "Did y'all miss me?" Their heads move up and down in rapid succession, reminding me of bobble head dolls since that's all I can see of them. "I missed y'all too."

Taking a few minutes with each of my girls, I pat them down, check their hooves, and chat them up some. "Who wants to go for a ride this morning, huh?" I decide to take Indy out since I'd ridden Liberty most recently, and she would be getting most of the practice today anyway. She was not going to be happy at being left behind.

After getting Indy saddled up, I lead her back through the barn and out into the yard. The owner had sort of shown me around when I dropped my horses off, but I'm not really sure how long the trails are or where they lead. That thrills me to no end because I can't wait to get out there when we don't have practice so I can explore. A quick ride would have to suffice today. Putting my foot in the stirrup, I pull myself up and swing my leg over Indy just as Ransom comes walking out with his beast of a jet-black horse, the white star between his eyes in stark contrast to the shiny darkness of his coat. He is one of the proudest, most beautiful horses I've seen in a long time.

Of course, the thrill-seeking, bull rider John Ransom rides a stallion. I ask, "How many hands tall? He's massive."

"He's about 16."

"A little over, I think." He just nods at me. "Hey, stud, what's your name?"

Ransom laughs as his horse starts nodding at me. "Watch out. He's a flirt."

"Yeah, I bet."

Stopping a good distance away, Ransom calls his name and tells him to be still. "Ah, Night as in dark or Knight as in warrior?" I ask.

"Warrior," he says as he swings into the saddle. I have to take a deep breath to calm my erratic heart when he throws his leg over the powerfully muscled animal.

"I like it. It's fitting. He seems noble."

He nods toward Indy. "I see you've got your own version of Trigger there."

I laugh and nod, giving her a pat down. "She does look like Trigger, but prettier, huh Indy?" She gives me a whinny and tosses her head. She has that same golden coat with a blonde mane and tail like the horse Roy Rogers made famous. And Liberty is a larger version of her. Me and palominos go back a long way.

"Wanna head up one of the small trails?" Ransom asks.

I try for nonchalance, even though my heart is about to beat out of my chest at the thought of being alone with him. "Sure, but is your stallion gonna mind his manners with my mare?"

Ransom laughs lightly. "Yeah, he's pretty calm. And I don't think Indy's in heat or he'd be prancing around for her as we speak, wouldn't you boy?" He thumps Knight's neck. "He's older, but still has a way with the ladies," he says with a wink at me.

I don't respond because my mouth's gone dry imagining Knight's owner having his way with the ladies. Scratch that—one particular lady. He could have his way with me any day. Where the hell did *that* come from?

As he spurs Knight into action, Indy and I follow.

For several minutes, the trail is narrow, and I ride behind him, studying him quietly and thinking through things. Last night, Greer had me pretty shaken on my belief that I can't commit to something more with him. I came to college seeking a change. I thought I could find someone to hang out and forget with. Someone who'd leave his feelings out of it like I do. But, what if, accepting everything Greer has to offer may be the change I need?

The burning question now, though—is it too late for there to be an *us*? I always hoped that, when I felt strong enough for a real relationship, Greer would be the one. Then I went and caused us both so much pain. Would he really be able to handle us just picking up and moving forward? Was I good with that? None of it could be erased, but could the hurt lessen with time?

When the path widens, Ransom slows Knight down until Indy and I are next to them. He strikes up an easy conversation about school and the different titles I won over the years. He asks me about all the records I set. It's funny because each time I give him a fact, he nods like I'm confirming it for him—like he's long since known the answer. Our conversation flows easily. He asks how I'll be getting to all the competitions, and when I tell him I'll be driving my horses and myself since my mom runs our ranch, he frowns at me. I backtrack and assure him that she'll probably attend some of them, just not all. No one really needs to be privy to the ugliness that is my home life.

And that's enough about me. "How'd you know you wanted to be a bull rider?" I ask.

"Ah, I don't know that it was so much a want as a need. It ate at me until I did it. Now it's got such a hold, I can't imagine doing anything different. I always loved everything about rodeo, but there was just something special about watching bull riders get ready to take on the beast. And the high I felt when they hit that eight second mark?" He shakes his head, seemingly with reverence. "It was indescribable. *Is* indescribable. Anyway, my dad took me to rodeo a bunch when I was a little kid. It was our thing." He looks pained for a minute, making me sense there's more to that story.

I'm curious but don't want to pry. To distract him, I offer up my secret desire. Changing the subject, I tell him about my sheep-riding dalliances of days long ago.

He gets a kick out of that. "Mutton Bustin,'" he laughs lightly. "I can see you holding your own."

"I did," I brag. "I wanted to be a bull rider when I was little," I add. *Still long for it.*

"Oh yeah?"

"Yep, like I said, I used to ride sheep at junior

rodeo, but that's as far as I got. Barrel racing is as close as I can get to that kind of high. I do love it, but that never stopped me and Greer from rigging up a barrel between some trees and trying to stay on for eight seconds while the other one pulled and yanked on the ropes. For the record, I generally stayed on, and Greer did not."

The laugh I hoped to elicit from him still shocks me because it's unguarded and genuine, and I'm ecstatic like I just won a huge prize. "I can only imagine. So ... you and Greer? Just friends?"

Now I'm the one who is uncomfortable. I shift in my saddle a bit and try to be as honest as possible. "We were a little more than friends for a while. He wants that back. But no matter my decision, he'll always be my friend."

"Sounds like you have a tough choice ahead of you."

"That I do."

After a few minutes, the trail loops around to take us back to the barn. We take the rest at a light canter. When it opens up to a field, Indy and I scoot past Ransom and Knight. When I look back, Knight is nudging Indy's hindquarters with his nose. Indy gives an indignant snort. I can't help the giggle that escapes me.

"That'll teach you to sway your ass in his face," Ransom says with a wicked laugh, making me laugh harder.

"Don't blame her," I say with mock indignation. "She's just minding her own business. She can't help it if she's sexy."

I look toward the barn and spot Greer sitting on his

tailgate with Shadow saddled up and ready to go. His eyes are pinned, not on me, but on Ransom, a curious expression in them. I don't even pretend not to know that he's jealous.

"Thanks for the ride, Ransom. I'll see ya," I throw over my shoulder. Kicking Indy into a trot, I head toward Greer. "Hey, Greer! Wait till you see the trails," I call out, hoping to distract him. It works. His eyes shift toward mine, and a smile lights up his face as he takes me in.

"MAGGIE, THAT WAS an incredible ride," I praise, as she joins me outside the arena. She just completed practice runs on her new back-up horse that she's been training. He's an impressive red Quarter Horse.

"Thanks," she says with a grin. "Coming from you, that means a lot."

"You're doing a great job with him. With a little more experience, he'll be hard to beat."

"Yeah, I'm proud of him. I trained him from a colt. My dad trained Starlight." Starlight was the strawberry roan that she rode earlier. Together, they are unbeatable. When I tell her that, she just laughs at me.

Liberty and I make our way to the arena. The closer she gets, the more she prances, and I'm raring to go too. I lean down and murmur, "This is what we live for, huh girl? Wanna show 'em what we got?" I run my hand over her neck to calm her a little of the flurry of emotions she displays from her pep talk.

Once inside the arena, we do a couple of tight circles while I gauge her readiness. When I feel it, I let her go. Liberty darts to the first barrel on the right. I shift the reins so that she knows we want a tight pocket. Her head slides to the left, and I remind her to keep it right. I sit my heels back in the stirrups as far as they'll go and squeeze with my legs to hold on as we round the first barrel. A whisper of the barrel brushes against my calf as we head toward the second.

She does much better on the second barrel, which is great, but she knows how important that first barrel is, so we'll be going again in a minute to get that one right. As she rounds the second, I click my tongue for speed. She immediately obliges me.

As we approach the third barrel, I turn her just a smidge too wide and scold myself. She snorts at me. "Sorry, girl," I apologize, as we correct and sprint around barrel three, completing the cloverleaf pattern of the barrels. As soon as she's cleared it without even a hint of touch of barrel, I lean in as far as I can go to lessen as much wind resistance as possible. When we clear the timer, I glance over and read it. *Shit.*

Chapter Six

Ransom

SHE'S WITHOUT A doubt the most beautiful rider I've ever seen. And her spunk? Holy shit. It's not arrogance. She's just that good and is that confident about it. I can't think of anything sexier.

When I saw her ride in Texas last spring, I was intrigued. When I officially met her last night, I was encouraged. But ever since I saw her checking out my truck this morning, I'm convinced she's the girl I want to break all my rules for.

Last night, when she got pushed into me, all I could smell were daisies and sunshine ... and those eyes. I shake my head at myself. I got lost in those warm, honeyed eyes of hers. We just started to have a promising conversation when she spotted Greer. Sucks.

As she prepares to take her second practice run with Liberty, I watch in awe as I recognize the same sort of pattern that I take up with my bulls. She waits, she feels, she assesses, then she fucking goes for it. She's intuitive yet knowledgeable. When she senses Liberty's readiness, she doesn't hold back. She rounds the first barrel, with a grin this time. I could tell she wasn't quite happy with her first run, which is amusing, because she outrode everyone who came before her, and not by just a little bit. When she takes the second barrel even faster than she took it the first time, my eyes widen. She never touches the saddle horn. She hangs on with her feet and her legs as Liberty almost lays them flat going around the barrels. Liberty digs so deep that chunks of dirt spray the fence in her wake. Her tiny grin gets a little bigger as she sprints off to the third. This time, she has the right space between the horse and the barrel to make the perfect pocket. She knows it, and I know it. And as she turns back toward me to head out, her grin is full blown. Denver and her mare make a pretty picture with their blonde hair flowing behind them as they sprint toward the gate. I don't even look at her time because the smile on her face tells it all. She beat her last time.

An elbow jabs in my side, and Austin whistles. "Holy fuck," he chimes in wonder. "That girl. That girl's good. And F.I.N.E. fine. A fine piece of ass, I tell ya. Oh, I bet she'd give me a wild ride." This is close to what he's been saying about most of the girls all morning. But when he says it about Denver, it's a lot more enthusiastic.

Before I can say anything or punch the shit out of him, the anger radiating from Greer, who's been standing a couple feet away, surrounds us. He was engaged in a conversation before Austin's loud proclamation. I stay quiet, curious to hear what he has to say.

"Hey, peckerhead," Greer calls out.

"What, man?" Austin answers, unruffled. That's

because he knows he is, in fact, a peckerhead. I can't help but grin and have to firmly bite my tongue to keep from laughing.

"See that girl there who just rode?" Greer asks with a gesture in Denver's direction.

Still oblivious to Greer's pissed-off tone, Austin shouts, "Hell, yeah! That's who I'm talking about. She's shit-hot."

Greer strides over our way a bit but doesn't lower his voice, wanting, I'm sure, to make his stance known to every horny cowboy within a hundred mile radius. "That girl is special," he says. That throws me. I expected him to say she's mine and stay away. That's what most guys in his position would say. "She doesn't need a no-count peckerheaded cow*boy*"—the way he emphasizes boy almost makes me lose it again—"like you leering at her while she goes about her business. You got me? Keep your eyes to yourself. Keep your hands to yourself. Most importantly, keep your dick to yourself."

Austin throws his hands out like he's indicating his innocence. "Aw, now. No harm in looking, Greer. You didn't say shit when we were checking out those other girls."

"Like I said, she's not just another girl. So hands off."

"Well, cowboy, let me assure you," Austin says as he gestures toward his manhood. "When it comes to my hands and my dick, they only go near the girls who are wanting it. So if it gets that far, it's 'cause she's asking for it. And I don't think I'll need to be answering to *you* when it comes to that."

Greer lunges toward Austin, but I step between them before he can get in Austin's face. "All right, that's enough. Austin, quit trying to start shit." I glance over my shoulder at Greer. "Greer, Denver's tough enough to take up for herself. And I'm sure she wouldn't appreciate you standing guard around her." I pat Austin on the shoulder and turn him back toward the arena to watch the next cowgirl.

"Yeah, boss," Austin grumbles. I turn toward Greer and raise my eyebrows when I see him staring me down now.

He has the nerve to hold a finger up in my face. "Don't kid yourself thinking you know what she would or would not want. You had one ride together. That's it."

My eyebrows shoot up further in surprise. "Whoa now, you sound like a jealous boyfriend. And from what Denver told me, y'all are just friends." For some reason, the fact that he considers Denver his foregone conclusion rubs me the wrong way. Probably because I sensed her doubt about them as a couple when we were talking, not to mention the little fact that I'm set on making her mine.

His jaw clenches and unclenches. "You know nothing about her and *will* know nothing about her. It'd be best if you just steer clear." With that, he turns on his heel and stalks off to where his horse is tied up. I turn back to the arena and wonder what kind of screwed up situation I'm about to get myself involved in, and if it's worth it. Rephrase—is *she* worth it?

Chapter Seven

Denver

THE GIRLS AND I gather around the fence to watch as the bull riders get ready to do some practice rides on a few bulls who were turned out to pasture. It's not as effective as practicing on rodeo bulls, but it will get them back in the swing of things.

Austin is up first, and he gives an impressive ride, even making it to the buzzer his first go-round. I noticed his free hand touching the bull's neck, which earned him a lot of booing and ribbing from the other cowboys. Tall riders like he and Ransom have to be careful not to "slap" the bull because it results in disqualification, even if they've stayed on for the full eight seconds.

A few other cowboys ride who, even though we met, I couldn't remember their names. A couple of them looked like they just started riding bulls and got bucked off quickly ... and not prettily. Another one had a decent ride.

While Pete's getting situated for his ride, I look instead at Maggie. She's studiously ignoring me and has a feigned look of disinterest covering her features. Her only tell is the focus of her electric green eyes. They dance with energy as she watches him pound his fist closed and nod. I hear him say, "Let's go," and he's off.

Turning back, I watch as he hangs on to the bull's every move and does it with grace and fluidity. When the bull spins, he spins with him, steady and sure. The buzzer sounds, and Pete springs off, landing on all fours. He snatches his hat off the ground and swipes the dirt from his knees as he laughs and jogs toward the fence. The other boys take turns congratulating him with slaps on the back and crude talk as they help pull him up and over the fence to safety.

Last to ride is Ransom, and a buzz runs through the small crowd as everyone who's paying attention spreads the word that he's about to ride. He's that big of a deal. There hadn't been a bull rider like him in a long time, and we are all quite aware that we're in the presence of greatness.

I laugh to myself when I realize his bull is, by far, the feistiest of the day. I'm sure that was no accident. I suck air through my teeth when the bull jars Ransom's body forward trying to ram Ransom's head into the metal bar in front of them. Fortunately, Ransom is able to jerk his head back in time. Bulls may be known for their brute force, but they're no dummies. After a few more minutes of preparation, Ransom nods with a quiet, but powerful, "Go," and his bull blows out of the chute.

When the beast spins, Ransom hangs on. When he cuts left, Ransom hangs on. When he kicks his back legs up and is perpendicular to the ground, Ransom hangs on. But he doesn't *just* hang on. His form is perfect. His arm stays powerfully straight and extended at a ninety-degree angle. His frame never slouches. His face never shows fear.

The buzzer sounds, and he dismounts, landing on his feet with his hat slightly askew on his head. He jogs to the fence and climbs up as everyone greets him with awe-infused congratulations.

I shake my head as I try to clear myself of my own John Ransom-induced haze. All the girls standing around me erupt into claps and squeals of delight. They immediately start in on praise of his ... uh, finer aspects. Just when I get used to hearing all the different ways to describe how tight his butt is, how strong he is, how commanding he is, one comment jars me from watching Greer take the arena. My eyes widen.

Maggie must've heard the harsh remark too because she asks the girl to repeat herself. I turn around to determine if it was a slip or if she was, in fact, bragging and realize it's Becky, the bitch who has a hard time keeping her mouth shut. She flips her long brown hair over her bony-ass shoulder, and I can tell she's getting a kick out of being the center of attention. "I said," she begins again. "If you think he's perfection here, you should see him in the bedroom. And no worries—chances are you all will since he's never with the same girl twice."

"Ransom wouldn't want you talking like that," one of the other girls scolds.

"Yeah, in fact, he pretty much demands that you don't talk like that," another says.

Oh my God! He has rules for his whoring around. Well, so do I, I guess, but I only whore around with one person. Great! And I now feel like a hypocrite but can't help myself. I mean, I know I brag about being a slut, but only when I'm provoked, and I don't drag other people through the mud with me.

I catch Becky's knowing eye. It's like she's daring me to comment, and I can't help but say, "Pretty hypocritical of you to stand out here and talk about whoring around with Ransom after what you said to me last night, don't you think?"

She just laughs and glances around at Ransom's other conquests. "If you were ever with Ransom, you'd know it wasn't whoring around. Oh, but wait, Ransom will never be with you because you really *are* a whore. He does have standards."

I give a short laugh and run my eyes up and down her skinny frame. "Clearly they're not very high if he's willing to settle for a prepubescent-looking girl who puts out for a known manwhore. And, trust me, if Ransom was ever with me, once would never be enough. I've proven that a time a two."

"You little bitch," she seethes.

"Don't be confused, Becky. I'm the biggest bitch you'll ever meet. So you'd best steer clear." I laugh and look around at the girls who've circled around us like we're about to put on a show. "And, just for the record, I'm immune to backstabbing, jealous harpies like you. So you're wasting your time trying to put me in my place. It's not gonna happen."

The other girls laugh at the righteous indignation radiating from her pores. I'm sure they all heard how she confronted me last night, and how it had backfired. And now she made it clear that she was the one with issues. No one here knew for sure about my past. I really wish I knew who'd told her, but I won't give her the satisfaction of my curiosity. I raise my eyebrows as I wait for her comeback.

I'm sorely disappointed. "Everyone believes those stories about you, Denver. You're the whore, not me," she screeches before stomping off with Amber in tow.

"'Cause everyone knows you can trust a lying, troublemaking bitch like you!" I call out after her, eliciting more laughter from our group.

One of the other girls—Lauren, I think—nudges me and says that Ransom isn't what Becky had made him out to be and that he obviously had a lapse in judgment by "fooling around" with the likes of her.

Her defense of him does nothing for me because nothing turns me off quicker than a manwhore. Ugh, how many girls has Ransom been with exactly? I really thought … *what did I think?* That Ransom was different from most of the guys out there? That maybe I liked him? It hits me then, that's exactly where my thoughts had been headed even though I was supposed to be thinking about Greer and whether or not I can give him what he wants. Somewhere in the back of my mind, I've been toying around with the idea of Ransom, and it stings to know that I will never have the chance to explore that. I promised myself I'd never let myself be used. And that's what manwhores do—they use, and then they move on.

Our attention turns to Greer as he and his calf sprint from their respective chutes. Greer swings the rope over his head in a near-perfect circle before releasing it from his powerful frame in a fluid movement, successfully roping the hind legs of his calf. Once he secures the rope around his saddle horn, he springs from his horse and sprints toward the struggling calf. Shadow does his job of keeping the rope pulled tight until Greer flips the calf over and ties him up. I flash a grin as he jogs back to his horse, mounts, and waits for his score. He executes his ride with textbook perfection. That's the cool thing about his event. Calf roping is something that can be perfected in everyday farm life, and Greer had been working cattle on my ranch for years.

After he's finished, he joins the other calf ropers to watch his competition, so I turn and make my way to the barn. I unsaddle Liberty, brush her down, and make sure she's comfortable before taking Indy back out to the area behind the barn. I work on some voice commands with her and do some quick sprints. She's holding back a bit on our last run and seems to be favoring her front leg, so I jump off to check her over. Tapping on her lower leg, she lifts her hoof for me, and I hold it between my knees while I use a stick to clean it of debris. "I don't see anything big going on here, girl. What's got you feeling bad?"

"I love the way you talk to your horses," declares that damn voice. The one that washes over me and has my entire body quaking.

Still holding Indy's hoof, I glance up and spot a grinning Ransom leaning against one of the giant oak trees that shades the round pen. I can't help my traitorous grin even though I'm put off by earlier revelations.

I'm the last person on earth who should rush to judgment, especially based on rumors. I wonder if his situation is similar to mine and all that talk is blown out of proportion. Or am I just making excuses because I'm interested in him?

"Oh, yeah?" I ask, feigning indifference.

"Yeah, I was watching you. You barely have to kick your horses, you definitely don't take a crop to them, and you don't shout or holler. So, what's your secret?"

"Hmm ... no big secret. I have the best horses around."

He kicks off the tree to walk over next to me. "True, they are amazing, but they're not amazing on their own."

I shrug and move around Indy to check her other hooves but don't see anything alarming. I'm about to shift to check her bridle when Ransom says, "Check her bit. It's pinching."

Trying to tamp down my annoyance at being told what's wrong with my own horse, I just nod and check it out. Sure enough. "That was my next guess," I mutter, as I remove her bridle and make some adjustments.

He keeps Indy still by holding onto her halter. I'm not real sure how I feel about him touching my horse. "I'm sure it was," he says with a laugh. "You don't like anybody telling you your business, do you?"

I grimace a little at being so transparent. "No, sorry about that. I'm, uh, kind of used to doing things on my own."

"I get that. You can't do everything on your own, though. There's no harm in taking orders every now and then."

Pfft. The thought of taking orders puts such a bad taste in my mouth that I mentally applaud myself for refraining from spitting. "Taking orders? I've never taken orders from anyone in my life."

"No?" He runs his hand up Indy's nose and ruffles the hair resting above her eyes. He's got that gleam in his eyes again like he's silently laughing at me.

"No," I confirm.

His hand leaves Indy's forelock to brush the hair from my shoulder. "I think you might like it in the right context," he tosses out, his voice turning gravelly. My head snaps back because I don't think we're talking about horses anymore. Before I can ask what he means, he changes direction. "How is it that a young girl like you finds herself in that situation? Not taking orders from anyone?" His hand moves from my shoulder to my cheek and cups it, his fingertips press against the back of my neck. I suck in a surprised breath just as he removes his hand. "Driving herself across the country all on her own? Handling horses like she's been doing it for twenty years rather than just a handful?"

My eyes make contact with Indy's as if to ask her if this guy is for real. She's no help as she just blinks at me. I see him mirrored in her eyes, and I imagine the intense stare he's leveling at me—the one I'm too chicken to return. "I, uh, grew up on a ranch," I stammer, as I busy myself with putting her bridle back on.

"A lot of people grow up on ranches. They don't act like they *run* a ranch when they're only eighteen."

I give a jaded laugh and, having had enough of his meddling, finally turn to him to snap, "Well, I *am* almost nineteen, and age ain't nothing but a number." I snort. "I know plenty of so-called adults who act more like twelve year olds caught up in the latest Facebook drama."

He laughs lightly and brings his hand up, grazing my cheekbone with his thumb. "I like you, Denver Dempsey." And with that simple declaration, he turns on his heel, leaving me staring after him like a dumbstruck fool.

"YOU 'BOUT DONE in there?" Greer calls from outside Indy's stall.

I peek over her and see his straw ivory cowboy hat. "Yep. You all set?"

"Yeah, uh …" Ducking under Indy's neck, I pop up next to the stall gate when he pauses in his answer. His expression is wrought with nerves.

"What's the matter?" I ask, as I reach a hand out to soothe the puckered skin between his eyebrows.

He immediately relaxes and grins at me. "Everything's perfect now."

I flick his hat down a bit and wink at him as I turn back to finish rubbing down Indy.

"Denver," he calls out, as I look over my shoulder at him.

"Yeah?"

"I'd like to take you on a date tonight."

He wears his nerves on his sleeve, but hope gleams bright in his eyes. Could it be that simple after everything that has happened? Can we just go on a date like normal college freshman do? One where your hopes and worries are no more than *I hope he holds my hand*, or *how do I eat pizza without getting sauce on my shirt?*

He folds his arms on the wooden slat to peer at me with a half-smile. "Don't over-think it. No pressure, no past, no future. Just tonight."

I feel myself nodding because that actually sounds amazing. "Yes, I'd love to," I answer with a small smile.

Chapter Eight

AFTER I GREET a breathless Maggie fresh from the shower, I jump in under the spray, and we babble (as in Maggie) and grumble (as in me) about our respective dates. I'm not worried about it or even nervous. I just don't expect much.

Maggie, on the other hand, just about barreled over me telling me about Pete asking her out right before she and Stephanie pulled out from the barn. They are going on a double date with Stephanie and another bull rider named Gage.

"You sure you don't want to make it a triple and tag along with us?"

"No, but thank you. I don't want to ruin Greer's plans," I explain, as I put my make-up on. I am really looking forward to seeing what he has planned too. I've never been on a bonafide date. All my previous ones had been ruses to keep up my shady arrangement with Greer, and I've seen him in action enough to know that he is a romantic. Will he put that kind of careful detail into our night even though it's just me? Pulling my hair into a low, side ponytail, I slip on my tight black jeans. When I walk into the room, I'm greeted by a cotton candy confection version of Maggie.

"You look great," I tell her. And she does. On anyone else, her shades-of-pink outfit would look ridiculous, but it fits her. "Pete's not gonna know what do to with himself."

"Oh, you think?" she gushes excitedly.

"Definitely. I reach into the closet and pull out my turquoise boots with black angel's wings emblazoned on them. The outline is filled with tiny black sequins that shimmer in the right light. I snag a black button-up to go with it.

Spinning around, I set about pulling my boots on and tucking in my pant leg as Maggie walks back, admiring my boots.

"Girl, those boots are gorgeous," she squeals, but then frowns as she looks at my shirt. "Nuh, uh. You're not wearing all black. You'll look like you're in mourning. Dates are happy things, Denver."

"Really, this is fine. I'm not into a ton of color." It's true, and now that I think about it, my wardrobe consists mainly of black, red, and white. I infuse color with one of my many sets of boots from time to time. She just keeps digging in her closet, ignoring me. "Seriously, I'm good."

My protests die out quickly, though, when she spins around with a turquoise cowgirl shirt with black stitching and black snaps. With a knowing grin, she edges closer to me, and I see the ropers embroidered with black threading on each of the shoulders. "Oh," I whisper.

"Yeah, oh. Greer will have a fit."

Yes, he will.

A few minutes after Maggie leaves, I slide my ID, some money, and my phone into my pocket and head out. When I hit the front stoop, I smirk at Greer's back as he leans into Pete's truck. I'm glad Maggie let me borrow this shirt. If not, Greer and I would have looked like twins. I'll let him be the Man in Black tonight.

He taps the top of the truck as they pull off and turns to me. I really do love him in black. His golden-blond hair and skin stand out against it, making him really earn the nickname I gave him. As he gets closer, I realize the color makes his blue eyes appear brighter too.

"You must be ... Denver Dempsey," he says with a crooked grin.

My forehead wrinkles. "What?" I mutter.

"Yeah, I sure am glad our friends suggested this 'cause you seem like a girl I could have a lot in common with," he continues, unabated.

Ah ... "Yes, me too. Greer, right? Greer Tanner?" I ask, playing along.

He tips his head. "Yes, ma'am. And you sure do look pretty tonight." He reaches out and brushes the roper on my right shoulder. "I see you like ropers. Well, this just so happens to be your lucky night," he boasts. "I happen to be a calf roper."

"Oh, really?" I snort. "Well, I've always thought they were a little too cocky for doing something as easy as bringing down a defenseless baby cow. I hope you have more than that going for yourself."

Greer's grin turns into a loud laugh that seems to echo off the buildings. "Hmm, you're a feisty one. I like that. I'd also like to show you how much more there is to me. I'm quite complicated and multi-layered, I can assure you," he teases. "You up for that?"

Amused, I look at my wrist like there's a watch there. "All right, Greer Tanner, your clock's ticking. You better get this show on the road. And fair warning, I'm not easily impressed."

"I think our roles are reversed. I suddenly feel like my truck is gonna turn into a pumpkin if I don't impress you fast enough."

"Better get moving, cowboy."

Greer takes us to a local diner that is known for its steak. He acts like he doesn't know anything about how I take my food or what I like to drink, and as he's "getting to know me," asks me all sorts of questions—like my favorite color (red), my favorite food (avocado), my favorite sport (duh, rodeo), my favorite animal (again, duh, horses). Of course, I ask him all these things in return like I don't know. He surprises me when he says his favorite sport is NASCAR, though. I know he loves it, just not more than rodeo.

"So, how is that a girl like you doesn't have a boyfriend back home? I can't believe no one has snatched you up yet."

I twirl the straw in my drink for a second before sitting back in the seat and leveling him with my gaze. "I had an amazing person who tried to snatch me up, but I'm not good enough for him."

Greer narrows his eyes at me. He loathes my self-abhorrence. "I find that hard to believe. You are the whole package—talented, determined, smart ... beautiful."

"He's all that and more. He's loyal, kind, compassionate … freakin' gorgeous," I add with a slanted grin.

"Gorgeous, huh?" He shakes his head. "Hmm, he does sound amazing. But I think you're his equal in all ways." He narrows an eye at me. "Maybe even better than him since you see your own 'faults' so clearly. I think someone who can criticize themselves and try to better themselves is far wiser than those of us who can't."

It never fails to piss me off that he only sees the positive in me. He ignores the open, festering wound that is my nature. "So you think I can bounce back from being a slut?"

His wince and indrawn breath don't surprise me, but his closed fist pounding on the table startles me a whole lot. When the dishes clink and clatter, I'm hurled from the little imaginary world he lulled me into. "I hate it when you call yourself that. You're no slut," he snaps.

"You don't know me, remember? And you sure as hell never see me for me. You have Denver-colored glasses on where I'm concerned." I reach over and grasp his fist. "But I've always loved that about you. You make me better even if it's only temporary, and only in your eyes."

I rub his hand for a few quiet moments while he calms himself.

"That's pretty impressive for a guy you've just met," he finally jokes. "If you're determined to believe the worst about yourself. Tell me … what is it about you that makes you a slut exactly?"

I try to pull my hand back, but Greer flips his over

and laces his fingers through mine, holding tight and running his thumb over my wrist. I study them as I confess, "I used my best friend for years to escape my shitty reality. When he was nothing but good to me, I shut down and lost myself in our moments together, effectively blocking him out from ever experiencing something real with me."

"You sure he wasn't a willing accomplice? Maybe escaping his own reality? 'Cause I can't imagine anyone having an issue with being used by the likes of you," he says with naughty grin and a twinkle in his eyes.

"He was willing, but that's still not fair. He felt things I didn't, and that hurts when someone doesn't return your feelings, even if he protests and promises that it doesn't. That took the edge off my guilt for a while, but the truth of the matter remained—he continually put himself second to me, but he was the only person on this earth who truly loved me. He allowed me to trust, to hope, to dream. And I hurt him—repeatedly. I was so addicted to him and what he offered me I couldn't see straight."

A frown mars his features. "You're not addicted to him anymore?"

"No, I conquered my addiction. I need to get through this world on my own without hurting or using others."

"So this guy? This guy loved you, and you didn't love him back? Not even a little?"

I pinch my lips together because, of course, I loved him. Just not the way he loved me. My love came with conditions and ultimatums and trappings. His love was pure and unconditional and free. Mine was twisted and dirty.

"I want to love him," I whisper, "but I don't know how to love him the way he deserves."

He nods and starts to speak, but our server brings our steaks over, and we eat in companionable silence for a while.

"Why do you think you don't know how to love?" he asks, breaking the silence.

I think for a moment before answering. This is something I've been trying to figure out for … forever. I didn't know if I could put it into words, but for him, I'll try. "Because real love is a learned behavior, and I've never had anyone teach me. My mother's version of love is that it's a tool wielded to get you what you want, and once that's acquired, you set your sights on the next objective, and repeat. If that's not enough, my dad taught me that when you let love in, it destroys you and spoils everything good about you."

"Sounds like this guy was teaching you, though," the always-optimistic golden boy murmurs.

"He was, and then I went and blew it. I took that ugly version of love and corrupted what he offered me."

Greer sits forward and steeples his hands against his chin. "OK … I know I don't know you well," he starts, making me laugh lightly as I recall the game he's playing. "But here's my diagnosis. Quit trying to determine that you know what is best for this *amazing* man who's lucky enough to have whatever you're able to give him. Quit pushing him away. Just quit all that. Now." He clears his throat, and I like this take-charge version of Greer so much that I find myself leaning in and struggling to grasp at whatever ridiculous straws he might suggest to get *us* back. He reaches over and runs his fingers through my ponytail. "Instead, allow what he freely gives you to mold your screwed-up concept of love." He pauses for a second and runs his hands over mine, holding them again. "You came here looking for a fresh start, yes?"

"Yes."

"All right. Close your eyes."

That's not what I expected. "What?"

"Close those wide, sunny-colored eyes of yours, Denver."

"OK," I mumble, as I close them lightly. His hands tighten on mine.

"Everything you've ever known about love has just been washed away from your mind like heavy dust after a long, rainless summer. You look around, and it's gone, but then you wonder ... what was I looking for again? But you don't know because, whatever it was has just ... disappeared. When you open your eyes, you'll be looking at the man who's forgiven you for whatever wrongs you *think* you've done him. The man who's going to show you what love is and show you how to return that love. Now, open your eyes."

When I do, all is I see is the breathtaking man sitting across from me. Gone is the paranoid, needy boy who had begun to let my ugliness taint him. All that remains is my chance, my shot at figuring out how to love with the only person who has ever seen that worth in me.

Nothing about our date is romantic. It's a date of cold, hard truths but also of bright, shiny promise. Greer really does know what he is doing because it is perfect and just what we need.

When I finally lie down for the night, I decide to, once and for all, purge all those polluted memories of who I was and how I became that way. Maybe when I see Greer again, the memories wouldn't cloud the vision of what we were trying to become. I've let my bad thoughts run amuck in my head long enough. I know that I can never forget them, but I think browsing through them and filing them away is the only way this can work.

Chapter Nine

Then

ONE WEEK. MY mother was able to last one week until Blake was allowed to come back home.

Vodka. Orange juice. Cup. *Check, check and check.*

I dash out of the house and into the barn, snatching a couple of horse blankets from their holders and climbing up into the loft. Spreading them out on the hay, I lower myself to my knees and make myself a strong drink.

Vodka, flood my brain and drown all those pitiful excuses my mother spouted at me.

Perhaps, you made it out like you were willing.

He's learned his lesson.

He cut back on his drinking.

I love him, Denver, and he'll be around long after you're gone.

He's promised to steer clear of you.

Just don't do anything to encourage him.

I whimper loudly and shove my fist in my mouth and scream around it. Why am I surprised? That woman had done nothing to protect me for all these years. I am responsible for my own protection. The only reason she kicked out the other husband who tried something on me was because she was finished with him. She used him for everything he was worth, and she was ready to move on. I was kidding myself to think it was about protecting her daughter.

Talking to my dad hadn't been any better. I broke my own rule, called him, and practically begged him to let me come and stay with him and my grandparents for a while. It was something I had never done, and said I'd never do. He left me, damn it. He didn't deserve me wanting to be with him, so no matter how tempted I had been over the years, I always resisted. I sucked up whatever fresh hell was being doled out around here by the supposed adults in my life and dealt with my own shit. But knowing that I'm forced to face Blake every single day makes me want to crawl out of my own skin and slither away in a new form never to be heard from again.

How can I exist in that house with people who are supposed to love me and protect me and do everything but?

So I broke down and begged and explained that to my dad without telling him exactly what had gone down with Blake. I can't imagine ever telling anyone how close I came to being raped, and in my own damn barn, to boot. This is my sanctuary, where I am the strongest. I practically run this place. The thought that he could have ruined me here of all places is ludicrous.

Work it out, my dad said. My mother was hard to deal with, he declared. Then he told me that I wasn't exactly a walk in the park either, that she and I were two peas in a pod. And that it would pass, petty teenager rebellion and wanting to have what you don't have. It's hard to live with someone who is a carbon copy of you, he explained.

A carbon copy of my mother.

My biggest, most terrifying fear that causes me to wake up panting, confirmed in under two minutes by the man who knows better than anyone. The man who was so broken when his beloved wife used him for all he was worth, screwing his loaded brother, all while taking what she needed and wanted from both of them. The man who was supposed to love me unconditionally but couldn't because, in his eyes, I am an exact replica of the woman who destroyed him. The woman he now hated.

I am the woman he hates.

I close my eyes on that thought. I'm not though, right? I'm not her. I've done everything in my power *not* to become her.

I'm beginning to understand what a childish notion I entertained by thinking I could change that. God decides who has blonde hair, who has brown ... and who has slut DNA. Now there's nothing more to do but face the facts that are painfully visible in front of me. Because, despite all my hoping and all my praying, I've become her anyway. Someone not worthy of respect. Someone not worthy of loyalty. Someone not worthy of compassion. And ultimately, someone not worthy of love.

Unlovable. And if you're unlovable, you're incapable of love too. How could I ever know how to love if my own parents don't love me?

My phone rings, and, pulling it from my pocket, I

see that it's Greer. I hit ignore. I can't. I just can't. He's going to freak when he hears my plan. God, he deserves so much better than me. It rings again. *Ignore.* I toss it to the side and down my drink. Pouring another one, I situate myself against a bale of hay so that I can continue to drink in relative comfort. My phone chirps, signaling a text. I pull it up and sigh. He'll be here in just a few minutes. Maybe he'll look around, not find me, and leave. I gulp down my drink, wiping my chin of the dribble.

Pour another drink.

Chug.

Burn.

Fade.

Repeat.

After a while, I hear his utility vehicle pull up and cut off right outside the barn. His steps on the ladder have me laughing like a fool. Did I really think I could hide from him?

"Denver?" he calls when he gets to the top step. I laugh louder. "What the hell are you laughing at?"

"You," I slur.

He climbs up the rest of the way, stretches out beside me, and stares for a minute. "Shit. You're drunk."

I shake what's left of the vodka. "Join me, why don't cha?"

Giving me a disapproving look, he motions toward the open bottle of vodka. "I hope that wasn't full when you started."

"Wasn't. Only had two." I don't mention that they were mostly made up of alcohol. He reaches out, takes my cup from me, and downs the little that's left in one gulp.

Grabbing the orange juice, he pours us a cup of juice to share. "I saw Blake's truck here," he says after a few minutes of our back and forth with the drink.

"Yep."

"Unfuckingbelievable."

"Is it really?" I ask, my voice laced with sarcasm.

"No. Your mother really shouldn't surprise me anymore. But damn. What about your dad?"

My laugh is stilted. "He doesn't give a shit about me either."

Greer just shakes his head in disbelief.

"Did you know Blake wasn't her first husband to come after me?"

He shakes his head at me, and I see pity in his eyes.

"Don't pity me, Greer. I can't take it." I'm two seconds away from crying, and I need to be tough now. Useless emotion is not my friend. He nods at me and looks away. "Yep, her lover when she was married to husband number three was just looking for a peep show. Pretty harmless stuff. I could never get my mom to catch him or believe me, but I knew." I blow out a deep breath.

"Husband number five came after me. He was such a coward, trying to keep me quiet, but I screamed bloody murder, and she actually responded. Caught him in my room, red-handed. But you know, if she hadn't been done with him, she wouldn't have sent him packing. I just got lucky. Then, there was husband number seven's brother. Now he was younger, but dead drunk, so I overpowered his ass before he did more than cop a quick feel. I didn't even bother telling anyone."

I finally look back to Greer and see him wiping his nose on the edge of his shirt. *Shit.* "Greer, don't cry for me. Please." A lump forms in my throat, and I know I'm about to lose it too.

"Greer, look at me." His head swivels around. "I need you do something for me."

"Anything, Denver," he whispers brokenly.

The solution to my problem had been but a blip on my horizon for quite some time. Only recently had it started to come more into focus, and although slight, it is my only solution. My certainty begs for me to spit it out, but I tamp down the impatience that bubbles up because I know I'm going to have to warm him up to the idea.

I focus on his eyes the best I can so that he will see every word I'm about to utter is undeniable truth. "It's the element that she attracts. The only good man she's ever had was my father, and she destroyed him." I hesitate, taking a deep breath. "All these men of my mother's ... it's not gonna stop. And their sole purpose is to possess one thing."

"What's that?"

"My innocence. It's like a fucking beacon for pedophiles and perverts. And if I weren't so innocent, they wouldn't want shit to do with me. I know it."

"I'll do anything. What can I do?"

He's going to hate what I need. I know it. He's so good. I just pray he doesn't hate me. "I need you to take my virginity."

He sucks in a breath and his eyes go wide. "No," he says, sounding final and definite.

"Yes, and you wouldn't be taking it anyway. I'm giving it to you."

"No, Denver, not like that. I love you. You know that. I want you. You know that too. But not like this. Not because you feel backed into a corner. That's not right."

Crawling over him and kneeling between his knees, I take our drink and set it down beside us. I fit my hands around his face and pull his mouth to mine, kissing him deeply and tenderly. Our being together wouldn't be wrong, right? I just have to show him that.

I straighten up on my knees and he comes with me, our kiss exploding. I move my hands to his shirt and fist my hands in it, fitting him to me. His hands move down to my backside, grabbing and kneading. I groan. Reaching up to my shirt, I start unbuttoning it, and he freezes.

I move my mouth down his neck, kissing and sucking. "Come on, Greer."

Suddenly, I'm on my rear, and he's up and moving away. "I can't, Denver. I'm sorry. I just can't."

Tears fill my eyes, and rage floods my veins. "If you won't have it, I'll find someone else who will!" I shout. He freezes at the top of the ladder. *Would I really do that?* I think I would. I'm that desperate to rid myself of this burden, this curse.

"Please, don't do that," he begs, staring straight ahead like he can't even look at me. "Don't even think like that."

"I don't have a choice, Greer. If these sleazebags think I'm yours in that sense, they'll back off. They don't bother with girls who aren't innocent. I know. I've watched and observed. And if I'm with you, they won't try to make me exactly like my mother. Are you going to help me or not?"

His head drops to his heaving chest. I wait patiently for his answer. Does he understand I've spent years trying to figure out why I am targeted, and now that I know I'll stop at nothing to remove the threat?

Finally, he turns back to look at me, and I smile at the look he gives me. It says I love you and I'll do anything for you. "Denver ... I'm sorry," he murmurs, as he propels himself down the ladder. I don't start crying until I hear his vehicle crank up and him peel off down the driveway.

Chapter Ten

Then

"So, Keith, what do you think of our little town?" I ask, leaning in and running my hand up his arm for a second. I'm an impostor, but I've made my decision, and I need to stick with it. I'm nothing if not determined.

"Uh, it's nice. You have a real nice place here. How long have y'all been ranching?" he asks, nerves reigning supreme in his voice. Maybe I'm laying it on a little thick. OK ... so don't *act* like a slut. Guys came after you the way you were. Remember that. I lean back against the doorjamb and clasp my hands in front of myself, hoping to strike a more demure pose. Keith seems to relax a bit.

"Oh, I'll be the fifth generation to run this ranch," I tell him. I wonder now if he's a good choice. Keith starts rambling about farm life and how wonderful it can be, so I survey the guests here for my mom and Blake's little anniversary party. I guess he'll have to do since I don't see any other options that don't repulse me. A bored sigh escapes my lips.

Just as I'm about to direct my attention back to

Keith, I see him enter. Oh, and he looks so good. He's sporting his black Stetson, the one with the band of silver adorning it. A couple of the pearl snaps are undone on his black western shirt, which goes nicely with his black dress boots. His jeans are faded and frayed in all the right spots. He's a delightful combination of perfect gentlemen and rugged cowboy.

Showtime. I turn my attention back to … Keith. *Right, Keith.* "So Keith," I begin, cutting him off, "what do you say we get out of here? I can take you for a walk along the property," I suggest in what I hope is a sexy voice.

"Umm … I, uh, I don't know. We just got here and …" Great! I've picked a pansy-ass.

I run my finger down the front of his shirt and try again. "I'm looking to have a good time tonight." I bite my lip since that seems to turn guys on. "Don't you wanna show—"

I can't finish my suggestion because I get the breath knocked out of me when I'm pulled into the angry wall that is Greer. This time when I bite my lip, it's to keep from full-on smiling. I sense victory.

"Excuse us," he mutters to Keith.

Keeping hold of my elbow, he pushes me through the crowd, and I can still feel the rage radiating from him. Angry sex. I don't think that will be good for my first time. I snicker at that thought.

"There's not a damn thing funny here, Denver," he seethes.

I purse my lips but end up laughing loudly, turning a few heads as he leads me out of the house and around to the space above the garage that doubles as game room and my ex-step-sister's bedroom.

"Greer," I toss over my shoulder, "I really like this caveman thing you've got going on, but if your intention is a friendly game of pool, I need you to let me go. I've got an agenda tonight."

"Shut up, Denver." I shut up.

Once we get upstairs, he propels me into the room and throws the lock behind us. He tosses his hat on the pool table while turning to me. The look on his face is pure torture. And I feel so badly for goading him that I yearn to take him in my arms and say, "Forget it. I'm sorry," but I can't afford feelings right now—his or mine.

He finally speaks, and each word punches itself out of him. "Denver, I'd give anything to be with you but not because you feel threatened or like it's a last resort. I. Just. Can't. But don't you see I want to? Can't we just pretend we do and go on like we were?"

"Do you think this is how I want it to be, Greer?" I throw my arms out like my joke of a life is splayed before me. "Do you think I enjoy being hunted like an endangered species? Because that's what it feels like. Like there's a fucking prize on my head, and my days are numbered! Did you know that the night Blake came home I lay on the bathroom floor sobbing for hours in between my bouts of throwing up? That when I was finally able to pick myself up and go to bed, I propped a chair under my door, and I went to bed fully clothed? That I lie there most nights wide-awake and cursing my existence? When I'm finally able to sleep, that it's been with a gun?" My voice hitches, and I curse myself. "That I considered turning that very gun on myself?"

Ripples of pain transform the cold fury marring his features. "No, don't talk like that."

"Why not? It's the truth. I'm tired of this. I'm tired of feeling this way. I'm tired of watching my back. Every day, he leers at me as if he's preparing me for the inevitable. I don't want him or any other pervert to be my inevitable, Greer. I want it to be you. The first man who touches me like that has to love me. You love me … please, love me," I whimper. Greer stares at me, assessing me and my pleas, and I try to remain quiet to let him decide, once and for all.

He has to see what I see because all of these fears and the subsequent paranoia have manifested themselves physically as well. I can't remember the last time I had a full night's sleep. My nightmares wake me up with paralyzing fear. I know it's bad when I realize my favorite dream is the one where Blake puts a bullet in my stomach after he has his way with me. I've resorted to wearing concealer over the darkened skin under my eyes—eyes that return a dead stare when I look too closely in the mirror. My hair falls out in clumps when I wash it or brush it. I have no appetite, and when I force myself to eat, the food morphs into a brick inside my mouth, gagging me as I try to swallow it. I quit weighing myself when I lost eight pounds, but I know I've lost more since then.

The worst part has to be the paranoia, though. I can't even find peace in my barn. Every shadow, every noise has me whipping out my knife and spinning to attack. Our ranch hands give me sidelong glances, and I'm not sure if those are out of concern or if they're gauging and planning their own attack on me.

I'm tired ... so utterly tired. My eyes drift closed before Greer shifts on his feet and blows out a deep breath, the movement not enough to pull me from my stupor.

"Denver," he calls. I force my heavy eyelids open. "You think us having sex is going to fix all that?"

"Yes, I do."

"I—"

My patience snaps, and my blood heats and rushes through my veins, lighting a fire under my purpose. "Everyone is downstairs celebrating my mother's marriage to a man who was a scrap of cloth away from raping me. I know I sound desperate. And I am. But I'm desperate for you. I need you. I want you. I want you to be my first ... and wouldn't I be yours?"

He gives me an incredulous look. "Of course you would. You know there's no one else for me, but this isn't about you and me. This is about you being scared and trying to control this situation in a screwed-up way."

I lower my voice so that he can see I'm serious and I'm done. "We've gone round and round about this for the last two weeks. You're out of arguments. This is what I need, and I want it to be you, but—"

"Don't you fucking threaten me with that again." I wince. He's never directed that word at me before. "I'm sorry, chicken." He reaches and grabs my hand, putting it over his heart. "I didn't mean to say that to you."

"It's OK. I say it to you all the time."

"It's different. You're more valuable to me than that common word. You're also more valuable to me than a quick roll in the hay. Do you have any idea how many times I've dreamt of taking you? But every single time I do, you're surrounded by clouds of white lace and rose petals. We're laughing, and we're happy. I've always wanted to make you mine, but not until the day you become my wife."

That's the most beautiful thing anyone's ever said to me and the most beautiful, pure idea anyone's ever had about me. What's pathetic about it is the fact that I don't deserve it. I've never deserved this person standing in front of me. And, suddenly, I can't do it. I won't convince him to take my virginity. It will kill him. Kill who he is at his core. And I know this now more than ever.

"Why are you crying, Denver?" he asks, his voice a jagged instrument, gouging at my heart. So full of the pain that I've put there. Why can't I be what he needs and deserves? I reach up and wipe away tears I wasn't even aware I was shedding. I look at them on my fingertips like they contain the answers to all my problems. "Denver?" he prompts.

"I have to go." It sounds like I've taken sandpaper to my vocal chords. "I can't do this to you." My eyes snap to his. He looks so confused yet hopeful. "And I can't see you anymore."

I try to move around him, but he drops to his knees, grabbing my hand as I try to pass. "I knew it. I knew you would win. You always win," he chokes.

"No, Greer, my acceptance is not my final act of manipulation. I truly do accept your decision. More than that, I respect you for it. I'm not going to beg or coerce or try to make any more deals with you. And I'm *not* going to hold it against you. I just ... I just don't want to hurt you, and I don't trust myself to be around you right now." I run my hands over his curls. "Everything about me is designed to hurt you. I—I'm sorry." I want to tell him that I love him too much to do this to him, but saying those three words will make it all that more difficult for him to say goodbye to whatever is left of the girl he's come to love.

Squeezing his hand one last time, I try to release it, but he grabs both of my hands and holds harder, pulling me around in front of him. Without a word, he drags me down to my knees so that we're face to face. He grasps my face with our entwined hands, and his eyes roam over me. When he brings them back up to mine, I whimper at the raw pain I see in them.

"Do you remember me telling you once that you're the only one I see? If I let you go, I'll go blind. I'll see nothing, want nothing, *be* nothing."

He moves his lips over mine in a tranquil way, like he's trying to hypnotize both himself and me. I'm subdued. He doesn't rush, but it doesn't feel like one of his savoring kisses either. It feels like a final kiss. Is he kissing me, or our innocence, goodbye? I clear my mind and take myself back to the stream for our first kiss. So beautiful, and so perfect.

His fingertips move to my waistband, so I move mine toward his, and we slowly undress each other. When we're both free of clothing, he tells me how beautiful I am. He gets a nervous look in his eyes, and I think he's going to back out. "I don't have any protection."

I laugh bitterly. "My mother's had me on birth control since I got my first period. We're safe."

"Oh, OK, want to get on the bed?"

I shake my head. "Right here is good."

He eases me to the carpet and settles over me, covering my face with kisses as his finger slides inside of me. His tongue explores the inside of my mouth. It's not bad.

I moan because that's what I think I should do, but I really don't feel the need to. I just want him to do it and get it over with, but I'm afraid to push. So my mind goes somewhere else until he's prodding at my entrance.

He takes it slow, probably afraid that he's going to hurt me. It's uncomfortable, but it doesn't hurt. It just feels awkward, and even though he fills me, I am …

nothing…

empty…

numb.

I wrap my arms around him tighter, pulling him closer until he's pumping in and out of me at a steady pace.

The emotions I'm supposed to be feeling taunt me. Am I supposed to be overcome with even more love? Turned on? Because I'm neither. And the more I try to force myself to feel those things, the further I am distanced from them. Like a dinghy that's gone adrift, I watch helplessly, as the lighthouse beacon gets further and further away. A seeping numbness overcomes me.

He buries his face in my neck, and his hot, rushed breaths coat me. It doesn't last long. Greer groans and stills over me while I turn my head to the side and focus on a print of dogs playing poker.

He rains little kisses on my neck and moves up to my jaw, my cheek, and my mouth. He professes his love for me while pecking away at my lips. And I just want him to be done so that I can get dressed and go back to the fraudulent party. I belong with all the other counterfeits. I kiss him back with a tenderness I don't feel, and tears spring to my eyes because he deserves someone so much better. Not someone who is numb to everything.

I don't feel like me anymore. So what does that mean? If I'm not me, who am I?

The answer hits me with such force I throw myself into the kiss I don't really feel, to mask the terror that has jolted me….

I'm transforming into my mother.

OVER THE NEXT two weeks, we have sex twice more. Once in the barn, and once more in the room above the garage. Never once in a bed. I don't know why that is exactly, but I'm sure it's symbolic in some way because it's not that we can't get enough of each other or are out of control.

I thought I'd feel a sense of relief with the unshackling of my innocence. I thought my steps would be lighter. I even went into Blake and my mother's room late one night when I heard them up talking and told them that I was having sex with Greer. Blake huffed a surprised breath, and my mother shook her head. "I always thought you'd go for Lawson. He has such aspirations," was her only real comment other than reminding me to take my pill regularly. And that was that.

I question why I had sex with him twice more when it was no good the first time. All I know is that it's the only time I don't feel, I don't think, and I don't hate myself. But, after I take him, it all rushes at me with a vengeance.

A few days before school starts back, and we begin our junior year, Greer broaches the subject of what we will tell people. "Nothing," I say, because we *are* nothing. I don't say that last part aloud though. I tell him I don't want to be his girlfriend. I want to be his friend and have sex, and that's all. I don't want to change anything.

Greer barely looks at me, and I swear I hear him mumble, "Everything's changed."

Our junior year proceeds like that—our "friendship with benefits." But he's right, it's all changed. Neither our friendship nor our benefits are any good, and I often find myself wondering why we're torturing ourselves. Why are we trying to maintain our damaged friendship? And, even though we don't do it often, why do we think continuing to have sex is a good idea?

I finally convince him to start dating other girls. He protests at first because he's still Greer, even though he's a miserable Greer. I tell him if he doesn't, then what we do have will cease to be. It's an empty threat because I can't let him go, but thankfully, he doesn't know that. Why do I do this? I hope that Greer will meet someone amazing and break things off with me permanently since I'm not strong enough to do it myself. I hope that Greer will compare me to someone normal and finally see me for what I am—toxic—and flush me from his system.

That's what he should do, but he doesn't. He dates other girls, hangs out with me, and screws me when he's in-between. Except it's not screwing for Greer. He never fails to try to make it beautiful and romantic, but the harder he pushes, the more I retreat. And, even though our friendship is an atrophied limb, neither of us is strong enough to amputate it.

Chapter Eleven

Then

ALL THAT AWKWARDNESS changes our senior year.

"I want you to go on a double date with me and Alyssa."

My eyes give an exaggerated eye roll even though Greer can't see me through the phone. "I don't think that's a good idea, Greer. And I don't date."

"I think it would be good for you. You need to get out and hang out with other people. This guy goes to another school, so he doesn't know …"

Doesn't know that I'm known as the school slut even though nothing could be further from the truth, is what he doesn't say. My golden boy is too polite to bring up my sordid reputation. It's ridiculous though. I've had sex with Greer and Greer only. And I could count the number of times we've done it on both hands.

Of course, the rumor is that I have sex with my friends—many friends—and I require nothing from them in return. They use me, I use them. I was sure that rumor had been spread by the one girlfriend I had. I had a moment of weakness and confided in her about my twisted relationship with Greer. Next thing I know, everyone's whispering about me being a slut, she's no longer friends with me, other girls are openly hostile, and other guys, the guys that are worth a damn, think I'm repulsive. The clichéd double standard is alive and well in Anaconda, Montana. The guys I'm "screwing" certainly fair no worse. If anything, they're fucking legends, and they don't even exist.

Greer falls for the rumors and confronts me, asking if I'm screwing somebody else. I assure him that I'm not. Everyone speculates over exactly who I'm sleeping with. I spent the second half of my junior year defending myself and attempting to curtail rumors before trying to just ignore it and pretend like I wasn't bothered. I was done with all that.

For a girl who claimed not to care what others thought about her, all this actually hurt. How could it not? I've never had many friends, but to go from someone who was simply considered different, to being the school pariah, it fucking sucked. And that's the key. Being different, I could handle. Being hated, though, I hadn't handled that well.

Defending with words quickly morphed into defending with my fists, and I found myself suspended from school more often than not in the course of a few short months. But what's a girl to do when she opens her locker and condoms come spilling out? Or when she goes to get in her truck and it's papered with STD pamphlets and filled with genital wart cream? Something had to give.

Many tears, a lot of alcohol, and a shit-ton of assurances from Greer, helped me gain a new outlook—

The Fuck 'Em All Perspective.

Now this helped tremendously with my implementation of a new approach this school year. I accepted the role everyone had put me in and was relishing in it. Someone calls me a slut, I agree and move on. I am a real bitch about it too, but that's the least I can do. It gets rid of them faster, and pretty soon there isn't anything to taunt me with. When someone openly admits to and owns up to rumors, it just slap takes the fun out of everything. Oh, except the sly looks and the social pariah aspect of it—that still exists, but it's much more tolerable. I was given a wide-berth rather than openly sneered at and attacked.

"Denver?"

I snap out of my mental torment. I've become comfortably numb to all that, so why does Greer want to open old wounds? "He doesn't know that I'm the school slut, huh? Nice. What do you get out of this, Greer?" He doesn't even like me talking to other guys. Never has, come to think of it.

He exhales deeply before he admits sadly, "I get to see my best friend live like a teenager for a night."

Completely selfless. Who could say no to that?

Date night arrives, and I'm looking good. Why? Because I literally have never been on a formal date and figure I should put some effort into it. We are going to a Kenny Chesney concert, so I paired my favorite black, red, and ivory floral, floaty skirt with a black, long–sleeved, lacy shirt, a blue jean vest, and my new red boots that had black fire running up them. I pulled up portions of my dirty blonde hair to braid around the crown, but the length cascades down my back in soft waves, and I lined my honey-colored eyes in kohl and smoothed on a smoky gray eye shadow.

Greer and his friend, Tyler, pick me up first. It. Is. Awkward. What was I expecting? Once we pick up Greer's date, things become less so. Tyler is nice. Not into rodeo, but I guess everyone can't be. When he says he hasn't ridden a horse since he was twelve, I shoot daggers at Greer in the rearview mirror. He's had it trained on me the entire time and chuckles when he sees my response to Tyler's confession.

Since it's last minute, we end up in the nosebleed section, but we have a blast dancing in the aisle. When a slow song comes on, I decide to sit it out, and I can only watch, mesmerized, as Greer holds Alyssa tight in his arms and nuzzles her neck. When his hands sneak down to her ass and he pulls her tight against his front, the bitter taste of bile floods my mouth. Jealousy turns my stomach sour, and hot tears flood my eyes. My eyes find his, and they are smiling as he mouths, "You."

I wonder what that means as I turn unseeing eyes to the stage, tears threatening to spill over. Greer's been giving me exactly what I wanted. Sex, no strings. Friendship. He's been dating other girls for over a year. Why am I jealous all of a sudden? Is it because I never had to see it first-hand? Why is he rattling around in that little box I put him in, damn it? I look down quickly, swipe at my eyes, and plaster a smile on my face.

Thankfully, the song ends, and he and Alyssa return to their seats. Kenny's wrapping up, so I'll be able to end this misery soon.

When another slow song kicks off during the encore, I groan aloud as Greer stands. I'm thinking I'll go to the restroom because I can't endure *that* again, but then he puts his hand out to me and says, "I've gotta dance with my best friend." My beaming smile works its way up all the way from my toes, and the small smile he wears morphs until it mirrors mine.

The theme of this song resonates with me, and I wonder if he waited and picked it on purpose. "Why'd you ask me to dance to this one?" I ask as he twirls me in his arms.

He closes his eyes tight for a few seconds, and when he opens them, they sear into my very soul. "Because I'd rather be somewhere with you, over anyone and everyone else in this world. Because when it's not you I'm with, my mind makes it so. Because I'm sick of playing games. Because it's always been you, chicken. I want you beside me in my truck. Beside me at school. Beside me in life. I want you. Every single day."

I can't breathe. The old me wanted that. The new me didn't deserve it and didn't know if she was capable of it. I glance over his shoulder at our dates and feel so naughty. We're having this conversation while Greer's hand rests, tantalizingly-so, around my hip. As his fingers dip down a little to stroke me, our dates sit ten feet away, completely oblivious. It just ... does something to me.

"I want you too, Greer," I whisper in his ear, but I know it's not the same *want* he feels. "But—"

"No buts. Not tonight. Just let me pretend."

His words pierce my heart. I let out a deep sigh. "I hate myself for a lot of things, Greer, but by far, I hate myself the most for hurting you. I'm sorry I'm so screwed up."

"I wish you wouldn't say things like that. You don't hate yourself, and I'm a big boy. I can handle myself." My eyes wander down to stare at his chest. I wish his simple words of confirmation could change the fact that I hate myself more than he knows. A finger slips under my chin to bring my gaze back to his. "And you're different—not screwed up—but I'll tell you right now, it wouldn't matter to me anyway if you were. I'll take you whatever way I can get you. I'm in love with you just as you are. But I won't lie either. I want us to get the old Denver back." He gives me a mischievous grin. "The one who was mostly carefree, and somewhat innocent."

I laugh a little at his qualifiers before a quiet sob erupts as his beautiful words sink into me. "We'll never get that back," I choke out.

"We can try." I just nod, hating to burst his bubble. It's never going to happen.

We drop his girlfriend off first since Greer explains that he and I live next to each other, and it just makes more sense that way. She pouts all the way to her house. I imagine she doesn't trust me alone with Greer. She has good instincts.

I cringe as I watch them make out again when he walks her to her porch. She actually walks to her front door backward, devouring Greer with her eyes as he makes his way back to the truck. The grin he directs at me makes me want to smack him upside his perfect face. He knows exactly what he's doing. We drop Tyler off, and I step out of the truck and give him a quick, awkward hug as I make my way to the front seat.

I close the door behind me, and the electricity that charges through the cabin is palpable. I haven't felt this need for him since before we started having sex. Does he feel it too? It's pretty sick that I need jealousy and the sinister aspects of cheating and sneaking around to fuel my sex drive, but I know that's what has done it.

Stupid, stupid, stupid slut! I denied it for over a year, and then accepted it like the joke was on everyone else because I knew differently. But now, instead of thinking about my slut potential as an inactive volcano brewing well below the surface, I finally feel like a slut.

It's an idea I've been toying with, but this makes me realize that being a slut has nothing to do with the number of guys I've been with. It's a mindset. The sad thing is, I have no remorse. I want him all the more for that very reason, and I'm unapologetic.

The drive from Tyler's house to the main road is only about a half a mile, but it's an enlightening and life-changing distance because it forces me to admit what I've failed to recognize—I am a slut.

When we get to the end of Tyler's driveway, I'm jarred from my mental chastisement, and subsequent awakening, as I hear my seatbelt buckle unsnap and feel myself being pulled to Greer's side. I grin and bite my lip as he fastens the middle belt around me. "This is where you belong," he breathes against my neck as he tugs on my ear with his teeth before placing a small kiss on the sensitive skin behind it. The noise that erupts from me can only be described as a mewl because it literally works its way up from my core and propels itself out of me of its own accord.

"Can you get us home quick?" I beg.

"I'm on it, babe."

I laugh and reach over to turn the stereo up. It's

playing a Toby Keith number that I absolutely love about lost loves. I wonder if that's how Greer and I will feel about each other one day because, deep down, I know we'll never last. He deserves so much better than the small piece of myself that I'm able to give. He deserves to find someone who is his everything, but more than that, he deserves to *be* that someone's everything. A pang of regret twists and pulls at my stomach because I'd give anything to be that someone.

Even though I love the song, it's settled deep in my belly like the heavy weight of lead. I reach up quickly and change the station. Classic rock. Let's go with that. Eric Clapton's "Wonderful Tonight" fills the truck. I relax a little and rest my head on his shoulder. I close my eyes and yawn. This is what happens when I finally slow down ... I crash.

Greer lifts his arm and maneuvers me to lay my head in his lap. I curl my legs on the seat, and being here feels so good that I sigh. He runs his hand over my hair soothingly. The truck comes to a stop, and I sense his eyes come to rest on me. Tilting my head back a little, I capture his eyes with mine. But he's not looking at me; he's looking at my hair. As Clapton sings out about her brushing her long, blonde hair, he lifts a lock of mine, leans down, and kisses it. And I just want to cry. I wish I could show him the same tenderness with the same meaning behind it.

He guns it, and we shoot off toward my house. I reach up and change the station again, and some Katy Perry bumps through the speakers. I think I'm safe from all the hearts and flowers shit. Glancing up, I see Greer roll his eyes, but he doesn't call me out on my avoidance technique.

We make it to my house in record time. He cuts his engine and edges out of his truck, dropping to the ground before turning back to help me out. Scooting me to the edge, he reaches around and grabs my ass and squeezes hard. My legs instinctively widen and he leans in and places light kisses on the insides of my knees.

"Ah, Greer," I breathe. My thighs tingle, and the tingling shoots directly to my core. "That feels amazing." Moving his hands around to my front, he bunches my skirt up and kisses a blazing trail up one leg until he gets to my center. I fall back on my elbows as he drags me to the edge. If he let's me go, I'll slide right off the seat.

He doesn't let go. He buries his face between my leg and kisses me hard … there. I blush, fall back, and cover my face with my hands. He's never done that before. He resumes his kisses on my other leg. The entire bottom half of my body is aflame.

I groan and tell him how much I want him.

"I want you too. So much," he whispers in that gravelly voice.

He slides my underwear down over my boots and places them on his floorboard as he guides my body out of his truck and onto the ground.

I put my hands on his shoulders to steady myself and look up into his molten blue eyes. It's all there, and all for me—love, desire, compassion … He didn't look at what's-her-name like that. I've never seen him look at anyone else like that. I'm two halves of a whole. Because as much as I ache to return that look, I know I never will. Is this knowledge enough to force me to behave myself? Unfortunately, no.

Greer moves in to kiss my mouth, and I turn my head quickly. "Save your kisses for your girlfriends, Greer. I want everything else."

"You're not going to kiss me?" he asks, astonished.

My little laugh is jaded. "After watching you kiss her all night? Not hardly. I'm fine with it. I'm just not going to be a follow up act. I want what you hold back from them though. Is that enough?"

"So nothing's changing?" He presses his lips together.

I shake my head and trail my lips over his throat. He's swallowing hard like he's trying to overcome something. "Nothing's changing, Greer, except how much I want you. Like this. Now. I need you to make me forget. I need you so much." My kisses turn feverish as I work my way down his chest. One of his hands comes to rest on the hollow of my back while the other works its way up the inside of my thigh. One finger slips in to tease and get me ready but is soon followed by another because I'm already so wet. I was as soon as I thought about the fact that we were going to drop his girlfriend off and go at it.

I fist my hands in his hair and pull as I devour his neck. His pace between my legs increases until I'm shaking. Letting go of his hair, I thrust my hand down his jeans to find him hard and ready for me. I palm it roughly and work its stiffness with my hand.

"Whoa, Denver, slow down. What are you doing?" Greer is used to me just kind of going through the motions, and not really showing any pleasure or desire. All that's about to change—I need something more from him, but I don't quite know how to ask for it.

"Greer, I don't want you to be tender with me. OK?"

"What do you mean?"

"I just want ... want you to be rough."

He grins and looks at me knowingly. Spinning me around, he pushes my chest down on his truck seat, tells me to spread my legs, and is inside of me before I know it. A gasp erupts from my open mouth as he drives in and out of me at a punishing pace. Instead of just taking him, I thrust back into him and meet him move for move.

I. Love. It. I feel ... alive. And from the sounds that Greer is making, he loves it too. I sense him close to climax, and something powerful works its way through my body. I hold my breath so that I can concentrate on the sensation that starts to overtake me.

"That's it, Denver. Give it to me," Greer demands.

My toes curl in my boots, my mouth falls open, and my breath leaves in a whoosh as I come apart underneath him as he empties himself inside me. The brilliant fireworks that had gone off in my body fade with a satisfied shower that continues to resonate throughout my limbs.

Suddenly, all the wrong we've been doing feels so right. And what's supposed to be bad, makes me feel oh-so-good.

He collapses against my back and kisses my hair. "Denver, you're amazing. That was amazing." And I think ... so that's what an orgasm feels like. And can I have more please?

"It was amazing," I agree. "And so were you." He

kisses his way down my spine and straightens my clothes as he stands. I grab my underwear and slide them on. He's not going to like my suggestion. Well, maybe a little. But mostly he's going to hate it.

I try for a businesslike tone to deliver my proposal. "Greer, I think we need to revise the parameters of our relationship."

"Oh, yeah?" he says, as he buttons his jeans and runs his hands up my thighs before fitting them around my waist.

"That was hot. Right? Going on a date. Flirting with each other right under their noses and ditching them, all the while knowing that, at the end of the night, it'd just be us."

He narrows his eyes and gives me a begrudging, "Yeah."

"So, let's continue to date others—I will too if I want." I shrug. "Then we'll have each other. And I want it like we just had it. No more trying to make it something it's not. We each do what feels good. Us and mind-blowing sex."

"That's how you want our relationship to change?"

"Yes, I think the reason we've been struggling and things have been awkward is because we try to make it something it's not. Our expectations didn't meet our reality, and it sucked." He looks affronted. "I'm sorry. Did it meet yours?"

He just shakes his head no. "So, you still won't be with me," he grunts. "That's the bottom line."

"I'm sorry. I'm just not ready for that. What do you think?"

Grabbing my waist tighter, he spins us around so

that his back is to the truck as he sets me away from him. "I think I'm done with this and with you," he barks, as he runs his hand through his hair. "I ... I can't be like that anymore. Like you. I. Love. You. You may have turned your damn emotions off, but I'm not capable of that where you're concerned. I'm not pretending this is something it's not. This *is* everything to me. And I've done everything and anything to prove that to you. Looks like you're determined to live down to your reputation. Congratulations."

He practically slams the door on me before peeling off down my driveway. I stand there stunned for a few minutes before slowly walking up to my porch. Numbly, I stumble to the porch swing and replay the night.

I was so wrong on so many levels. He was right to push me away. I congratulate myself on finally having done the thing that made Greer realize that I'm no good for him. Who knew? Over the past year, I've tried so many things. Flirting with other guys, setting him up with other girls, ignoring him at school, being a complete and utter bitch, ranting and raving like a lunatic ... OK that part was not feigned by me. I really felt like a lunatic.

Even though I did all of these stupid things hoping to drive him away, I've always gripped tightly to the sliver of hope that I wouldn't actually do it. That one day, I'd wake up healed from being such a soul-sucking mess. Greer and I would go back to being like we were when we first got together. I'd finally be all he deserved.

Now I wonder, since I've lost Greer, will I become the slut that everyone already sees? Will I start sleeping around on a regular basis? How can I not when it's the only time I don't *feel* ... when it's the only time I can escape all the dark thoughts that plague me, and it's the only thing that sends a hands-off vibe to the men who want to use me.

A buzzing snaps me out of my reverie. A glance shows a text from My Golden Boy displayed across the screen. I don't want to open it because he's going to apologize and accept my conditions, and I'm going to let him. And then my torturing of him will continue unabated. But, just because I don't want to open it, doesn't mean that I'm capable of resisting.

I'm sorry. I shouldn't have said those things. Just like I thought.

Don't be sorry. Everything you said is true.

Not all of it. But you're still my best friend. And I never want to hurt you.

You can't hurt someone who is so riddled with holes that nothing can fill her and make her whole. And you can't hurt someone who is not whole. **I'm fine, but I'll miss you.**

Nothing to miss. I agree to your terms. Before I can respond, he buzzes again with ... **No sex with anyone else though.**

Shit. I shouldn't be so relieved. I should tell him the offer's off the table, but I know I won't. **Of course not. And no kissing when we are having sex.**

Umm…OK? But we can still kiss other times?

Yes. Our friendly kisses don't bother me.

Chapter Twelve

Then

AS MY NEW ranch hand walks away with his tail tucked between his legs, I throw my hands up in the air, spin around, and run right into a smiling Greer. His hands shoot out to steady me while his chuckles ring in my ear.

"Don't laugh at me," I snap.

"I can't help it, chicken butt. I love to see you all worked up. But why are you yelling at your new ranch hand?"

Shaking off his hands, I cross my arms across my chest and cock my hip. "First of all, I wasn't yelling. I was speaking in a stern tone. I was speaking in said tone because I told him exactly how many cattle needed to be on the front twenty, and instead of following my instructions, he went behind my back and asked my mother. She didn't know the answer and put him off, and now I've got an overeaten pasture and some hungry livestock," I finish almost out of breath. Greer just stares at me, so I state, "I've gotta get up there and help get 'em moved." I scoot around him and out of the barn, turning back when I get to the utility vehicle, only to see him grinning and leaning against the barn door. My brows pinch together. "Are you gonna stand there gawking at me all day, or are you gonna make yourself useful?"

His eyes drop from mine and run down my black t-shirt, over my frayed, holey jeans, and all the way to the tips of my black work boots, his scorching look setting my body aflame. Finally, his gaze meets mine again and he shrugs. "I can't help it if your farmspeak turns me on."

Laughter rings out over the hubbub around the barn. "Really? That's what does it for you?"

He straightens himself and saunters toward me, stopping a few inches away so that his fingertips graze the outside of my thighs. The light, fairly innocent touch somehow causes my stomach to clench and my center to throb. "Are we still on for tonight?" he rasps.

I groan, and not in a good way. "Ugh ... my mom made me promise to show up for dinner tonight with her and Blake or else she'd take my door off the hinges again. He's not worth losing my privacy, so I'm going, but I did get her to agree for us to just eat here." A mischievous smile overtakes my face. "So, I've decided that me and *mi amigo* would be in attendance."

His brows pull together since he knows he is my only friend. "Mi amigo?"

"Jose Cuervo!" I say, trilling my *r*.

"Oh, shit. I do not think that's a good idea. You forget the last time you two spent quality time together?" he says with a frown and a shake of his head.

No, I sure didn't. I tried to pick a fight with my mom, but when she didn't bite, I hopped in the John

Deere and drove all over the property at midnight ... with no lights on. It's pitch black in the Montana countryside, so I ending up running through a couple of gates. Greer laughed his ass off as he watched me repair them the next day, refusing to help me because he thought I needed to learn a lesson and remember my stupidity. "Hell, no. I haven't forgotten. That's the point."

His fingers come up to hook my belt loops, and he jostles me side to side, sporting that lopsided grin. "You wanna make trouble."

"Well, I wouldn't want to be a bore," I deadpan, as I get in the John Deere. I pat the seat so he'll join me.

"Got room for one more at dinner?"

"Will you get drunk with me? It'll be more fun if we're both wasted," I singsong.

He just laughs at me, slides into the driver's side of the Gator, and punches the gas so we can go straighten shit out on the front twenty.

"SHH," I WHISPER loudly, which is probably more a shout than a whisper. Then I lose it because I'm incapable of whispering since I can't feel my teeth, my throat or my vocal chords.

"I'm being quiet," Greer replies. "You're the one kicking shit over."

I snort laugh. "Who the hell puts gardening tools in the path to the door?"

"Well, they weren't exactly in the path," he says with a laugh.

I prop myself on the garage wall and watch Greer's

strong backside as he examines my mom's Lincoln. And what a sight. His curls are shorter than usual right now from the cut he got over the summer. This tequila may have numbed some of my body parts, but others are on fire. "Come 'ere, Greer" I call out, with a chuckle. Hey, that rhymes.

He straightens up and turns to me. He pins with me with those striking blue eyes. "Did you do this?" he asks as he thumbs at the long, angry scratch on my mom's car.

I lose myself in those eyes for a minute. God, I just … "Greer, come here," I demand, a little less slurred this time.

A slow smile works its way up to his eyes as he strides toward me. He's far less drunk than I am, I think. "What, chicken?" he asks when he's a hair's breadth away.

I don't answer him with words. Pulling his face down to mine, I thread my fingers through his short hair. I kiss one corner of his mouth and pull back to smile at him before kissing the other corner. He releases a shaky breath and trembles against me. He loves it when I kiss him. If it were up to him, I think that's all we'd do. That and maybe second base since he loves to worship my tits. I giggle with that thought. He stares at me like I'm too good be true.

When he doesn't move to kiss me back, I kiss the tip of his nose and move my lips up the bridge, placing more light kisses until my lips meet the center of his forehead. I kiss one side and then the other. With a sigh, he brings his arms up to plant themselves on the wall behind me, like he has to hold himself up. I run my lips down his temple, over his cheekbone, and back toward his mouth.

When I'm a kiss away from his lips, he turns his head and presses the soft, plump flesh against me. A groan escapes me, and I swear I almost climax on the spot. He doesn't open his mouth, nor do I. He just moves his lips over mine, slowly, tantalizingly, until I almost come undone again. I can't take his teasing anymore, so my tongue darts out to taste him. His mouth opens immediately, and he nips at my tongue with his teeth. The once throbbing pulse in my center swells into a vigorous tattoo.

His hands come up to frame my face. "God, Denver, I love you so much," he rasps.

And I respond as I always do. "My Golden Boy," I whisper.

I wrap my arms around his waist and lay my head on his shoulder as I try to gather some strength to see my mother and Blake. Greer folds me in his arms and runs his hand over my hair. I've done everything within my power to avoid the both of them. I can't avoid my mother near as much as I'd like, as we do have to discuss the ranch from time to time. Any time I can get by with leaving a note on her computer, texting her or emailing her, I do. Blake's pretty easy to avoid, though. If he isn't stuck up my mother's ass, he's out with his friends or passed out in their bedroom. Any time I do see him, he still has that perverted glint in his eye, like he's imagining what I look like without my clothes or what it's like to be inside me, although I don't know that he'll do anything to me now. He's caught me alone a few times over the last year and hasn't tried anything. The looks, the stalking, the creepiness are all meant to terrorize me ... and they do. I'm jumpy. I'm paranoid. I'm a fucked-up mess.

"You ready?" Greer finally asks.

"I guess," I mumble, freeing myself from his arms.

"Denver, did you key your mom's car?" he asks me again.

I chuckle and run my tongue along the inside of my cheek. "What do you think?" I flash my eyebrows at him.

He whistles through his teeth. "I can't believe you did that," he whispers in awe.

"Why not? I told you I've been doing all kinds of vindictive shit to her. She's too stupid to figure out it's me."

The truth of the matter is I want to get caught. I want to hurt her. I want her to *know* that I want to hurt her. And then I want her to rant and rave and throw shit and cuss me out. Well, you know what they say ... people in hell want ice water, but that don't mean they're gonna get it. And I'm in hell.

"What do you think she's going to do when she figures out that you're the one behind all her flat tires, her many lost sets of keys, the scrapes down her car, the nest of rats in her linen closet ..." He fades out, probably trying to recall the rest of my pranks.

"Nothing. Absolutely nothing. You have to give a shit about someone to let the things they do rattle you. Whether its love or hate ... doesn't matter ... they both show you're affected. But nothing kills a soul more than indifference," I toss over my shoulder as we enter the house.

My buzz has worn off a little by the time we enter, so I go into the kitchen and make us another drink. My mother enters while I'm pouring a generous amount of Jim Beam in our glasses since we plowed through the tequila. She just cocks her at head at me. I slide my chin up and give her a shit-eating grin, daring her to chastise me. She doesn't.

"Denver," she says patronizingly, "I'm so glad we're gonna sit down and clear the air, honey." And her tone drips, saccharine sweet.

I clench my teeth and nod before grabbing our drinks and heading to the dining room. When I hit the room, my stomach twists free and drops. Blake is sitting at the head of the table, pointedly ignoring a vicious stare-down from Greer, who is standing next to the wall.

I steel myself and move toward Greer. I give him a fake smile and say in a haughty tone, "Dear, here's your cocktail." That earns me a laugh. A stilted laugh, but a laugh, nonetheless. I smile warmly at him and reach up to kiss his cheek.

He looks surprised, but I need him to know how much I appreciate him.

"Let's get this over with," I whisper. He inclines his head once.

I didn't think about how hard this would be on Greer, having to sit down with Blake and play nice. But I've already decided I'm not playing nice, so maybe that will take his mind off things.

My mom strides in wearing her low-cut black sweater dress with the wide rhinestone belt. When I hear her heels clicking, my eye is drawn to her feet. I gasp. She's wearing brand new shiny, red boots that look exactly like mine. I didn't notice them in the kitchen, but seeing them now makes my blood boil.

"Did you help yourself to my boots?" I bark.

Her head snaps back at my tone, and not a single Clairol #9A curl moves from its strategically placed position. She envies me my naturally, dirty-blonde hair. Her brown eyes narrow at me. "Do not speak to me that way, young lady. And for your information, these are *my* new boots."

That actually pisses me off even more. "You went out and bought the same boots that I have?" I shriek. "Boots that are meant for a *young* girl?" I mentally pat myself on the back. My mother hates anyone insinuating that she's aged past twenty-five.

"I saw these months ago at the Boot Depot, Denver. I just went back and bought them recently."

"You saw them when you met up with me and paid for my pair, is more like it. You just can't let anyone else have anything for themselves, can you?" I huff.

She slides into her chair next to Blake and places her hand on his, effectively ending our conversation, because I don't speak to her once she's attached herself to him.

"Greer," my mother finally acknowledges. I down some of my drink.

"Mrs. Brown, uh, Mrs. Tipple." My cheeks bulge with liquid since I can't swallow over my laugh and risk choking. "No, wait. Hold on. I got it. Mrs. Smallwood. No, that's not right either." He shakes his head, feigning confusion. "Damn, I can't for the life of me recall your *latest* married name."

"It's Mrs. Turner," she seethes, shooting daggers at Greer. "Your mother put up with that kind of sass, Greer?"

"My mother would applaud me for any insults I throw your way," Greer boasts.

My eyes widen, and I finally gulp down my drink. "Greer," I whisper, feigning outrage. "Is that any way to speak to your elders?"

He turns his focus back to me and shakes his head in disbelief. I lean in and whisper even lower, "Well played, sir."

"I've learned from the best," he says with a laugh.

Ms. Louise makes her way around the table serving up my favorite—Southwestern Enchiladas. Her eyes meet mine as she serves Greer, and she grins big. I love that woman! She made my favorite because she knew my mother was making me have dinner with her and Blake. She's not privy to all the details, but being as she's a live-in housekeeper and not blind, deaf, or dumb, she picked up on his nefarious demeanor and our issues. I want to kiss her, so when she gets to me, I do just that.

"Denver," my mother snaps.

"Yes?" I ask innocently.

She shakes her head at me. Giving her a dumbfounded look, I turn my attention to Ms. Louise, "Ms. Louise, how's your grandkid doing since his surgery?" I ask as I cut into my food, not waiting for anyone, knowing it irritates the shit out of my mother.

She gives me a knowing grin before she beams, "Oh, Ms. Denver, he's doing just fine. And he told me to tell you thank you for that generous gift basket too." She puts her hand on her hip and tsks. "You shouldn't have gone and sent that boy all that junk to get him through his recovery." Ms. Louise is definitely in on some of the ways I try to get under my mother's skin. She mostly just knows about the ridiculous shit I charge on her credit cards. My long-suffering mother was constantly having to cancel subscriptions to all sorts of crazy ass magazines—*Girls and Corpses*, *Bacon Busters*, and my personal favorite, *Miniature Donkey Talk*. But when Blake got his subscription to *Beefcakes a Go-Go*, I decided that nothing would top the shitstorm that ensued after the magazine catering to a hairy, gay men fetish arrived with his name all over it, so that was my final hurrah in unwanted magazine subscriptions. I promptly upped my game to renting seedy pay-per-view movies.

"Tell him he's welcome." I giggle when I imagine the sugar high he's been on. And strapped to a bed to boot. I bet his parents were ready to kill me. I look at Greer and confess, "I went online and ordered the biggest basket of candy I could find, and had it delivered to his house to aid in his recovery from his broken hip and leg." I grimace as I recall Ms. Louise telling me how he was dragged across her son's property while trying to break his new colt. I couldn't imagine being cooped up like that. I've been lucky as far as injuries go. The most I've ever had were sprained ankles, a couple of black eyes from getting head butted, and a sore rear end from having been thrown more than a few times.

My mother cuts through my memory in her annoyed tone, "And how, pray tell, did you pay for this extra-generous gift, Denver?"

"Your black Am Ex, of course," I mumble around a

mouthful of food.

"Young lady, I told you no more charges on that. I'm still paying off the arcade pinball machines you ordered that were nonrefundable," she bites out.

"And I just can't thank you enough for those. They are the most fun." I crack on the word fun as I make eye contact with Greer. Boy, had we made that machine go *Ding! Ding! Ding!*

My mother cuts off our laughter as she snaps, "Money's getting tighter, Denver. And besides, we have some news." Suddenly, I'm thrilled with our dinner. *Please be divorcing, please be divorcing.* She takes Blake's hand in hers again, and her face softens. *Yes!* How many times had I watched this scenario play out? "Blake and I are trying to get pregnant."

Have you ever been so instantly furious that your ears ring and your vision blurs? Yeah ... that. And it's not the tequila that I shot or the Jim Beam that I've been nursing that makes the room feel like it's closing in on me. Claustrophobia claws at me, and I want nothing more than to rip my clothes off and dart outside to be able to absorb oxygen through my pores 'cause there's no way I'd be able to breathe around this knot that's formed in my throat.

"A baby?" I hear someone whisper, and when all eyes fall on me, I realize it must've been me. I swallow hard. "How can you? Why would you?"

"Well, that's why money's tight, honey. We're having to use a reproductive specialist," she purrs. I glance to Blake and see the gleam in his eyes directed at her. *The worship.*

"He was gonna leave you, huh?" They both stiffen.

"He's gotten bored with you." She sucks in a breath, and I know I'm on to something. "He's just gonna leave you with *another* little brat to pawn off on the help and soak up your booze and whore herself out," I predict, knowing she'd have to survive like I had.

"Watch your mouth, young lady," she says.

I level my gaze on Blake. "You do realize that if you use all her ill-gained money on producing a kid, that you'll lavish your attention on instead of her, your marriage will be over? Your gravy train will derail. If she needs money, she'll move on to the next payday. If you're not worshiping her, she'll be on to the next sucker. This is lose/lose for you. You may as well start packing your bags." The extreme satisfaction I get from watching Blake squirm with what he knows is truth doesn't quite offset the hurt that consumes me, but it does help.

"You have no idea, do you?" My mother calmly asks.

I fix my stare on her. Not answering, knowing she will explain herself.

"This ranch was going under, Denver, when my momma and daddy died. The things I did, I did for you and your ungrateful self. All that money you spend on your horses, the traveling, the equipment, the clothes ... you think that just falls out of the clouds?"

Bullshit. "I give you every penny of my winnings to cover my expenses. And I work this ranch like a dog. You may be the one paying the bills, but it thrives because of me—my blood, my sweat, my desire to see it succeed."

"Pfft ... and that's not enough. You have no idea

what it takes. You have no idea what I've had to endure … and all for you. This," she covers Blake's hand again, "is my shot at happiness. I want to give Blake a child. You could try being happy for me for once."

Greer's hand squeezes mine, and I wonder how long he's been holding onto me. My eyes meet his to see tears shimmering in their blue depths. The skin around his eyes tightens, and he turns to my mother and says, "You don't even love the kid you've got. Why would you go and have another one? Just to save your sham of a marriage to the piece of filth who tried to rape your daughter?"

"He explained that. She—"

"She did nothing! She was innocent!" he roars.

The look my mother gives Greer can only be described as sorrowful—but not real sorrow, mocking sorrow. "Greer, you can't honestly believe that, can you? You've known Denver more than long enough to understand what she's made of. Ah," she whispers and smiles knowingly, "you're completely blinded by her."

Squeezing his hand, I pull his attention to me. "Greer, if my mother and Blake want to spawn a child, who are we to criticize?" My voice sounds detached, dead. I turn back to them. "I can only hope that you two have a boy. I wouldn't wish this kind of existence on what could be a fragile little girl because she wouldn't survive it." My eyes don't leave hers. "Greer, it's rare that I get to sit down and enjoy a meal. Let's finish eating."

Most nights, I microwave leftovers and eat in my room since I work the ranch or my horses as late as possible just so I can avoid situations like this. I'll be damned if they're going to keep me from enjoying my favorite dish. I don't know how I do it, but I chew and savor every bite even though Greer's comment rings in my head, *"You don't even love the kid you've got."* I think it. All the time. But to have it said aloud ... cuts deeply.

Greer and I clean our plates, and I'm up and moving while still chewing my last bite. I swallow a hunk of food because I can't resist getting in one last jab. Turning, I mockingly assess my mother's appearance. "Mom, you've done something different," I revere. She doesn't catch the not-so underlying sarcasm.

She touches her perfectly coifed hair, and then her hand flits to move around face. "Is it my new make-up?" she replies seriously.

"No," I hum, pretending to ponder. "Oh, I know!" I snap, slapping my hands together. She preens. "Your roots are showing," I deadpan.

I see her snort but can't hear her over Greer's roar of laughter.

GREER WALKS ME to my room after our disastrous dinner. When we're just outside my room, he pulls me back by my elbow and pushes me against the wall with his body. Intertwining our fingers, he rests his forehead against mine. "Jesus, I don't know how you live like this. You know, I already admired you," he confesses as his lips make contact with my forehead. "But seeing all that firsthand, I have a new level of respect. You're eighteen. You could ... leave."

"I can't leave. I have too much invested here." Lord

knows, I thought about it. "You're the only way I'm able to get through it," I whisper. "You and my horses. If it weren't for y'all ..." We're standing outside my bedroom. And I need him. I need him to make all that go away.

I push my butt off the wall and collide with him, rubbing myself against the front of his jeans. He hardens immediately. He's so weird about having sex when my mom and Blake are in the house, so I know he's going to take some convincing. I run my lips up his throat, teasing him with my tongue as I drop back down. I unravel our fingers and unsnap a button. Kiss. Another button. Lick. Another button. Bite. His hands trail around my hips to my behind, and he squeezes me to him. One hand runs down my thigh and latches onto the back of my knee as he brings my leg up to rest around his hip. I grind against him. "Mmm ... Greer. You feel so good sliding against me. I want you inside me."

He pauses from nipping at my ear. "Oh, yeah?" His smile presses against my throat.

"Oh, yeah," I moan. "Come in my bedroom with me?"

"'K," he readily agrees. *Yes!*

Opening my eyes is my first mistake. Glancing down *his* body is my second. "You sick fucker," I fume.

"Denver, what the—" Greer jerks back.

"Blake's the fuck. That's what." Greer spins around, but by then, Blake has his arms folded across his chest, the lustful look having disappeared as well.

"Denver, I don't think your mother would appreciate you bringing your boy toy into your room this late at night."

Greer slides in front of me, blocking my view of him. "You were told never to speak to her. I'm pretty sure we made that clear."

I slide my arms around Greer and pull him to me, standing on my tippy-toes to glare at Blake. He gives me an all too-knowing, all too-satisfied look. I see red.

I run one hand up Greer's chest and the other down until I reach his belt buckle; he stiffens under my hands. I plant a kiss on the side of his neck before looking back at Blake and offering, "Want to join us, or you just wanna watch?"

"Denver," Greer hisses.

Blake's look falls, and he suddenly looks disgusted.

"Oh … I get it," I hum. "Now that I'm Greer's whore, I'm not good enough to be yours."

He jerks back, blowing a quick breath through his nose, spins around, and heads back to his room.

Greer's head drops to his chest before he mumbles, "That wasn't right."

"What? Making him feel uncomfortable? I live for that." I run my hand down his jeans and try to bring him back to life.

His hand clasps mine, throwing it off. "I'm not in the mood anymore."

"C'mon, Greer. I need you," I beg in between the kisses I rain on his back.

Jerking out of my hold, he spins around and narrows his eyes at me. "Look," he demands, pointing his finger at me. "I know you're using me. I accepted that a long time ago. But not like this. I'm not fucking you like this."

"Like what?" I ask, playing dumb.

"While I feel this way ... while I feel this ... *used*."

ROLLING OVER, I groan as the beat in my head throbs harder. When Greer left me in an embarrassed, yet turned on, heaping pile of emotional shit, I went down and finished off the bottle of whiskey before stumbling back up here to collapse and pass out—fully dressed and spread-eagled across my bed.

God, I've said and done some stupid shit to Greer over the years, but last night I had really taken the cake, lined up my baseball bat, and smashed it to smithereens. I've stooped to an all-new level of low. Allowing others to control my emotions was stupid and pointless and unforgivable. *I* should be in control of how I feel, how I behave. I'm going to be out of here in four months. Controlling myself for that long shouldn't be a problem. First up, no more using Greer. Of course, I knew I was using him. I knew he was aware of that too, but he's never called me on it quite like that before. And after everything he's done for me, I can't continue to hurt him like this. I have to find other ways to numb myself. I whisper a prayer of thanks again for the fact that he's going off to Wyoming for college. I'll miss him. Every single day. But I know this is what's best for him. And for me.

Reaching blindly for my nightstand, I hear several things crash to the floor before my hand curls around my cell.

I pull up his contact information and stare at his face for moment. I've never figured out how someone could look so angelic and so rugged at the same time, but he always manages to pull it off. His look is so unique, so striking, that it didn't matter where in the country we traveled to, people always paused to appreciate it.

I snapped this picture of him while we were lying alongside one another down by our creek. It was our traditional first ride this past summer. I dozed off for a few minutes until I stirred, feeling overly heated from him devouring me with his eyes. I peeked out at him with one eye, and the look I'd felt him giving me didn't change.

"Don't move," I whispered, sliding the phone out of my pocket and snapping his picture.

"Why'd you take that?" he asked.

"Because I've never seen anyone else look at me like that ... and I don't ever want to forget it."

"Like what?"

"Like I'm the most precious thing you've ever seen."

"I'll never let you forget that," he vowed, sealing it with a kiss.

That ever-endearing look disappears as my phone times out, and I unlock it quickly to bring him back up.

How 'bout mending fences?

I have to wait several minutes for him to respond. **Meet you by the barn in 30.**

K

Once he shows up, I've got the Gator packed and

ready to go. He jumps in without a word, and I whisk us off to the back forty. The sounds of hammers, the rough-cut saw, and the wildlife that teems back here, usually undisturbed, are the only noises that ring out for hours. Without even discussing the process or who will do what, Greer and I work side-by-side, in sync with one another while repairing the fence that runs between our properties.

Again I find myself wondering why I can't accept all that Greer offers me. Why I can't be whole. Why I can't be normal. I remind myself that, while he thinks himself in love with me, it's only because he doesn't see the real me. If he saw the real me, he'd run for the hills. Well, he did get a glimpse of the real me last night and did run.

When we've run out of materials, I drive the John Deere into the little meadow that is surrounded by a circle of trees. The barrenness of winter has crept over the land, leaving trees to look like they're made of only sticks, and a wide-open space filled with dead, brown grass. When the wildflowers bloom back here in the springtime, it looks like an alternate universe. How can something so utterly dead be brought to life like that?

Killing the engine, I sit for a few minutes before breaking the engulfing silence. "I'm sorry, Greer." I don't even look over at him.

"Me too."

"Are you kidding me?" I finally glance at him. "You have nothing to be sorry for. You've never done anything but be there for me. God, what a curse that's been laid upon you ... I can't believe He burdened you with me."

"If you're a curse, then I'm gladly damned," he whispers, running his calloused thumb along my jaw. "I shouldn't have said that last night about you using me." I start to speak, but he silences me with a look. "You can't use someone who is willing, Denver. That was stupid of me. I knew what I was doing when I got into this with you. You laid all your cards on the table. I just always hoped that you'd move beyond all that pain, all that self-hatred, and see me. See me, waiting here for you. Accepting you. Wanting you." His thumbs sweep up to run under my eyes to catch my tears.

The pain-riddled words ... kill me ... but make me stronger at the same time. "We can't do this anymore, Greer. I can't use you like that anymore. What you saw last night ... that is the real me. I still want us to be friends, but no more screwing around. I can't be the cause of all *your* pain anymore," I punch through my tear-laden voice.

He opens his mouth, looking determined to argue with me but snaps it back closed before mumbling, "Shh ... come on. Let's eat." He climbs out of the front of the Gator and walks around to the back.

While we're eating Greer regales me with story after story of our youth and all the trouble we stirred up around here, which soon has me laughing the sweet kind of tears. He says he's getting sentimental since our time is getting short.

"Do you think you'll come back here?" I ask him.

His brow furrows. "Of course I'm coming back here." He hesitates for a second. "Are you thinking of not coming back?"

"I don't know. Sometimes I think it'd be best not to.

If I win enough money on the circuit, I can buy my own place and start over. I don't know if I even want to have a place this big and run a cattle ranch on my own. I'm thinking I'll just stick to breeding and training barrel horses."

"On your own …" He leaves the words hanging in the air.

"Greer," I whisper. He has to know that we'll never be together.

"I'm not dating anyone," he states. I turn to him and see sheer panic burning in his eyes. I tilt my head, wondering where he's going with this, and his mouth slams down onto mine. I wince and cry out. His hands are in my hair, pulling me back and drawing me in simultaneously. For a moment, I revel in his rough but worshipful assault. His tongue thrusting in and out of my mouth reminds me of what I am trying to break off with him.

I pull back slightly. "Greer, no. We can't. Not anymore," I mumble against his lips. He pulls my head back by my hair and works his lips down my throat while one hand begins to unzip my jacket. He's so practiced with me that in seconds, he has my shirt unbuttoned and my lace-covered nipple in his mouth.

"Greer," I groan, as he tugs and pulls with his teeth. "Please. Stop."

Both of his hands move to cover my breasts, and I hear a rip before his rough hands massage me. My head falls back, and I whimper, my reasoning for not doing this quickly evaporating. I grasp at the vapors of my argument once more. "No, I don't want to do this anymore," I try again. It sounds weak, even to my own ears.

"Do what?" he murmurs around his sucking and his kissing.

"Use you anymore."

He tilts his body to the side and shoves his hand down my jeans, his finger sliding into me with ease. "Then I'll use you," he rasps. My resolve shatters as his finger works in and out of me, rotating and pinching over my little bud before he pushes back in again and again until I am an incoherent, writhing mass beneath him. He slips his hand out and stands. "Take your clothes off," he tells me.

I shake my head at him. "You do it."

He shoves his jeans down to his ankles. Grasping my boots, he tugs them off and yanks me to the edge of the tailgate. Standing me up, he unzips and whips my jeans down, making me step out of them. My body burns with the heat of a thousand suns. Grabbing our jackets, he lines the bed with them.

His eyes find mine, his look piercing me. "If having you like this is all I get, then I'll take it. Haven't you realized that I need you too? If you're using me, I assure you that it's a two-way street."

"How exactly are you using me?" I gasp.

"I use this—" he runs the back of his hand down my neck, between my breasts, over my stomach, and flips it to lightly cup the vee between my legs "—to be close to you. To be a part of you."

Grabbing his hand, I force him inside of me. "Use me, Greer," I groan.

Before I see him moving, he's thrown me back into the bed and has my legs splayed open before him. He hooks one leg around the roll bar and slams into me at the same time. I grind myself against him as he hammers into me. "Use me," I demand over and over again until my voice grows hoarse, and it becomes a pleading whisper. And every time I do, his thrusts grow harder and harder. Just when I think it can't get anymore intense, he loops his arm under my other leg and drapes it around the other bar. Clutching my hips, he relentlessly drives into me until I shriek his name and lose myself in an aching cloud of ecstasy.

WE DON'T SAY a word until we're both dressed and sitting back in the front of the Gator. If it weren't for the cold settling in, after the incredible things he made me feel, I'd still be lying back there, panting for air. As it is, I'm trying to calm my breathing and my hands before I drive us back to the barn. I turn to see how Greer's holding up. His head is resting on the back of the seat, a content smile on his full lips. I can't resist. I lean in and give him a little kiss on his bottom lip, making his mouth twitch. He gives me a wide-eyed look.

"What?"

"Surprised me," he says.

"Sorry," I grumble.

He pulls me by my neck back to him and gives me a better kiss. "Don't be sorry. I've got one thing going for me that means everything," he whispers against my lips.

"What's that?"

"You find me irresistible," he says with a smug grin. I chuckle against him for a second before straightening back up. He is so right, but the thought that plagues me rears its ugly head—is it him that I can't resist or the escape he offers me?

Just as I turn the ignition key, a random thread from last night's conversation tugs at me. My head darts his way. "What did you mean last night when you said 'we' told you not to speak to her? Who's 'we'?"

Bracing his foot on the dash, he brushes an almost-invisible piece of dirt from his knee. "I was hoping you didn't catch that."

"Greer," I warn.

"Chicken," he says with a catch. "My dad and I confronted him. My dad threatened that if we got word of him messing with you again, or so much as speaking to you, he'd trump up some charges and have him arrested."

Turning away from him, I stare out over the field for a few moments as I let that sink in. "You told your dad … what he did."

He blows out a resigned breath. "I tell my dad everything. I only wish I'd told him before …"

"Before what?" I ask, looking back at him.

Giving me a rueful smile, he whispers, "Before we made our arrangement."

It hits me that neither of us ever thought to tell another adult besides my mother. We trusted her to keep me safe, which, in retrospect, was beyond naïve. When that didn't work, I took matters into my own impulsive, immature hands, and now look at the damage I've caused him. Could all of that have been prevented if we had gone to Judge Tanner first? The thought is too depressing, by far, so I dismiss it.

I glance over at Greer, who is warily regarding me,

and joke, "You owe me a bra."

"What?" he laughs.

"You ripped my bra, sir," I say with flourish. "A true gentleman would replace it."

He doesn't miss a beat. Giving me an impossibly naughty look, he reminds, "You don't like it when I'm a gentleman, remember, dear?"

"On this, I will have to insist," I say proudly.

Chapter Thirteen

Then

"I'D DO ANYTHING for you. Haven't I proven that time and time again?"

I run a hand over my chest, trying to catch my breath, before pulling my bra over my breasts and fastening the buttons of my shirt. "Yes, you have. And what you just did for me was ... incredible."

I hear him zip before he props himself up on his elbow. Leaning over me, he kisses me softly on the cheek. "It's empty. Meaningless. What we have. We're getting ready to go off to college, go our separate ways for a while. I don't want anyone else. I'll never want anyone else ... I want us to go our separate ways—but together."

I laugh when he nips my chin with his teeth. "Greer, what does that even mean?"

"It means that I'm yours, and you're mine. We may be a few hours away from each other, but we'll see one another on the road and when we come home to visit. And we're ... together. Like a real couple. That's what I want. And I know somewhere deep down that's what you want too."

My eyes mist over as I take in his earnest look. I don't respond.

"Dammit," he says softly before he sits up to put his boots on.

The sane, rational part of me screams, *Yes! Yes, I want to be yours, and I want you to be mine.* But the damaged place that's in control says, *No. No way. You'll destroy him just like your mother did your father. And here's your chance to end this. Out of sight, out of mind. He'll meet someone amazing and move on.*

He springs up, picking his shirt up along the way. Exhaling, he brings it up over his head and stretches it out with both hands. He's grown taller but remained lithe, and his muscles were compact things that were way stronger than they appeared. My eyes run down his frame and linger on his trim hips for a second before his shirt hits me in the face.

"Quit objectifying me," he barks out. "I already feel like a piece of meat to you most of the time."

"You shouldn't feel that way," I protest.

"Don't tell me how to feel, Denver."

"I—"

Whatever I was going to say dies out as he shouts, "Life or death!" I sit up and start to ask him what he means, but he's moving quickly to the opening of the loft. "Life or death situation," he says as he teeters on the edge. "You have to choose. Be with me, or watch me bite it? What's it gonna be? Come on, Denver," he cajoles me with a laugh.

I laugh loudly at his over-the-top ultimatum.

His face falls, and his eyes bore into mine. "I'm

serious."

I shake my head.

"Choose."

"No."

"OK," he says with a shrug before propelling himself backwards from the top of my barn.

"No!" I scream, as I scramble to the edge. I mean, it's not a big enough drop to kill him, but it could hurt him.

When I peer over at him, he's lying in the middle of the corral on a pretty large chunk of the bales of hay that we threw out for the horses earlier. He looks like he's about to make a snow angel, or hay angel, as the case may be. I giggle at him. Idiot. "Denver Magnolia Dempsey, will you be mine?"

"Go home. You're drunk!" I joke, trying to distract him.

He shakes his head at me. "I'm serious."

I want to scream at him for pushing me. But I don't have the right. And he wouldn't understand my truth anyway—I can't be his when I'm not mine to give. I'm a slave to my emptiness. It's stolen into every aspect of me and owns me so thoroughly.

"I'm giving you as much of myself as I'm able, Greer," I say, slightly above a whisper.

He closes his eyes and nods. "Your body will have to do for now," he says after a minute. "Can you come help me up? I think I broke my ankle."

I shimmy down the ladder and make my way over to him. "You're crazy you know that," I say as I take his hands in mine.

"Crazy for you," he whispers. He winces when I

pull him to his feet. "I really did hurt myself," he mutters, astonished.

"Idiot," I say aloud this time.

A PERSISTENT BUZZING wakes me up. Pulling my phone from my nightstand, I hold it in front of my one opened eye before rolling them both at Greer's smirk on the screen. "What Greer?"

"Hey, Denver. It's not Greer. It's Walt."

Wide-awake, I sit straight up. "What's wrong?"

"Umm ..."

"Is he hurt?"

Walt hesitates for a second, but it feels like a year. "Not like you think. He's just drunk. I can't bring him home or to my house. He told me to call you."

"Of course he did."

"Want me to take him home anyway? He can deal with the consequences."

"No," I say running my hand over my hair as I think fast. "His parents would freak. Bring him to the barn. I have a bed in the tack room. He can sleep it off in there."

"'K. Thanks, Denver."

"Yep," I say quickly before disconnecting. It's my fault he's acting like this anyway. After his ultimatum in the barn, he left to go hang out with his buddies since I had to pack to go to my dad's. He told me he was going to go drink me off his mind. I begged him not to. We usually reserved drinking for hanging out in my barn where nothing bad could happen. He told me there was only one thing that could keep him from going and doing just that. I didn't respond. And at my silence, he left.

I texted him on and off throughout the night, trying to check on him. He ignored me all night until he sent me a picture of him with his tongue down some random chick's throat with the caption. "I'm good. Real good."

Asshole.

Bitch, I promptly remind myself.

After throwing on some boots and a hoodie over my pajamas, I grab an extra blanket out of the closet before heading out to the barn.

Walt's pulling up as I open the door. Greer swings from the truck as soon as it comes to a stop. "Hey, baby," he shouts. "My ankle don't hurt no more. All healed!"

I roll my eyes. More like too drunk to feel. Walt jumps out and steadies him as he walks him over to me. "You sure you can handle him? I can call my mom and make something up so I can stay."

I blow out a breath and look at Greer's now-slack face. "No, it's fine. I'm just gonna put him down in here, and we'll both go to sleep."

"You make me sound like one of your horses, Denver. Not your property," Greer slurs.

"Whatever, Greer. You know what I meant."

Walt helps me get him situated, and I walk him out so that I can close up behind him. He thanks me again and tells me briefly how out of control Greer had gotten that night.

"Y'all having problems?"

"No. Why?" Lie.

"He kept saying 'If your best friend doesn't love you, nobody will.' Then he was taking polls on how many people had been broken-hearted and all kinds of shit. I've never seen him act like that."

I nod because I have, to some extent. He can't hold his liquor. Beer? He was good. Not so much with the hard stuff. "We had a little fight. He's not happy with our going to different schools. And I'm leaving for Mississippi tomorrow."

"Ah. Well, he, uh … he loves you. If you should ever stop … um, you know, he'd be there for you."

Walt is a good guy. He's the only one of Greer's friends who'll even speak to me. So I feel about two inches tall when he hints at my reputation. "We'll be fine," I say with a pasted grin. "He just needs to sleep it off."

We say our good nights. I lock up and find my way back to the tack room. I have a daybed in there for when one of the animals is sick or due to have a baby. I'm glad it's big enough for me to crash with him. I really don't want to leave him alone.

I lock the tack room door behind me and move through the room, grateful for the moonlight guiding my way. I toe off my boots and climb under the covers with him. Wrapping my arm around him, I fit myself to his back. Curling up to Greer is the most natural thing in the world. I kiss his neck before laying my head down beside his. Closing my eyes, I allow myself to drift to one of my favorite daydreams. The one where I'm not evil, Greer's not bitter, and we're happy together. I'm only happy there for about thirty seconds.

"Did you kiss him?"

"What?"

"Walt? Did you kiss him?"

"No, Greer," I snap, my annoyance seeping

through. "Go to sleep."

"Why not?"

"Because I had no desire to."

"I tried to fuck that girl in the picture I sent you," he confesses, pain lacing his words.

I take in a swift breath. That's not Greer. He doesn't talk like that. He doesn't think like that. And in that second, I know beyond a shadow of a doubt that I've thoroughly damaged him even though keeping him at bay was supposed to protect him. I've made him paranoid and needy and insecure. These little moments had been coming with more frequency of late, and I could no longer deny the facts.

"I take it you weren't successful," I mutter.

He shakes his head. "I wanted to. I wanted to so bad. I need to be rid of you. Couldn't do it."

Despite my numb state, that hurts. The pain flips on me, though, and twists into what looks like hope. He's breaking things off with me. Finally, he'll end this. He's stronger than me. He'll do it, and then he'll be free. And I'll be … I don't know exactly. I guess I'll be free too. Free of guilt, free to float off into the ether, free to figure out what the hell I am.

"I'm sorry, Greer," I whisper. He just grunts. And we both slip into sleep.

I smell leather, oats, and horse. Why? Ah … I'm in the tack room with Greer after his drunken night. Him ending things with me punches me in the gut. I shift a little under the pain. Better me than him, I remind myself.

I sense him staring at me. I let out a shaky breath. This is going to hurt. I hate to lose my best friend, but

I've done it all by myself, so I was going to have to bite the bullet and deal. And he's going to be so much better off without me. Ah ... I chant—*Greer is better without you, Greer is better without you*. And repeat.

"I know you're awake," his whisper raspy.

My eyes fly open. I smelled it on him with the booze, but thought it was *on* him not *in* him. "Were you smoking last night?"

"What the hell do you care?"

I narrow my eyes at him. "You know I care about you."

"I do?"

"Of course."

"Just not enough to act like it."

I close my eyes tight so that I don't give in to the hurt I'll see there. "I want you to leave here today and forget about me. Go to college and find someone amazing. Someone who deserves you. Someone who would never hurt you the way I do."

"Let me guess. You're off to find someone else too. I'm not enough for you somehow."

I open my eyes so he can see the truth there. "It's not about you, Greer. You've never been the problem. It's about me." My hand subconsciously moves to where my heart should be. "I don't have it in me."

"You did at one time. I remember. I saw it when we looked at each other. I felt it when we kissed. I heard it in our conversations. It was so strong that I could taste it. Hell, all my senses fired with it. You couldn't have faked them all out, so I know it was real." His voice had gotten louder with each word. He pauses to calm himself, but I have nothing, so he continues, quieter now. "But that's not there anymore. And I want that back. Don't you? How can we get that back?"

I swing my legs over the side of the bed and throw my hands out in despair. He's beating a dead horse, yet again. "I'd give anything for that to happen," I say through gritted teeth. "But I'm not that girl anymore. I wish I were. But I'm just … not." One hand stills while the other beats at the empty hole in my chest as if I can massage it back to life. "If I could do it for anyone, Greer, please know that you are the one person I'd do it for."

A single tear slips down his cheek. "If you wanted it bad enough, you'd make it happen. Look at everything you've accomplished with little to no help from anyone. You're the strongest person I've ever known."

But I'm not strong. That's just it. I'm too weak to allow myself to feel—that is what's wrong with me. Fear claws at my throat, and I rush out, "Not when it comes to this! I'm not strong enough to let you hurt me!"

He drops his head, shaking it. "I'd never hurt you on purpose."

A jaded laugh cuts across the room. "Did you catch your little qualifier? 'Cause I sure did."

"So where do we go from here?" he asks, jerking his hands through his hair.

"We go to school and recover from how I fucked up our once beautiful, once perfect relationship. When we see each other over the holidays, we'll be reset, reborn."

"And …"

"And that's it," I whisper, wearied. "Friends, Greer."

"Back to just friends."

We sit and stare at each other for a few minutes before he stands and puts his hands on his hips. Finally, he walks over to me and bends, placing his lips on the top of my head. "Tell your dad I said hello," he murmurs against my head. I nod under his touch. "Don't forget me while you're away." I shake my head fiercely. "I'm not saying goodbye. OK? So … I'll see you soon." And with that he strides out of my life.

Chapter Fourteen

Now

"YOU JUST SIGHED an entire cloud. Thinking about me again?" Austin whispers in my ear.

I throw my head back and groan as he slides into the seat next to me, cackling like a fat kid on a chocolate high.

"You've got to be kidding me," I complain. I had three classes today—all of which Ransom's cousin, Austin, is in. He spotted me every time too and sat right next to me. He spent half the class writing me dirty notes and the other half giving me naughty looks.

"Aw … come on. You love me. Admit it," he says as he spins my desk toward his. "I'm gonna venture to say that this is fate at its finest."

"Oh, yeah. How's that?" I can't help but ask. He is kind of funny and endearing in a most annoying way.

"Denver." He points at me. "Austin." He thumps himself and raises his brow.

"You, Austin. Me, Denver. You swing from vine lately?" I quip, in a weird cavegirl voice.

He bursts out laughing. "Ah, good one," he cries.

"No, seriously." His smile drops just as quick. "We're both named after two legendary U.S. cities. Obviously, we're meant to be together and have children named Dodge, Las Vegas, and Amarillo."

"Las Vegas?" I say with horror.

"So you're good with Dodge and Amarillo then? I can compromise on the other," he deadpans with a shrug and a mischievous grin.

"Denver!" Maggie squeals from the door before rushing toward us. "Hey, Austin!"

"What's up? Hey, how'd I end up in so many classes with you two freshmen anyway?"

"They're called Advanced Placement classes." He gives me a blank look. "We took college level classes in high school so we could get a head start?"

Recognition dawns in his eyes before they brighten with mischief. "Aw, shit. I just aced three of my classes. Fucking sweet!"

"You're not cheating off us," Maggie and I cry together.

"C'mon," he cajoles. "Doesn't matter, since this is my last year anyway."

"Why? Aren't you a sophomore?" Maggie asks.

He blows out a breath. "Yeah, but I'm not college material. The only reason I'm here is 'cause Ransom didn't want me on the pro circuit without him. He graduates in May. I'm sticking a fork in my college experience. And we're hitting the road."

"Why didn't Ransom want you going pro without him?"

He gives me that already-infamous Austin grin. "Thinks I'll get in trouble out there. Can you believe that shit?" he asks, dumbfounded.

"Yes," we answer in unison.

"Anyway, I don't want to cheat off of you." He takes on a faraway, dreamy look. "I'm seeing lots of study sessions where y'all only wear those cute little boy shorts that no real boy'd ever wear, and those tops that look like bras. Oh," he moans, "and pillow fights and back rubs that turn into—"

"Speaking of sports bras," Maggie cuts in, taking the focus of Austin's wet daydream. "We're working out after class."

"Uh ... I don't work out."

She gasps. "How do you keep that fabulous body?"

"Mmm, that's a cornbread-fed girl right there, Maggie," he declares as he slaps the side of my thigh. I kick him in the shin. He better be glad I wasn't wearing boots. "Ow!" His voice drops down an octave and his eyebrows shoot up. "I just meant don't change one ... healthy ... inch."

"You're incorrigible."

"You say that like it's a bad thing," he smirks.

I turn back to Maggie. "I don't know. I don't work out though."

"You worked your ranch, didn't you?" I nod. "You're not doing near as much here. You don't want to get flabby." She peeks around me to eyeball Austin. "Even if you do have wonderful curves."

I'VE NEVER BEEN so miserable in my life. I'd rather load a hundred bales of hay, drive cattle for two weeks straight, and deliver fifty colts single-handedly, than run on another damn treadmill for an hour. At least when I did my farm work, I had shit to show for it. I just ran in place for an hour. She *made* me run on it for an hour. *An hour!* I scream in my head as I push the door open to the locker rooms. Then she wanted me to get a bicycle that went nofreakingwhere for—an hour! Umm ... no, thank you. I stumble into the locker room, wiping a towel across my sweaty face.

Dropping the towel to my neck, I glance around and see guys. Lots of hot guys in various stages of undress, standing around, and in what is clearly a boxing ring. Oh, sweet goodness. I gawk for a couple more seconds before slowly beginning to back out of the room.

"Denver?" a familiar voice says.

Shit, shit, shit. I glance over to my right and see a half-dressed, sweat-drenched Ransom standing by a big bag suspended from the ceiling.

"Hi, Ransom," I say with confidence, like I belong here.

"You box?"

"Oh, sure," I reply, stepping toward him.

"Really?" He cocks a brow at me.

"No, not really. Is it a good workout? 'Cause I never wanna see another treadmill in my life. Why would people torture themselves like that? You just run in place, staring at the same thing. For. Ever."

He laughs at me. "You should just run outside then. Campus has pretty running trails."

"I think I will," I groan, blowing out a resigned breath. "I can't take that again."

He bumps his gloves together and suggests, "You can take up boxing too. It's never boring."

I consider this for a minute. It does sound like fun. "I don't know how. Do they have a class?"

"I think so," he says, as he looks back at his bag and scratches his head with his gloved hand. "I could show you a few moves."

"That'd be cool. But I don't have any gloves or anything."

He motions me over. Bending toward his bag, he retrieves a pair of lightweight gloves.

"These are wrap gloves. You can use them for now. I can help you pick out some real gloves if you want to continue."

He pulls off the ones he's wearing and shoves them under his arms while he helps me with the extra pair. His eyes shine bright with excitement.

"Have you ever hit a heavy bag before?"

"No, but I punched a cow once."

He grins. "Only once?"

"Yeah, she was standing on my foot." I shrug. "Self-defense."

He laughs lightly. "All right," he says as he pulls his gloves back on and repositions himself in front of his bag. "You want to stay light on your feet. Basically, that means your balance and your focus is on your core. That's the first thing you focus on 'cause that's most important. Every punch you throw comes from here," he grunts as he hits his abs with his gloved hand a couple of times. Now my focus is on *his* core. Good Lord. He's freaking ripped. Why didn't I notice those first? Ah! The eyes. The eyes get me every time.

He throws several punches, talking me through each one.

"Your turn," he says. His voice has dropped an octave, making him sound all hoarse and sexy.

Moving behind the bag, he holds it for me while I imitate his stance and his punches. "Good," he calls out. He names the punches and gives them numbers. Then he calls out a series of numbers. I rapidly punch them out as quickly as he calls them. "You're a natural little fighter," he says with admiration. I can't help but flash a cheesy smile.

Stepping away from the bag, he circles behind me and runs a gloved hand over my stomach, reminding me to balance and keep my core tight. My breath hitches in my throat when his hand comes to rest lightly on my stomach. He calls out another series of numbers. If I didn't want to impress him so badly, my arms would flop like limp, cooked noodles. It's everything I can do to focus on my actions and not on that tortuous, gloved hand.

"You're a quick learner," he praises.

"Maybe you're a good teacher," I choke out.

"I doubt it," he says with a laugh as he drops his hand and steps away. "It took Austin months to learn the numbers. By the way, he won't shut up about having so many classes with you."

I chuckle at that. "We just got done for today."

"Oh, he's been texting me all day ... trying to make me jealous, I think." He winks at me.

He. Winks. At. Me.

"Oh," I utter, suddenly embarrassed. "He wants to have a bunch of babies with me and name them weird city names," I blurt out.

He shakes his head and grins. "Not surprised ...

Denver? That is an unusual name." Ransom leans against the wall and, snagging a bottle of water, squirts some into his mouth. I swallow hard as a few drops trickle down his chin and to his neck, drawing my eyes to his thumping pulse.

"Yeah, not named after the city though," I mumble, distracted. Observing the drops of water and his sweat collide over his beating pulse has me yearning to lick him clean with my tongue. *Holy shit*.

He motions with the bottle of water. I reach for it to get my fill, but he shakes his head at me.

"Tilt your head back," he insists. When in Rome? I can't believe I don't choke as he shoots water into my mouth. I'm sure I don't look half as sexy as he did. I'm thirsty, but it's hard to swallow past my other craving. "So … you're named after …"

"John Denver, the musician. My mom was a huge fan, which is odd 'cause she's like the antithesis of poetry and hearts and flowers. Anyway, she wanted me to have a strong name. You know, strong name for a frail girl." I lean in. "She really wanted a boy."

He laughs. "I'm glad she didn't get her wish."

"Why's that?"

"It'd be kinda weird for me if you were a guy," he declares with a shrug and a look that says everything. Cue the butterflies. Massive swarms of them. "What kind of middle name would go with Denver?"

I groan and pinch my lips together. "Well, my dad wanted something girly and something to represent his neck of the woods, Mississippi." He gives me a go-on look. "Magnolia," I say with my head up. I secretly love my middle name, but that love hadn't come until about two years ago. I thought it weird, and not in a good way, so I always wanted Jennifer or Stacy or Michelle. Something feminine and normal. But then, I figured I no longer gave a shit about normal, and embraced it.

He squirts some more water in his mouth before he replies. "You're just full of contradictions from the start, aren't you?"

"What do you mean?"

"A poet ... a flowery tree ... a fighter."

"A fighter?" I ask, trying in vain to ignore the thrill that races through me at the way he analyzed my name and my personality.

"Oh, you have to know who Jack Dempsey was."

I suck air through my teeth and nod my head up and down but squeak out a, "No," since I can tell it means something to him.

"Oh, Denver Magnolia Dempsey," he chastises. "We are gonna have to fix that." And I like the way he says *we*.

After we say our goodbyes, I, in essence, float to the locker rooms. I replay every look, every uttered word. Everyone and everything is a million miles away, and I'm suspended in a fog of desire and intrigue. Oh my God, I'm such a girl. But, it can't be helped; he's just so ... dreamy. I roll my eyes at myself. Looking across the room, I see the same exact look I imagine on my face, mirrored in Maggie's. Her eyes meet mine in the mirror, and she grins big.

"I ran into Pete," she beams.

"And I ran into Ransom," I don't beam. I narrow my eyes and try to shake my hazy state.

Chapter Fifteen

Ransom

"NO WAY SHE'S gonna jump from that rope swing. It has to be over thirty feet in the air," Becky grumbles.

"Thirty-two," I mutter absentmindedly.

"Jesus, and not even covering herself. It'd serve her right for her to lose her bathing suit," Amber says, seeming not to notice my comment. I start to consider their open hostility toward Denver, but I get distracted.

Utterly fascinated, I stare as Denver hikes her bikini clad ass up the slope to climb the ladder, intending to do what most guys never think twice about, most girls would never consider doing, and what could likely get her hurt. A miscalculation of when to let go—too soon, too late, too high, too low—of course, the threat of danger is the appeal.

I should stop her, but I won't. I'm itching to see what she does, as messed-up as that is. What's more, I still haven't been able to take my eyes off of her delectable ass. That ass moves like it knows it's the best thing around. It. Just. Is. She's not even working it like so many girls do, vying for attention. I finally pull my gaze from the very generous half-globes. My eyes work down to take in her toned calves and slender ankles. One of them has a silver chain looped around it. Looking back up, I skim over her body. She's pulled her hair from its braid and has shaken the dirty-blonde locks loose. It hangs in long waves and sweeps the middle of her shoulder blades—I want to wrap it around my fist.

When she gets to the top, Denver turns to scale the rungs to the platform. That's when I get the full view of the tiny red triangles covering her beautiful, full breasts and the vee between her legs. My jaw ticks, and I almost call out to her to get the fuck away from the platform ladder.

Why? Fucking Austin is right behind her, licking his lips and laughing up a storm. I glance around for Greer but don't see him. He'd be freaking the fuck out right about now.

"Oh, Denver," Austin moans, exaggeratedly. "Will you marry me?" All the rest of the guys headed to the platform laugh and carry on.

"For the fifth time today, yes Austin, I will marry you," Denver says as she reaches the top and grabs Austin's arms, hauling him to the sturdy wood that she will catapult herself from in just a moment. My damn heart is about to beat out of my chest—98% excitement, 2% fear. "Just remember I like to spend lots of money, I don't bathe, take orders, give head—" she pauses "—massages." Unfurling the rope, she walks it to the back edge of the platform.

"Baby, you could just stand there for all I care. I'd be happy just to call you mine."

"What the fuck?" I hear from behind me.

I glance over my shoulder at Greer. "You gonna stop her?"

"And get my ass kicked?" he laughs. "Hell, no. She's knows what she's doing. I would like for Austin to get his slimy eyes off of her, though."

"He's harmless. She knows that."

"Didn't you tell me he's your cousin?"

"Yep," I say with a shake of my head. "Sure is."

Greer throws me a grimace. "Too bad he doesn't act more like you."

Laughing, I look back to Denver. He *should* be happy I'm not like Austin. Austin's on the up and up about his desire for Denver. Mine is secret, making it all the more real, and all the more dangerous.

She's pulled the rope back to the jumping off point and looks confused. "Austin," she says, cocking a hip and putting a hand on it. "How did you say this goes again?"

"Oh, just let Austin get behind you, so he can tutor you." He moves behind her. "I'm a believer in hands on instruction, Denver. You good with that?"

"Touch me, and I'll elbow you in the face."

"Aw, you're sucking the fun out of the whole experience. And that's one of the few times that sucking happens to be frowned upon," he grunts since Denver has made good on her threat to throw an elbow. Fortunately for him, she aims for his stomach not his face. "OK … you're gonna step back to gain some momentum before you throw your legs around the rope and hold the knot between your feet." He puts his hands out and looks like he's mimicking stroking his dick and not giving her instructions on how not to maim or kill herself. Denver looks at his hand placement and just shakes her head. "Once you get those legs around that rope, you're gonna clench your butt cheeks real hard. I need to see those muscles moving from here. Got it?" She nods. "When you feel like you're about to swing back in, that's as far out as you're going and ... let go. You can fold your arms around your legs so as not to hurt your ... pretty pink taco," he finishes with a wink and grin.

Everybody cracks up except for the girls who mutter, "Gross." He steps back and scratches his head. "On second thought, odds of you coming out of those bottoms are greater if you don't bend your legs."

She throws her head back in laughter and shakes her hair around so that it's all out of her face. "Thanks, Austin. Anything else?"

Austin slaps her on her ass and says, "Don't forget to scream my name."

"Got it."

She steps back, gets her momentum, and swings out over the creek. Her hair streams straight back, looking like stardust as the light filters through it.

Austin groans and yells, "Denver, please know I'm picturing you naked right now, and I'm the rope you're wrapped around."

I hear her laughter over all the others. When she peaks, she throws herself backward, tucking her legs in the tight circle her arms have formed. "Hell, yeah!" she shouts as she somersaults doing not one but two flawless back flips. She straightens at the last possible second to dive under the water.

"Argh!" she howls as she pops back up like a cork.

"This shit's cold! Two perfect back flips. Beat that, boys!"

"You big tease," Austin shouts from the platform as all the guys below cheer and whistle. "You said you were a virgin."

"You made it feel like my first time all over again, Austin," she teases and blows him a kiss.

For the record, I've never before in my life been jealous of my cousin. I want nothing more than to be on the receiving end of her laughter and her kisses.

I hear Becky and Amber start giggling like schoolgirls, and I glance at them before my gaze finds its way back to a water-drenched Denver whose fucking bikini is clinging to her every curve. Blood rushes and pounds in my ears violently before getting the fuck out of Dodge to rush its way down south. I find myself wondering if her bountiful breasts will fit in my unworthy hands. Bountiful, there's a word I'm sure I've never used, but … Fuck. Me.

Believe it or not, I'm able to tear my eyes away and take in her gently rounded stomach and belly dancer hips. She may be only eighteen, but she has the body of a voluptuous woman. And, thick as she is, I've seen her muscles working in the arena and on the rope swing just now. Yeah, she's hot.

"And here I thought I was special," Austin throws down.

When she reaches the sandbar, she glances up at Austin and yells back, "You're a fabulous teacher."

Greer picks that moment to catch her off-guard as he rushes forward, hoisting her up on his shoulder and charging into the water. She does that girly thing where she protests and shrieks for a minute. Then she springs out of the water, and as the rivulets of water trickle down her body, she dunks Greer, which is not very girly. My respect for her is restored.

Still in the water, she and Greer watch Austin swing. "Kowabunga!" he yells, right before he does a single. He pops up and kicks over to Denver, encircling her in his arms and spinning her around. Greer dodges the wake her legs make.

"You're a little smarty pants, aren't you?" She nods. "Denver, will you marry me?"

It's Austin's turn for a dunk.

"Ugh!" I hear Amber curse softly. "What a tramp. Look at her. She's got them all eating out of the palm of her hand."

"Well, of course she does, Amber," Becky says dramatically. "They already know her reputation and will play nice until she puts out. Just you wait, she'll be outcast as soon as she's been ridden hard and put up wet. She'll be finishing her college experience either knocked up, fighting off various STDs, or hooking up with desperate married men because they're the only ones who'll have her at that point."

Amber cackles at the crude speculation. "Do you really think she only does the booty buddy thing? I mean, I've never heard of a girl not wanting a relationship and sleeping around like that."

"You heard what I heard," Becky snickers. "And straight from the horse's mouth. She's a well-used fuck buddy."

My vision has been trained on her the entire, revelatory time that Becky and Amber shared Denver's sexual practices. And what I see, I no longer like. What was beautiful and lively and strong just withered and died right in front of my very eyes. Where I saw a red string bikini, porcelain skin, blonde hair, and eyes that reminded me of Black-eyed Susans, I now see grayscale and worn edges and imagine a giant red "X" stamped across the entire picture. A slap on my shoulder jars me, and I turn to see Pete and Maggie just arriving. Maggie's eyes dart around me to find Denver.

"Man, you all right?" Pete asks. "You look like someone just said you've drawn Bullzeye to ride in the finals."

I nod for a few seconds before I can form syllables. "Uh, yeah."

"Let's go show 'em how it's done, brother."

Nodding is all I'm good for now. A couple of more guys take turns going off the rope swing while Pete and I make it to the platform. "Tandem?" he asks. Again, nodding. "Dude, shit, what's wrong with you?" I shake my head at him.

Pete and I swing out over the water and, throwing ourselves backward, complete singles.

When I resurface, I swim over to the opposite bank rather than to the group now playing and splashing in the water, everyone oblivious to the fact that my wildest fantasies had just imploded, leaving me nothing but a smoking carcass. Damn, she captivated me these past couple of weeks, watching her around campus, in team meetings, at practice around the arena. She is, by far, one of the most fascinating women I've ever laid eyes on, and as odd as I thought it was at first, she reminds me of my mom. Self-made, honest, hardworking, focused, talented, and so fucking strong. All of that, combined with her quick wit, determination, and sure-fire beauty, had me thinking that she was the girl for me. Not just the girl for some fooling around. *The* girl.

I'm reminded of the time my mom made brownies for her class and left them on the counter to cool. She caught me standing over them licking my lips and chided, "Nuh, uh, Johnny! Those are not meant for you. I had just enough to make for my students. You'll have to sit this batch out, mister." I wanted those brownies so bad that I had to convince myself that they were disgusting and were really made of my mud that just looked like chocolate. Underneath the trappings, nothing but dirt and water.

My mom knew it and, being the compassionate woman she is, made me a bowl of Cocoa Puffs as a consolation prize. Sweet, but it wasn't the same. Likewise with Denver, from what I'd seen, Denver was my shot at a rich, decadent fudge-covered brownie, making everyone else look like soggy Cocoa Puffs— diluted ... processed.

My attention is drawn from the playful group to Maggie and Pete making their way back up to the platform. I decide to quit pouting like a little boy who just had his brownies snatched away and swim back over to our group.

Pete really does have to instruct Maggie on how to swing from the rope. Denver shouts up her support before Maggie plummets toward the creek. Her blood-curdling scream is likely heard for miles. She literally screams until she hits the water, and I find myself hoping she closed her mouth in time.

I start small strokes to move in closer in case she needs help, but she pops up, laughing and talking simultaneously. "That was amazing!" she yells at Denver.

"Told ya," Denver agrees.

Pete shouts, "Baby, you did good," before he gathers the rope and swings out after her.

Eventually, pretty much the rest of the team makes it out to the creek. Today had been a long practice since we were getting ready to begin our season next week, and we were deserving of an afternoon of tallboys and swimming. Retrieving our ice chests from the trucks, we make a small campfire to roast some hotdogs. When the sun sets, everybody gets changed real quick into hoodies and jackets and jeans. Montana is no joke when it comes to changing temperature.

After we eat, we all stretch out around the campfire on our blankets. Talk turns to rodeo as usual, and the guys and I shoot the shit about the competition. When I hear Denver talking to the other barrel racers, I get quiet and tune in to what she has to say.

She's stretched out, talking about technique. The girls are complimenting her on her speed and accuracy. She downplays it for a minute until she realizes they're sincere. Her brow furrows, her eyes taking on a distant look. I can tell from the way her body has frozen that she doesn't receive many compliments and is struggling with accepting them.

She finally murmurs a, "Thanks, y'all," to Lauren and Stephanie. They ask her if she has any tips for them. Then she does something else that gets my attention and my admiration, and I see another hue of her colorful personality. "Well, one thing I noticed that you can work on, Stephanie, is your feet. You keep your feet flat when really you should be digging in with your heels. You can gain a couple of tenths by being able to spur your horse quicker. When you waste time turning your feet, it shows up on the clock."

"What about me, Denver?" Lauren asks, "You see anything I can work on?"

Denver sits up and pushes her hair over her shoulders, seeming to warm to the discussion. "I noticed something, but it's actually something we all need to work on and that's keeping that barrel positioned behind our leg when we make those turns. If your horse's shoulder is at the barrel, which I saw a bunch of today, he gets spooked 'cause his peripheral is screwed and will throw his hip out. When he does that, his butt end springs out. Once he's out of alignment, he either knocks over a barrel, getting five seconds added to your time, or adjusts himself by stopping before cutting in, which again wastes valuable seconds. You've got to keep your eye trained on your back cinch to prevent that, which boils down to trusting your horse with his front end. That's what he's trained to do, though, so you're in good hands."

Hearing her talk confidently like that is like dousing lighter fluid on the smoldering heat she's been stoking in me all week. And, holy hell, is it hot. Just one more thing that adds up to her being unbelievably perfect for me.

She can't be that strong, that intuitive, that intelligent, that willing to help her competition, *and* be a girl who allows herself to be used, can she? That just doesn't match up. My instincts scream that I am right about her, and leaves no doubt that I have to find out for myself.

Abruptly, like she can read my thoughts from across the fire, her honeyed eyes meet mine, locking on them, and that stinging bite that starts at the base of my spine and works its way up—the contradicting, yet perfect, combination of fear and confidence I get when I'm about to take on the beast—makes itself known.

Pete slings his arm around my shoulder. He claps me on the shoulder, awakening me from the spell she cast over me. "Bro, you been quiet all day."

"Always am."

"Nah, you're quieter than usual. What's up?"

"Nothing, man. It's all good," I say, taking a pull from my beer.

"You hurtin'?"

I laugh once. "Yeah, but no more than usual. None of us are sitting here pain-free."

"True."

My attention is drawn to Denver again as she heads up the trail to the vehicles. I glance over to see Greer engaged in conversation with the other ropers and decide to go see about her.

"I'll be back," I tell Pete.

Pete's gaze has followed mine. "What are you doing, Ransom?"

"Going to see about a girl."

He glances over to Greer. "Greer's a good guy, and any fool could see he's in fucking love with Denver. Sounds messy."

"Would you have held back from pursuing Maggie

just because someone else had feelings for her?"

His eyes find her across the campfire. He doesn't answer me, though. He just gets up and moves behind her, sliding his legs around hers and pulling her back to his chest. She turns her face up to his, and he captures her lips hungrily.

"That's what I thought," I mock with a laugh and a decisive nod. He raises one hand very slowly and flips me the bird.

Chapter Sixteen

Denver

LOWERING MY TAILGATE, I hoist my ass up on it and lie back, exhaling like I just ran a marathon. Looking up at the stars, I laugh at myself and my cosmic joke of a life. Who the fuck gets teary-eyed and overwhelmed when people are nice to her? It's not like I wanted those high school assholes to be friends with me 'cause, obviously, they're assholes. But it had sucked not having anyone besides Greer all those years. You always need at least one back-up friend. I swipe a wrist across my eyes before my body actually resorts to shedding tears. God, I'm such a loser.

The truck sinks as someone slides next to me. I turn my head to see who's joined me, only to meet clear, green eyes gazing back at me, practically daring me to say something about his brazenness.

"Hi," he whispers with a smile. "Whatcha doing?" A playful Ransom? That throws me off-guard.

"Lying here cursing the cosmos for being such a loser," I whisper back before I can stop myself.

His brows shoot up as he sucks a breath through his

teeth, and my mouth widens into a smile. I can practically smell the sarcasm rolling off of him. "Yeah ... I didn't want to mention it before, since we haven't known each other long, but I did notice that you were of the loserish variety."

"Well, thanks for not harassing me about it," I laugh.

"Yeah, I mean, I'm pretty sure you're the biggest loser I've ever met."

"Don't sugarcoat it now. Give it to me straight. I can take it."

He folds his arms behind his head and turns his head to the stars. "Well, there's the fact that you are, without a doubt, the worst barrel racer in the world. I've never seen anyone who is as mean to her animals as you. I heard you were really dumb too. Oh, and let's not forget how disgusting you look in a bikini. Did I leave anything out?"

"Nope, I think that about covers it," I murmur.

"Ah, wait," he muses. "I forgot a few things."

"Well, let's have 'em," I mutter.

He rolls and comes up on his folded arm, resting his face in his palm. His face must be a foot away from mine, but it feels like an inch. His scent hits me full force—fresh like the water we swam in, strong like the kind of man he is, and absolutely unique. I focus on those scars again and find myself wondering about him. What makes him tick? What drives him? I have this insane urge to discover everything that makes him—him.

"Everything I just said?" I'm drawn back to those reflective depths.

"Yeah?"

"The opposite—you're the best barrel racer, the kindest horsewoman, the most intelligent, the sexiest." His fingers move to play with the wildly mused hair resting on my shoulder. I have to swallow hard before I can speak.

"You don't even know me."

"Call it a hunch," he says with a shrug. "I have excellent instincts. But I do have the strangest desire to know everything about you."

He's just like Greer in that regard—only sees what he wants to see in me, or more like, what I want them to see. Even though his instincts are off about me, I'm dying to know if his other instincts are as excellent as he claims. I need to know that just like I need to know everything … about *him*.

The slut in me wants to start with his lips. I make the mistake of dropping my gaze to his mouth. His bottom lip is thick and full while his top is a little less so. I have the strangest craving for him, for those lips. How can you crave something you've never tasted? My tongue darts out to lick my bottom lip as I imagine sitting up and testing the softness of him. Would he be salty, sweet, spicy?

I prop myself up slightly on one elbow. My hand reaches up and flattens itself on his neck, my fingertips running over the collar of his shirt. Those full lips curve into a small, inviting smile. My mouth reciprocates. I can feel my eyes shining with unshed tears, and now excitement, so I seek out his to see where he stands. They're brighter and more alive than ever.

Blue eyes flash through my mind like the blinding

lights from a police cruiser. I've caught myself red-handed. My smile falls, and the hand that was touching him experimentally, now pushes him away. I sit up quickly, an apology on my tongue.

"Uh, I'm so sorry, Ransom. I, uh—"

"Yeah, I'm sorry too, but only because you didn't follow through. I'm not gonna beat around the bush, Denver. I've been wanting to kiss you since the first time I saw you, but more than that, I'd like to get to know you."

"Umm ... Greer," is all I can mutter.

His brow pulls together. "I thought you said you weren't together."

"Well, we're not technically, but I told him I'd consider it. I don't think it'd be cool for me to run around kissing other guys while I'm supposed to be giving him a fair shot."

His eyes zero in on me like he's trying to piece together all parts of the puzzle. *Good luck with that, buddy.*

"I'm gonna go out on a limb and say anyone who has to be 'considered' is probably not the best option." Massaging his shoulder with his palm, he confesses, "I'm also gonna say that just being around you makes me feel more alive than I've felt in a long time." *Oh my. Me too*, I want to say. He needs to stop, but he doesn't. "I watch you. And I know you watch me too." One side of his mouth quirks into a slanted grin. "I can't even imagine what else we can get into if we move past that chapter. Tell me it's not my imagination."

Every word he uttered has clawed its way into me in the most painfully, delicious way. Of course I want he wants. Of course I feel what he feels. But … again, that's just the insatiable, gluttonous succubus that I am. And he should steer clear. "It's not your imagination," I voice stupidly.

"Denver?" I hear Greer holler. *Shit!*

"H—" I clear my throat. "Hey, Greer, over here."

Greer rounds the hood of the truck parked behind mine. His eyes go from me to Ransom in a single heartbeat. He tenses slightly before forcing himself to relax again.

"Everything all right?" he asks without taking his eyes from Ransom.

"Yeah, it's all good. I just …" *have no words to finish that statement.*

"Can you believe she's worried because she's only beat her own record once in the past couple of weeks?" Ransom expertly covers. My head swivels toward him, though, because I *had* been secretly worried about that. He's been watching and learning. "I told her I think it's pretty crazy to sweat that. She's still almost a full second ahead of her closest competition."

"That's true," Greer agrees. He steps up to my tailgate, his thighs resting along the curved metal. Before I know what he's about, he snakes one arm around my waist and pulls me into him. My legs divide, sliding around his. His other hand grabs my hip and fits me to him. I can't help but gasp as I feel him against the inside of my thigh. He's not completely hard, but he's not soft either. My eyes dart up to his, and he looks so damn smug, practically daring me to say something, to move away. *I'll be damned.* "But, if you knew anything about Denver," he continues, his eyes blazing into mine, "you'd know that she won't rest until she beats her own record. She's that damn competitive. Hell, she's so competitive she was born three weeks premature, just so she could be thirteen hours older than me," he jokes.

I can't help but laugh. He loves telling that story. "Not my fault you were asleep on the job and were two weeks late, momma's boy," I say, placing my arms on his.

Suddenly, Ransom is the intruder on our private moment, and he needs to leave. Oh, God. He had me all worked up, and now Greer's here to finish the job. Old habits die hard.

Ransom clears his throat and has my head swinging toward his with his next comment. "Well, I'll let you two reminisce about days gone by and whatnot. I just wanted Denver to know that I admire her. Telling her competition how to be better and how to possibly beat her was mighty big of her. It takes a special kind of person to care about others' success."

The soft look in his eye—it makes me buzz. I'd give anything to bottle it up and get drunk on it every day for the rest of my life. He really does admire me. How 'bout that?

"Well, don't be confused. I still wanna win. I still *will win*," I brag, trying to derail my conflicting thoughts. "I just want everyone else to run a real close second."

Greer laughs. "That's my girl. It's no fun beating them out if they don't challenge you, is it?"

I just shake my head.

Ransom shifts and propels himself from the truck. "See y'all in a bit," he says.

I turn my attention back to Greer. His eyes harden a bit. I wait him out. I don't have to wait long.

"What are you doing, Denver?" His humor gone, his voice steely.

"What?"

"Flirting with Austin all day? Out here in the dark, alone, fooling around with Ransom? Is that the way you wanna play this? Teasing me with other guys? I can sure as hell go get me one of those cute cowgirls down by the fire to rub in your face. Stephanie? Lauren? One of them's bound to be more than willing to spend some time with me if that's what you need."

I push at him a little, but his arms just tighten. "It wasn't like that, Greer. We were just talking. And Austin? He's just my friend. I have, like, four classes with him, and he's grown on me, kinda like a fungus," I joke, hoping to distract him.

"I get the Austin thing. But Ransom? Just harmless talking? I don't think so. You're attracted to him."

Shit. I am. The more I deny it, the guiltier I'll look too. "I am," I concede. He tenses under me. "But I'm *more* attracted to you." And that's true … right? Running my hands up his arms, I loop my arms around his neck and pull myself flush against him.

"I was serious when I said I was done playing games, chicken. It's just you and me now. No other guys. No other girls. We're done using others."

"The girls were being nice to me," I blurt out.

"Really?" he asks hopefully.

"Yes," I mutter. "I'm so pathetic. I was overcome with fucking emotion because they were asking my advice and treating me with respect."

He gives me a lopsided grin. "Baby, I'm not surprised. Everybody's finally seeing all that I see."

"I really don't understand what you see in a slut like me, Greer." His eyes flash, but I don't let him argue with me. "But I am grateful." And on that note, I bring his lips to mine. It's been so long since we've tasted each other. We've been "seeing" each other for two weeks. Sweet, platonic dates that have ended with a sexually frustrated Denver.

I moan the instant our lips meet. I meant it to be a quick, reassuring, friendly kiss, since we agreed to refrain from that physical side of our relationship for a while, but my body has other ideas. She knows who's been responsible for her pleasure in the past, and she wants some of that now.

Threading my fingers through his curls, I pull him in and shift my mouth, fitting my lips to his. My tongue darts out to tease his bottom lip, and he opens for me. "Oh, Greer," I murmur before teasing him lightly. He's so wet and so delicious. His now hard length rests against my thigh, and I groan. Oh, I want him. I want him now. "Greer, I want you," I whisper against his lips before kissing him lightly. "Have you been with anyone else?" I screw my eyes tight because I hope not, but I would understand—we all have needs.

He stiffens against me for a second before he whispers gruffly, "Hell, no. Denver, you're it for me, you know that." His tongue tangles with mine, searching, destroying. He pulls back and utters, "I want you too. So bad."

"Let's go somewhere," I coax. "There are lots of little trails for us to go get lost on."

"Mmm … how 'bout I make you feel good right here?" He nips at my bottom lip. "Right now?"

"What?" I breathe through my haze. "We might get caught." He recaptures my lips with his and works me over with his tongue. Suddenly I'm reminded of the time we sneaked off during our prom. Oh my God. It was … mind-blowing. The thrill of getting caught. The thrill of our dates waiting for us in the ballroom of the hotel while we fucked each other hard, up against a wall in the housekeeping closet. Yes, please. I want that.

I'm jerked from my thoughts as he pulls me from the truck bed. I latch my legs around his waist, not certain where we are going, but along for the ride, nevertheless. He doesn't take me far. His truck is farthest from the little party on the creek. He doesn't open the door though. Just pins me to the truck and lets me slide down, drops one of my legs, and pulls the other high on his hip. He nudges my free leg between his and squeezes me tight.

"You ready? Hold on," he commands before I can answer.

"What? What are you doing?"

"Trust me," he says, as he buries his mouth in the hollow of my throat. His hands slide in my back pockets, grasping and squeezing. "We promised. No touching like that. No sex. Even though I can't wait to be inside you again, this is gonna have to do." He drops his forehead on mine. Those fiery eyes meet mine, igniting a blaze. "The best non-fuck fuck of your life." And those words douse it with kerosene, creating an inferno. A tremble works its way through me, and I almost come right then.

"Move yourself against my thigh," he says. I don't even think. I just start moving. Oh, that feels good.

He clutches my hips and grinds me against him harder, making me gasp. Ahh ... that feels better than good, it's incredible. I groan at the friction our jeans create against my needy core. "Oh, yes, Greer, yes."

"You like that?" He thrusts against me. His length against my belly, pressing the metal button of my jeans into me. "Imagine my cock sliding over your clit."

Whimper.

Grind.

Tremble.

Our bodies move together—rhythmic, knowing.

"Yeah, just like that. Over and over again. It's so tight. That little bud. That needy little bud. I work it with my hard dick, my cum drips all over it, and we slip and slide together. Electricity zips through your nerve endings 'cause you're getting close. *We're* so close."

Whimper.

Grind.

"Greer, please don't stop."

He thrusts his tongue in my mouth and simulates what I know I would feel if he'd allow himself inside me. "Who's been in this mouth?" he demands against my lips.

"You. Only you."

"Who's been inside you?"

"You, Greer. Just you." I drop my mouth to his neck and kiss and suck and bite while he works my body with his.

My nerve endings pop and crackle like live wires until I don't think I can take anymore. It's too intense, too overwhelming. I open my mouth to tell him to stop, but his naughty words kill my would-be protests.

"Just when you think you're going to explode, I slip inside you," he whispers gruffly. I moan. I can feel him inside me like a phantom.

"Greer," I beg.

"You're so tight, so wet. My dick stands at full mast in honor of your perfect fucking pussy," he praises. His shocking words create a fierce pull deep inside. "Ah, God. It's so hot. It wants me so bad."

Groan.

I throw my head back and ride him, surrendering myself completely.

Cry.

Hand over my mouth. I bite it.

Grind.

"Oh, baby, clench that sweet pussy around my dick. Wring every bit of your pleasure from me ... and give me mine."

And with that, I detonate, exploding from within and all around him. My body is hit with wave after wave, as I come and come and come, pulsating and coming apart simultaneously. My head falls to the side, and I melt into him and his truck. The three of us just became one. Someone's going to find us here and have to scrape us off of it.

My other senses start to return. The night air nips at my face, the voices from the creek echo over the stillness, and Greer and I hold each other tight in our naughty interlude. I imagine the picture we must make, and can't help but giggle. His forehead rests on my neck. His breath comes fast and heated against my chest. I lean in and kiss the top of his head, languidly.

I'm in awe of him and what he just did to me. He's never been like that. "Greer? What the—" I pause to catch my breath. "You've never talked to me like that. What got into you?"

He laughs lightly. "Too many nights fantasizing about what I was gonna do to you once I had you again. My imagination took over."

"And what a deliciously naughty imagination you have," I praise.

He just sighs and resumes breathing hard.

"Are you OK?"

"Umm … no. Why *do* you think they call it dry humping?" I giggle lightly. "Good thing I have extra pants in my truck." My laughter comes hard now. His finger skates over the seam between my legs, which quickly shuts me up. "Laugh all you want. You're wet too."

Then I'm laughing again so hard I'm crying. I pull his face to mine and kiss him softly through it all.

Chapter Seventeen

Ransom

I CAN'T GO back to the creek and everybody just yet, so I grab a flashlight out of my truck and comb through the woods looking for some extra branches to keep the fire going. Finding a weathered branch that would make for good kindling, I place my hands on the ends and my boot in the middle. I pull up until it snaps in half. I continue to ignore the thoughts raging in my head for a few more minutes while I complete my mundane task. I'm not able to fight them off for long, though.

I really shouldn't have stood around and listened to them, but when I heard Denver and Greer openly discussing me and Austin, and using other guys and other girls, I couldn't have moved if a herd of buffalo had been stampeding my way. I had to know. Now I wish I hadn't.

I really don't understand what you see in a slut like me.

God, what did that even mean? She's the slut Becky and Amber accused her of being? What kind of girl openly admits that about herself? What kind of arrangement had they had? I'm not naïve to unusual sexual preferences, so I know about open relationships and shit like that. But they're eighteen, almost nineteen. A little young to be flirting with that kind of trouble, which makes me wonder exactly how fucked-up the two of them are.

I know in that moment I want nothing more to do with them or her. Most especially her. And just like that, I am bitter, vile feelings overtake the ones I entertained these past weeks. Hell, I haven't even fooled around with any other girls because I was so set on her. So set on having her. So obsessed with the thought of breaking my own rules for her and what exactly that would mean for us. Oh, I was determined there'd be an *us*. I know my intentions weren't the purest, but at least with me, she would have control over how things went down. Sounds like she and Greer just flat-out use each other, and others, without thought of consequence.

I hear a branch snap to my right and throw my light to spot Pete. "What are you doing, man?" I ask him.

He ignores my pissed-off tone and strides over to me. "Just checking on ya. How'd it go with Denver?"

"Not good."

"Yeah, I figured that when I saw you heading in the woods alone, looking like somebody kicked your dog. What happened?"

I find myself a sturdy Black Cottonwood, set the wood down at my feet, and lean against the tree before answering. "She's not who I thought she was."

Pete scratches his chin for a second. "What's that mean? Maggie loves her. And Maggie's amazing."

He's my best friend, my brother, and I don't hide

anything from him. But I don't want him to feel awkward or whatever around his girl's best friend. "Have you heard of anything being ... off with her?"

His gaze drops to his boot as he kicks a rotten log. "Um, yeah. A little something."

I still. "And?"

"It's just a stupid rumor."

"Rumors usually have some nugget of truth, don't they?"

He looks up, his hands finding their way into his hair. It's his tell. Folding his arms, he cups the back of his neck. "Shit, I haven't seen any proof."

"Just spit it out," I demand. I need to hear it again. Third time's a charm to keep me from getting confused about her again.

"She, uh, sleeps around. That's the rumor."

"Yep." I pull away from the tree and knock it a couple of times with my fist. "Well, I just heard her admit it."

"Really? Kind of odd for someone to openly talk about that, don't you think? Maybe you misunderstood."

"Yes," I retort, sarcasm dripping from my words, "because there are so many ways 'I really don't understand what you see in a slut like me' could be taken."

"Damn."

"Yep, I'm just gonna keep my distance. It was stupid of me to think she was worth it."

"You could try to talk to her about it. Get her side of it. See if it's as bad as what you're imagining. I mean, I've never seen you so hung up on a girl before. I know you're usually the observant one, but I've been noticing you notice her."

Part of me knew that I hadn't been so subtle. That part also didn't give a shit. "That's all over," I grind out.

"You fucking smile at her, and you don't smile at anyone."

"Fuck you," I laugh. "I smile."

"No, you don't," he maintains.

"I'm not arguing with you over a non-issue. And that's what she is. Bottom line—I can't be with someone like that."

"You know, you're not exactly a choir boy, Ransom. I'm thinking maybe you need to withhold judgment," my easygoing best friend snaps.

"Fuck off. You know it's not like that. And those words I quoted? Straight from her lips. It's done before it even got started. And you know what? I'm actually relieved. So let's drop it," I bite out before stomping toward the fire with the measly amount of firewood I collected. I'm not quick enough to escape his parting comment, though.

"I think that's a copout, bro. I'm gonna go ahead and call it. You're scared of the shit she makes you feel."

Stopping, I take a deep breath and release it before continuing on my path. Why don't I respond? Because I know he's right.

Chapter Eighteen

Denver

MY EYES FOCUS and unfocus while I stare out the passenger window of Greer's truck as he and I make the trek to Wyoming State. Fall plays out before my eyes on the road. All the colors changing, all the shapes morphing into differences—all in stark contrast to the little cocoon of life that we've had to sculpt for ourselves. It's become rote, but I love it.

Rodeo. The road. Stolen moments with Greer. Late night talks with Maggie. Drinking. Raising hell. And classes. Those definitely take a backseat when you're an athlete, though. My job here is to be the best rodeoer on the college circuit. Not that I'm not doing well in school. It's just not what takes up the majority of my time.

These are the things that have consumed me for the last few weeks, and I've loved every minute. I almost feel like I've invented a new life for myself. Becky and Amber shoot me spiteful looks as often as they are able, and I grin as big as I can when they do. Other than them, everyone has been incredibly good to me. Asking my advice. Seeking me out to hang with. At first I thought it was Maggie, but when she started spending most of her time with Pete, and they were still coming around, I had to revise that opinion. Everything was good. Everyone was good.

Except Ransom.

He hadn't spoken to me since that night in the back of my truck. It was odd. Before that night, he sought me out constantly, even if it was in a small way. And here I thought he got me. Thought he was interested in me. Yet he hadn't spoken to me in three weeks. Or even so much as looked at me. We're a small, tight-knit group, traveling together, eating together, partying together, so he's had to have some interaction. It's how I learned that people could talk to you and even look at you without *really* talking to you or looking at you. I was used to people ignoring me, but this is different. He's fucking fabulous at making me feel like I don't exist while subjecting me to his larger-than-life personality. Even in our team meetings where he has to address me—he may as well be talking to the fucking wall.

I tried to convince myself this was a good thing. If Ransom isn't talking to me, I wouldn't be tempted to screw up things with Greer. And he had become a temptation for me, but Greer is nothing but *good* for me. It's become pretty clear that he's everything I want him to be, everything I need him to be. And he assures me constantly that he feels the same way about me.

The prospect of building something real with him excites me. I daydream about our future together, something I haven't let myself do since we were sixteen, when life was beautiful and bright and shiny. Well, the most beautiful I've ever known anyway.

So why then, does it haunt me knowing that anything I could've had with Ransom died that moonlit night?

The answer to that question comes as easy as the whore who springs to mind. No matter what, I'll never be able to let down my defenses. My whore gene is alive and fucking well.

It doesn't help that, for weeks, I've watched Ransom dominate the bull riding circuit everywhere we go. Texas, Oklahoma, Missouri … no one can touch him. Other cowboys can stay on their bulls sure, but Ransom does it with such ease, yet such intensity. It is the hottest thing I've ever seen, and the Baby Buckle Bunnies agree with me. Every city we rodeo in sees its own share of fangirls who are more than willing to forgo their morals for a night with one of our guys—Ransom being on the top of their lists. And, from what I've gathered, he has done his fair share of sampling what each city had to offer. He is the manwhore that I suspected. And, of course, that bothers no one else. So it sure as shit shouldn't repulse me. It shouldn't matter. But it does. I can't quite explain the why of it to myself.

As for Greer, he continues to amaze in the arena and out of it. He is fabulous, and don't think for a second he doesn't have his share of girls trying to get with him. He is so adorable about it. He does his meet-and-greet, takes pictures, and signs autographs. I've watched girls shove scraps of paper in his pocket, but as soon as they walk off, he reaches in, balls it up, and chucks it. Doesn't even look at them. He caught me grinning about it once, threw me one of those irresistible grins of his and mouthed, "You're my girl," while I was posing for a picture with our mascot for the team Facebook page. That's the prettiest picture I've ever seen of myself.

His parents come to most of the events. His mother still doesn't speak to me outright, just kind of talks around me like I'm not even standing there. His dad isn't so bad. He at least says my name and tries to make some conversation until Mrs. Tanner gives him a "What the fuck?" look, and our would-be conversation dies an awkward death. My mom may have the whore-market cornered, but Greer's mom is the biggest bitch I ever met. Greer assures me that they'll come around once I've proven I am nothing like my mother. In my head, that translates to—they will never like you; you are your mother.

I am thankful that my mother hadn't shown up at any of my events. I just have no desire to be around her. She's sent me a few text messages, mostly asking about different things for the ranch. No word on whether or not I am going to be a big sister. I wonder, if I don't go back, will she eventually forget that I even exist? Both are a real possibility because, once I got over not being on my ranch on a day-to-day basis, the thought of returning made my stomach twist. Me, the one who dreamt of nothing but running it one day. I've started seeing other options for myself, and it's freeing.

Greer's hand in my hair brings me back to the here and now. He runs it through his fingers for a few minutes while I close my eyes and delight in his touch. "Hey, Denver?" he calls eventually. "We're almost there."

I clear my throat and turn my head toward him as he drives, his hand resting on top of the steering wheel.

Looking at him never fails to resonate with me. He's just that beautiful. His long, blond curls rest in charming disarray around his strong features. Those bright blue eyes, those thick eyebrows and long eyelashes, his long, straight proud nose. You could cut diamonds on those cheekbones. And that mouth. I happen to know how soft and warm and incredible it feels. My own mouth waters, and I'm beyond tempted. I unbuckle and scoot to the middle, buckling quickly before I curl one arm under his chin to thread my fingers through those soft curls. My touch elicits a groan from him. I nudge his hair up with my nose as I plant a lingering kiss behind his ear, which earns me another moan.

"Baby, you better quit if you don't want me to lose control. The horses would not be too happy if I just whipped off the road."

"No, but I would," I purr.

"Ah, Denver, I wish. We're, uh, kinda in a caravan. We'll be in Laramie soon, though."

"Good," I whisper, as I continue to torture him. I run the tip of my tongue down his neck, and on my return path to his ear, I taste the tiny goose bumps my touch has erected. Moving my hand from his hair, I circle his thigh and squeeze. I lay my head on his shoulder and breathe in his familiar scent—horses, leather, and Greer. Warmth spreads throughout my being, and I feel ... content.

"Maybe we'll sneak off and find a quiet spot before the madness begins," he breathes, as I make little circles on his jeans.

"I'm in," I rush out. He just chuckles at me. I move my hand to his chest so his laugh moves through me too.

Our rodeo here is a big deal. They're our rivals in every sense of the word. We are continually swapping places with them—we'll be first for a while and then they'll take over, and we'll trade places again. Currently, we are number one. Mostly because of Ransom and me, but everyone plays a part in making sure we bring it home. This weekend is an event stretching over three days, and then we're off until the spring. I can't even imagine what I'll do with all that free time. I'll have to work my horses, of course, but that still leaves a lot of time. Ransom has warned us not to get complacent, and we'll have a ton of charity events too.

I hear my phone buzz. Pulling it from the holder, I grin as I read the first little bit and click to read the rest.

I'm DYING...to be alone with Pete. You're DYING to be alone with Greer, so I made it happen. You and G can have our room to yourselves for a while. I'll be with P. ;)

You read my mind. You rock! :D You're not gonna...

No! Even though I really, really want to!!!!!! Are you?

No!!!! Greer still won't give it up.

OMG! A guy who won't give it up. What a refreshing change!

Shut up. I don't feel refreshed. :P

I slide my phone back in the holder next to Greer's, just as his lights up. Pulling it out, I smile at the picture on his lock screen. I flash it toward him. "Your favorite girl?"

He laughs and squeezes my thigh. "Not my favorite girl, but one of them."

"Do you miss her?"

"More than you know. Frisco's a slobbering, snoring mess, but she's my mess."

I bite my lip, trying hard not to say it. "Good thing you have a penchant for … 'messes,'" I quip.

He gives me a warning look.

I slide his phone back in beside mine before turning back to him. "Guess what?" I tease.

"What's that?" he asks, as he plants a kiss on my cheek.

"No sneaking around. No backs of trucks. No feed trucks," I finish with a laugh at the thought of that ingenious spot he found for us in Texas. "Maggie's going to hang out with Pete in his room for a while, so you can come to my room with me." I resume what I hope is my slow, sweet attack on Greer's resolve.

"Mmm … sounds perfect. Are, uh, Maggie and Pete …"

"No, everything but. She wants to wait. And he's being crazy-patient."

"Good for them," he grins.

"Kinda like you and me, except reversed," I groan.

Frowning, he runs his hand between my thighs as he teases, "Mmm, hmm, but I've been taking care of you, haven't I?"

"Yes, you have," I admit, as I continue my assault on him.

AFTER THE NATIONAL anthem, the fireworks, and the team introductions, we get down to business.

Maggie takes first in Pole Bending. Greer's second in Calf Roping. He and his rival from WSU are always swapping places. The rest of the guys and girls hold their own.

Liberty and I finally beat our record-holding tie. I'm over the moon. Of course, she and I end up with bunches of flowers and take lots of pictures and sign tons of autographs. Liberty gets spoiled with her loot of carrots and apples and sugar cubes. They adore her.

Once we're caught up with our duties, Maggie and I crawl up in between the bull chutes and the fences so we can get an unfettered view of the bull riders. One of the coaches tries to run us off, but we're not having that.

When Pete slides down on his bull, Maggie grabs my hand and holds it tight. "I get so scared, Denver. We've had such a good season so far. Very few injuries, very little drama."

"I know," I agree. It is scary because it's not *if* we will get hurt, it's *when and how bad.* And bull rider injuries are the worst of them all. The thrill of danger is in our blood, but actually dealing with that chilling reality is not something any of us focus on.

Pete wraps his hand up tight and pounds it closed with his fist while the men struggle to keep him from getting crushed in the chute before unleashing Holy Terror. Yes, that's the bull he's drawn.

Pete looks up, catching Maggie's gaze and winks before pulling his white straw hat down tight over his shaggy brown hair.

After Pete and his bull get situated, Pete gives the call, and they're off. Holy Terror rips from the chute, his hind legs immediately thrown into a ninety-degree angle in an extreme dive-bomb, and Pete is quite unceremoniously catapulted over the head of the bull to face-plant in the dirt. "Oh, ladies and gentleman, not even a full second on Holy Terror. Holy Terror 1. Pete Ford 0," the announcer quips and hits play on "Another One Bites the Dust." Asshole.

Maggie and I stand up to watch for Pete as the bullfighters get the bull shooed out of the arena. "He's not moving," she whispers and turns her face to mine. Her normally cheerful grin and sunny demeanor slip behind the gray cloud that is the eventuality of getting hurt in bull riding.

I grasp her hand tighter and look back at the scene for her. He's so still. "I know. He's probably stunned. They're checking on him now." I can't see what they're doing, so I stand on my tippy-toes and crane my neck. When I do, I catch Ransom's eye, as he is sitting atop his chute, waiting for his bull. He's looking at Maggie, concern evident on his face. When his eyes drift to mine, they crystallize, and he turns away.

Finally, after what seems like forever, the little crowd clears, and I see Pete stumbling to his feet with the help of the trainers. "Maggie, he's OK. Look, he's getting up on his own."

She lets out a startled cry before finding him with her tear-filled eyes. "Oh, Denver, cowboy up," she whispers. "Look at him. He's just so ..."

"So?" I ask with a grin.

"Mine," she says with a smile. "I need to make him mine."

That cracks me up, causing everyone to look back at us. "Well, nothing like a close call to get your libido going, I suppose."

She slaps at my arm while waving to Pete with the other. He snatches his hat from the ground and waves it around at the now cheering crowd. The announcer calls for everyone to give him a hand, and one of the bullfighters drapes his bull rope over Pete's shoulder. Pete finds Maggie with his eyes and winks and kisses at her. "Oh, I've always wanted him, Denver. I'm just more highly motivated now than ever before."

I just laugh again.

She scrambles down from our perch. "I'm gonna go see about him. You OK here?"

"Yeah, go. I'm good." I let out a deep sigh. That was terrifying.

I turn back to Ransom and his bull Gladiator. Gladiator hasn't been ridden all season. Of course, Ransom's hoping to change all that. Most of me would like to see that happen, but a very tiny part of me loves to see his smug ass get bucked. That's a rare event, though.

Watching any bull rider prepare to take on the beast thrills me to no end. But I'm captivated as Ransom runs through his routine, which is why I haven't been watching him prepare these past couple of weeks. I know it's wrong to lust after someone when I'm "dating" someone else, but I can't seem to help myself when it comes to him.

As he pulls his red glove on tight and flexes his fingers, I imagine what it would be like to feel those strong, capable hands on me. When he makes his wrap and weaves the rope between his ring finger and the pinkie on his left hand, I gulp as I realize just how hardcore he really is. Not many cowboys use the "suicide wrap." Sure, it makes it harder for the bull to pull out of his hand, but it also makes it more difficult for the rider to let go when need be. I can't help but imagine what all that intensity would feel like transferred to me as he worked my body.

I obviously need to get laid. Too bad Greer's holding out on me.

Ransom nods once and grunts out a "Go," before the chute gate swings open, and an angry bull charges out. Ransom leans forward, his arm extended into a 90-degree angle, and looks poised to have a great ride. That is, until Gladiator spins hard to the right, away from Ransom's hand, and doesn't stop spinning until he kicks high and jerks him off center. Ransom spins like a rag doll until he's lying flat over the bull's head and horns. I hear a gasp and realize it's me. Shit. I secretly wanted him to get bucked off, and now look. I stare down at my boots in shame until I hear the announcer.

"Oh, boy! Ransom's caught up in his rope, ladies and gentleman. And Gladiator's taking him for a wild ride."

I worry my bottom lip with my teeth as Ransom's body dangles from the bull like a crash test dummy. I barely register the announcer telling the crowd that he's "Down in the well." I can't hear it when it snaps, but I know that something has, when his arm extends at an odd angle. Dislocated and not broken is the hope. His face contorts with pain, but somehow he's managing to stay on his feet and out from under the bull. Holy shit! How long can he be dragged like that? It must have been three seconds by now.

Finally he comes loose and falls heavily on his side in the fetal position. But the bull isn't done with him. He turns and drops his hind legs on Ransom's side, forcing his body to unfurl with the blow. Almost immediately, Ransom is up with the help of a bullfighter while the bull flounces off through the gates, snorting and sputtering.

"Oh, God," I groan when I spot Ransom's arm hanging limply from its socket. Dislocated shoulders are commonplace for bull riders, and I'm hoping that's all this is. The crowd goes nuts for Ransom, chanting his name. The announcer has "Tubthumping" cued just right so that it boasts cowboys may get knocked down, but they get back up again.

"Ladies and gentleman," the announcer booms, "it's a rare day to see a bull get the best of Ransom. Everyone give this cowboy a round of applause. You can bet he'll be back with a vengeance on Sunday, looking for redemption."

Even though Ransom walks out on his own merit, I can see him wincing with every step. When he gets to the gate, he drops his good arm from the bullfighter's shoulders and salutes the cheering crowd with this hat before turning and heading back to the locker rooms. That's two close calls today. I finally sit back down and stiffen my spine for the rest of the rides.

"YEAH, AUSTIN!" I holler as loud as I can for his ninety-point ride. He hadn't been doing too hot lately, so he was due for a good one. As soon as he hears his name, he turns and runs at the fence where I'm standing.

He sticks his head in between the bars and shouts, "Kiss me, Denver, for good luck."

"You've already ridden," I say with a laugh, as I tip his hat back with my boot.

"Luck for next time," he persists.

He's so silly that I can't resist him. So I slide down from my perch and give him a peck on the cheek.

I have tears in my eyes from laughing at him when I straighten back up. Someone grazes my elbow, so I peer sideways to see what's up.

"Hey, Coach," I say.

"Hey, Denver. We need you down by the locker rooms for a quick interview with ESPN."

"Oh, sure thing." I turn back to Austin and give him a wink before following Coach through all the cowboys and cowgirls in their various states of getting ready, getting checked out, and interviewing until we get back to locker rooms.

I'm told to wait along the wall opposite the boys' locker room, and when the door opens, I spot Ransom lying face-down on one of the tables. His shirt is off, his ribs wrapped up. The hand on his good arm clenches and unclenches on the table. The door tries to close, so I move in quick and keep it cracked open so that I can watch him.

"Hey there, Ransom. Heard you had a hard time

saying goodbye to your bull today," Doc jokes.

Ransom grunts a response and sort of laughs. "Don't make me laugh. It fucking hurts."

"Yep, we're gonna get you squared away right quick. How are the ribs?"

"Broken," Ransom deadpans.

Doc looks at his assistant. "How many?"

"Three," he answers and turns back to his current patient.

"Whew, no wonder you've been a model patient today and haven't popped your own shoulder back into place. All right, ready?"

"Yep," Ransom answers clearly.

Doc straightens out the lifeless limb. That simple act is enough to make my toes curl and my own hands clench. When he pulls and rotates, the loud pop it makes causes me to jump and my stomach to pinch. A wave of nausea rolls over me. Ransom doesn't even flinch. I'm not normally squeamish, but something about him just lying there and taking it like he's so used to pain and injury doesn't sit right with me.

"How's that, cowboy?" Doc asks.

"Ah … much better," Ransom breathes, sitting up like there's nothing to it. "I'm all set, right?"

Doc nods.

"All right, thanks, boys. Gotta get to my interview," he says, as he shrugs on his shirt. I take that as my cue to back myself up against the wall and allow my breathing to return to normal. I run my thumbs over the little half-moons from where I dug my nails into my palms.

After another couple of minutes, Mark, the rodeo correspondent for ESPN, joins me and mikes me up. I look past him, as I see the locker room door open, to watch a grinning Ransom's face fall as he makes eye contact with me. So he can deal with all that shit with a sense of humor, but just the sight of me puts him in a foul mood. Fantastic. I just don't get it. I hadn't done anything to him. We had so many promising conversations, and then nothing. He just quit talking to me. I'd ask him why, but that would do nothing but show him I give a shit. Then a thought hits me. Maybe it wasn't even about me. Maybe he had other shit going on.

"Ransom, we're ready for you," Mark tells him.

He steps over next to me, careful not to touch me as he gets miked up too.

"Great. You guys are both at the top of your game, so we want to do an interview, getting your take on the other's success. Since you guys are both number one in your event and at the same school, we thought it would be interesting."

I nod, but inside, I'm dying a slow, painful death. I was going to have to talk about Ransom? And he about me? This sucks. As far as I can tell, he hates me, and I worship him. This interview is going to be a little lopsided.

Mark situates himself between us and talks into his microphone while the camera guy zones in on the three of us. "Mark O'Neal here with ESPN at the Collegiate Rodeo Quarter Finals taking place at Wyoming State. I'm here with the current number one barrel racer, Denver Dempsey, and the current number one bull rider, John Ransom, who both happen to be from Montana State," Mark finishes and turns to Ransom. "Ransom, we'll start with you. This is your senior year, your last hurrah as a collegiate performer. You've seen lots of rodeoers come and go over the years. What's your take on Denver Dempsey and her record-setting runs?"

Mark thrusts the question at a thoughtful looking Ransom, who finally makes eye contact with me. His eyes are crystal again, cold and hard. "Uh, Denver's unlike any other cowgirl out there today, Mark. You think you're getting one thing with her, but looks are, indeed, deceiving."

What the fuck is that supposed to mean?

Mark gives a fake laugh and tries to clear up Ransom's comment, "You mean Denver's small but mighty, right?"

"Yeah, she's small and may look fragile and all girly. But that's not the case. I've never met anyone as cold and as willing to put herself out there for everyone as she is."

Cold? Willing to put myself out there? What the hell?

Mark ignores the cold comment. "What do you mean by 'put herself out there'?"

Ransom doesn't miss a beat. "You know, with her fans. She's always giving pointers, signing autographs, and she's just really put herself out there as a tool to be used by anyone and everyone." He smirks at me.

Oh. My. God. Why is he being such an asshole?

"Well, all that aside," Mark starts, "what do you think her reason for success is inside the arena?"

Ransom's smirk gets even bigger as he declares, "She's the fastest girl I've ever seen. Deceptively so."

"It takes more than just speed, doesn't it?"

"Absolutely. She's seductive too." My mouth drops open on that one. So far all his comments had been filled with double meaning. No way could that little comment be interpreted any other way.

"Umm ... seductive in the arena, how so?" The more clarity he asks for, the worse it gets. Someone please put me out of my misery.

"You've watched her. She seduces you into enjoying her, making you forget she's the enemy. Makes it seem effortless. She gets in there, glides around those barrels, barely looks like she's hanging, not even breaking a sweat. Then bam! She just whooped your ass. Never saw her coming. Seductive." When his eyes meet mine this time, they're filled with something other than the mocking look he's been giving me throughout his entire interview, and I'm not sure I can place it before it evaporates. If I didn't know better, I'd call it hurt. I haven't hurt him though.

"Ah ... I see," Mark says. I don't think he does.

Mark turns to me. "Denver, you've been rodeoing with the best of the best in John Ransom. What have you learned about competing from him?"

My blood burns so bright I can only see red. Just give him a couple of quotes and then you can get to the bottom of this once and for all. "Basically that you have to make snap judgments and never doubt yourself. You have to really commit to decisions and believe in them. See them through. Even if it's not the right one."

"Umm ..."

I show mercy on Mark. I want to end this and put us all out of our misery. "Ransom's the best out there. He may have had an off day today, but he's standing before you just moments after breaking three ribs and dislocating his shoulder. He's as tough as they come. Stupid or not, he's not backing down. I really admire that level of commitment. And he's already taught me a great deal. In … and out of the arena." I chance a glance at Ransom. He looks like he wants to strangle me. *Bring it on, cowboy.*

Mark does his wrap-up while Ransom and I stand there smiling at the camera like a couple of paid buffoons. As soon as I hear "cut," Ransom and I snap the mikes off and thrust them at the camera guy. Mark mutters, "Hope you two get your lovers' spat worked out quickly enough," before they traipse off to their next interview.

"God, you're an ass," I seethe as I move in close. It's everything I can do not to knock the smug look right off his face.

"Right back atcha, babe," he smirks.

"Don't *babe* me. You haven't spoken to me in weeks." My finger is in his face, but he doesn't even acknowledge it, which pisses me off more, so I go up on my tippy-toes. "You send me dirty looks left and right. And then you discuss me like … like I'm some joke on national television. Are you proud of yourself? Showing everyone the many nuances of your asshole behavior?"

"Nuances?" he questions with a quirked brow.

I throw my hands out to the side in frustration before resting them on my hips. "Yeah, nuances. Now everyone knows you're a jerk of a thousand shades."

He has the nerve to laugh at me. "I did no such thing. I praised your ability to be attainable by everyone, your deceptively smooth side that allows you to blindside the competition, and the speed with which you get those things done. Sounds like you can do no wrong in my book," he reasons innocently.

"There you go again. All those backhanded compliments can be taken out of context and be misinterpreted, and you know it. What I don't know is why. I haven't done a thing to you."

"Not for your lack of trying," he murmurs and tries to turn away from me.

I grasp his arm and spin him back to me. He glances at my hand like it's a bug he wants to squish. "What's that supposed to mean?"

Bracing a hand on the wall beside me, he leans in and says with deadly calm, "I don't know. Why don't you tell me what you're up to? From what I've seen, you're pretty smart for a whore."

I gasp at the talons slicing at my heart. He's trying to hurt me just like everyone else. And it does hurt because I never saw it coming. I thought I moved beyond this these last few weeks. I can't speak for a minute. Part of me wants to deny it. To set him straight. His opinion of me shouldn't matter, but for some reason, it does. It matters a lot. The other part wants to resort to her old ways and claim it. I'm torn, so I stand gaping at him.

"You can't even deny it. Can you?" He straightens and lifts his chin, looking down on me with complete disdain.

And that does it. I lean in and capture his eyes with mine, hoping to instill conviction with my look. I shake my head before I confess, "No, I won't deny it. You're only half-right, though." I pause for dramatic effect. Oh, this comes so very easy. "My mother's the whore in the family. I'm just your average, everyday slut," I finish with the smile I've perfected over the years. The one that says I'm proud of who I am regardless of whether or not I should be. The one that sends jealous bitches on their scampering, ill-intentioned ways.

He just nods at me like he knew all along I'd never deny it. Like he knows me somehow when, in actuality, he doesn't know shit. Then he mutters, "Such a waste," and walks away backward before giving me a regretful look and turning away.

Salt in an open wound. I never had anyone feel sorry for me when I told them off. Never. People usually reacted with shock or indifference. Never pity. He pitied me, and that killed me.

Chapter Nineteen

Ransom

"Come on, Ransom," Maggie begs. "We need an even number. You have to ride."

I look at those bright green eyes and bouncing red curls and look to my buddy, whose look smirks, *go ahead and try to deny her*, and I know I'm getting no help from him.

"Fine, I'll ride," I grit out. I want to tell her to make sure I don't draw Denver, but figure that will actually ensure that I do draw her.

Since we have the day off between competing, we decided not to go out and party but instead spend time with the horses. We've done all different kinds of fun exercises with them. They needed a good workout, but also needed to be reminded that it wasn't all work and no play, so we took a short trail ride. I stayed as far away from Denver as I could.

The last competition we'll hold, before heading back to the hotel, is cowgirl pickup. The girls tie up their horses and head to the other end of the arena, waiting their turn to climb the barrel. The boys line up their horses outside the arena and wait for our numbers to be called.

Pete's number one. At the other end, surprise surprise, Maggie hops onto the barrel. He dashes in, and once he gets close enough to the barrel, he reaches out and Maggie grabs his hand while swinging herself onto his horse behind him. Pete rounds the barrel and sprints back out with the time of 11.2.

Everyone cheers and talks shit simultaneously. Austin draws Stephanie. He does much the same as Pete, but Stephanie hesitates and costs them a second. When they clock a 12.2, we boo and talk even more shit. Suddenly, I hear Stephanie smacking Austin and letting loose on him. "Austin, we're done riding. You can take your hand off my ass now," she complains.

"Oh, my bad," he says innocently. "Just protecting my precious cargo."

"Yeah, right," she says with a laugh, as she slides down from his horse.

When my number's called, I approach the arena cautiously. Of course, I watch in silent horror as Denver's back goes ramrod straight as she's told she's drawn me. I'd bow out gracefully, but everyone would wonder why, and that would lead to an uncomfortable line of questions. She must think the same thing because, after a few seconds of hesitation, she turns and makes her way to the barrel. She doesn't look at me until she's standing tall on top of it with her long blonde hair blowing. Then her demure moment is gone, and her look is one of pride. My dick stirs. He doesn't seem to mind that she is a slut. Her bright yellow eyes dare me to back down. *No such luck, sweetheart.* I find I'm actually looking forward to making her squirm on the back of my horse.

I dart off toward her, barely slowing when I approach the barrel. I throw my arm out, and she grabs it without hesitation as she swings her ass behind me, throws her arms around me tight, and whispers a, "Go," in my ear.

We both lean in as we sprint for the finish line. I hear our small crowd explode with an "11.0" chorus. That would be difficult to beat. I gallop Knight in a circle outside the arena while I savor the feeling of Denver's breasts pushed against my back. Up and down. Up and down. The motion nearly pushes me over the edge as I imagine her riding me, up and down, up and down.

Her whispered words are what do it instead. "Let me the fuck off this horse," she fumes.

Wrong edge. I don't think so. First, I don't like to be told what to do. Second, I'm quite enjoying having her on the back of my horse, even though I'm not supposed to.

Rather than slow down, I call to Pete that we're heading to the barn as we rush past him.

"What the fuck do you think you're doing?" she shrieks into my ear.

Now instead of going to the barn, I'm nudging Knight toward one of the trails. Her hands tighten in my shirt when she sees where we are headed. "I swear to God, Ransom," she bites out.

I surprise myself by rolling with laughter, and it hurts like hell, but I don't care. I haven't really laughed in forever. I swear I can feel her temperature rising by degrees behind me, which makes me cackle like a mad fool. I don't really know what I'm doing here. The one thing I do know is that I want her to pay for the way she made me feel before she outed herself to me and ruined everything. I know it's childish. She was never mine. No promises were ever made. But that didn't stop me from convincing myself of the promise of her before it was snatched away. I felt deceived. Then lonely. Lonely led to pissed. And now here we are—me being a childish asshole, and her surely about to take my head off. And hell if my dick doesn't stir again with that thought.

When I hit the open area, I slow down to a trot. As soon as I do, her hands slip away from me, and she slides from the back of the horse with a curse. I twist around in my saddle and watch as she drops and lands—hard—on all fours.

"What the hell, Denver? I wasn't going slow enough. You could've hurt yourself." I swing down and go after her. Before she has the chance to fully stand up, I grab her elbow and spin her toward me. Her blonde hair covers her face like a veil. I run my hands over her face and separate it to reveal an angry expression staring back at me.

"What do you care whether or not I get hurt? You've been nothing but a cold jackass to me for weeks before yesterday's delightful fucking Q & A where you basically called me a slut in front in the entire country." She puts her hands on my chest with the intent of pushing me away. I grab her arms harder and crush them between us instead.

"I do care about you, dammit. I think that's why I'm so pissed off."

"Oh, wow. Way to deal with your feelings in a mature way," she mocks.

Fuck, I don't need her to tell me that. "I don't understand this," I confess.

"It's not complicated. The attraction to the unattainable—it goes back to the beginning of time. You want me. I'm a slut who can't be 'had' by any one person. A guy like you? It pisses you off."

"What do you mean 'a guy like me'?" I ask, afraid to really hear the answer.

"A manwhore, a hypocrite, a guy with double standards. I piss you off because you wanted me, just for the night, as usual, but when you realized I was the female version of you and would feel the same way about hooking up and wouldn't want more from you, the tables were turned. Then, lo and behold, here's someone whose panties you can't get into and leave her worshiping you, and it chafes your ass," she finishes, gasping for breath.

Her chest rises and falls against mine. I can't help my eyes as they fall from hers to her breasts. I swallow hard and lick my lips as I see the tops of what I can imagine are the most perfect breasts known to man. When I glance back up, I catch her running her tongue over her bottom lip. I want to suck on it and bite it simultaneously. I want to fist her hair in my hands and have my way with her. I want it like I've never wanted anything else in my whole life, which gives me the strength to do what I know I need to do.

I tighten my grip on her arms and pull her even closer to me, if possible. Her eyes widen as I do. Then I conjure the strength to do the impossible and push her away with everything I've got. She stumbles back a few steps before catching herself, a knowing smile on her face. I want to wipe that smile from existence, but I won't because the way I want to do it will have her writhing underneath me, moaning and taking me. My dick begs again. *Shut the fuck up!* I refocus my anger. "Don't pretend to know anything about me, Denver."

"I know what I see, unlike you, believing what you hear. And what I see is a guy who uses girls for his own pleasure. I know what Becky—" she sneers the name like it leaves an ugly taste in her mouth "—told me. You don't have the same girl twice. That's pretty fucked-up. And it's enough to make me keep my distance."

A noise distracts me from what I was going to say, which was to tell her to mind her own fucking business. When I look toward the noise, I see Greer.

Shit. I don't need this shit. What the fuck was I thinking? Oh yeah, I wasn't.

His eyes find Denver. "What the hell's going on here? Denver, are you all right?"

"Yeah, I'm fine."

He looks back to me, and he doesn't mince words. "I don't know what you're playing at here, Ransom, but stay the fuck away from her. She doesn't want anything to do with the likes of you. You're a user, and she's better than that, better than you. Do you understand?"

I don't like his assumptions about me either. Neither of them know anything about me, dammit. Instead of denying anything, my irrational, dumb ass decides to egg him on. "I think Denver should be the one to decide who she associates with, don't you? She doesn't seem to be the kind of girl who likes to be told what to do. I don't exactly see her protesting my attention either."

He ignores my taunting. "You know nothing about the kind of girl she is. All you need to know is to stay away from her. She is *mine*. And I'm not gonna let some asshole like you get in between us." He turns back to Denver. "Get on my horse," he demands. My eyes flash to Denver to see how she handles that order. She doesn't disappoint. Her arms are crossed over her breasts, her legs braced like she's ready to fight.

"*She* is sick of being talked about in the third person. *She* can speak for herself. *She* is not yours." She points at Greer. "And *she* is definitely not yours." She points at me. "And *she* thinks you're *both* assholes."

She stalks toward the trail, away from the two of us. "*She'll* find her own way back to the barn," she grinds out over her shoulder.

"Come on, Denver, don't be so damn stubborn. I came to help you out."

Her head snaps back. "I don't need your help, Greer. I don't need to be rescued. I don't need a knight in shining armor. I can take care of myself. Just leave me the hell alone," she asserts before stomping off down the trail.

My laughter gets his attention. "Looks like you need to tame your pussy."

Greer's eyes look like they're about to pop out of his head. "We're not finished," he seethes.

"What the fuck does that mean?"

"It means you don't get to run off with my girl, upset her, and cause problems with us without answering for that."

I decide to piss him off some more. "Lapse in judgment. Won't happen again. She's definitely *not* worth fighting over," I say casually before mounting my horse.

"Maybe not today or tomorrow, but I will be beating the shit out of you," Greer sneers at me before taking off after Denver.

Denver

I CAN'T BELIEVE them, talking about me like I'm some object. How ridiculous. I feel like shit for talking to Greer like that, though. Ransom already had me so pissed off and got me so worked up, that when Greer started bossing me around, I just lost it. I hang my tack up in front of Liberty's stall and turn to go find Greer. I don't have to go far.

I throw myself around him before he can utter a word. His arms engulf me, and I know this is where I belong. I'm safe with him. "I'm so sorry, Greer. I was furious with Ransom for acting like that, and I took it out on you. I hate myself for talking to you like that." I lean back and run my hands over his jaw. "Do you forgive me?"

"Of course, Denver, I'm sorry I was jerk. I just want him to leave you alone."

"You weren't a jerk. I was a bitch. And I don't deserve you."

He tenses against me, his arms squeezing me tighter like he's protecting me from some imaginary threat. "It's not that I don't get it. You're fucking amazing, but you do know he's fixated on you, right?"

"Fixated on me? No he's not."

"Oh, he is. He thinks he's kept it secret, but I can tell. He watches your every move. He wants you even though he pretends otherwise. It goes beyond liking though, and I'm afraid it's not one-sided. He thinks he has a chance with you ... does he?"

I can see the fear in his eyes, and I'm afraid he can see the truth in mine. The truth is that, despite the anger Ransom provokes in me, he provokes other feelings too. Feelings similar to what I once had for Greer. Feelings I've been trying to get back for him. That wasn't working out so well since they seemed to re-route themselves toward Ransom. You think all these weeks of him being such an ass would've dulled what I feel. No, just the opposite. They've only intensified it.

Great! Not only did I have the slut gene, but I also had the asshole-magnet gene.

I don't answer quickly enough. "He does," he mumbles and drops his arms from around me like someone just dropkicked him. Turning from me, he puts his hands on the wall and leans in like he's catching his breath.

"Oh my God, Greer. I'm—" I throw my hand over my mouth. I'm what? Sorry? Fucked-up? Stupid? All of the above.

He drops his head further. "I remember me and you watching him ride on TV. I know you are fascinated with him, but I thought I had a shot. I don't stand a chance, do I?" he asks, resignedly.

Moving behind him, I wrap one arm around his waist and the other around his chest. "You're the only chance I need. I don't want to be with Ransom. I want to be with you." Translation—I don't *want* to want to be with Ransom. I *want* to want to be with you. But I'm still working on those nagging details.

"You mean that?" he asks.

"Yes," I whisper without hesitation.

He spins in my arms, his eyes search mine for a moment. "I love you, chicken. I'm not going down without a fight," he declares.

Chapter Twenty

Ransom

"DENVER, YOU'RE STILL in first," I snap, as I head off a furious cowgirl. "Damn, woman. Stop," I demand, as she rams right into me.

"That's bullshit, Ransom, and you know it," she yells in my face. *In my face.* She's on her tippy-toes and pointing at the scoreboard. "Did you see it? That little shit added almost a full second to my time." She's back to gesturing wildly.

"You look like a damn windmill. Rein it in, Denver."

She folds her arms and cocks her hip. I stare down at her for a minute, my eyes scanning her, pretending I'm gauging whether or not she's calm. In truth, I'm committing her to memory. She stands about a head shorter than me, her long, blonde hair is windblown from her ride, and her eyes are wide and bright with fury.

"You calm?" I finally ask.

"Yeah, *boss*," she sneers and rolls her eyes.

"Good. Go get your horse. She's in need of a cool

down same as you." I move past her quickly to head to the locker rooms because, frankly, that fire in her eyes that reminded me of a burning sunset had me beyond hard. I push my sleeves up and feel a little proud of myself for having disarmed the ticking time bomb that was Denver Dempsey. Holy shit. I've never seen someone so pissed-off. When she exited the arena, she dismounted quickly, throwing her reins and hat to Maggie. I watched, amused, for a minute until I saw her rolling up her sleeves and heading for the judges' podium. Some kid had waved his cowboy hat in front of the motion sensor, setting her clock off before she was ready. She didn't realize it until she was already racing, but she bounced back, of course. She still came in first overall, but that just isn't good enough for Miss Dempsey. She wanted those judges to let her ride again.

"Did you set her straight, boss?" Austin asks, as I make my way down the platform.

"Yeah, sure did," I grumble, unhappy with myself for letting her get me worked up. I need a distraction.

"Oh, so that's what set straight looks like, huh?" he says and promptly bursts out laughing along with Pete, who's also amused at whatever he sees behind me.

I spin around just in time to see one of the judges frantically waving security over.

"Shit. Really?"

"Way to show her who's boss, Ransom," Pete jokes with a chuckle and slaps me on the back.

"Fuck, y'all," I call over my shoulder, as I head back up to talk her ass down.

Denver

"AH! THE BIRTHDAY girl has to sing," I hear a buzzed Maggie squeal from behind me. I straighten up from taking my shot at the pool table to see her careening into people as she makes her way to me. Pete's laughing and trying to hold her up. Maybe she's more than buzzed.

"Denver!" she shouts, as she sweeps me up into a hug like she hasn't seen me in years, rather than thirty minutes. "Can you believe that they not only let us drink here, but we haven't had to pay for the first drink either?"

Pete wraps his arms around her and nuzzles her neck. "That's because we're fucking rodeo gods, sweetheart," he boasts. And it's then I realize they're both wasted. Great! I'd be on duty tonight. Our conversation about how bad she wanted Pete, but how she didn't want to lose her virginity just yet, is still fresh on my mind.

"Pete, should you be drinking with a concussion?" I ask.

He gives me a slanted grin. "I haven't drunk that much, and I'm no worse for wear." He knocks on his head. "Takes a lickin' but keeps on tickin.'" Maggie and I both roll our eyes.

For the most part, we wrapped things up quite nicely for the first half of our season. Maggie and I are number one in our respective events, despite my being cheated out of almost a half of a second. Ransom had ridden today with his three broken ribs, got a ninety-two-point ride, and finished in first place. Pete is number three, having ridden with his mild concussion. Greer is number two. Everyone else is still in the chase, even if they aren't in the top five. They'll have plenty of time to rest up and come back in the spring ready to take care of business. Since we didn't party yesterday, we're letting loose tonight.

"OK, you two, I realize you're both inordinately horny," I say, causing them to laugh in between the kissing and the sudden semi-inappropriate fondling that's going on right in front of me. "But you're making it look like our night's going to end in a sure-fire threesome." Greer's pool stick brushes against the inside of my thigh as he moves in behind me. I shoot him a knowing grin over my shoulder, but he doesn't even acknowledge his little teasing.

Pete's head pops up, and he has look of wonder on his face. "Is that like something you girls are into? Because, holy shit, that'll be hot!"

I hear Maggie gasp, and she spins around slapping him on the chest and pushing him off her at the same time. Pete stumbles a bit, laughing. "I'm just kidding, sweetheart. You're all the woman I need."

"Whatever," she snaps out. But since she's drunk, it's not near as pissed-off sounding as I'm sure she intended. Putting both her hands on her hips and spinning back to me, she says, "Let's go show him what he's gonna be missing out on, Denver. Come on!" She's grabbed my hand and is pulling me toward the karaoke corner before I can resist.

"I'm not drunk enough to sing," I protest.

"I've heard you sing. You have a lovely voice," she shouts back to be heard over the girls on stage now. I glance up and can't help but roll my eyes hard at Becky and Amber. They don't sound bad, but they're trying to be sexy and it's ... ugh! You're either sexy or you're not.

Stephanie is throwing darts, and Maggie smacks her on the butt as we pass. She misses the target and jerks around looking like she's going to take someone's head off. When she sees me and Maggie, she just laughs. "I had no idea, girls," she says, as she waggles her brows at us.

"Oh, no," Maggie protests, "You're a hottie and all, but I just want you to sing with me and Denver. Anyway," she sighs, "I'm saving myself for Pete. His tongue and his fingers are like pure magic, so I can't even imagine what he can do with his—"

"Oh my God, Maggie. Really?" I interrupt. "What have you been drinking?" My shy friend will crawl up in a ball and die tomorrow when I tell her how loose she'd been with her tongue tonight.

"Pete and I were doing tequila shots. And I sucked lime juice from his lips," she brags.

"Girl, you're gonna feel that tomorrow." I hear the Dastardly Duet come to an end, and then Maggie is pulling on both Stephanie and me.

I glance at the screen, wondering what we're singing. I almost let a squeal as I see "Only Prettier" queued up. "Oh, Maggie, you're too good to me," I say as I lean in and peck her on the cheek, much to the delight of all the cowboys who've gathered around.

Austin calls out, "Yeah, baby! I'd much rather watch y'all make out than sing."

We're laughing so hard that we actually miss our cue and have to jump in on the second line. Somehow

I've ended up in the middle with both girls dancing on me like we are, in fact, trying to simulate some hot girl-on-girl-on-girl action. I can't help but play along, so I shake and shimmy and make suggestive glances while trying to keep in time with the music. Karaoke may be meant for having fun, but I won't do Miranda Lambert an injustice, so when Stephanie and Maggie forget to sing and end up doing more of a striptease, I'm the only one left singing.

I glance to the corner booth that Ransom's been hanging out in to see if he's watching me. I don't intentionally watch for him, but my body instinctively knows where he is. It's pretty eerie, come to think of it, but he's not looking at me. He's just staring at his beer with a look of concentration. I close my eyes and will myself not to give a shit what he does or does not notice about me.

When I reopen them, my eyes find Greer. He's kicked back on the wall by the pool table just taking us in with a slight grin on his face. He loves it when I sing.

Our song winds to an end, and when I belt out the line, "I'll just keep drinking, and you'll just keep getting skinnier," I can't help but direct it at those skinny bitches, Becky and Amber.

As the music dies down, the cheering and clapping reach a fevered pitch. I look to my left and to my right and crack up at my singing partners' astounded expressions. "We were good, huh girls?"

"We? What we?" Stephanie questions.

"Holy shit, Denver! You can really sing!" Austin yells.

"Denver, I'm gonna be sick," Maggie cries. I grab

her mike. Luckily, Pete's right next to her and sweeps her off the stage before she can embarrass herself.

Stephanie and I holster the mikes and start to make our way off stage, but Austin grabs me and pushes me back on stage.

"No way, you're not getting off that easy," he says as he wiggles his brows at me. "I didn't mean that like it sounded. Or … maybe I did," he jokes. I can't help but laugh at him.

He backs me up to stand me in front of one mike and announces in the other, "Ransom? Where's Ransom?" My laughter dies out quickly, and I cringe and swat at him to get his attention. I don't know what he's about, but I don't want to be anywhere near Ransom. Or more like I really *do* want to be near him, and that's a problem. "Stop hitting me, Denver. You're gonna sing with Ransom."

I throw my hand over the mike. "It'll be a cold day in hell when I sing with Ransom," I grit out.

Austin shivers and says, "I just got goose bumps. You feeling that chill?" He turns back to the mike and calls for Ransom again. I see movement from his corner, and I'd bet anything Ransom is trying to get out of the bar unnoticed.

"Ugh, Austin!" I try to jerk away, but he's got a good hold on me. And then Ransom moves in behind me, but I stiffen rather than lean into him like my body practically demands.

"Yeah, buddy!" Austin shouts and turns to his mike again. "Y'all are in for a treat tonight. Ransom's practically a singing cowboy, and since we've just heard Denver's sexy pipes, we know she's gonna give him a run for his money. Put your hands together for Denver and Ransom!" He dramatically fades out and removes himself from the stage as I stare daggers at him. My killer look loses its effectiveness when I burst out in laughter at his enthusiastic expression.

Ransom slides a hand across my lower back and hip as he moves to his mike. My skin tingles in its wake. I take a deep breath to steady myself, but instead of approaching his mike, he ducks down to my ear and rasps, "You're even more beautiful when you laugh."

My heart has lodged itself in my throat, but somehow I manage to squeak out, "What are we singing?" trying in vain to take my mind off that telling comment. You don't say things like that to someone you hate, do you?

"Probably some Kenny Chesney. Austin knows that's what I like to sing."

Sure enough, the first chords of Kenny and Grace Potter's duet "You and Tequila" ring out over the bar. My palms go clammy, as I haven't sung this one in the shower very much. "You got this," he assures me. "I'm pretty sure there's nothing you can't do."

Is he drunk? I giggle at that thought as he sings out the first line. My giggling is short-lived, though, because he has a stunning voice. So stunning that when my line comes up, I almost miss it. I recover quickly and sing out softly since that's what this song demands. And I suffer those lyrics with every fragment of my pathetic existence—not being able to resist those who are bad for you, you keep going back for more even though you should know better—mmm, hmm, that's what I've been doing with Ransom, constantly tempting myself.

Unconsciously, we've both angled our bodies toward one another, and we end up singing to each other rather than the crowd. And, even though I can hear them catcalling and dancing and moving along with us, I block them out and focus on the man in front of me.

When I turn my full attention on him, he does the same to me. The moment we both let go is palpable. The intensity in his normally soft green eyes burns through me as they focus on my lips. My eyes drop down to his lips, and I love the way he wears a smirk as he sings about me making him crazy. Even if he's not singing about me, I'm pretending he is. I'd give anything to feel those lips on mine, making me crazy, making me his. God, I want him. When he sings about your favorite sin doing you in, I fight the urge to throw down my mike, drag him off the stage, and show him sin in the best way possible.

Somehow, someway, I'm able to finish the song without embarrassing myself. As the music quietly fades out, Ransom replaces his mike, gives me a strange look, and stalks off the stage, leaving me by myself to receive the praise we earned together. I'm afraid everyone will have noticed how much he hates me and how bad I want him, so I do what I do best—I take the attention off of my discomfort. I stick my boobs way out and curtsy deep, which elicits more hooting and hollering.

When I spring back up, my eyes meet Greer's, and what I see there almost causes me to cry out. He's hurt and pissed, and that's not a good combination. Pushing away from the wall, he storms out of the bar.

Great! I hear someone moving in behind me to take his turn at the mike, so I move off the stage. I get lots of slaps on the back, and someone smacks my ass. Gasping, I turn to see Austin with a mischievous grin. "He went that way," he deflects, as he lifts me up and jostles me in a bone-crushing hug. "Y'all were amazing. You're amazing. Will you marry me, Denver?"

"And deprive all these ready and willing cowgirls of all that is Austin Ransom? Not a chance," I joke, slapping the brim of his hat down.

"Aww ... shucks, ma'am," he says, angling his head back to smirk at me. "We aim to please."

"Oh, I bet you do, cowboy." I can't help but place a playful kiss on his cheek since he's put me in a generous mood. Even though Ransom had stormed off, seeing inside him with his defenses down for a moment had been fascinating and well worth the ensuing awkwardness.

I snap back to reality as I see Austin's chocolate-brown eyes heat to molten from my little unguarded moment. I throw my hand up as his lips make their way toward mine, causing him to kiss my palm. "Ew, Austin," bursts from my lips since he gave it a little lick too. He erupts into loud laughter.

"Oh, Denver, the fun we could have," he cajoles as he lifts and spins me around. My heels whack some people, but they don't seem to care, and neither does Austin. "When you realize what pussies all these other guys are, I'm your man. Got it?" With that declaration, he sets me down to totter off toward the bathroom. I don't get far before I am yanked into a hallway.

The wall at my back, his hands on either side of my head, his lips at my ear ... I liquefy into the wall as Ransom just holds me there, intense green devouring bewildered gold. The moment I've been anticipating … yet dreading. I swallow hard. I won't be the first to speak, I promise myself. He's been so hateful to me.

He breathes me in and nudges the hair from my neck as he runs his nose down it. My hands form fists against the wall as I fight the urge to pull him into me. I want him. So bad.

"I know you do." His breath tickles my throat. I groan as I realize I said that aloud. "You have no idea what you do to me," he continues, as the vibration switches to coming from his voice, to coming from his tongue. I want to weep with relief when it sweeps back up my neck lightly. When he gets to my ear, he places a playful little bite. "Or, maybe you do know. I can't decide how culpable you are in bringing about my downfall."

His words confuse me, but I don't have to wonder long.

"I promised myself I'd never be with anyone like you. Someone who uses others. Someone who finds pleasure in other's pain. Someone not strong enough to be herself." My hands fly up between us, and I push him with all my might. He chuckles as he finds himself a foot or so away from me. We both ignore the fact that he let me push him away. Raising an eyebrow, he tilts his head and boasts, "I could do a lot with that spunkiness, though."

"Why are you such an asshole?" I demand, as I use my shirtsleeve to wipe away the now-cooled trail he left on my neck.

"Why are you such a slut?" he counters.

"I'm …" My voice dies out. I can't deny I'm a slut,

just like he can't deny he's an asshole. But, if I'm going to stand for him labeling me a slut, I'm going to earn it and get a little pleasure out of it at the same time.

Springing from the wall, I put my hands on his chest and back him up against the opposite wall. His eyes widen, and his mouth drops as I catch him by surprise. I take that moment to lean into him and thrust my tongue into his open mouth. I moan as I finally satisfy that curiosity—spicy with cinnamon, bitter from beer, and ripe with his excitement. Desire explodes deep in my belly, and I can't control myself.

He doesn't take long to join me, and our mouths work each other's over at a fevered pace. My hands travel down to fit themselves around his hips as I pull myself into him. His hands match mine as he fits them to my ass and squeezes me hard against him. I feel how turned on he is, and I whimper into his mouth.

I pull back and nip at his bottom lip as I taunt, "You want me. Slut or not. Asshole or not. You. Want. Me. And I want more than anything to see that precious control of yours crack when you finally take what you want, what you've been fighting."

I see his eyes snap to attention before I am flying backwards. I throw my hands out to catch myself against the wall as I laugh lightly and right myself. I've just hit the nail on the head. I make him feel out of control, and he can't stand it. For some reason, I'm different to him, and that's why he hates me. That, coupled with the fact that he can't control me, pisses him right the fuck off.

He schools his features before stalking calmly toward me. And his calmness actually frightens me more than his being out of control. Frightens me and fires me up. Putting one finger under my chin, he moves my mouth up to rest just a centimeter under his. He stills, holding there for a moment. Instead of stilling, my breaths come fast and hard as I anticipate what he'll do or say next to insult me to put me in my place.

He throws me for a loop when he leans down and swipes my bottom lip with his tongue. "You taste so good," he murmurs. "Honey ... daisies ... and ... sunshine." I can never keep my sense of balance around him. My hands move up to pull him further into me. "No, no touching. Put your hands against the wall." They hang in the air for a second before I feel myself complying. "Good girl," he breathes. The way he praises me, excites me and makes me more eager to please him because I have a feeling, if you please Ransom, the rewards he will lavish upon you will know no bounds.

One of his hands comes up to lay itself flat on my neck. His calloused fingertips sweep lightly over my jaw. "Open your mouth," he breathes against my lips, and I do. He slides his tongue teasingly against mine. He pulls back, sucks on my bottom lip, and then he's back inside me. And it's a sweet torment, as he is dedicated to his craft. My heart hammers in my ears, and I am dizzy. He pulls back and bites my bottom lip again, but harder this time. A desperate sob barely escapes me before he's back in my mouth, sweeping and exploring. I relax and feel him, really feel him. The walls could come crashing down around us, and I wouldn't have the faintest idea. Finally, I join in. As soon as I do, he pulls back with another bite at my already swollen lip, and what he says almost causes me to melt on the spot. "I'm tired of fighting this." He smiles against me before he lays his forehead on mine. "But I'm not tired of fighting with you. When you get bored fooling around with those little boys, you know where to find me. Until you're mine, and mine only, I won't touch you again."

His words paralyze me so that it takes me a few minutes to register that he's long gone. I didn't even see him walk away. I stumble out of the little hallway and make my way to bathroom. What the hell did that mean? I know where to find him? He practically said he hated me. Why would he want to be with me? Ah, the answer hits me with such force, I release a strangled breath. I glance up to see my surprised reflection. Despite the way he feels about my reputation, he wants me for a one-night stand. God, and the way he hates me and wants to use me—that's my attraction. Just what my self-destructive nature needs, a heaping pile of burning hatred to enflame my compulsion. *Self-hatred seeks match so that she can, once and for all, burn herself to the ground.* Fuck that. I've spent my whole life making sure that never happened.

When I emerge from the restroom, I feel like a new person. No longer torn. No longer divided. My eyes search the crowd. When I spot Greer next to the bar, I make a beeline for him. He's leaning against the bar on one elbow, sipping his beer. One boot, propped against the metal footrest. His stance says *relaxed*, but his face says *wounded*.

My eyes follow his to the current performer, and my jaw drops as the singer, and the noise he's making, registers. I want to yell at him to quit butchering Alan Jackson, but Austin looks like he's having a blast as he bounces completely out of time with the beat. I just shake my head and continue my path.

When I'm standing in front of Greer, he finally turns to me. I can tell that he saw me coming but just didn't want to face me. I take his beer from him, and keeping my eyes trained on him, I drain it. Even though the music's bad, I pull him out onto the dance floor and wrap myself around him.

"I hated that. Every minute," he says, pain coating his words.

"Don't think about that for another second. I'm yours."

"What?" He stops dancing and holds me at arm's length.

My eyes pierce his for a moment, hoping he will see the truth in my words. "I'm yours, Greer. Always have been. Always will be."

"You mean it?" he whispers brokenly.

I pull him back to me, and threading my fingers through his hair, I pull his mouth to mine. "I mean it," I whisper against his lips before I kiss him lightly.

Over his shoulder, I glimpse Ransom. He's smirking at me, all-knowing.

I keep my eyes on his as I run my lips over Greer's for a second. He goes from smirking to scowling. Smiling against Greer's lips, I finally close my eyes and lose myself in our kiss.

I pull back, suddenly realizing something. "Hey, what time is it?"

He pulls his phone out, grins at it. "One minute till midnight."

"That's how you got me to kiss you the first time, do you remember? You told me our birthdays kissed each other so it was only fitting that we did. You were only six, smooth operator."

Grinning sheepishly, he admits, "Yes, but it was only a peck for years."

"Think you can kiss me for a full minute and bring in our birthdays like old times?"

With a shimmer in his pretty blue eyes, he places a light kiss on my lips and whispers against them, "Definitely."

Chapter Twenty-one

Denver

WE'VE BEEN BACK from Wyoming for a week, and he still won't give it up. He told me he was gonna make me work for it—make me prove I haven't said yes just because I want to use him for sex. Whatever would give him that idea?

The stress of all this back and forth with Greer and Ransom—that's what I'm blaming. I know better than to do shots of tequila, but I'm on a mission to drown out my every thought, my every feeling. I know when my teeth get numb I should stop, but I don't. It doesn't help that Greer has matched me shot for shot, which is pretty rare. He doesn't usually drink so much. I can barely handle tequila, so I know it must be kicking his ass.

I move myself against him to the beat of the song, and I realize that there is one feeling the tequila has amplified. I'm horny as hell.

"Hey, I'm gonna step outside for a minute. I'll be right back," he yells in my ear over the noise of the party.

Turning, I pull him in tight to me. I can feel him

against my stomach, and I know that all our dirty dancing has him worked up. Maybe I will get lucky tonight. "Greer, I can feel how bad you want me. If you touch me right now, you'll know how bad I want you too."

He just laughs at me and gives me a quick peck before leaving me feeling lonely and turned on in the middle of the dance floor. I can't even imagine the sad state I appear to be in.

I don't stand like that for long. Austin barrels into me, almost knocking me over, since I'm pretty damn drunk. He reaches down and grabs me around me knees before lifting me and spinning me in a circle. "Nobody puts baby in a corner," he yells at no one.

"What are you talking about, Austin? Put me down." I slap at his shoulders.

"You looked so sad over here all by yourself," he says as lets my body slide down his.

"You're taking this Patrick Swayze thing a little too far."

"I may not be able to sing, but I can dance," he declares as he grinds his hips into mine and sways me back and forth. He actually can dance.

Our moment of fun is short-lived when I spot an angry Ransom staring at us from across the room. I stiffen up and look to Austin. "Why does your cousin hate me?"

He looks over his shoulder and then back at me. "'Cause he wants you so damn bad he can't fucking see straight. But, he's got those damn rules of his. Poor fucker."

"What rules?"

"Ah ... not for me to discuss," he says. "I know I like to flirt with you and give you a hard time, but I'd never fuck around with you either."

"Umm ... thanks, I think."

"I don't mean it like that. I'd love to fuck around with you. Nothing would *satisfy* me more. But not when Ransom's got it so bad for you."

"He doesn't have it so bad for me. You're mistaken."

"Yeah, you're wrong about that, sweet thing. I've never seen him so hung up on a girl before. Even Victoria, who he pledged his undying love for back in high school, didn't have a hold on him like you do."

"Well, he just wants what he can't have. Much like every other guy—no big mystery. It's not me he's hung up on, it's the idea of me not falling over myself for him with stars in my eyes and air in my head."

A tap on my shoulder has me turning to see Greer, eyeballing Austin. "Nuh, uh. No jealously. Austin's a lover not a fighter," I joke. "Right, Austin?"

"Right!" he shouts as he leans in and gives me a peck on the cheek.

"Oh my God, this has gotten beyond ridiculous!" someone screeches. The three of us turn to see a drunken Becky and a wide-eyed Amber standing beside us. "I mean, are you just gonna have a three-way right here on the dance floor so that everyone can see for themselves what a slut you are?" she practically screams in my face.

Suddenly, I have a wall of men in front of me. "Get out of my way. I want to punch that lying, hypocritical bitch right in her face," I screech.

"Whoa, now," Austin says calmly, throwing his

arms out. "Nobody needs to go hitting anybody."

"What the hell's going on over here?" Ransom appears behind Becky and Amber.

"Oh, Denver. Here's another one for you. Perhaps a four-way is in order tonight?"

"I've had about enough of your shit," Greer jumps in before I can say anything. "You are a hypocritical little thing, aren't you? You think guys don't talk? You think we don't all know about how quick and willing you are to get on your knees for most of the cowboys in this room?"

I hear her gasp of outrage before she explodes, "I've done no such thing." She looks around desperately. A grin works its way over my whole face, and I am helpless to stop myself from snorting with laughter. "Don't you laugh at me, you little skank!"

"That's enough." Ransom grabs her arm and starts pulling her backward. "Come on. Let's go walk it off," he says.

Greer shouts out over him and the crowd, "At least she's honest about who she is. Not one person standing in this room can say that. We all have our secrets. We all have our hidden faults. Not Denver. You'll never hear her deny who she is. You'll never hear her claim to be perfect. She's the most honest person here!" With that, he grabs my hand and wraps me in his arms, resuming our dance.

After a few more shots and a little more dancing, he pulls me behind him and drags me from the party, and up the stairs toward his apartment. We're both swaying back and forth, so it's pretty slow going. Curiosity finally gets the best of me. "Was that true? Does she really give out free blow jobs?"

Greer laughs roughly. "No, but it doesn't need to be true, does it?" He sobers for a minute. "All it takes is an accusation, a murmur. And you know, firsthand, how people rush to judgment and want to believe the worst."

"Greer, I can't believe you said that if it wasn't true." I've never seen him act like that before. And he witnessed those kinds of confrontations plenty of times. "I'm glad you did though. That little bitch deserved to be put in her place for a minute."

I stop him and tug him down to my stair without breaking eye contact. "Greer, that really turned me on. What you did for me. I'm done waiting. I need to be with you."

Leaning in, he grasps both sides of my face, and his mouth moves hot and fast over mine. My lips tingle as he kisses the feeling back into it. "I'm going to put you in your place now," he threatens as he kisses the corners of my mouth. I groan against him.

"You think you're the man for the job?"

"You better believe it," he declares, sweeping me up and carrying me down the hallway to his apartment.

He puts me on my feet, and we both stumble before falling into one another, using the other for support. Laughing, we stagger into his room, frantically groping each other. All my pent-up desire for him comes rushing to the forefront, and I can't get enough of him. He makes quick work of the snap buttons on my shirt, tugging so that they open in rapid succession. *That was hot.* I can't help but giggle. I meet his big, blue eyes, and the look I see there causes my laughter to die quickly. He has always been so in love with me, and all I've done is push him away and block him out, only giving a little piece of myself—the piece I deemed unimportant and detached. Am I finally ready to give him all of me?

Greer runs his hands down my arms and clasps my hands in his. Pinning me against the door with his body, he kisses and sucks my neck until I can't breathe. I pull my hands free and fist them in his curls to direct him over me. I can smell his stolen cigarette and the tequila, and in my drunken haze, it fuels me. "God, yes, Greer," I say with a moan.

My head drops back, and I'm gone as my zipper flies down, his hand down my jeans in seconds. Oh, those fingers. They play me and rub me like a delicious torrent, until I'm chanting his name and spouting gibberish. His eyes widen and revere me like he's just cracked the safe on the Crown Jewels. I become putty in his hands as he works me to climax in mere seconds. He's an expert at my body. "You are amazing," I breathe.

"You feel incredible. I can't wait to be inside you again. You've been starring in my naughty fantasies for so long." My laughter bubbles out and around us, wrapping us tight.

Bracing my hands on his shoulders, I gaze at him as he removes my boots. When he slides my jeans down, the friction from the crisp material sends tingles down my thighs, over my calves, and over the tops of my feet. He grins when he notices the goose bumps and looks up at me as he kisses his way up my thighs to the crease in my leg. Hooking his thumbs in my panties, he slides them down slowly, his hot kisses trailing behind them.

Rising, he quickly slides my shirt from my

shoulders. I help him out by unclasping my bra. Once they are exposed, Greer stares appreciatively at my breasts, and I heat under his gaze. Without warning, he dives and devours them while inching us over to his bed. I gasp as his hands and mouth work themselves over my tender nipples.

"We're finally gonna do it on a bed," I joke. He laughs before pushing me back to topple on the mattress and takes on a serious look as he kicks off his boots and clothes. When he is standing naked, I let my gaze wander down his strong, lean body. I give him a mischievous grin when I get to his manhood. My eyes work their way back up to his. He is so gorgeous. Every. Single. Inch.

"You are so beautiful," he echoes my thoughts. "I've waited forever to have you again."

My mouth widens into a soft smile. I've wanted him too. I feel terrible for making him wait for my commitment. He's always been so good to me. And he waded through all my bullshit, making him the only person I could ever truly count on. The fact that I almost threw him away is sobering. "You're gorgeous, Greer, inside and out," I breathe. "I can't believe you're mine."

He runs his teeth over his bottom lip and gives me a lopsided grin. "Yours?" he questions.

"Mine," I confirm.

"Yours."

Bending, he picks up my foot and runs his lips over the top of it to my ankle. As I try not to squirm, he kisses his way up my body until his lips hover over my belly button, then he dips in to tease and play while I run my hands through his hair. "Denver, you have no idea how much I've wanted this. How much I've wanted you. How much I've *needed* you."

"I need you too. I've missed you," I admit that truth. I hadn't really understood the depths of it, but I had missed him terribly since I closed myself off to him. I missed his tender touch. His pure friendship. His sweet attention.

Under my hands, his jaw tightens, and he swallows hard. "Watching you talk to *him*, to those other guys, has been hell on me. I'm done with all that teasing. I'm afraid you don't understand." He pulls back to make eye contact with me. "Do you understand?" I'm puzzled, seeing something I've never really seen directed at me before. Anger. Ferocity. Before I can say anything, he tells me, "You. Are. Mine. Do you understand that? No one else can have you." His hands tighten in a pleasurably painful vice on mine.

"Greer?" I question.

"Denver, I ... I mean it." He grinds his hips into mine and moves down to my mouth. I jerk my head to the side. I can't let him kiss me yet. This doesn't feel quite right. My stomach pinches. Something's off. "You back to not kissing me? What else do I have to do?" He attacks my neck, biting and sucking. "You want him too, don't you? I knew it. You're still not gonna commit to me? I don't want you talking to him anymore. I can't take it. I see the way he watches you like you're a seven-course meal. I won't have it." He spreads my legs with his knee and presses his length against me, rubbing up and down against my tiny bundle of nerves. I close my eyes and moan. He feels so good. "I've worked too hard for this just to let him come along and fuck it all up. Do you get that?"

I try to reason with him through my drunken haze. "Greer, we're barely tolerant of each other. I want to be with you. You're being ridiculous."

Anger flashes again in his eyes, reminding me of a tornado with its scary quick power. "You're not going to speak to him anymore," he orders.

I bristle and buck against him, which only serves to bring him closer to me. I don't even really like talking to Ransom half of the time, but no one is going to tell me what to do, especially Greer. "Greer, I'll speak to whoever I damn well please," I bite out, remembering all too suddenly why I don't like drunk Greer. He's making me uncomfortable. "You know? I think I need to go. This is a mistake."

His grip tightens even more, but there's no more pleasure mixed in. It's just painful, and it scares me a bit. I remind myself that Greer would never really hurt me, and I force myself to relax. "No, you're not going anywhere. I'm not letting you shut me out again."

"Greer, you're being a jerk. You're just drunk. This is not you. Let me up, please."

His eyes narrow at the word *jerk*. "Do you remember Drew from high school?"

My breath leaves me in a swift rush. Drew, come to find out, had been responsible for much of my humiliation and torment. "You know I do. You're the one who told me that he started all those rumors about me."

"He started them because of me. Because of what I had to do to make sure you were only mine."

My brow draws together in confusion. "What do

you mean?"

He drops his lips to my chest and runs them over me lightly. Then his kisses turn heated. "I'm sorry. I'm so sorry I hurt you," he rasps. Tequila makes his mood swing like a pendulum, every single time. I shouldn't have let him drink that with me, but I was so frustrated. His words make me snap to attention. "I didn't know it would take on the life that it did, though. I only told him one tiny thing so he would stop trying to take you from me. When I saw how the guys started ignoring you and the girls warned everyone away from you, I couldn't help myself. I made sure everyone knew that you were willing to fuck your friends—" he stresses the plural "—with no strings.

"I had to make sure no one stole you away from me. Do you see the lengths I've had to go to? I'll be damned if I'm going to let all that hard work, all those years of waiting to truly possess you, go to waste. I would do anything to keep you. That's love, Denver. That's how much I love you. Can't you see that?"

His confession freezes everything inside me, and all the hateful and vindictive things that had been hurled at me over the last few years come at me with lightning speed. They strike at my heart until I lie there, a tattered, frozen mess.

How many nights had I cried myself to sleep? How many days had I spent trying to figure out a way to get everyone to see I wasn't like my mother? I've endured years of accusations of being nothing but a slut.

I've only had one person to comfort me and know me and watch out for me.

And that one person had been the very root of all

that pain.

He set up a slow drip of poison and watched as it oozed into every aspect of my life, coating me in every way, until I didn't know who I was anymore.

Years of pushing everyone out of my life so that they couldn't hurt me even more. Years of pretending to be something I wasn't so that it wouldn't hurt all that bad. Years. *Years!* I've had to put up with that shit, and all because of *his* insecurities, of *his* possessiveness? I can't believe it. I can't believe he could hurt me like that.

When my shock wears off, I realize that he's kissing my breasts and murmuring how happy I've made him. But I want him off of me. Fury throws a fiery blanket over my frozen state, and I'm boiling instantly.

"Greer, get off of me." I struggle against him, but he just tightens his hold again and switches from his two hands holding me to just the one. The tequila's made him stronger while it seems to have made me weaker.

He focuses his mouth on one of my breasts, while his other hand runs down me and massages the other before going down to play between my legs. I feel sick. He repulses me. Do I even know this person? "Greer, get off of me," I repeat with more force. "I want to leave. I don't want to do this."

"Your body's singing a different tune, baby," he breathes against me as his fingers slide inside of me. His thumb plays at my bud of nerve endings. "You are so wet, so turned on for me. I'm about to take you hard. Just like you like it. I've needed you for so long."

His fingers continue to pump in and out of me, and my quiet refusals become enraged protests. "Greer, you make me sick. I fucking hate you! Stop! Get off of me!"

I struggle against him again. Tears spring to my eyes.

"You don't hate me. You may not have told me you love me, but I've seen it. I don't need the words. You love me. You want me. Only me," he says as he sinks into me.

"Ah!" I cry out and my tears pour forth in earnest. "No, Greer, I hate you! Don't do this!" I scream again. I start to struggle even harder, but it just forces him further inside me. I hear myself whimper. I'm crying in earnest now. I've had him many times, but he feels foreign and unwanted in this moment. I try to push him out of me. I want him out of me.

"Oh! I can tell how much you hate me. You're so hot, and you fit me like you were made for me. Only I've been here. I'm the only one who'll *ever* be here. Don't you feel how much I want you? 'Cause I feel how much you want me." His eyes zero in on my mouth for a second before he mutters, "Fuck your rules."

I open my mouth to scream again, but he slams his down on mine and sucks my words into his mouth with a punishing kiss. I can't breathe. I can't think. I don't know what to do. Silent sobs wrack my entire body. And all they serve to do is make it feel like I'm participating in this. I finally think to bite him, but he has my mouth pried open and pinned back. I can't even do that. With his legs sprawled on top of mine, he has me completely trapped.

I can't breathe. Light-headedness overtakes me, and a seeping numbness spreads through my limbs. He drives in and out of me, and I want to die. His thumb come back to work me. And, to my utmost horror and shame, an orgasm works its way through me. How is that even possible? Now my tears are for my own body's betrayal. I hear him groaning and feel him straining. Finally, he fills me with one final thrust and collapses on top of me, his hands finally releasing mine, and his head coming to rest on my panting chest. And I can't move. I'm frozen again. Stunned.

After what feels like forever but is probably only a few minutes, his breathing returns to normal, and I realize that mine has too. He pushes up on his palms, and I see his gorgeous, smiling face go from blissful to pained. Dropping down on his elbows, he uses his thumbs to wipe under my eyes.

"Baby, why are you crying?" he asks with concern.

I just stare at him. I can't speak. *Why am I crying?* You just ... just. "I told you no," I whisper brokenly.

"Denver, I thought you were kidding around. We've played that game before. But you know I'd never hurt you," he soothes, as he runs his hands over my hair.

"You did hurt me, Greer. You've been hurting me for years. I just didn't know until now and I—" A sob breaks through before I can say anymore.

He leans and kisses the tip of my nose and my forehead. I don't turn my head quick enough. "Let me get you some water," he says as he eases out of me and rolls out of bed. I watch dispassionately as he slips on his boxer briefs and leaves the room.

I lie there for a second. Wondering ... did he just ... did he just do what I think he did? That's the way it feels. I snap out of my stupor and spring from the bed. I'm shaking as I pull on my clothes and grab my boots. I sling the door open, forcing it into wall with a loud bang. Greer's leaving the kitchen to come back to me when I spot him.

"Baby, where are you going? I—"

He can't finish his statement because my fist slams into his perfect fucking face. Water sloshes to the floor. "What the fuck?" he roars, grabbing his nose and pinching. He removes his hand, looking at the blood. "Fuck, Denver, you busted my damn nose!"

"I said, 'No! Stop! Get off of me! I fucking hate you!' And you wouldn't stop," I storm. "You've hurt me so badly over these years, Greer. I can't even …"

He sets the glass of water on the bar and grabs a paper towel to staunch the blood that trickles from his nose. "You liked it," he insists. "You always like it like that." He grabs my arms and tries to pull me to him. I'm not budging. Does he think I'm playing some kind of game? "Denver, I'd never hurt you like that." I see the sincerity in his eyes and hear it in his tone, but I … I just don't know. Maybe that's not what happened. I waver. "I swear to God, Denver, please know that I was messing around. I'd never hurt you like that."

Maybe not like that, but he damn sure hurt me in other ways, and on purpose. "Not only that, but you'd ruin me for every other guy so that I'd have no other options but you, right? That's sick. I meant what I said, Greer, I hate you." I jerk my arms from his and start toward the door.

"Please don't leave like this. Let me make this right."

I throw my arms out in exasperation. "Nothing you could *ever* do would make any of this right!" I screech. "You. Betrayed. Me! After everything we've been through. And I did NOT want to have sex with you after you told me how you did me wrong, and you … *you made me!*" I take a deep breath, trying to calm myself. "I told you no." My voice cracks, and I hate it. I finally see a little something register in his eyes. I need to get away from him. Just being near him makes me want to vomit.

"Oh my God. Oh my God, Denver! No."

That's the last thing I hear him say as I turn and fly out of his door and run toward the stairs, taking them as quickly as possible. Adrenaline courses through me, and I make it down the stairs in record time. When I near the bottom floor, I'm shaking uncontrollably. Greer was supposed to be my ride home, and Maggie is still at the party with Pete. I can't go in there.

I wind myself around the banister and duck under the stairs. Pulling my legs to my chest, I wrap my arms around them and perch my head on my knees. I'll just sit for a few minutes while I get myself together. I just need five minutes.

Chapter Twenty-two

Denver

CLOSING MY EYES, I try to clear my head and rid myself of all thought. I envision my mind as one of my open fields back home. It's green and lush. It's springtime. Having just rained, it smells fresh and unused. Teeming with new life and new possibilities, it awaits my next move. Will I ride out across and embrace this hand I've just been dealt? Or, will I sit back in my saddle and let this happen around me, unspeaking and unmoving?

How many times have I had to pick myself up and move forward?

How many more times would I have to?

I shake my head as black ink spills all over my perfect landscape. A single tear slips down my cheek. I don't know if I can do it this time. At least all those other times, I had my best friend. Now, I have no one. I sniff a little.

Deep breath.
Release.
Hiccup.
Tears.

Shit.

The music from the party gets louder for a minute, and I hear a couple shuffle past me to sit on the steps. About that time, I hear angry footsteps coming down the stairs.

"Hey, Molly, Luke, have y'all seen Denver?" Greer asks.

"No, man, not since she left with you."

"Molly?"

"No. Is everything OK?"

Greer starts walking again and says, "Not really. I need to find her is all." I hear the door open and slam behind him. He's had too much to drink, so I hope he's not going to drive. *Ugh! Why do I care?* Letting out a shaky breath, I feel as though I've just been granted a reprieve.

I don't know how long I've been sitting here, but my legs are cramping up. My hand is throbbing too. I pull it up and examine my swollen knuckles. I punched him hard right across the bridge of his nose. I guess it'll be sore for a while.

I see a few more feet pass by me and leave the party.

I will myself to get up, but I just ... can't. I can't.

I've been with Greer before. Many times. Why am I so upset? Even though we used each other for years, I never actually felt used. Until now.

I feel used now.

My brain cannot wrap itself around the fact that he is the cause of so much of my pain. The one person I trusted to keep me safe. Keep me from being hurt. He was my secret tormentor, and I did that to him. He may have been the nail, but I was most definitely the hammer. I drove him to desperate measures with my rules and my boundaries and my unwillingness to do the simple thing he asked of me—love him back. He was nothing but good to me before I tainted him.

My golden boy. Gone.

I guess a toxic relationship like ours couldn't die a quiet, dignified death. It had to go out with a bang—a spitting, sputtering, gut-wrenching bang.

I gasp for air on this thought, and another whimper leaves me. I try to stifle it, but it can't be helped. My tear ducts seem to use this slight sound as permission to allow a waterfall of tears to escape. Damn it! I need to stop, get it together, and get out of here. I use the back of my hands to dry my face.

"Well, if it isn't Denver. What's wrong, sweetheart? Couldn't find someone's boyfriend to steal tonight?" I hear Becky taunting me. "Look, Amber, it's Denver and she's crying. I didn't know sluts had the emotional capacity for tears."

Amber snickers and mutters, "Will wonders never cease? Come on, Becky. We'll miss our ride."

They move to leave, but Becky turns back. "And don't think for a second that Greer's little outburst against me had any effect whatsoever. Everyone knows the truth about you and about me," she scolds before she prances off.

When the door slams, my quiet sobs become louder. And I literally shush myself. Oh my God! Why can I not stop crying? I haven't stopped crying since he … since he was on top of me. I can't think about that. I can't think about him being inside of me.

After all these years of making sure that never happened to me ... I never thought he'd be the one to ... no, I'm not ready to consider that.

I relax one of my legs and rub it for a moment before tucking it back in and doing the same to the other. I consider making the short walk back to my dorm, but I'm weak and afraid he'll be there. As I pull in the other leg, I hear a muffled curse.

"Denver?" Oh, no! Anyone but him. I'd rather be ridiculed by all those hateful girls than see him. He hates me. He will take so much pleasure in seeing me brought down to the level he's already put me on. Sobs wrack my frame. He crouches in front of me. "Hey, now. Shh ... what's going on? Why are you crying? Are you hurt?"

I shake my head side to side, close my eyes tight, and bite my lip. His hand brushes my hair aside, and I flinch.

"Easy now. Can I do anything? Can I get someone for you?"

"Ye-yes ... Maggie?" I manage.

"Oh, um, Maggie and Pete left a while ago. She said you left already. Is there anyone else?"

"No," I whisper. And I did that to myself. Well, I had a little help from Greer. With that thought, I'm overcome with tears again.

I hear Ransom let a long sigh and feel my hands being pulled until I am on my feet. Looking up, I take in his set jaw and piercing, green gaze. Will he know? It has to be written all over my face. "Come on, Denver. Let's go upstairs and get you cleaned up."

He reaches down to grab my boots for me. "Is this

all you have?" he asks. I nod. He motions for me to lead the way to the stairs, and I try to head that way, but my legs don't work. I almost crumple, but I feel myself being lifted in the air before I can actually fall. "I've got you. I don't know what's going on, but you've got me scared."

"Just need another minute," I sob.

Chapter Twenty-three

Ransom

MY DOOR'S UNLOCKED, so I tell her to open it before easing us both inside. She's a compact little thing and fits perfectly in my arms. I don't really know what to do with her, but I've got it in my head that if she gets cleaned up she'll feel better, and I can take her to her dorm and be done with her. So I head toward the bathroom.

Bending over, I set her on her feet and glance at her. I saw she was a mess, but like a solar eclipse, looking directly at Denver is painful, so I didn't until now. Her mascara is running down her face. Hair's a complete mess, like her hands were fisted in it and she was pulling on it. Those eyes, though, the ones I thought were the strongest I've ever seen—they look … weighty. Like it's everything she can do to keep them open. What are they weighted with—that's the question. *Shit.*

"Umm … I'll get you a washcloth. You'll be OK here for a second?"

"Yeah, I'm fine," she chokes out.

Yeah, no you're not. Shit.

When I come back from the hall closet, she's laid her forehead on the door and is just standing there focusing on breathing. At least that's what she looks like she's doing. She's not crying anymore. That's a plus. I almost mention that to cheer her up but think better of it. Don't want to set her off again.

I lean her back and reach around her to open the door. I follow her in, flip the light on, and toss the washcloth on the sink. I glance around, wondering if it's clean. It looks like two guys live here. I push our shaving gear and other stuff into a compact circle. I grab Pete's clothes off the floor and back out.

"Ransom?" I barely hear her call.

"Yeah?"

"Umm ... do you mind ..." Her voice catches. "Do you mind if I take a shower?" Another sniff.

Shit. A naked Denver in my bathroom? Can I handle that? No. "Yeah, of course," my manners speak for me. Shit.

"Thank you."

After I get the water right for her, I step out quickly, but linger by the door. Does she want clean clothes to put on? She didn't look dirty, just rumpled. I start wondering what exactly happened with her. She and Greer left the party after he made his stupid announcement. Did he hurt her? I don't see that happening. First off, she's tough as nails and wouldn't let anyone hurt her. Second off, Greer may be a lot of things, but I don't see him hurting her. Unless it's her heart that's hurting. I guess she does have one after all. Whatever happened, she seems a shell of the Denver I've come to know and hate and ... as much as I wanted to deny it, love. I'm sure this Denver is temporary. She'll be back to her caustic self in no time at all.

My brow wrinkles from what I don't hear behind the door. I turn my head and press my ear to the wood to make sure. The shower runs steadily, telling me that she didn't get in it.

"Denver?"

"Yeah?"

Yep, she's right behind the door.

"You're not in the shower."

"No." Hitch. "I'm not."

"Coming in. You decent?"

Hesitation. "I guess."

Another brow wrinkle. I crack the door and peer through it, starting at her feet just to be safe. My eyes wander up to see she's completely dressed and staring at the water falling from the showerhead.

"Do you still want to wash up?"

Her honey-colored eyes that are still tinged with sadness slide from the shower to me. "Yes."

"Why aren't you getting in?"

Her face falls, and she looks down at her hands. I'm at a complete loss with how to handle this Denver. "I … I—"

"I can't take this indecisive shit anymore, Denver." I hear the mean tone in my voice, but I've got to get her out of my apartment. I can't be around her much longer. I know my bad attitude will spur her into action. "Do you need my help undressing?"

"No," she barks. Her head flying back up. Mission accomplished. I see a little spunk behind the sadness. I can't help but grin. There she is. Even if it's just a bit.

"All right then." I nod. "Get your butt undressed, and get cleaned up. Want some clean clothes?"

"Yes, please."

I shut the door on her niceties, which are beyond confusing, to go in search of something for her to wear.

When she emerges from the bathroom, dressed in my sweat pants and too large t-shirt, I leave my position of leaning against the wall with my cell phone in hand and start toward her. She cowers a little bit, and in that moment, I know something awful has happened. This is bigger than hurt feelings.

"I sent a text to Pete so he could tell Maggie you're here with me, and I'd bring you to your dorm in a bit." She just nods.

I need her to talk to me. I know that now. Figure out what I can do to help her and whether or not I need to kick someone's ass. First things first, though. "Are you hungry? Thirsty?"

"Some water would be good."

Since I need answers and don't want Pete interrupting us, I guide her to my room and tell her to wait there for me. When I come back with some ice water and Motrin, she doesn't even notice me until I'm standing directly in front of her. She takes the medicine without even asking what it is and swallows it with her water. She reminds me of a machine that's forgotten its programming. Going through the motions with prompting, but still not quite right. When she finishes gulping down most of her water, she just holds the glass at an odd angle in front of her like she doesn't know what step comes next.

I take the glass from her and set it on the nightstand,

pulling up my desk chair in front of her in the process. I swallow hard. Other than our sometimes flirting and usual bickering, I don't know her all that well. Then I wonder if anyone really knows Denver. Does she even know herself for that matter?

Rubbing dampened palms over my thighs, like I'm getting ready to ride the beast, I brace them sideways on my knees and lean into her space a little. She's been busy staring a hole in my wall. "Denver?" I say softly. Only her eyes move to find mine. "I need you to tell me what happened tonight."

She shakes her head at me. "Nothing I didn't deserve. I'll be OK, Ransom. I just need—"

"Another minute?" I finish for her.

She exhales shakily, and the cinnamon smell of my toothpaste engulfs me. "I guess. I don't know." She finds her palms interesting in that moment. I glance down and take them in. They're small but steady and strong. "I don't know how to recover from this betrayal."

"Betrayal? Who betrayed you? What happened?"

She traces a pattern on her hand before sighing. "It's not important. I'll get over it. It just ... hurts."

Surely it couldn't be as bad as all that. "Maybe it's not as bad as you're thinking. Maybe you got your wires crossed. A misunderstanding?"

Nodding, she looks back up at me. "Yeah, that's it. A misunderstanding."

She's too quick to agree with me. I frown at her. "Bullshit."

"Yep, that *was* bullshit." And I earn myself a tiny grin.

I narrow my eyes. "You just don't want to talk

about it. And would say anything to get me to drop it, right?" I joke.

Another tiny grin. Why did that make me feel like I hung the damn moon? I somehow refrain from grinning with pride and continue, "I guess I really only need to know one thing. Did anyone hurt you ... physically?"

She maintains eye contact, her eyes hardening before she mumbles, "No." She doesn't like look she's lying, so I just nod and relax. I didn't realize how tense I was, waiting for her answer. I was ready to kick some necessary ass on her word. I may not like her very much, but I wouldn't let that pass. "But I did," she confesses and flips her hand over, showing me her swollen knuckles. "You'd be proud. I threw the punch from my core."

"You hit someone?" I marvel, as I run my thumb over her hand.

She shrugs. "Yep. Deserved it. And it wasn't my first time to throw a punch at a face."

"We'll get you some ice, and then I guess I can bring you to your dorm." Her semi-relaxed state morphs right before my eyes. Her eyes shift from mine. She takes a deep breath and folds in on herself a little. That scares her for whatever reason. I can't imagine why. It's just a bunch of girls. Then it hits me. It's the girls who've hurt her. Not a guy. They must have upped their game. I guess a person could really only take so much. "Unless you want to stay here," I hear myself utter. Her eyes dart back up. *Shit*. Really? What the hell's wrong with me?

Her relief is even more visible than her tensing a second ago. "Yeah?"

"Yeah, I'll sleep on the couch. You can sleep in here." Her eyes tighten, but she nods her head.

"Thank you, Ransom. For everything. I know you … don't like me much."

My hand finds her knee and gives it a quick squeeze, but not quick enough. It registers immediately that I like how soft she is. "Hey, don't worry about any of that. Water under the bridge."

"Really, Ransom?" she says with hope this time.

"Really. Let's call a truce, yeah?"

"Yeah." She nods her head somewhat enthusiastically. "I'm sorry for being a bitch."

"I'm sorry for being an ass. Or … what was it?" I tap my chin thoughtfully while a little blush steal over her cheeks. *Holy shit!* A blushing Denver? That has to be a first. And that does more for me than the bikini-clad Denver or even the badass, barrel racer Denver. "A jerk of a thousand shades." I laugh, remembering her insult. "Can you really think of a thousand nuances?" She opens her mouth, her nerves practically bubbling out. "Hey, I'm kidding. I thought it was funny. Later. Much later." That actually gets me a little laugh.

Pete comes home before I can text him. I ask him to let Maggie know what's going on while I brief him on the situation.

After I get settled on the couch, I realize it's around four in the morning. I don't think much else because I promptly pass out, but not before a pair of sad, honeyed eyes float through my mind.

I don't know how long I'm asleep before a blood-curdling scream jars me from my dream.

Sprinting toward my room with a pronounced limp,

my heart is lodged firmly in my gut when I get to her. Pete meets me at the door, looking wild. I shrug and throw the door open. She's quieted herself, so I don't turn on the light. The moonlight casts a glow over a very still Denver. A too-still Denver, for someone who's just released that scream. If I didn't know any better, I'd think I'd dreamt it. Once my eyes adjust better, I can see that her eyes are moving steadily and her body is frozen, yet stretched completely out on my bed. I hobble over to the bed and sit beside her, reaching out and trying to wake her.

"Hey, Denver, you're dreaming. Wake up," I say gently. I don't want to scare her any worse.

She thrashes around a little at the sound of my voice. I run my hands up and down her arms and hear her murmur the name Blake, which makes my teeth clench. Who the fuck is Blake? Another one of her "friends"?

I shake her a little harder on that thought. Did I think things had suddenly changed between us because of her vulnerable moment? If so, I'm stupider than I thought. "Denver," I say gruffly. Finally, her eyes edge open.

"Greer?" she asks, obliviously confused. Fuck, how can she keep all their names straight?

"Nope, Ransom," I mutter and hear the door close behind me.

"Ransom?"

"Yeah, you're staying at my place. Remember? Bad night filled with evil bitches?"

Suddenly, she sits straight up and wraps her arms around me tightly. I hold my arms out to the side until she whispers, "Oh, thank God it's you, Ransom."

I am high at her relief that's it me. I shouldn't give a damn, but ... damn. She whispers my name like a prayer, and it goes straight to my head like the purest form of oxygen. I wrap my arms around her and drop a kiss on the top of her head and know that I'm screwed. All that I buried for her is, not-so slowly, fighting its way to the surface. I can feel it clawing and scraping and freeing itself. "It's all good. You're OK." I squeeze her in response to her squeezing of me. She turns her face and buries it my chest, breathing deeply. I shudder and gently push her away from me. I can only take so much.

"You good?"

She nods but then says, "Stay? With me. Please."

"I don't know—"

"It's OK," she rushes out, and panic registers in her eyes as she starts pushing me off the bed. "I don't know what I meant, saying that. It's fine. I'm fine."

I chuckle. She's anything but fine. I grab her wrists and still her arms. "I'll stay." I contemplate putting a shirt on, but don't decide quickly enough because she's flipped her wrists and is pulling me down next to her.

Chapter Twenty-four

Denver

KEEPING MY EYES closed upon waking, I pray that when I finally do open them, I won't be in Ransom's room, his won't be the warm body I'm wrapped around, and I won't have forever lost the only person who's ever tried to love me.

Lost.

Destroyed.

Scorched into nothingness.

I just don't get how he could hurt me like that. That's not true. I so got it. I was the lost one. Destroyed him in the process. And scorched us into nothingness. His actions were merely reactionary. A wrecking ball only goes the direction you send it. It was only fair that it had come crashing back into me full force.

That acceptance didn't mean his betrayal hurt any less.

I can't wallow in that though. I've got to get up and move on. Both figuratively and literally. What was I thinking last night? I practically begged Ransom not to make me leave and then begged him again to sleep with me.

Question is … how do I extract myself from him and make my great escape without waking him up? I look down our bodies and gauge how thoroughly we are tangled with each other. My bottom leg is thrown over his. His top leg snakes around mine. My arms are squeezed between our chests like I'm gearing up to box him, but his arms are wrapped firmly around me. One of his hands threads through my hair, and the other rests on my lower back. Ransom's a cuddler? Who'd have thought it?

And it makes me feel … safe. I feel so safe in this moment. How I can feel this way in his arms after he's been so damn mean to me, truly boggles the mind. I shake my head back and forth a little, and thoughts of how good he was to me last night rattle around. The way he helped me had been kind of funny. I could tell he really didn't want to, but his manners had won out.

I am so numb though. Under normal circumstances I'd have given all that attitude back, but I just couldn't last night. That had worked out in my favor since I can't imagine anyone else would've helped me without a ton of questions. Questions I just wasn't ready to answer yet. I don't even know the answers myself right now. I just know I hurt.

Greer.

My golden boy.

Gone.

Tears spring up again. Damn. I can't believe I have any left after last night. *Suck it up. You've got to get out of here.*

Slipping my legs from his, I twist my middle and

scoot. His legs and one arm fall away, but his one hand is still twisted in my hair. I wind my hand through and work to free his. *Ow!* It's like his hand is fisted back there. I finally extract myself. Easing down to the end of the bed, I look over my shoulder at him.

He's stretched out on his back now. The sheet had fallen, exposing him from the waist up. His is such a strange attractiveness. It's like God had put together all the imperfect qualities he could think of to make this perfect-looking human being. Then Ransom had gone and adorned that perfectness with his own works of art—those glorious tattoos.

I've never really been able to study them before, but boy had I wanted to. Dark black barbed wire stretches across his biceps, and scrolls lick their way up both of his arms in an arrangement that didn't make much sense to me, but, among them were representations of meaningful bits of his life—a bull, a cross, a cowboy hat, the number eight. I know there's more, but no more are visible from here. He has those gorgeous sleeves, but then his chest and the rest of his body, all that I'd seen anyway, remain untouched. My eyes roam across his bare chest that had been kissed by the sun quite a bit, making the silver scar running along his collarbone shimmer. Most people appear vulnerable in their sleep, but not Ransom. He still looks like the badass he is. I can't help the light sigh that my body releases.

I glance around the room, finally taking in my surroundings. It's surprisingly neat and clean with very little adorning it—a couple of rodeo posters and one of a boxer. His array of cowboy hats hangs from the pegs on one wall. Underneath a few of them, hang his bull ropes.

Slipping out of the bed and out of the room, I close myself in the bathroom and pick up my clothes from last night. I should put them back on, but I'm not going to. Ransom will have to be OK with me borrowing his clothes. I slide the phone out of my pants pocket to call Maggie for a ride. I could walk, I guess, but really don't feel up to it. I press the wake-up button but nothing. Great! I guess I'll be walking home after all. I pull my socks and boots on quickly.

Finally, I look in the mirror and I look … normal, but I don't feel normal anymore. Had I ever been normal though? Well, I don't feel my version of normal. My hair's a total disaster, so I quickly pull my fingers through it, combing it into submission. I splash some warm water on my face and run a toothpaste-covered finger over my teeth.

I should start my walk. Maybe I could find something and leave Ransom a note telling him thank you. He was incredible to me last night. I still can't believe that. A small smile plays at my lips. There are good people out there.

Somehow, someway, I had to allow myself to find them and move on from people who hurt me. But the fact that I am the common denominator here plagues me, and the little nagging detail about me being unlovable rears its ugly head. Once thing's for certain though—the way I've been trying to live my life wasn't working out so much, so I need some kind of change.

Quietly, I ease open the bathroom door, turning the light out as I close it behind me. Turning back toward the hallway, I startle at a dark figure standing a few feet away. My hand flies to my throat, and a nervous laugh bubbles up when I register it's just Ransom.

"Mornin,'" he greets with a small smile.

"Hi, umm ... I was just heading out. I didn't mean to wake you after everything you had to put up with last night."

"Well, you did wake me."

"I'm sorry," I murmur.

He cups the nape of his neck, and his brow furrows. "When I realized you weren't there ... it scared me. I needed to know you were all right. How 'bout that, huh?" He scratches his head and runs his hand back and forth over his cropped hair. "I guess I really meant what I said about bygones being bygones. I don't want you hurting. So, how are you?"

"I'm ... better. I really will be fine. I've recovered from worse than this." *Liar, liar.*

"Yeah, then why you think it hit you so hard last night?"

My gaze flies to the floor as the confidence in my ability to overcome such a betrayal wavers. I *was* hit hard last night, and I really *can't* imagine just getting over it. "I, um—"

He puts his hand on my chin, forcing me to look at him. Those green eyes knowing, yet unknowing. "Don't downplay how you feel. You were obviously hurt last night. I saw it, and you don't have to pretend otherwise. You don't have to pretend with me."

I swallow hard and nod. "Thank you," I whisper.

"You're welcome," he says with a smile and a nod. "I'm gonna jump in the shower, and then I'll make us something to eat before I take you to your dorm."

"You don't need to do that. It's not far, so I can

walk."

Ransom moves in close, his hand sliding from my chin to cup my cheek, his fingertips resting on the nape of my neck. "Nothing I just said contained a single question. You can wait for me in the kitchen."

Before I can respond, he's moved around me and into the bathroom. I go to the kitchen to wait.

AFTER RANSOM MAKES me breakfast, he follows through on his promise to bring me back to the dorm. Our conversation en route is much the same as it was throughout our meal—highly personal, yet somehow, light and comfortable. He won't allow me to give quick answers; he makes me explain *why* to my every response. He wants to know everything about me, like what I do for fun, my favorite songs, and my favorite candy, among other things. I suspect it is all a ruse to keep my mind off of what happened. It doesn't quite work out like that, since almost every memory of mine features Greer, and thinking about all that quietly kills me because most of them are beautiful.

I lose myself a little bit as I consider what not having Greer in my life will look like—bleak and dreary and hopeless. A deep sigh works its way out of me.

"You're going to be OK. You're a little fighter," Ransom says as he runs his thumb over the back of my hand. I glance at him in surprise when it dawns on me he hasn't stopped touching me since last night. And he swore he'd never touch me again. I can't help but laugh a little on that thought. He's become my knight in shining armor despite my spouting that I didn't need one of those. He's completely unaware, though, since he has no idea how much he helped me. "You're laughing—that's a good sign." His fingers thread their way through mine, and I stop laughing. I like that. Too much. I give him a squeeze and release him, placing my hands in my lap. He doesn't retract his hand from the seat.

"Yeah, I guess it is." I lean back against the headrest. "Thank you for everything last night, Ransom. I don't think you get how much you helped me. I ..." A sob has worked its way up my throat, and if I continue, I'll start bawling again. So I just shut up instead. God, I'm sick of crying.

The truck comes to a stop. "Hey, little fighter," he calls. I slant my head toward him and look up at him through my lashes because if I don't, he'll see the tears that have pooled in my eyes. I gaze in utter fascination as he swallows hard and stares at my lips. His eyes slowly make their way back up to mine. I love how alive they look. "You are one of the strongest, most bullheaded women I've ever met." My grin is smug. "You are going to get past this and be pissing everybody off, including yours truly, in no time at all."

I laugh in earnest at his assessment of me, and I bob my head in agreement.

He gives me one decisive nod, as though it will be that way because he has decreed it, and turns into our parking lot. I spot Maggie and Pete sitting on the steps. She's sitting in front of him between his legs with her head thrown back. He has her in a lip lock.

"They've sure got it bad for each other."

"They do," I agree. Since I already told him thank you about a million times, I just hop out with my bundle of clothes. After I close his door, I give him a small wave through the window. He ducks his head and gives me a wink.

"Hey, you two," I say, turning to the lovebirds I love so fiercely.

Maggie's head jerks up, bumping Pete's in the process. "Denver!" she screams as she propels herself off the steps and hugs me hard. "I was so worried. If I'd known there was trouble, I never would've left," she rushes out.

"I know that," I say as I hug her back. "It's all good. I had a fight with Greer, but I'm fine. Ransom was good to me last night," I assure her.

She pulls back, and Pete runs his hand over her wild hair as he moves around us to speak to Ransom. "I can't believe he let you stay with him after everything."

"I know. Me either. I was surprised, but he was … incredible."

She narrows her eyes at me. "Oh, Denver, are you gonna tell me what happened? I had to threaten to call the campus police since Greer wouldn't leave here quietly. I've been so worried about you."

I open my mouth to respond, but Pete cuts me off by calling her over to him. "Hold that thought," she says as she kisses me on the side of my head and skips over to Pete and Ransom. She leans in and gives Ransom a kiss on his cheek. A stunned Ransom laughs at her while Pete frowns. When they all glance at me, I cringe and turn, running up the stairs.

Exhausted and utterly spent, I collapse on my bed after a thorough shower. Pulling the covers over my head, I curl up into a ball. I grab my phone and pull it under with me. It has a little charge and has powered back up to reveal fifteen missed calls, four voicemail messages, and ten text messages—all from Greer, of course.

I exit out of all them without reading. I just can't. Not yet, maybe not ever. What am I supposed to do with this? Without Greer, I have no one in this world. On that thought, I hear Maggie stroll in. She promptly whips my covers back and climbs in with me. She covers us back up, and we are in our own little cocoon. I know, for a fact, that I've never cried as much as I did while that shy, yet spirited, fire-headed girl held me. And she never said a word or asked me a single question.

Chapter Twenty-five

Denver

SOMEONE IS GASPING and sobbing. I try to reach out and help her, but my arms are heavy. I try to kick, but my legs are heavy too. That's when I realize Blake's got me pinned down. I'm on my bed this time. I glance over his shoulder and recognize the trophies shelved and the ribbons hung in one corner of my room. Oh my God! Why am I here? I left all this behind.

"You'll never leave this behind," Blake seethes. "You thought you were safe from us, sleeping with that boy?" He gives a jaded laugh. "That boy used you just like everyone else in your life. Like everyone will continue to use you unless you get smart. Use or be used. That's the way this world works. You let him in for a minute, and look what you got—exactly what you deserved."

I recognize every bit of truth in his words, but there's one thing he doesn't get. "I know I deserved what I got," I shout. "If anyone gets that, it's me. But I did love Greer. I wasn't faking it. I didn't mean to use him or hurt him. I thought he could deal with my crazy."

"Yeah, he dealt with it until it broke him. You broke him. Ruined him. Do you have any idea how what he did to you is killing him?"

I hear those sobs grow stronger, relentless. Then I hear shouting. And my arms hurt, but they're not pinned anymore. I sit up, gasping. There are hands on my face, hands in my hair, so I just start slapping and kicking. I let out a piercing scream that startles my attacker, causing him to release me.

"Denver, dammit! Wake the fuck up!"

"Ransom?" I question, as my eyes fly open to take in my dorm room, an angry Ransom, a terrified Maggie, and a saddened Pete.

"Yeah, little fighter. It's me. What the fuck?"

"Oh, God." I shove my hands in my hair. It's dampened with sweat and sticking to my face. My dream comes rushing back in, and I remember how violent I'd gotten as I tried to free myself. "I'm so sorry. Did I hurt you, Maggie?"

"No," she says as she comes to rest on her knees in front of me. "Ransom told me to call him if anything wasn't right with you. The minute I couldn't wake you, I called him. It was like your nightmare was on repeat, honey. Over and over you kept saying the same things. And I couldn't wake you," she finishes with a sob.

Pete walks over and scoops her off the floor. "Come on, sweetheart," he coos.

My eyes find Ransom's again. He's studying me, and I don't have the energy to resist his scrutiny. I start to speak, but he beats me.

"Maggie, get her things together for a couple days. She's coming with me." His almost-translucent green gaze pierces me, daring me to argue.

"OK, Ransom," she agrees. Damn, I must have really scared her for her not to protest or question him at all.

"Don't, Maggie," I call, making her freeze like a deer in headlights. I ignore that and focus on Ransom. "I appreciate everything you did for me, Ransom. Really I do. But I'm not going over to your apartment. I'm a big girl. I can deal with this."

"Your friend was in hysterics when she called me."

Simple yet powerful argument, I had to give him that. I cross my arms over my chest because it's just dawned on me that my camisole is thin and my pajama shorts are tiny. "And I'm so sorry for that. Sorry you were troubled."

"Don't pretend like I told you that 'cause I was inconvenienced. Throw on a t-shirt and some pants and meet me out front."

I take a deep breath to try another angle. "Ran—"

He tilts toward me and a deceptive little smile plays at his mouth. His voice drops to a low hum. "If I get busted by your dorm mother, I'm gonna be pissed. If I lose my resident advisor status, I'm gonna be *more* than pissed, which will probably happen if I'm caught in here. If you're not out front in two minutes, I'm coming back in here to gag you and haul you out over my shoulder."

I stare at him, not really sure what to say.

"That's what I thought," the arrogant bastard says. When the door closes behind him and Pete, Maggie and I both sag and exhale.

MAGGIE WON'T HEAR of staying without me in the dorm, so off we go to Ransom and Pete's apartment. She kisses me on the cheek and follows Pete into his bedroom. I stand in the hallway, fiddling with the straps on my bag for a second before walking toward Ransom's room. I swallow hard when I see him propped against his headboard. Shirtless, of course.

I clear my throat. "Hey, I'm sorry to bug you again. But do you have some sheets or a blanket for the couch?"

"Yeah," he says, but he makes no move to tell me where or get them for me. I shift on my feet. Geez, he throws me so off balance. Or maybe it was last night's events that have me so off. Or maybe I'm just an idiot when it comes to him.

"Um, can you tell me where or what?" I snap.

"No, you're sleeping in here. We're talking before you go to sleep."

My back stiffens. This is bullshit. "Look, I feel like I owe you for helping me out, which is why I've let you get away with bossing me around, but I'm over being ordered around like some helpless child. I'm nineteen years old. I take care of myself. Always have, and that's not gonna change because I had a shitty night last night. I came over here tonight because I didn't feel like fighting with you in front of everyone, but I draw the line at sleeping with you. That's not gonna happen again."

He looks through me the whole time I'm speaking, which is part of the reason I kept ranting. I was waiting on some evidence that he was registering my words. "I wasn't asleep when Maggie called," he says softly.

"Uh, OK?"

His eyes focus on mine. "I couldn't sleep because I was worried about you," he confesses.

Oh.

"Please, come here." A request that still sounds like a demand.

I'm back to shifting on my feet. Shit. I drop my bag on his floor and close the door behind me. I hate sleeping in a bunch of clothes, so I comprise by stripping the t-shirt off and leaving the pajama bottoms on. I walk to the side of his bed. "Are you gonna let me in?"

"No," he says with a laugh. He motions his head to the empty side. "Climb over."

"Whatever." Instead, I scoot around to the end of the bed and climb up from the bottom. I crawl between the sheets while he situates himself on his side. I turn on my side and face him.

"So who's Blake?"

Fuck. That throws me, but I hear myself answer automatically, "My step-father."

He narrows his eyes at me. "Why would you be calling out his name from your nightmares? And what does that have to do with what the bitches pulled last night?"

"We're not gonna start with the easy stuff, are we?" I joke. He just stares at me. I have a feeling that any stories I fabricate will only lead me to eventually telling him the truth, and I'm exhausted. "He stalked me for years before he finally tried to rape me. And he got close to making that happen. Real close."

"Holy fuck."

"Yep."

"Is he still your step-father?"

"Yes. My mother fancies herself in love with him," I singsong.

"Fucking bastard. How far is it to your house?"

This makes me laugh. "It was a long time ago, Ransom. But thanks."

"According to Maggie, it was happening for you just about an hour ago."

Son of a bitch. It was. When I think back to my nightmares, it was a combination of what Blake did, what Greer did, and my bleak predictions of what my life would become without Greer. They felt so real too. "I guess what happened triggered those memories. I'm sure my tortured psyche will bounce back in no time."

His brow wrinkles. "Why do you think some girls being jealous bitches, which I suspect you've been dealing with for years, would set off dreams like that?"

I close my eyes. He's good. "I don't know."

"Bullshit."

Maybe it would feel good to say it, get it out of me. I can't tell Maggie. She's so sweet, and she'll never just let it go. She'll push until it's all out there, and then the disease of me will taint her too. Ransom's strong enough for me to lean on, and he doesn't really give a shit about me, so it won't affect him. I take and release a deep breath. "OK, so last night wasn't about girls being jealous bitches."

"That's what I fucking thought," he grinds out. "So?"

My eyes cloud over. I can't tell him about Greer's

betrayal—that's too raw, too hurtful. I'll tell him the lesser of the two evils. "Someone …" *OK … even that's hard to say.* God, I feel so weak.

"Someone?"

"Forced himself on me," I finish slowly. "But it was someone I've been with before, so I don't really know how to feel about it," I rush out.

He closes his eyes, and I see his jaw twitch before he grits through his teeth, "Forced himself how?"

"What other way is there?" I ask, confused.

"What the fuck?" he roars. He's out of the bed like a shot, ripping the covers off me in the process. I sit, pulling my legs up to my chest and wrap my arms around them because I'm suddenly freezing. "What the fuck?" he shouts again, and a look of pure astonishment crosses his face. "You lied to me. I asked you if anyone hurt you physically, and you lied."

"Shh … I didn't want anyone to know, Ransom. And I still don't."

He drops the volume, but his voice still rings with rage. "The fuck you don't want anyone to know. You're talking rape here, Denver. People have to know. The police need to know."

I flinch when he says *rape*, close my eyes, and start shaking my head back and forth. That's such a revolting word. And I don't know that it even applies to what happened. "I don't think so."

"What do you mean? You have to go after this guy. He can't get away with that." The bed sags, and I open my eyes to find a kneeling Ransom. His hands lightly coming to rest on either side of my face. "He needs to pay."

"Ransom, it would be my word against his. I was … we were already in that position when I said no. I'm not even sure if that's what it's called. I was ready and willing until about three seconds before—"

"I don't give a shit if he was already inside you. You say no. You say stop. He damn well stops. That's fucking Guy 101. Ends it. It's done."

I nod rapidly, agreeing whole-heartedly. But does that make him a rapist or just a shithead? The word rapist floats across my vision of Greer's face, and it just doesn't fit. Shithead? Totally fits.

"Will you tell me what happened? I need to know if I'm going to be able to help you, Denver."

This is the first time he's asked me anything. It's all been orders prior to this question. I wish he had ordered me to tell him because I don't know if I can say it otherwise. I laugh at the line of my thoughts, which causes him to frown. Here's his proof that I'm definitely not normal.

"Why are you laughing?" he asks.

"I wish you had ordered me to tell you," I blurt out. "You know? Like you've been ordering me around. It'd be easier to say if I didn't have to think about it."

Chapter Twenty-six

Ransom

I'VE ALWAYS KNOWN that I'm not like most people. Before I knew what it was called, I knew there had to be a name for it, and I knew that I couldn't be the only one. But even knowing everything I know about myself, and that I'm not a freak, I still reprimand myself over my reaction to her words. Honestly, it's the only time I've ever felt sick because of my preferences. I knew I was different, accepted it as a good thing, and owned it. I've never been ashamed. Never felt guilty over it until right now in this moment. And, of course, it's this girl who's made me feel this way. Of course, it is. I knew it when I saw her the very first time that she would change my life. I never thought she'd make me question myself though.

She's staring at me with those wide eyes that haven't stopped glistening with tears since last night, and all I want to do is wrap her up tight and hold her and make the world melt away.

I tamp all that down. It's not about what I want or what I need. It's about her right now. And hiding and trying to forget is not the best course of action. Facing it head on and dealing with it, that's what she needs. I lie back down and bring her with me, pulling the covers over her shivering form. Clearing my throat, I give her what she needs and command, "Denver, tell me what happened to you."

She smiles. She freaking smiles at me. This girl. This girl who's been through so much. She's so tough, my little fighter. I don't even understand how she's walking and functioning, let alone fucking thriving, with all the shit's she's been through. And I have a feeling I only know the tip of the iceberg.

She places her hand on my chest, and I shudder at her light touch. "I need to know that what I tell you won't go any further than this room. I can't have … my friends knowing, and I think it'd be good to talk about it, and you don't really like me, so it makes sense to tell you because you're, um, likely to be more objective when it comes to me. You know? You won't automatically take my side. You can give me better advice," she ends with a shrug.

I want to set her straight. I want to tell her that not liking her is *not* the problem. Liking her too much … even beyond liking her … is the real problem. But again, this isn't about me. I'm not really comfortable being the only person who knows this, but what am I supposed to do? She needs to tell someone. I can probably help her more than anyone else could. I don't know why I know that. I just do.

Running my hand over hers, I thread our fingers together. "I want to help you. I meant what I said about putting all that aside. I won't tell anyone if that's what you need."

She releases a shaky breath, and I prepare myself to hear some things that are going to make me want to kill some piece of shit.

Denver

THIS HAS TO be as brief as possible, but I can't tell him everything. I'll never tell him it was Greer. I won't do that to my golden boy. Despite everything, he doesn't deserve that kind of reputation or the punishment that goes with it. Losing my friendship will be punishment enough for him. I can't even imagine how he's hurting. I almost cry out at the thought of him in pain, but I can't focus on that right now. I need to focus on getting my own shit together.

My eyes shift to our intertwined fingers, and I breathe a sigh of relief. I can't believe how much he's helped me already, and here he is again.

I bring my eyes back to his, those aqua-green depths glowing with the moonlight, he is not of this world. "Like I said, I'd been with this person before. I left the party with him and went to his apartment. We were both drunk and fooling around. We stripped each other and were lying on his bed. He started … talking about my reputation. Taunting me. It made me uncomfortable, but I was still … aroused. But then he got … rougher than I like, and I could tell he was angry. He said some really hurtful things. I told him to stop and get off of me. He wouldn't, and I told him I hated him." I shake my head at the memory of his beautiful, twisted face not understanding what he did to me, or how he hurt me.

"He was so furious with me. He said he wanted to possess me. He wouldn't stop. I tried to fight him off, but it all happened so quickly. And like I said, we were already in that position, so it was easier to ... I should've been able to fight him off," I cry out.

"Shh," he whispers. "Don't blame yourself. You're strong, but he's stronger. If he was angry and drunk, that only intensified it. Like an adrenaline rush gone bad."

"The worst part?" I choke out.

He just nods and tightens his fingers around mine.

I'm mortified, but he needs to understand why I can't tell anyone else, and why I'm not sure that it was ... rape. "When I realized I wouldn't be able to fight him, I went limp and kinda accepted my fate even though I was still crying. And then ... I ... I climaxed." The shame of that, of my body's betrayal, forces my eyelids closed. "I don't understand that. I don't understand how my body could still find pleasure after everything he said, after I didn't want him inside of me. But ... now it's very clear. Crystal fucking clear."

"What did you figure out?"

I open my eyes back up, needing to own it. A rueful smile forms. "Through and through," I whisper in awe. "I am a slut. Through and through."

Chapter Twenty-seven

Ransom

I'M NERVOUS ABOUT leaving a sleeping Denver, but lying here wondering what I can do to help her isn't in me. And I'm afraid I'm out of my depth. Extracting myself from her grip without rousing her isn't easy, but I'm able to after a minute. I tell myself that I'm standing over her and looking down on her to make sure she's sleeping peacefully, but I call bullshit on myself. I don't make a habit of lying to myself, ever. I'm staring at her because she's beautiful and hurting and ... just so damn lovable. I tried to fight that after I learned all that shit about her, but it was too fucking late. And it didn't change a damn thing for me. Lord knows I'd tried. If anything, my feelings have intensified, knowing that she's a hell of a lot stronger than I ever imagined.

Am I fated to be another one of Denver's victims? Loving what can never be mine, like fucking Greer? God, just the thought of that seems so ridiculous, but I'll be damned if it's not true.

How can she truly give herself to someone if she's so messed up, not even whole? She can't. And that's gonna be a problem for me. That goes against my every instinct.

Enough pondering shit that can't be figured out tonight. I lean in to brush my lips over her hair before I leave the room. But then I feather my lips over her forehead. Over her cheek. Over her nose. I move in for her mouth, but I catch myself and hover. I can barely feel her lips, and the energy that buzzes between us, but I hold myself there, not completing the kiss. What the fuck? She's like a drug. I just had a little taste and couldn't get enough. I'm supposed to be better at controlling myself than this. Again, this is gonna be a problem.

I force myself from the room, and after firing up my laptop, put on a pot of coffee before sneaking back into the bedroom to check on her and grab a hoodie. I prop the door open so I can get to her quicker if she needs me.

Moving back into the kitchen, I steal the first offering of coffee before situating myself on a barstool. Just like when I needed to figure out how to handle my own unique set of issues, I Google.

When I've got enough information to get us started, I hover the mouse over my favorites button. Ah ... my addiction calls to me even though it feels wrong right this minute. I wage an internal battle, but finally, I tell myself that I'm going to look because I need to see her like this. That is, in part, the truth. The rest of it is that I haven't been able to get enough of her since I first met her, and these videos have been like methadone to a heroine addict—just enough to keep the edge off, but never really satisfying.

I click and watch YouTube video after video of my

little rodeo queen, my little fighter. I watch her highlight reels, her interviews, and even her less than stellar moments ... so strong, so confident, so incredibly sexy. And I want so badly for her to feel that way in and out of the arena. Maybe I can help her get there.

A pot of coffee and three hours later, I stand over her, armed with my newly found knowledge I pray will help her sort through this.

Denver

RANSOM SAID WE would talk tonight after classes. My mind wanders to what exactly that could entail. I don't want counseling from him. I just need some time is all. I will get over this, and I'll be much stronger for it. That has to be the bright point.

I've been sitting in a quiet spot I found while waiting for class to start. I was afraid if I waited right outside, Greer would've found me, and I'm just not ready to face him yet. I couldn't stay in Ransom's apartment another minute, though. The walls were closing in on me. I finally pull my cell out to check his messages since I've got so much time to kill.

My finger hovers over Greer's string of text messages before I press it. I scroll up to the first one from that night.

Please call me.

I'm freaking out. I'm sitting outside your dorm. They say you're not here.

Where are you?

Please Denver.

I'm an idiot. I love you. I'm so sorry.

If you'll just let me explain, I promise that it's not as bad as it sounds. I chortle at that. How could it not be that bad? He ruined my reputation. He ruined me for others, even though I've never even wanted anyone but him.

I know you think there's no explanation that could make it right. And you're right. I can't make it right, but I can make it better.

Let me make it better, please.

I'll do whatever it takes, Denver. Please know that.

Do you want me to turn myself in? Would that make you feel better? I will fucking rot in prison if that makes this all better.

Please call me.

I can't call him yet. I'm afraid of my reaction at hearing his voice. I'm trying to figure how to deal with my own shit right now. I can't worry about what he's feeling right now. Hearing all that in his voice will kill me. But, I can't not answer him.

I'm OK. I'm safe. I'm trying to figure all this out. No, I don't want you in prison. But I DO want to be left alone. I'm NOT ready to see you. I'm NOT ready to talk to you. I need you to accept all that.

I wait a second to see that he's read it before I click out and quickly power my phone off. I can't read his response. I hope that he understands what I'm asking for and that my text sets his mind at ease.

I lay my head back on the brick wall and close my eyes for a few minutes, gathering my strength and clearing my mind. Finally, I stand up and brush myself off. *I've got this*. I've got some energy in my step because now I'm going to be late if I don't find my way back out of the maze of hallways I took in my attempt to hide out.

When I round the corner, my step falters as my eyes meet Greer's. I shake my head at him. He looks terrible, but I can't focus on that right now. I move quickly to enter into the classroom, but he blocks my way.

"Denver, please," he whispers.

I close my eyes tight and throw my hands over my ears. "I can't. I can't. Please don't make me right now," I cry out.

An arm wraps around my shoulder, and I jump. "Hey, good lookin.' What's up?" I relax at Austin's voice.

I open my eyes and move my hands down. Austin's eyes dart from me to Greer and back. His look tells me he knows something's not right and asks me if I need him to intervene. "Hey, Austin. Greer was just leaving," I manage.

I've never, I mean, *never* seen Austin do anything other than smile. I keep my eyes pinned on him as his features sharpen before he looks back to Greer. "Good to see ya, Greer. You were just leaving."

"I, uh, can I just have a minute, Denver?"

Austin doesn't let me answer. I'm grateful. "I'm pretty sure your minute's up."

I hear Greer blow out a breath before I sense him moving to the side. I can imagine his tortured look and him running his hands through his hair, but I still can't look. I can't see that pain on him. I can't hear it. I just can't deal with it.

Austin's arm falls from my shoulder, and his hand comes to my elbow. "Come on, Denver. Class is about to start."

"'K," I mumble and tuck my head down to go into class.

"I don't know what I'll do if you don't forgive me," Greer rushes out in a trembling voice as he turns away.

My head flies up, and my hand finds his jaw to turn his head toward mine. "You're already forgiven, Greer. It's me that I'm working on. It's *me* that I can't forgive."

Chapter Twenty-eight

Denver

I DON'T KNOW how I've been able to avoid him coming and going from Ransom's apartment, but I am grateful. After we pass Greer's floor, I relax somewhat. Austin and I make our way up to the top floor, and I stand outside the door wondering how I'll be able to get in.

"So why am I delivering you to Ransom's doorstep?" he finally asks. I told him I'd walk back to the apartments with him after our classes, and he shrugged and graciously kept quiet.

"Umm … I'm staying here."

"'Cause that's not weird. Why?"

"Well …" My mind latches onto the only probable excuse. "Pete wanted Maggie to stay, but she didn't want to come alone. I'm sleeping on their couch."

He nods his head slowly but narrows his eyes. "And Ransom's OK with that?"

"Yeah, why wouldn't he be?" I play dumb to the fact that, up until this moment, Ransom has made no secret of his disdain for me.

"Uh … I don't know. Maybe 'cause he's in—"

Ransom's door swings open, pulling my attention from Austin. "What's up, y'all?" Ransom asks. He leans casually against the frame, his glorious, bare chest on full display.

Like a tightly coiled snake, my patience snaps. "Do you own any shirts?"

He just chuckles and looks at me like he knows exactly the torture he's inflicting upon me. He turns back to Austin. "Austin?"

"Oh, nothing," Austin mumbles. "Denver here was telling me how she's sleeping on your couch since the lovebirds can't get enough of each other, and that you're all right with that." His voice turning from curious to taunting. I look from Ransom to him and see a teasing glint in his eyes.

Why would he tease Ransom about me? Ransom hadn't come right out and told everyone he hated me, but if you know him at all, it has to be obvious.

"Well, I am fine with it," Ransom states after a second. "Matter of fact, I'm great with it." My gaze shoots back to his. "Thanks for walking my girl home, Austin."

Thanks for walking my what ... where? I don't understand what he's playing at. He stands aside and opens the door wider, motioning me in. I glance up to say goodbye to Austin and see a huge grin on his face. "Well, all right then," he says while clapping his hands together loudly. As I move past him, he grabs me by my waist and pulls me into him. "No wonder Greer was so pissed," he whispers. "You sure you know what you're doing, sweetheart?"

I nod my head *yes* but murmur, "Hell, no."

He chuckles at me and knocks his knuckles against my chin. "As long as you're aware of that."

"You 'bout done hugging up on her?" Ransom demands.

"Ah, yeah, bro. She's all yours." He leans in and bites my cheek before he licks it.

"Ugh, nasty, Austin!" My reaction makes them both howl with laughter before Austin moves away to go to his own apartment.

"*Nasty* Austin," he calls over his shoulder. "Has a nice ring to it!"

My lips twist, and I can't help a small laugh as I move past Ransom and into his apartment. "I kinda love your cousin," I admit, as I sling my book bag onto an empty chair.

His brows rise.

"Not like that. As a friend."

If possible, they go even higher.

"Not like that kind of friend. I'm capable of more than just that," I bite out.

"I was kidding, Denver. I know you and Austin are just friends. He wouldn't …" His voice trickles to a stop.

My back stiffens and my hackles rise. "Wouldn't what? Be with a slut like me?"

"No … I wasn't gonna say that."

"Not gonna say it, but definitely thought it. Got it. I'm not good enough for your cousin. No problem," I seethe over his low opinion of me, despite the fact that I'd earned it, and he's still willing to help me. Which brings me to, "And why'd you call me that?"

"I—" he cuts himself off. "Call you what?"

I notice he doesn't correct my assumption about not

being good enough for Austin. "You told Austin I was your girl. Why?" *God, why did I love that so much?*

He swallows hard before throwing himself on the couch. "I've come up with a plan, and I think it'll be easier if people just think we are together."

I cock an eyebrow at him and rest my hands on my hips. "Easier how? What kind of plan?"

"Well, it'll be easier to explain why you're here, even though I'm not planning on advertising that. It's a co-ed building so you won't stick out or anything, but when people ask, that'll be our response."

I nod as I wait for the rest of his explanation.

"Come sit," he tells me. I move to the couch, sitting on the edge. "Relax, Denver. It's nothing too painful." I reluctantly lean back on the couch. "I've done some research, and I think I can help you since you want to keep this quiet. As a matter of fact, that's my first condition. You want me quiet, you stay here."

Now I'm really intrigued. How *does* one research moving past being fucked over by her best friend even though she totally deserved it? Oh, wait. I didn't tell him that part. "What exactly are you 'helping me' with?" I ask instead, ignoring his condition for the moment.

He doesn't mince words. I guess I need to get used to that if I'm going to accept his help. "Dealing with what happened with your body while you were being assaulted." He throws his hand up when he sees my head shaking. "Nuh, uh. No argument," he says. "You were assaulted. You're going to learn to accept that too."

Deep down, I know he's right. It's just hard to fully accept that when you know the root of the problem resides solely with you. "Umm ... OK," I mumble.

"Anything else?"

"Yes, we're going to figure out why you see yourself as a slut, and why you're OK with that."

Oh, that's easy. "Well, I'm a slut because I use others for sex without remorse," I state. "So, don't get your hopes up on finding out anything to contradict that little fact 'cause what looks like a snake in the grass is usually just that."

His eyes sadden with disappointment, and a pang of regret twists at the thought of letting him down. "So you enjoy sleeping around and hurting people and don't want that to change?"

Wasn't that what I was seeking when I came to college? A way to escape all that? I didn't think I would find the man of my dreams or any fairy bullshit tale like that, but I thought I could find a guy who would help me forget, one who didn't love me, and wouldn't be hurt by me and my … need.

He snaps me out of my reverie. "Daddy issues?" he jokes.

"Daddy issues?" A jaded laugh rips through me. "Daddy issues is the side item. Mommy issues is my main course."

"Great. Fuckin' double dose," he mutters.

That causes me to laugh harder. "Yeah, you may have your work cut out for you, so let's just focus on the first thing for now."

He gives me another disappointed look and pulls some papers from the table next to him. "I was awake pretty much all last night researching. In my experience, even if it feels like you are alone, you rarely are. Whether it's how we feel, or our experiences, or our …

dispositions, chances are, someone out there in this great big world has felt it, gone through it, and acts like us. So I Googled it."

I pinch my lips together to keep from cracking up. "You Googled it?"

"Yep," he says with a grin.

Oh my God. I'm going to die, but I have to hear him say it. "*What* did you Google exactly?"

"The possibility of whether or not one can orgasm during an assault," he states.

Wow. He said it. And I burst out laughing. "I—" Nope, I'm still not done laughing. My laughter bounces off the walls of the living room. Tears leap to my eyes. I don't know why it's so funny. But it's just ... so funny.

"She laughs at me," he murmurs, while staring at me like I'm an alien.

"I'm ..." Wheeze. "So ..." Cackle. "Sorry." He waits stoically for me to calm down, and I'm so close. But then he cocks an eyebrow, and I'm off again.

"This shit's from *Science Today* and *Psychology Now*," he deadpans. "I printed up some online discussion forums that I thought were enlightening too."

"You've got to admit that's funny," I say, wiping a tear from my eye. "You. In the middle of night. Googling whether or not it's unheard of for someone to get off on being raped. That's hilarious," I cajole, as I tap his knee. "Picture it, John."

I suck in a breath; my laughter dies a quick death. I'd just called him John, and he'd never invited me to. I'd never heard anyone call him that. And it seems so intimate, but so natural too.

His look goes distant, and he taps the papers on his

leg before thrusting them at me. "Your first assignment—go in the bedroom where it's quiet, since I'm sure Pete and Maggie will be here soon, and read over these things."

"SO, GOOD NEWS." I wave the articles in the air. "I'm not alone in my freakiness," I tell him with little enthusiasm as he lies beside me on his bed. I'd finished reading quite some time ago but stayed here trying to process it all. According to multiple sources and multiple definitions, I'd been date raped. But who are they to say what happened with me and Greer? I mean, I don't totally buy into that.

And, according to experts, the number of both females and males who report arousal or orgasm during an attack are around 2 out of 5. That's pretty significant when you think about it. Most of those occurred in a date rape situation that involved either drugs or alcohol. So check and check for me, right? "They" also stated they believe that number to be even higher. They feel most people experiencing this would be ashamed to admit that little detail since the victim fears being viewed as a freak who enjoyed being raped or even fantasized about being raped beforehand. Of course, they explained arousal and orgasm as natural physical responses to a stimulus. Nothing at all to be alarmed about.

Reaching out slowly, he runs his hand up my arm and squeezes my shoulder before I curl into him. It feels good here, wrapped in his arms. It shouldn't, but it does. Apparently that's my MO. I'm the girl who enjoys things she shouldn't.

"You're definitely not a freak," he says as he runs his hand over my hair. He always does that. I like that. Scratch that. *I love that.* "Everything they said makes sense. The trick will be accepting that, little fighter."

"Nope, I've already accepted it. I'm healed. Thank you for everything, Ransom."

"Whatever," he mutters, and I can imagine him rolling his eyes at me.

"I'm serious. I get it. You're right; they're right. It makes total sense. A physical reaction to stimulus—like a fear response or adrenaline rush can't be controlled—neither can an orgasm."

"Yes," he agrees softly.

"Welp, there we have it. I can go back to my dorm now. Your work here is done. Thank goodness for Google." His hand stills.

After a few seconds, he states, "The nightmares."

"Yeah?"

"You're not leaving till I know you're nightmare-free."

"But—"

"Shh, no buts. I told you I'll help and keep quiet. You agreed. That's that." He resumes his petting of me. I'm proud that I resist purring.

"I don't know that I ever *really* agreed," I mumble, as I inch a little closer. "Why do you want to help me? You hate me, remember?"

He blows a breath, ruffling my hair. "If I hate you, you know my intentions are pure. Hate is pure. It's love that's corroded." I stiffen in his arms. "But I don't hate you. It's what you're doing to yourself, and how you see yourself, that I hate."

"OK ... SO MY parents would freak if they knew, but I have to admit I'm loving staying here," Maggie says as she slides up on the counter in the bathroom. We'd had pizza and watched a little TV before Maggie and I sneaked off for girl time in the bathroom. "I loved waking up with Pete this morning and knowing that we would come back here together and have dinner together and go to bed together," she finishes with a dreamy sigh.

"Did you hear how many times you said the word *together*?"

"Yes, that's the whole point—together, together, together."

I grin around my toothbrush.

"So how long do you think we'll be here?"

"Umm ... indefinitely?" Her mouth drops, but I seriously cannot remember a time when I hadn't had at least one nightmare a night. Granted, they didn't usually make me scream and cry like these last two nights, but I have a feeling that part will persist until these particular demons are exorcised.

"Really?" she breathes, all wild, green eyes and bright smile.

"Yep, really. Do you think you'll be able to resist Pete's charms and maintain your, huh hum, chastity?"

I gape in utter fascination as Maggie burns a bright red. Even on her arms and chest.

My mouth drops with a gasp. "You didn't?"

She fidgets and bites her lips. "Well, let's just say technically I'm still a virgin but ... Pete's happy. Pete's satisfied. And so is Maggie," she finishes quickly.

"Well, OK then," I laugh.

"What's going on with you and Greer?"

"We're done." God, that hurts.

"I was afraid of that. No way would we be staying here if you were still seeing him."

I want to tell her what he did, but if I start talking about that now, we may never leave this bathroom. "I want to tell you, Maggie. But I'm not ready to talk about it."

Her eyes are sincere as she smiles slightly. "I understand that, but you're talking to Ransom about it, right? I can't bear to think you don't have anyone to talk to even though I'm not quite sure why you'd confide in him. I mean, a week ago, y'all were ready to kill each other. ESPN, anyone?"

Was that just a week ago? That's crazy. My life had completely upended itself in just a few days. Funny how it had seemed to last longer. "I didn't exactly confide in him willingly. He found me when I was wrecked from what happened, and he didn't give me much choice. Then, I thought it would be good to tell him since he doesn't really give a shit about me. What I had to say couldn't hurt him."

"Oh, you're so wrong about that." I open my mouth to protest. "I'm serious Denver. Pete hasn't said anything directly because that would be betraying Ransom, but he's made a couple of off-handed remarks. That coupled with the way he looks at you." She shakes her head. "Girl, that boy's got it bad. You know, much like you for him," she says with a nudge.

My eyes tear up. Here's the crux of my problem. "I tried to fight it. I was supposed to be working on my relationship with Greer, and I kept thinking about Ransom and flirting with Ransom and talking to Ransom. Greer saw all that too, and my fickleness is partly to blame for what went down with us."

"You know, sometimes we fight battles we have no business fighting," Maggie says with a nod of her oh-so-wise little, red head.

Chapter Twenty-nine

Ransom

UNFURLING MY HAND from the mass of blonde hair that I wake up entangled in each morning, never fails to make my heart still. I prop myself up on an elbow and grin as I glance down at our entwined limbs. It doesn't matter how we fall asleep, I always wake to the heat and security of our bodies vined around one another. Surprisingly, instead of her threatening to choke the life out of me, she is winding her way into my every thought, triggering my every instinct—loyalty, protectiveness, and ... love. She makes me feel stronger and more alive than I've felt my entire life, and those are two things that have never eluded me.

I stare down at the porcelain beauty who, while damaged, is anything but fragile, and I try to figure out exactly how I let that happen. I guess that's the thing with Denver, though, she doesn't ask to be let in. She ran roughshod over my heart. Then just stole her way right in there, like it's where she was always destined to be.

I've never let a girl sleep in my bed, and yet, here I am, knowing I never want to wake up any other way but with her at my side. *It's a little too soon to be thinking forever*, I chastise myself. But again, I have no control over my desires. And, I'm old enough to recognize the difference between lust and desire. I lusted after girls before, no doubt. I never desired one, though. And I desire to begin and end my day with this girl and share every moment in between.

My fingertips tingle, missing her touch, so I run them down her bare arm and watch, fascinated, as little goose bumps spring up in their wake. Even in her sleep, she responds to my touch. My eyes dart to hers to see if I've awakened her, but I'm safe, for now. She caught me ogling her yesterday, but I just played it off, for fear that I make her uncomfortable with my intense line of thought. I'm sure she can see every emotion in my eyes, since she's proven pretty good at reading me, so I'll have to guard those closely.

Bringing my hand back up, I run a lock of her hair through my fingertips and wonder how soon is too soon? When will she be ready to accept us for what we are? Accept what I have to offer her? What if she doesn't want anything to do with me? What if, when she heals, I'm just a painful reminder of all that she's gone through? I shake my head of the negative thoughts, and promise myself I won't let that happen. I'll take it slow and ensure she feels nice and safe with me.

I know she feels something for me too. I felt it the night we kissed. I think back to the way she surrendered herself to me. If I could undo anything, it'd be walking away from her that night. If I hadn't, if I had taken what I knew deep down was mine, she wouldn't be struggling like she is right now. Or, maybe it was too soon then and now that we are kind of forced together, it is all playing out like it should. Hell, I don't know. All I know is that I'm never letting her go. I grin when I imagine her fiery temper trained on me when that time comes, if that's not what she's ready and willing to admit. That fires me up almost as much as her acceptance.

My hand has made its way to her hip and is tracing a pattern on it when I sense her rousing next to me. Slowly withdrawing, I shove both arms under my head. "Denver?" I whisper.

"Mmm, hmm," she responds without opening her eyes.

"Mornin,' you awake?"

"Mmm, hmm," she purrs, as she runs her leg up mine and frees it. I have to pinch my lips together and curl my fists to keep from doing something stupid, like throwing her on her back and devouring her.

"You're done with classes at noon, huh?"

"Yeah," she finally whispers.

I want her to myself today. I'd had to share her with Maggie and Pete every day. "I want to get an early start today with the horses. I'll pick you up right after class, and we can leave from there. Ballard building, right?"

Her sunny eyes finally meet mine, and like always, the warmth that look generates spreads through me like wildfire. I have to force myself not to smile like a fucking clown. "Yep, I'll be ready," she mumbles, as she licks her lips.

The things I want to do to that mouth and that body are dirty, dirty, dirty, so I propel myself from the bed after I mutter a strangled, "Good deal," and hop into an ice cold shower. It's just one of many this week.

SHE BOUNDS FROM the building with excitement rippling from her in waves. Her strength and tenacity always surprise me. Just when I get used to how strong she is, and I think she can't top that, she barrels over my assumptions and proves me wrong. It gives me hope.

As she comes a little closer, I take in her simple appearance and know I've never seen anything sexier. White, button-up, long sleeve under a black, heavy coat. Her jeans are well worn and fit like a second skin, and she's got them tucked into black cowgirl boots that are stitched with white designs. My eyes travel back up to see her hair in a French-braid, a few strands escaping to blow around her make-up free face. I have to start thinking about shoveling manure from my horse's stall, and other mundane tasks, to fight off my rapidly growing need for her.

I push off the side of my truck and turn toward the door and covertly, I hope, adjust myself.

Opening the door wide, I glance at her as she sidles next to me, her arm brushing mine. "Hi," I say.

"Hi," she replies softly, as she climbs into my truck.

I close the door and make my way around to the driver's side. She sits forward and pulls her coat off, since I have the truck warmed up for her already. I slide my aviators on and glance over to see her do the same. She looks up and laughs at our similar tastes in eyewear.

"You think it's gonna snow on us?" she asks.

I pop my truck into gear and whip out of the parking lot. "They're calling for it later this afternoon. We should be able to get some exercise in."

"Hmm … do you mind?" she asks, gesturing to my collection of eight-tracks.

"Nope, go for it," I tell her, curious to see what she'll choose.

She puts a tape in, and I fight the urge to peek at it. She fast forwards a bit, presses play, and the Allman Brothers sing out a little before she presses fast forward again. "This is the only thing about eight-tracks. No instant gratification. You have to be patient," she laughs. "What made you install one anyway?"

I tap my fingers on the steering wheel. "Instant gratification is highly overrated, and never underestimate the power of anticipation." I can hear the double meaning in my words, so I quickly add, "And anything worth listening to came out before 1980, so it just made sense."

My tactic works … I know she loves her modern country music. She gasps and her mouth drops open. "What?" She stops fast forwarding. "What about Garth Brooks, Bruce Springsteen, Miranda Lambert?" she demands.

"They play all that on the radio."

"I guess you have a point," she concedes, going back to searching for the song she wants.

She presses play and "Soulshine" floods the cabin. "Aha!" she cheers. "I do love that when you land on a song perfectly, you feel like you have superpowers!"

I can't help but laugh at her enthusiasm just before I open my big mouth again. "Like I said, the power of anticipation … delayed gratification … it's a heady thing."

Her head flies up on that comment. Does she

understand? She swallows hard, and then her gaze darts back to the landscape. The movements of her hands draw my attention, and when I glance down, I grin at their clenching and unclenching. *Oh, she gets it all right.*

My mood sobers pretty quickly when the lyrics start to infiltrate my brain. I wonder if she realizes how telling this song is for the both of us. She starts out on a low hum, but before I know it, she's singing along quietly. That night I heard her sing, I was frozen. I literally could not look up or speak to anyone when I heard her voice cut across the bar. I'd never heard anything prettier. When Austin called me on stage to sing with her, I had to talk myself out of running up there, spinning her around in circles, and serenading her. My thoughts made me feel like a ridiculous dipshit, but they were what they were.

When the song comes to an end, I turn the stereo down a little. "You really can sing," I tell her.

She giggles around a quiet, "Thank you."

As had been our pattern this week, I know it's time to talk a little. "Denver, the night of our interview," I begin. She tenses up. I know this isn't easy, but it's the only way.

"Yeah?"

"You said some things about your mom."

"Yeah."

I wait for her to elaborate, but she just stares out of her window. "Well, it's not every day someone calls her own mother a whore, so I guess it stuck," I joke, trying to lighten the mood somewhat. "What did you mean by that?"

Releasing a long sigh, she finally says, "Well, my

mom marries for money, hopping from one payday to the next, quicker than you can say prostitute. She's cold, she's calculating. She cares about no one but herself, not that the men she hooks up with deserve any kind of sympathy. She's on husband number seven; he's her boy toy. You best believe number eight will serve to replenish her bank account. So, in a nutshell, she's a whore."

Some of things she'd told me, combined with the way she sees herself, start to come into focus. "You're not your mother," I assert. I don't know how I know this, but I do. She may have been promiscuous, but she's not cold, not cruel. And that promiscuity bullshit is done, dammit, that doesn't have to be something that marks her forever.

"You don't know that," she whispers.

"Denver, you may be reckless and a little wild, but you're not cold. You're not calculating," I say with a glance at the back of her head.

Her gaze snaps to mine. "You called me those things in the interview. You used those exact words."

I grip my steering wheel because she's right. I'd said those very things, only I didn't mean them. Well, I did at the time, but I was just being a jackass since I couldn't have what I wanted.

"I didn't know you, Denver. And while we're on the subject, I owe you an apology." I hate that I'm driving right now, so I whip my truck to the side of the road.

"You've already apologized," she rushes out.

"Hmm ... I apologized for being an ass," I remind her, throwing the truck into park. "That doesn't even begin to cover it."

She gasps, as I toss my glasses on the dash, unbuckle, and jump from the cab. "Ransom, what are you doing?"

I round the truck, not breaking eye contact with her. Pulling her door open, I unbuckle her and turn her body to face mine. I ease her shades down and toss them on the seat. I mold my hands around her jaw. Her eyes are wide and searching.

This has been a long time coming, but I hadn't wanted to take the focus off of her. So, I've been biding my time and have been rehearsing the shit out of exactly what I'd say. Of course, the second my mouth opens and I stare into her eyes, everything I had prepared flies out of my damn head. *Gonna have to wing it.*

"I've never felt like more of a dick than the night I said those things to you, and that pissed me off so bad. The fact that I felt like that, the fact that you made me lose control and question myself, the fact that I knew you didn't deserve that ... I don't know how to explain this without scaring the shit out of you, but nothing I said that night, or the next day for that matter, was about you." I have to take a deep breath and force my fingers to relax. "It was about what *I* was feeling, and how *I* was hurting. You called me on my shit, though. You told me I was being childish and immature and a jerk. And you were right." I hesitate and run my thumbs over her cheekbones. "I am sorry I said those things to you, Denver. You've got an uncanny knack for blaming yourself for other's actions. You're gonna let that go, and put that on me, where it deserves to be. Understand?"

I watch disbelief flitter across her eyes before she bursts out laughing. Not the reaction I was hoping for, but I'll take her laughter any day of the week.

Raising her brow, she asks, "Are you seriously *demanding* that I forgive you?" She shakes her head back and forth as much as she's able. "Well, if that don't beat all."

I drop my hands and lean in to her. "I'm serious, Denver. Those things should've never been said. Yes, you've made some mistakes. Who hasn't? You didn't deserve that shit. I'm sorry you had to prove that to me to gain my respect, but you have earned it, over and over again. Do you forgive me?"

"You respect me?" she breathes out.

"Hell, yes. I respect you more than anyone I've ever met, and I've known you for all of a couple of months. What does that tell you?"

"I forgive you," she replies seriously.

"You gonna put that shit out of your head?"

She nods earnestly. "I'm going to try. Really try."

"That's all we can do," I say, and start to turn away, but she stops me with a question.

"Why'd you kiss me that night?"

Facing her again, I turn that back around on her. "You kissed me first," I grin.

Her face heats, and she grins back at me. "I did, but your kiss was … more. Why?"

There's so much to my reasoning, but only one thought sums all that up. "Because I couldn't *not* kiss you," I admit.

I turn around quickly because I'm feeling that same intense urge to do it again, right here, right now. But, I know she's not ready. Slamming my door, I pull back onto the road to take us to our horses.

Denver

WATCHING RANSOM IN his long-sleeve, black thermal, his faded jeans, and his dusty and worn cowboy boots as he shops for groceries is beyond fascinating. It's like watching Santa Claus shop for Christmas presents. Here is this larger-than-life, sexier-than-all-hell bull rider doing something mundane like putting bacon in a shopping cart. I offered to push the cart, since it's his fridge he's restocking. I quickly decided that this was the smartest thing I've ever done. I get to marvel at his backside every time he stretches and bends. He caught me a couple of times when he turned to ask my preferences for what we'll eat this week. I don't even remember my answers because I couldn't care less about all that.

Suddenly, translucent green eyes are staring into mine. "You seem distracted," he murmurs. "Matter of fact, you've been distracted all afternoon—all throughout our ride and now here. You good?"

My wayward thoughts revolve around how good he is, how well he treats me, and how ridiculously appealing he is. Can't mention any of that, though. "Umm ... yeah, I'm good," I choke.

He wrinkles his brow and frowns at me. "Well then, are you going to answer my question?"

"What question?"

Laughing, he asks, "Anything special you want to

get?"

"Oh, um, some avocadoes and chips would be good."

"That's it?"

"Yeah, I could live on those alone, I think."

"Well, I doubt it," he mumbles before leading me to the next aisle.

"Ransom?"

"Denver?"

"You know a lot about me. Probably more than just about anyone," I grumble.

"Umm, hmm," he agrees, as he tries to decide between two kinds of mayonnaise.

I'm dying to know more about him. More than what everyone else knows. What makes him tick? What drives him? Why has he decided to help me? But I'm scared he'll shut me out even after I've been pretty forthcoming with him. To know that level of trust isn't reciprocated would crush me. "I know next to nothing about you," I hedge.

He glances up and gives me that lopsided, roguish grin of his. God, if only I could be in his head to hear what he's thinking when he gives me *that* grin. "What do you want to know?"

Everything. I don't know where to start, but I find myself whispering, "Why don't you like to be called by your first name?"

He grimaces. "You don't start with the easy stuff, do you? No … what's your major?" he teases.

I laugh as I recall myself uttering those same words to him not so long ago. "Like someone else I know," I challenge. "So what's your major?" I quip, giving a brief reprieve.

"Agricultural Business," he says with a grin, knowing he's not off the hook.

"Mine too. Now, why don't you like to be called by your first name?" I don't want to cause him any heartache, though, so I add, "If it bothers you to talk about it, you don't have to answer."

His green depths pierce mine. "I'll tell you whatever you want to know, Denver," he stresses. I nod. I like that. "I don't like to be called John because that's my father's name."

I wrinkle my brow in confusion. "Umm … OK. But don't you have the same last name?"

"No, my mother is a single mom. They never married. She gave me her last name."

"What's wrong with your dad?" I push.

"First off, he's not my dad. He's my father. There's a difference. And, well, it's a long list, but suffice it to say, he's not a good person. I was about eight when I figured that out for myself and started insisting people call me by my last name. It stuck," he says, as he throws some lunchmeat in the cart. "And now with my 'fame' and his, that's all the more reason to keep it that way. I just don't want any kind of association."

I can certainly understand that. I always hated that everyone knew about my mother's reputation and associated me with it. Fortunately for me, she's only notorious in Anaconda. I can only imagine how much worse it would feel if she were famous. "Who's your father?"

Ransom rolls his shoulders, shifts a little on his feet, and stares down at the selection of cheeses. I don't think he's going to answer me, so I walk over to him, place my hand on his arm, and turn him toward me. I've never seen this strong man afraid before, but there's no doubting the fear that laces his features. He can face two-thousand pound bulls on a daily basis. Face an opponent in a boxing match. Help a girl he barely knows, or even likes, deal with her—my heart races as I admit to myself for the first time—rape. But, he's petrified to tell me who his father is?

"Ransom, if you don't want to tell me, you don't have to, but please know that I would never judge you or tell anyone else. Your secret's safe with me," I promise.

"I don't want any secrets between us," he whispers.

My heart squeezes painfully in my chest. With those little words, I know that I must mean something more to him. I wonder what he would do if he knew what that did to me. Taking the cheese from his hand, I toss it in the basket. I weave my fingers through his and squeeze them tightly, waiting for him to tell me.

"Ever heard of a bull rider named John Stone?" he asks, his voice raw with emotion.

My eyes widen, and I nod. If anyone else in any other situation had asked me that, my response would be, "Hell, yeah!" and then we'd commence to raving over what a badass legend he is, how many records he set, and how many times he cheated death at the hands of the beast. But, the only thought filling my head now is "What did that man do to you?" I nod my assent again because I don't trust myself to speak.

"He's not a good person," he repeats.

I give him a small smile and squeeze his hands before letting go to return back to the cart, knowing that standing in front of the dairy cooler at the Community Food Co-op is not the place for him to elaborate on that. "Will you throw some pepper jack in there?" I ask. He breathes a sigh of relief, and my smile widens. "I'll make you some of my famous Pepper Jack Mac 'n Cheese," I promise.

"Famous, huh? Sounds delightful," he says with a quiet laugh.

"Oh, it is. It's a flavor party in your mouth," I joke. "So, what's your mom like?"

"My mom is ... perfect."

Great! Another perfect mom to live up to. I shake my head at that thought. I don't need to start thinking about *him*. "Elaborate, please," I urge.

He runs his hand over his hair a couple of times. "Well, she's a teacher. She raised me all on her own. She made sure I had a good life despite her being dealt a terrible hand. I was only three when we got evicted from our tiny apartment 'cause she couldn't make rent, so I don't remember the details. But, I know that she didn't take that shit lying down. She found a rancher who needed house help and had a small trailer we could rent for real cheap. So, not only did she work for him and waitress full-time, but she also managed to put herself through school, two classes at a time."

I'm in awe. Money had never been something I had to struggle with, so our existence was easy. Of course, our so-called living was up for debate. "She sounds remarkable. Who took care of you, though, when she was working and going to school?"

"I was able to be with her while she worked at the big house, and she worked nights at the diner. I really don't know when that woman slept," he muses with a quiet but strong reverence. "But, when she wasn't able to be with me, I was with Austin's family. They treated me like their own. His dad is my mom's brother, and he's the only dad figure I've ever really known."

No wonder he and Austin were so close. "You grew up on a ranch?"

"Yep, a big one. When I was old enough, I started working it. I learned a lot. Made me realize that's what I want one day."

Yet another thing we have in common. "You're not going pro?" I ask, surprised. It's all anyone talks about.

"Yeah, but the career span is pretty short for bull riders, ten, maybe fifteen, years. So the ranch is long-term."

I nod and hop off the bar of the cart, making a beeline for a bag of Hershey Kisses. "Makes sense," I agree, as I toss the bag in the cart.

"Something sweet?" he asks with a raised brow.

"Yes, they're my weakness," I admit.

Grinning, he teases, "You deserve to have all the kisses your little heart desires."

And that quickly, I'm done contemplating ranching and families and bad parents, now completely focused on how badly I want for him to kiss me again. My hands feel slick on the cart, and my pulse races as I recall how thoroughly he owned me with that one kiss. It's everything I can do to put one foot in front of the other and finish our shopping.

When we hit the parking lot, I gasp in wonder at the steady stream of snow flurries making their way down to the pavement. I push off to get the cart going fast and jump on the little bar, riding the fast-moving cart to the truck. I hear Ransom laughing behind me. I know I'm being kind of silly, but I love snow, and we haven't seen in any in a while. I tilt my face up, and sticking my tongue out, I let the little tufts of snow melt in my mouth.

"Whoop!" I holler, as I propel myself off the cart and rein it in just before we crash into the truck. "What a ride," I muse.

"Nice ride, Dempsey. But cutting it a little close to my baby there, don't you think?" Ransom deadpans, as he starts loading the groceries into the bed.

"Hey, I was in control. I am a professional after all," I scoff.

I place the last of the bags in the back before stowing the cart in the corral and returning back to a waiting Ransom. He holds my door open for me, and I smile and mumble a thanks before moving to get in.

Suddenly, his hand is on my hip, stopping me. Looking up at him, I see so many emotions flit across his eyes—amusement, surprise, concern, uncertainty.

"Ransom?"

He takes a deep breath, his hand tightening on my hip. "Denver, I ... had fun today."

"Me too," I admit. Worry is the only emotion left in his eyes. "You're not worried I'm going to say something, are you? I'd never betray your confidence," I swear.

He gives me a look of disbelief and shakes his head. "No, I'm not worried about that."

"Well, you're worried about something." I frown. My fingers itch to smooth the doubt from his features. I don't like him looking less than his strong, confident self.

"You. Just worried about you," he confesses.

My heart thumps blissfully in my chest. And I marvel again at how incredible he is. Somehow, I know that no matter what happens between us, I've made a true friend in Ransom, and that has been exceedingly good for my warped mind. Tears spring unbidden to cloud my view of him.

"I'm sorry. I shouldn't have said anything. It's just—"

"No," I interject, "you didn't make me sad. These tears are grateful tears. The good kind. I don't know if you understand how much your friendship means to me, but it means a lot. It means ... everything. Thank you."

"Friendship," he muses, rolling the word around on his tongue.

"We're friends, right?" I ask, suddenly insecure that I've read too much into his actions.

He sighs. "Yeah ... no, I'm glad we've made friends."

Impulsively, I pull at his hand on my hip, bringing it around me, and gather him in my arms. I lay my head on his chest and feel him shudder against me. He's strong and warm under my cheek. There are so many things that I want to say in this moment—how amazing he is, how amazing he makes me feel, how I'd give anything to be with him if I weren't so screwed-up. Of course, the fact that I'm no good for people like him, that I'm incapable of more, and that, ultimately, I'm unlovable—keep me from saying any of that. Instead, my grip intensifies as I hold onto him. In the snow. Next to me. In a grocery store parking lot.

"I'LL GET THE other two bags while you unpack, all right?" I suggest, as he tries to head back out the door. My pockets feel a little lighter. I check them and come up empty. "I must've left my phone in the truck anyway."

"You sure you don't mind?"

Ever the gentleman. Well, mostly. "No, I don't mind. Be right back."

I head down the stairs, pausing as I always do before I hit *his* floor to make sure the coast is clear. I don't see any movement, so I double-time it until I'm safe outside.

When I reach the truck, I see my phone sitting on the seat and breathe a sigh of relief. It has all my music on it, so I'd definitely be lost without it. Opening the door, I snatch it off the seat and pocket it. I lock up and reach into the back to grab the last two bags. As I grasp the handles, I hear a pair of angry heels on the concrete heading my way, and I look over my shoulder to observe a furious Mrs. Tanner just behind me. *Oh my God.* What is she doing here? Did something happen to him?

I turn and open my mouth to ask her just that, but I can't get a word out before she slaps me right across the cheek. Hard. I gasp because that stings like hell. Blinking hot tears from my eyes, I try to muster the strength to look back at her. My eyes barely meet hers before she rears back and slaps me even harder. I vaguely register the bags slipping from my hands, and the cans crashing onto the concrete. Her ring catches my lip, and my tongue automatically darts out to catch the little dribble of blood that escapes the fresh cut. My breathing is garbled, even to my own ears, and I know I'm on the verge of losing it. Ransom kept me busy this week, so I didn't have much time to think about all the hurt, all the agony that Greer must be feeling, and her slaps bring it all back, bombarding me at full force.

Fisting my hands at my sides, I look back at her and plead, "Hit me again, Mrs. Tanner." The tremor in my voice causes copious tears to spill from my eyes. "I deserve it, so do your worst. But just know that no matter how many times you hit me, how much pain you cause me, you can't do anymore damage than I've done to myself."

She looks a little taken aback by my words, but a coldness schools her features before she spouts, "I begged him. Begged. Him. Not to follow you here. To cut ties with you, but he promised me that you were more than your mother. That you would never hurt him the way your mother hurt my brother, my brother-in-law, my cousin," she sneers. "The list goes on and on. But he assured me that that's not who you were." Shaking her head, she mocks, "But the apple hasn't fallen far from the tree, has it Denver? You're just as low as your mother. Matter of fact, lower even. You were best friend to my son. You've known him since birth. You knew exactly how terribly he would hurt at your betrayal, yet that didn't stop you, did it?"

Words seem to lodge themselves in my throat since I know that nothing I can say will make this right. I finally stammer, "I'm so sorry, Mrs. Tanner. And I know that'll never be enough for the pain that I've caused him, but ... I. Am. Sorry," I emphasize.

She raises her lip in disdain at my paltry offering. "So sorry that you'd shack up with the first man who shows you a little bit of attention, huh?" she challenges.

How long did I think I'd get away with him not knowing about that? "It's not ... it's not like that."

"Save it for someone who's not privy to your conniving, deceitful ways, Denver," she snaps and narrows her eyes at me. "You think I didn't see how you lined up my sons? First, you wanted Lawson. When he wouldn't have any part of you, you set your sights on Greer. And you used and played him to a tee, didn't you?" Her blazing eyes dart over her shoulder before they meet mine again. "He's coming out here, so make yourself scarce. I don't want him to set eyes on your lying, manipulative face. Understand?" she barks.

Completely humiliated, I mumble, "Yes, ma'am." She spins on her heel and stalks off.

Unlocking the truck, I throw myself inside quickly and make myself as small as possible.

Closing my eyes tight, I try to leave my head for a while. All the ugly thoughts about myself, my nature ... the ugly truth about what I'd set in motion, swirls the drain but refuses to go down.

I wonder what he's told her to make her that angry with me. Did he think I started sleeping with Ransom right after he ... did that to me? Betrayed me like that? I know I've done some awful things. Hell, I'm the first person to admit how fucked-up I am, but he of all people should know I'm better than that. And he's not completely innocent here. I tried to warn him away. I didn't even choose my college until after he picked his, hoping that would drive a wedge through our messed up connection.

Who am I trying to kid? I'd sunk my hooks so deeply into him he'd never stood a chance. I can sit here and try to justify it until the cows come home, but the truth of the matter is, I've brought all this on myself.

I shriek as the truck door suddenly flies open, but I breathe a sigh of relief when I see an angry Ransom staring me down. "What the hell?" he grinds out. Before I can utter a syllable, he rages on, "You scared the shit out of me. I come out here to check on you and find groceries all over the ground and you nowhere in sight. What the hell?" he repeats.

"I …" My voice is shaky to my own ears, so I try again. "I dropped the bags—"

"What's wrong with your face?"

"Same thing as usual," I quip. My lip burns when I smile.

"No, it's red." His eyes fall to my mouth. "Is your lip busted?"

"Yeah … I bent down to pick up everything, and when I came back up, I rammed my face into the side mirror." *That's believable, right?* Those things are massive and unforgiving. "I just sat down for a minute to get my bearings."

His fingertips graze my smarting cheekbone as he studies me. "That's gonna leave a bruise. C'mon, let's get you inside."

Chapter Thirty

Ransom

MY LITTLE FIGHTER had done well this week. Her nightmares were still there, but she was getting easier to wake up from them and didn't fight me as much. I think it's me who's not doing so hot. Constantly holding her, knowing I shouldn't want to take her and make her mine while she's dealing with all that she's dealing with—it makes me feel like a pervert. I'd thought of just taking care of myself, but I know I wouldn't be able to resist using her image, and that's fucked too. So by Friday, I'm a little snappier, a little short in temper. She called me on it too. I told her I was tired and stressed out and would try to stop being a jerk. She told me she wouldn't have me any other way. That made me laugh my ass off.

It's Friday evening, and we had a quick dinner. I can tell everyone is bored, but I fail to come up with anything creative because my mind is elsewhere.

"Let's go the movies," Maggie blurts out.

Denver and I both groan. She has a hard time sitting still for any length of time, and I'm not going to sit in the dark next to her while feeling this on edge. No fucking way.

"Come on, y'all. It'll be fun," Maggie cajoles. "We haven't left this apartment all week except for classes and working the horses."

"Whatever you want, sweetheart," Pete coos at her.

"So fucking whipped," I sneer.

"So fucking jealous," he quips.

"Whatever," I mutter. "Denver, movies?"

"I guess," she says with a shrug.

Perfect. I need some time away from her. "Y'all go to the movies. I'm gonna go out." I pretend not to notice her face drop. I call Pete back to my room and give instructions for watching out for her before I go.

I DON'T GO far. There's a party in the apartment building next door. And it's perfect since there are no rodeoers here. Our group is tight-knit, and I wouldn't trade them for anything, but sometimes it's suffocating.

After a couple of beers, a little brunette with shy, blue eyes approaches me. We chat for a while. I ascertain the things I need to know about her—she's no virgin, she's no slut, she'll leave shortly after, and she'll keep her mouth shut.

When I tell her what I'm interested in, what I'll do, what I won't do, she blushes, but readily agrees.

Lacing her fingers through mine, I lead her back to my apartment.

Denver

I BARELY OPEN my eyes when I hear the door open. I glance at the clock; it's too early for Maggie and Pete to back. It must be Ransom. I wait a minute for him to come to the bedroom before I stretch and go to the door. As my hand turns the knob, I hear two voices, and that female is definitely not Maggie. I cringe, and my stomach instantly knots. I know this whole "my girl" thing is an act. I know it is. But that's not helping, and I want out of this apartment. Right now. There's no way I can listen to that.

Slipping on my shoes and throwing a hoodie over my head, I ease the door open, hoping to quietly slide past them. I move out into the hall, but I'm too late for a quiet escape.

I retrace my steps and edge the door closed before I collapse against it. I'll never get that image out of my head. Her lying there naked, her arms stretched above her head, her legs spread before him. Him standing over her, devouring her with his eyes. I picture him getting her worked up and slipping inside her, and it makes my stomach turn. I'm jolted from my living nightmare when I hear her moan his name. I kick off my shoes and dive for the bed but can't get the pillows over my head before I hear her call out his name twice more.

After a while, I remove the pillows and listen intently. I don't hear anything more for a few minutes before I hear the front door close and then the shower running. That's when I lose it.

Ransom

I TOWEL OFF and stare at myself in the mirror, hating that I needed that release, but glad that I got it. I'll be much better at helping her without feeling constantly on edge. I don't kid myself in thinking that the little fix I just had will stave off my craving or my ache for her, but this should buy me some time.

A glutton for punishment, I find myself wondering again if she'd ever be up to exploring anything with me. I know I'm supposed to care about all that other shit, and despite the fact that I made a promise to myself, she overrides it all. It surprises the hell out of me.

If she's willing to give that up to be with me, I'm willing to overlook her past and be hers. And if anything, she's proven time and time again that she is the perfect woman for me in every other way. I just have to get her to see that she doesn't need all those other guys if she's got me.

Wrapping the towel around my waist, I make my way to my room to get some clean clothes. I open my door and the slim shaft of light lands on the lump in my bed, facing the wall. What the fuck? The blonde hair that I've spent countless hours running my hand over splays out over my pillows, and my jaw hardens. Stepping back into the hall, I pull the door closed quietly before stumbling back to the living room. What the fuck? Why the fuck is she here? I start to sit but change my mind and cross the hall to Pete's door. I knock, nothing. Opening the door, I see they're not here.

I shoot a text to him. Sitting on the couch, I put my head in my hands and curse him. I told him I didn't want her alone. I told him she wasn't ready for that, and he'd left her anyway.

Then I curse myself for leaving her. This wasn't Pete's fault. She isn't his responsibility. She's mine. *Mine.* I punch my palm several times before my phone buzzes.

Said she didn't want to be a third wheel and was tired. We tucked her in tight before we left. No worries, boss.

No worries? She probably heard me fucking around with another girl. She didn't need to hear that. I don't want her to think … what? That I couldn't keep it in my pants after what she just experienced? My mind races over everything I did to that girl, and I think about every moan, every groan, every time she called my name. There's no way she didn't hear. She'd have to have been comatose. This place is tiny, and the walls are paper-thin.

Time to stop being a pussy and go check on her.

I ease back into the room, slip some pajama bottoms on, and crawl in bed with her. I hesitate for a moment before curling into her. After I listen to her breathe for a minute, I whisper, "Say something."

Her breath catches and she sniffs. Hell. I'm in hell. "I have no right to feel hurt," she whispers, a voice thick with tears.

I squeeze my eyes tight, wishing I could undo the whole night. It should have been enough to sit with her tonight, to take her the movies, to crawl in bed with her and talk until we dozed off like we had all week. "Turn around," I rasp before clearing my throat.

Edging up on her elbow, she spins, and I wrap my arms around her. "I'm sorry. I didn't know you were here. I never would have—"

"It's OK ... really. I'm fine. It's just ..."

I wait for her to finish that statement. Tell me that she wants me like I want her. Tell me it made her sick for me to be with another girl. My blood boils, and my whole body tenses when I think of how I would've felt if she were with another guy while I lay in the next room. I'd have torn this fucking place to shreds.

"Just what?" I finally prompt. I need her to take my mind off her with another guy. Yeah, I'm a selfish bastard.

"I was jealous." My blood thunders in my ears. "I just wonder if, I mean, when I'll ever want to be with someone again. When I think of being with someone now, my whole body protests. And I hate it. I hate it!" She wants to be with someone again. Not me. *Someone*. I have to force that bitter pill down before I can speak.

I strive to give advice in a neutral tone. "When you're ready, you will want it. You won't run from it. You'll know when it's right. And maybe this is your chance to ... undo some of the past." That sounds like a bunch of bullshit, but it's the best I've got because ... *someone*. Might as well have said anyone.

"But ... you wouldn't understand," she mumbles.

That kind of pisses me off. "Has there been anything I haven't understood yet?" I demand, a little rougher than I meant to.

"No," she squeaks.

"Then try me."

It dawns on me, as I wait for her to confide in me, that she's not touching me. I've got myself wrapped around her like a second skin, and she's not touching me. She's got that pose, that fighter's stance, my little fighter. All the progress I've made with her, effectively erased with one selfishly stupid move on my part.

"You're not gonna like it," she finally whispers. "But I'm afraid I'll never want to be touched again. That terrifies me because I've come to rely on it." She shifts a little. "The sex. I used sex to forget everything. Hearing you ... it made me remember all that I've been trying to forget. It came on full-force. It rushed over me like an avalanche, and I was buried under the weight of it, starving for oxygen and light. That's what sex gave me ... an out. It infused me with oxygen and light for a while so that I didn't think about the darkness, the suffocation. I'm scared I'm never going to want it again. And I'm terrified that if I don't, I'll be consumed. That's why I did what I did. The sex with no strings. The other stuff ... the love and the commitment ... I don't deserve those things. But I need the oblivion, the peace."

"Put your arms around me, little fighter," I command softly. Reluctantly, she does what I tell her. I bury my face in her neck, and I squeeze her to me. "I'm sorry," I murmur against her neck. I say it a few more times before her tears wet my neck. "I would ... if I could, I would be with you. I would take it all away for you. But I can't ... not like that."

She stiffens against me and withdraws her arms, shrinking away before I realize how that sounded. "I understand. I'm gonna sleep on the couch tonight. I just ... I need to be alone."

"No," I bite out. I want to tell her that the timing's just not right. I want to be with her so much that it's killing me, but we can't yet. And now that an awkward silence has set in, she won't believe any of my reasoning anyway. I'll just have to show her. "I'll sleep on the couch. You stay here." In my bed, where I imagine you all day long. *In my heart, where I long for you.*

Chapter Thirty-one

Denver

I STUMBLE TO the bathroom feeling like I have the worst hangover, but not having had a drop of alcohol. When I stare in the mirror, I remind myself again that he doesn't want me. Or more accurately, wants me but won't take me. I'm not good enough for him. My unlovable nature strikes again.

I splash some water over my face and run my fingers through my hair. I missed his hand in my hair, and the way it made me feel, last night. Usually when I wake up, it's a rat's nest because he's fisted his hand in it sometime during the night. Not today. And that reminds me that I owe him an apology. I finish up in the bathroom before going to stand over him on the couch. He's all scrunched up. I notice his hair has grown out a little since we first met, and I can't resist running my hand over the soft darkness of it. Once I touch him, it's like I can't get enough. I run my fingertip over the lightening-shaped scar through his eyebrow. I smile as I realize the other eyebrow scar shoots like a falling star. Then I remember the crescent moon on his chin, and I move my finger down to run over that. He's otherworldly, my celestial being. Well, not mine exactly.

I glance back up to his eyes, and they're lit up like the stars themselves. "Don't stop," he says, his voice hoarse. His voice is intoxicating, and I am compelled to explore each scar.

Kneeling down in front of him, I move my finger up his jaw, down his neck, and over his collarbone, to finger the scar that cuts across. His hands are so scarred I could spend eons there. I take them in mine and run my lips over his knuckles, placing light kisses as I go. I sit back quickly on my heels as I realize what I just did. Touching him was one thing, kissing quite another. "I'm sorry," I groan.

His brow furrows, and he whispers, "I'm not."

"You confuse me," I admit. He shouldn't let me touch him if he won't have me.

He sits up abruptly and winces with a quick draw of air beneath his teeth.

"Ransom, what's wrong?"

"Oh," he says, as his hand massages his knee. "Just an old war wound," he kids. "I sat up too quick. I'm always so stiff."

"Your knee?"

"Knee, back, shoulder, neck, ribs … you name it."

He seems to have a handle on the knee, so I crawl up on the couch behind him and run my hands over his shoulders. He's done so much for me. Then I practically kick him out of his own bed because of my own insecurities. I couldn't feel any shittier. The tension in his shoulders vibrates under my hands. I work my fingertips around the knots, going deeper until each one fades.

"You should still have your ribs wrapped, huh?" He hums a *yes*. "You ever wonder why you do this to yourself?" I can't help but ask.

"Every damn morning," he jokes.

"You're so tense." I run my hands down the knobs of his spine, and he exhales and shudders with the movement. "Does that feel good?"

"Good, incredible, amazing ... I'm afraid you've just bought yourself a lifetime of rubbing my back."

My heart speeds up, prancing from his off-handed remark. His phone buzzes on the table, and I look over to see it blowing it up with messages. I stretch with one hand and grab it for him. My eyes catch on *Elizabeth*. Ugh! I hand it to him and start to get up, but his other hand comes out and traps me. "My aunt," he states.

He clicks through them and then jumps so quickly that I almost topple off of the couch. "Ransom?"

He knocks on Pete's door before heading to his room like a hobbled flash. "I gotta go home today," he calls out.

Pete stumbles out and looks at me questioningly. "He's in his room," I answer.

I'm not sure what to do, so I go in with Maggie and scoot her over into Pete's spot so I can lie on her side of the bed.

"What's going on?"

"I don't know. Ransom got some texts from his aunt, and he took off to his room."

"I hope nothing's wrong," she whispers.

"Me too, but I'm afraid there is."

Her brow wrinkles. "You OK?"

"Yeah, I'm good."

"Ransom was not happy about us leaving you last night. I feel terrible, but you promised you were fine."

"I was fine. I am fine." I glance over my shoulder to make sure the coast's clear. "He brought a girl back here last night," I mutter.

"Oh, no. What happened?"

"Nothing. I mean he ... did what he did, she left, and he climbed in bed with me. And I told him I couldn't sleep with him after that. I feel terrible making him sleep on the couch, but the thought of him holding me after he ..."

"I bet," she whispers before a grin overtakes her face. "He holds you?"

I bite my lip to keep from smiling. I don't trust myself to talk about the way that makes me feel, so I just nod and move on. "I have no right to feel jealous, but I was so pissed and hurt. He's just helping me through a rough patch, but I can't help it, Maggie ... I've fallen for him. And I've never fallen for anyone like this." God, I'd wanted to fall so badly for Greer. Why couldn't it have been Greer? And why couldn't that have happened years ago?

"I know you have, sweetie." She fusses over me as she pats my hand.

"I hope he doesn't know. How embarrassing," I groan.

"Why would that be embarrassing?"

"Because he doesn't feel the same way about me," I say it like I would say *duh!*

Her soothing voice is stowed, and she takes a tone of impatience. "I've told you before that Ransom feels—

"

Pete clears his throat while entering the room and grunts, "Ransom wants to talk to you." Worry mars his features.

I jump out of the bed and head back to his room, where he's zipping up his duffle bag. "Is there anything I can do?"

Grabbing my hips, he pulls me into him. Tension courses through him in waves. His eyes burn into mine. "Yes, you can stay with Pete or Maggie. I don't think you should be alone. I wish I could bring you with me, but it's not a good time. I'll be back tomorrow afternoon."

"Yeah ... no, I understand," I assure him. "I hope everything is OK."

"It's my mom, but she'll be all right." I hug him to me because he doesn't sound convincing.

"Is it a far drive?"

"Nope, little over an hour is all."

"I'll miss you," I whisper. I cringe a little at my admission, but I hold my chin up and maintain eye contact.

Some emotion I can't name shadows his eyes before he drops a kiss on the top of my head. "I missed sleeping with you last night, and now I have to miss it again. I'm sorry I was an ass. I wish I had time to explain, but my mom needs me."

"Don't worry about me, please. Finish getting dressed. I'll make you some coffee for the road, all right?"

He just nods.

PETE AND MAGGIE have worn me out. We spent the day working the horses and trail riding. After a mostly sleepless night, all I want to do is crawl in bed and pass out. Unfortunately, our stock of clothing needs to be replenished, so Maggie and I head to our dorm while Pete whips up something for dinner. We put some clothes in the washer downstairs before heading up to our room. After fiddling around the room a bit, I go back down to throw the clothes in the dryer. As I round the staircase, Stephanie catches my attention.

"Hey, girl. Where've you been hiding?"

Hiding was right. Come to think of it, I am done hiding. I've never hidden in my life. When Ransom gets back, I'll just have to tell him it is time for me to move on. Especially in light of last night's event and this morning's ... weirdness. I've been trying to process that all day. One minute, I'm so hurt that I can't see straight. The next, I'm tending to him like he's breathing his last breath and he's the most precious thing I've ever seen. That made no damn sense.

"Denver?" she prompts.

"Oh, sorry. I've been staying with Maggie and Pete."

Her eyebrows bunch up. "Doesn't Pete room with Ransom?"

Totally not an innocent question. Our little version of Mayberry—everybody knows everybody else's business. "Uh, yeah. We're just friends though." She doesn't look convinced.

She catches me up on the goings on of our dorm

life—it's like a bad soap opera. We walk upstairs, and I start to tell her I'll talk to her later, but she squeals, cutting me off, and spins around to run to her room, telling me to wait right here. She bounds back after a minute. "I can't believe I almost forgot, but Greer stopped by a few days ago and asked me to make sure you got this."

My heart bottomed out when she said his name. I'm pretty sure this is the longest I've ever gone in my life without saying or hearing his name. Tears spring to my eyes on that thought. A gaping hole in my chest makes itself known. God, I miss my best friend. I've tried not to think about him all week, and I had been pretty successful. I think that was Ransom's plan, surrounding me so that I had some distance to consider everything more logically. Pretty smart plan. I've been functioning well all week.

"Denver?" Stephanie waves the letter in my face. "You're acting so strange. Are you sure you're OK?"

I clear my throat before trying to speak and give her as much truth as I can. "Yeah, I'm gonna be fine. Greer and I had a fight. And you know, we grew up together and have been best friends since before we were born, so it's been hard."

She throws her arms around me. "You're so lucky to have that. I can't tell you how many friends I've had come and go over the years. To have Greer in your life like that ... I'm sure there's nothing you two can't work out. I will say, I thought you two were headed toward more than friends up in Wyoming."

That had been the night I told him that I was his, and we kissed on the dance floor for everyone to see.

What a silly little fool I'd been. Kissing Ransom and then giving myself to Greer? I deserve everything I get.

I avoid the more than friends comment. "Yep, I'm a lucky girl. Thanks for everything, Stephanie."

I'M ABLE TO make it back to Ransom's apartment and through dinner without reading the letter even though it is burning a hole in my pocket. I just don't know that I'm ready. What will it mean for us? Is this his goodbye? I know that I deserve it. He would be better off without me since I bring out the worst in him—jealously, insecurity, anger …

Or, rather, what I was unable to give him brings that out. But that's the kicker, I was so close, so ready to give him all of me, but since he's so used to me and my old ways—the flirting, the using others to fuel my desires, the mind-numbing sex—he couldn't accept, couldn't even hear, what I was offering him.

I opened myself up for him, and he never even heard me.

Even though I am royally fucked-up, I always held out hope that, in the end, it would be Greer and me. Even though I've been entertaining thoughts of Ransom, I can't imagine spending the rest of my life with anyone other than Greer or spending it not even knowing him. And just as quickly as the barriers around my heart had erected, reinforced, and welded themselves shut, they disintegrate, crumble, and crash down around me.

Despite all my protests and denials, I do love Greer. Not as just a friend, either. *I love Greer Tanner.* Regret rips its way through me. I wince and breathe deeply. I wish I had been whole enough to admit it before now.

Sometimes our first love isn't meant to be our last. Will that be our sad truth? Am I ready to say goodbye to Greer?

I get so overwhelmed with this thought that I sink down on my knees behind Ransom's bedroom door and imagine running into him on the streets of Anaconda ten years from now—a sweet, doting wife on his arm, a little boy perched on his shoulders, Greer with little laugh lines, evidence that he had been well-versed in happiness. That's what I want for him, so why does this image make me seize for air like my lungs are paralyzed?

Then I picture what he would see … would I be walking downtown, all alone? Would I be on the arm of husband number three because no *one* man could ever satisfy me? Would I have my men on the side too, just like my mother? Would Greer hear my name around town and feel sorry for me? Poor little slut, she never stood a chance.

Oh … maybe that's where I went wrong. I've been trying all these years to fight my natural instincts. I screwed myself, and I screwed Greer, trying to be something that I'm not. I used Greer and his body to keep me from becoming what I feared most, becoming one anyway, and I took Greer down with me, wreaking the worst kind of collateral damage—Greer and his innocence, Greer and his sanity, Greer and his goodness.

Getting up, a calm settles over me as I slip the note under my pillow. I ease out of the room and to the bathroom, splashing a little water on my face and taming my hair a bit. I slip past Pete's room and into the hallway, breathing a sigh of relief like a sneaky teenager.

I don't know where I'm going, but I know what I'm going to do, and that strengthens me. I know what I am, and I embrace it.

I am a slut.

Not just in my imagination. Not just in my DNA. Not lying dormant. I imagine it oozing from my pores, tangible and present.

I wonder if my mother had this same kind of epiphany, or maybe she never even tried to fight it. What a blissful feeling—freedom. When I came to college, I thought I'd find a friend and permanent hookup, much like I had with Greer, but without the possibility of hurting him. I wanted someone who'd fuck me into oblivion and curb my natural instincts. Someone who didn't care about me as much as the pleasure they could get from me. I laugh at myself a little when I remember that's exactly what I hoped for in John Ransom. How I ever thought I could control that man is beyond me.

Chapter Thirty-two

Denver

WHEN I REACH the bottom of the stairs, I hear loud music coming from our usual party locale, and I relax as I realize I won't have to go far. Walking into the room, I see all the familiar rodeo faces. Funny how they all look the same even though I've just undergone a life-altering realization.

I head for the drink table and make myself a stiff one before I look for a stiff one. I laugh at my pun, and a few people give me a questioning look. I shrug, lift my drink, and let out a rousing call. They cheer and lift theirs, and we drink in unison.

After draining the contents of my glass in record time, I decide dancing will be my siren's song, so I make my way to the little crowd of pulsing and shifting bodies. It doesn't take long. Someone moves in behind me, so I wiggle my ass and press back, putting my hands on his thighs. A clear invitation. We dance like that, anonymously, for the remainder of the song.

When it fades into another song, he spins me around and wraps his arms around me. Brent, one of the bronc riders, I think. His eyes bubble with knowing excitement. Oh, I bet he thinks I'm a sure thing based on my reputation—funny how a change of school setting makes me more appealing. In high school, decent boys wanted nothing to do with me because of that. Now, I guess, anything goes. And it's true. I've felt less judged here than in high school, with the exception of the two bitches and Ransom.

Ransom.

Nope, no thinking about Ransom or Greer. No thinking. I need to get to the sex part quicker for that to happen. I loop my arms around his neck and pull him in tight. He tries to go in for a kiss, and I shake my head.

I move against him meaningfully, and his eyes flare. I'm clearly a chick who wants to get right to it. Almost every man's dream, I would imagine. Will he consider me a total pervert when I tell him how I like it?

His lips run up my neck and over to my ear while I run through possible scenarios of me telling him to take me rough and make me forget the world. His hand grazing my tit makes me jump a little. I'm not used to public groping. Greer and I were always so clandestine in our naughtiness. But something about him touching me in front of everyone shoots off a tiny thrill. I press myself into his hand so he knows I'm game.

He squeezes me in his palm before two fingers pinch my nipple. I squirm and pull him in closer. Well, I certainly have his attention. I wonder if he lives in the building or if we'll have to go far.

Nuzzling my neck with his nose, he pushes my hair back until his mouth is at my ear. "Do you even know my name?" he asks, his voice pained.

"Do you know mine?" I retort.

"Touché," he murmurs. He definitely knows my name, and I'm pretty sure I know his, but it's fun pretending.

Again, anonymity fuels my libido. "It'll be better this way. You can screw me hard and then walk away, no problem. Yeah?" I never knew slipping into slutitude would be so easy. I giggle again at my pun, and his eyes light up, desire shining bright. He probably thinks I'm being shy about what I just requested, and that turns him on. My little power trip goes straight to my head. *Yes, you're the king of my world! Whatever works for you, buddy.*

"Let's get out of here," he suggests. I just nod against him.

Grabbing my hand, he pulls me off the makeshift dance floor and toward the door. My heart trips over itself as I fully comprehend that I'm about to have sex with some random guy, and not Greer. It doesn't feel as good as it should for a slut. I chalk it up to years of being with the same guy. I'm sure once I get this one under my belt, I'll be good to go. *Way to think positive, Denver!*

We head up the stairs, and I panic a little as I realize he's on the same floor as Greer. What if he's one of Greer's roommates? I can't remember their names. Just as we pass his apartment, I release a shaky breath. I made it. And just as I have that thought, another obstacle makes itself known. Austin.

His eyes light on mine as soon as he pulls his door closed behind him. It takes him all of three seconds to know exactly what's going on.

"Austin, don't lock up," my lay utters. Oh, shit.

They live together.

"I won't, but there's no way you're going in there with her, Brent."

Oh, good. I do know his name. "What? Why not?" Brent looks from Austin to me, worried about losing out on a sure thing.

"It's real simple. You're gonna turn around, go back to the party, and forget this ever happened." Brent looks prepared to argue more, so Austin finishes with, "She's Ransom's girl."

My mouth drops, but before I can say anything, Brent drops my hand like he just found out I have an STD and trips over himself to apologize to Austin. "Shit. I had no idea. I won't say anything. Don't tell Ransom, OK?" His beseeching gaze flies to mine. "It was a misunderstanding, right Denver?"

"Yeah, there's a misunderstanding all right. I'm not Ransom's *anything*," I sneer at them both.

"Well," Austin begins, not unnerved in the slightest by my sudden outburst. "Ransom wouldn't agree with that sentiment, so we're gonna err on the side of caution tonight since he's not here to clear it up."

I cross my arms over my chest, which is a woman's universal sign for everyone to back the fuck up. Brent takes off back down the hall and is on the stairs, uttering more apologies.

"I'm glad I didn't mistakenly sleep with a pussy," I yell out at his retreating figure.

Austin looks at me like I've lost my damn mind. "Have you lost your damn mind?" he demands, causing me to cackle.

"No, but I lost my good time. Thanks a lot, Austin."

I narrow my eyes at him. "I would have never taken you for a cockblocker. Oh, well. I guess I'll go find someone else," I say as I throw my hands up in the air and turn to head back to the party. Actually, maybe I'll head over to one of the frat houses where Ransom's name doesn't have the scary, repellent effect it has here.

"Not so fast," Austin drawls, as he slides one arm around my waist. With the other, he pulls me toward his apartment.

He slams the door behind us as I spin into the room, spoiling for a fight. "What's going on with you?" he demands.

Shrugging, I try for detachment. "I, uh, am just looking for some fun. And Ransom's gone."

"Yeah? Fun? Are you really that selfish to mess around on him while he's dealing with ..." He stops and leaves that hanging in the air.

"With what?" I finally prompt.

He rubs the back of his neck, staring at the floor for a second. "Family problems. He's got a lot on his plate back home, and you're just gonna cheat on him his first night away from you?"

"Look, we have an ... arrangement. We're not in a real relationship," I reason.

He waves his arms in a safe motion as he shakes his head so hard something probably rattles loose. "Nuh, uh ... bullshit. Ransom's never called anyone his girl before. Never. Not even Victoria. She was his girlfriend. Always."

"So what?"

His mouth gapes at me. "If you knew anything about cowboys, you'd know there's a huge difference between being a cowboy's *girlfriend* and a cowboy's *girl*."

"We're not together," I practically screech. "And maybe, Ransom's the opposite and 'his girl' is code for 'girl I'm trying to help' because that's all that's going on."

He crosses his arms over his chest and narrows his eyes at me. Is he trying to intimidate me? "That's not the way Ransom sees it, and until he tells me otherwise, that's the way of it. And now that I know you're unwilling to behave yourself, I'll be your shadow while he's away."

"That's ridiculous," I scoff. "I don't need you in protective, big brother mode. You know nothing about me or what's going on with us."

"Aha ... so there is an *us*." He grins like he just won the grand finale of the collegiate rodeo.

I decide to change tactics. Sauntering toward him, I widen my eyes, lick my lips, and gentle my voice. "You know my reputation, Austin. You've been gentleman enough not to say anything to me, but I know you know." He backs slowly to the door.

"Denver ..." His voice cracks.

"Um, hmm?" Grabbing his belt loops, I pull his hips into mine and put my lips on his Adam's Apple. He shudders when I touch my tongue to it gently. I swipe my tongue up to his ear and whisper, "Austin, I need ..."

"What do you need?" he asks, his voice turned husky.

"You." I bite gently on the lobe of his ear before I kiss a downward path on his neck.

"Umm ..."

"Oh, Austin," I murmur, hoping that if he thinks I'm turned on, he'll get turned on. His fingertips bite painfully into my hips. *Yes ...*

"Denver," he rasps.

"Yeah?"

"Back the hell away from me now," he bites out.

I continue my kissing and sucking. "Austin ... all that flirting. Come on. You want me."

"That was before," he says shakily.

"Before what?" I ask as I take another swipe at his throat.

"Before you." He pushes at me. "Belonged. To. Ransom!" he finishes angrily and pushes me backward a little.

I run a shaky hand through my hair. I'm not turned on, but I'm nervous as hell. I need ... I need to forget for a while. "I don't belong to Ransom." I soften my tone. "Austin, please?" I implore.

"I can't, Denver. I think you're amazing. You're a fucking knockout. I know *you* know exactly how turned on I am, but we'd both hate ourselves tomorrow. You told me Ransom's been good to you. You wanna ruin that? Risk one night of pleasure for what you might have with him? He's good for you."

He talks like he knows everything about me. My blood simmers for a whole other reason. "What did he tell you about me? About why he's helping me?"

"Nothing really. I've just known him my whole life and can read him. I've known you long enough to know this is different for you too. Just because I like to cut up and have fun doesn't mean I'm not paying attention."

Stupid, stupid fucking tears burn at my eyes as I

digest all he's just said. I need to get out of here. "Let me pass," I mutter angrily.

"You need to take a minute and calm down. And what's the plan now that I've thwarted your others?"

"I just ... I need to go to bed." And that's the truth. I want to get away from everyone and just sink into oblivion.

His dark brown eyes pierce mine. "If I move out of the way, you're gonna go up to Ransom's, right?" I nod. "Alone?" I nod again. He steps out of the way, swinging open the door as he does. I storm past him, but he calls out after me. "I'm calling Pete in two minutes just to be sure!"

Great! I'm being monitored like a fucking nut job. I feel like one right now, so that actually fits. I hurry up the steps and into Ransom's darkened apartment. Dashing into the kitchen, I throw open the cabinets until I find what I need. If I can't forget the way of my choosing, I'll forget this way. I have a quick recollection of doing just that when Greer was unavailable back home.

Armed with my sweet oblivion in a bottle, I escape into Ransom's room. I stash the bottles under the bed and pull off my clothes quickly. Since Ransom's not here, I crawl under the covers in my bra and panties. I'm just tucking myself in when the door cracks open. I know it's Pete because Maggie would call out to me. He stands still for a second while I focus on regulating my breathing. Finally, he closes the door. I sit up and fish the bottles from under the bed, putting one on the nightstand and pulling the stopper from the other. I don't even bother with a glass. I visualize my problems being swept away by the surge of whiskey rushing through my system. *Yeah, fuck y'all!*

After seven or eight good swigs, I get up, turn the lock on the door, and search my pockets. Pulling out my phone and earbuds out, I scroll, searching for some mind-numbing music. Thumbing through, I land on "Inced the End" and hit play and then repeat. I push the buds in tight and turn up the volume to maximum. No thinking, not even to choose another song. Picking up my bottle, I guzzle the rest of it even though my throat burns like I'm pouring hot coals down it. My eyes burn like I've already consumed so much there is nowhere else for it to go.

After I drink the bottle dry, I slam it down and jerk my hand to the other so quickly that the empty teeters and falls to the floor. I'll get that in a second, right after I get some more alcohol in me. I take a long swig before realizing it's tequila. Oh, yeah. That's fucking perfect. *Goodbye, everyone and everything! Denver out!* I snicker at my stupid internal asides.

Shifting the pillows against the headboard, I scrunch down and pull my knees up, but I don't have the energy to keep them up. They just fall languidly to the side. I chuckle at them like they're not even a part of my body. I move my right leg a bit just to test it. It moves and brushes up against something crinkly.

Reaching down, I pull the offending object from under my leg. I should read it. I'm too gone to give a shit right now, so it's the perfect time, right? I set my bottle on the stand, being careful not to knock this one over and shift my phone to shed light on the letter.

I honestly can't comprehend much of it. He's to

blame. He's sorry. He wants to help me. Blahfuckingblah. I wrap it around my bottle. Me and tequila, we will rid ourselves of this too.

Several gulps later, I forget what I hold in my hand. I forget what I'm doing in this bed. I forget I tried, unfuckingsuccessfully, to screw two different guys tonight. I push my phone around, tired of this song, but I can't get my fingertips to work.

Damn.

"I tried so hard … it doesn't even matter," I try to sing out. It sounds more like a pathetic whine.

Another swig.

At least they're still useful for that movement.

I giggle at nothing.

Chapter Thirty-three

Ransom

CRACKING THE DOOR open to the apartment, I drop my bag by the door before locking back up. It's still early, so I'm sure she's asleep. As soon as my aunt showed up this morning, I kissed them both and took off. I needed to get to her after I read Austin's texts. He was vague, I'd get to the bottom of that later, but he said enough for me to know that she's hurting. And she's been doing so well. I guess setbacks are part of the healing process and to be expected. I scowl as I recall the pain in her features from own stupid action the other night, and I can't help but feel responsible for her setback. She always comes across as so tough; it's easy to forget that she's got all that shit going on in that pretty little head.

I try the handle, but it's locked. I really want to curl up with her, so I pad back to the kitchen and grab a butter knife before going back and picking the lock easily.

It's barely dawn out, so my eyes have to adjust for a second before I can fully comprehend the scene before me.

I'm a guy so, of course, the first thing I notice is the breathtaking sight of her lying there in her red lacy bra and panties. My eyes don't linger there for long because there's a bottle wedged between her thighs. I quickly realize that she's not just lying there. She's passed the fuck out, propped against the headboard, her legs and arms at odd angles. Almost like she went from thrashing to comatose in a flash.

I close the door behind me and move toward the bed, not really sure how I should handle her just yet. When I hear a thud, I realized I've kicked something. My eyes find an empty bottle of Jim Beam. Shit. This was half-full. I pick it up and set it on the nightstand.

Glancing back at her, I see she has her earbuds plugged in. I pick up her phone and grimace at her selection. It must have been a bad night for her to resort to that noise. I hit pause and give in to the urge to lean in and place a kiss on her forehead, easing out the earbuds. She's freezing. I reach down quickly to pull the other bottle from her legs and see something wrapped around the bottle. I cover her quickly and decide to get in bed with her and warm her up. God, if she had any idea how many times I thought of her lying here in my bed in the short day we were away from one another, she'd run for the hills.

When I set the bottle down, the paper sticks to my hand, so I bring it up and, tilting it toward the light, begin to read. I glance down and see Greer's name signed to it. Is this what set her off? I tell myself I'm reading this for her own good. To help her. It's definitely not because I'm a nosey, jealous bastard.

Denver,

I've written five letters and shredded them all. "It's me that I can't forgive," constantly repeats in my head since this afternoon, and that's when I knew what I needed to say. <u>I beg you to forgive yourself.</u> God, it's killing me that you're blaming yourself for what I did. And I should've known that it wasn't my forgiveness that needed begging ... of course, it's yours. That's what you do. Shoulder everything yourself—good and bad—it's what you've always done. You have to forgive yourself, Denver.

You think how you treated me led me to making not one but two terrible, for lack of a better word, mistakes, but it's just not true. I have my own flaws. One of them being that I never saw you clearly even though you begged me to. I think that's what drove you the way it did. Not ever having anyone see you. Or, more accurately, see what you see in yourself. I see you. I've always seen you. I know you're not perfect, but I've always loved you just like you are—which is what makes you perfect in my eyes.

I know what you're afraid of becoming. I know you feel unloved. I know that you feel like no one could ever love you. And I know you think I could never truly love you because I don't see you for who you are. I told you before I've never seen anyone but you. I stand by that. Just because I didn't let you focus on your flaws doesn't mean I didn't see them. Maybe I should have let you talk about them, explore them more. Maybe then we wouldn't be in this mess—you hating yourself because of what I did.

You say you've forgiven me already. I can't tell you

what that means to me, but I haven't forgiven myself. I should've never said a word about you. And I should've stopped when you said no. Those things are on me—only me. I fucked up so bad. Put that blame where it belongs—on me.

God, sometimes the things we coulda, shoulda, woulda are the easiest path to choose, but for whatever reason, we don't. I could have done the right thing, I should have protected you, and I would be with you right now. So simple, making me the world's biggest fool.

I can't imagine that you would ever want to be with me again, but you have to know that I want to work through this in whatever way you'll let me. I backed off when you said you needed space. I'll keep my distance for as long as I can, but some things that I need to tell you can't be done in a letter, and I know they'll help you heal. I'll wait for your lead, chicken. Please don't make me wait too long.

Greer

My eyes run over those lines again and again, and I know that Greer's the one who raped her. That sick feeling I had that night she told me what happened washes over me. Her word of choice that first night—*betrayal*. You can only be betrayed by someone you truly trust, and all the pieces start clicking into place. She told me she didn't want her friends to know. Feared their judgment. I should've known it was more than that. Her friend did this to her—her best fucking friend. My mind races, and my hands tremble. The paper crunches in my fist as I take in her sleeping form, so strong in so many ways, so vulnerable in so many others. I talk myself down a bit and try to focus on what's important.

I'm scared that I won't be able to help her, but that fear doesn't control me. I'd walk through fire for this girl. Sometimes I wonder why. Why her? All I know is that she consumes me. For months, I've tried to block her from my every thought, and no matter what method I've tried—ignoring her, pushing her away, hating her—there she's been tempting me. And I know I'll do whatever it takes to get her through this.

But, first things first.

Turning on my heel, I stride into the living room and spot Pete in the kitchen. "You're back," he says, surprised. "Man, I had no idea she left outta here after we went to bed last night. Is she OK?"

"She's sleeping. I need to go out for a minute. Keep an ear out."

He just nods at me as I exit the apartment.

"Thanks," I mutter. I can't believe how calm my voice is while I'm feeling this kind of rage. It actually scares me a bit because I've only ever felt this furious one other time in my life, and that didn't turn out so well for the other guy. I hope I don't kill him.

I take the stairs slowly in an effort to calm myself a bit because all I can think is, *I'm going to kill that motherfucker,* and I can't help her if I'm in prison. But Greer's going to be thinking about this for a while, not a few measly hours a day. Every time he moves, I want him to think about the girl he violated and what a piece of shit he is.

I round the staircase to his floor, flexing my fists and stretching my neck. And it's like the god of retribution is smiling down on me. His eyes meet mine, and I grin. It's the most evil grin I imagine has ever been grinned because that bastard knows right away that I'm here to kill him.

He doesn't utter a word, just nods at me like he's going to accept his fate quietly. That might change another man's mind, knowing his prey isn't going to put up a fight, but I think about Denver crying and screaming and begging him to get off of her, and it's all the fuel I need.

I point my finger at him. "You should run, motherfucker," I bark, rage finally filling my voice as well. He looks determined to hold his ground, but as I continue toward him, he falters and takes a couple of steps backward.

"You like to hurt women?" He shakes his head no. "You must!"

"That's not exactly what—" he begins.

And *that's* exactly what I need, a hint of a pathetic excuse. I bring my right fist back and connect with his jaw. He stumbles, but not before I get another right in.

Right.

Eye. It splits.

Left.

Nose. It spurts.

Right.

Eye again.

I don't stop pummeling as he goes down, and I go down with him, his hands curled up by his side.

"Don't look at her." Right. Ear.

"Don't write her." Left. Mouth. Blood gushes.

"Don't talk to her." Jaw. Crack.

"She's mine." I can't get another hit in, but it's not

for lack of swinging. Someone's got me underneath the arms and is dragging me backward. How the hell is someone able to get me off him? I finally look up and see two someones—Austin and Gage. Some of the other guys are checking on Greer.

"What the hell, Ransom?" Austin asks.

"He hurt Denver. Bad," I snarl, as I spit blood. I think I knocked my mouth on his elbow as we went down. He sure as hell never threw a punch. Wouldn't even defend himself. That's how I know he's guilty as hell.

"What? What do you mean?" I look up at Austin and hope that my eyes communicate how serious this is and that I'm not just another jealous boyfriend. He nods at me. Understanding, I hope. Or maybe he just sees the rage in my eyes and is agreeing with me to keep me calm. He pats me on the back, and they pull me to my feet.

"He's gonna need stitches," someone says. "Busted eyebrow."

I hope I broke his fucking nose too. I hope he has to eat through a straw till Christmas. I hope I deafened his ear. I hope he hears a fucking buzzing noise for the rest of his pathetic existence, and every time he hears that buzz it makes him think about the beautiful girl he hurt.

They haul Greer past me, and I spit again on his path. "You got anything to say, you piece of shit?" I growl.

He shakes his head, and blood drips from his eyelashes. "I know I fucked up, but just don't hurt her. Take care of her."

He fucked up? That's it? "Oh, that's rich. Thanks

for your meaningless blessing," I sneer. My fists ball up. I want to hit him again.

"All right, Ransom," Austin says as he moves in front of me and pats my shoulders. "Calm down, man. You've made your point."

I let Austin walk me back up to the apartment. Pete and Maggie sit on the couch. I collapse in the chair across from them.

Austin blows out a breath and puts his hands on his hips, staring me down. "Well, I think it's safe to say that Greer is out of the picture, Pete."

Pete sits up straight as I examine the cuts on my knuckles from where they tore against his teeth. "Is that blood on your shirt, Ransom? What the hell did you do?"

I stare down at my hands, finally feeling the pain from my knuckles radiating upward. My ribs are throbbing. My knees hurt. Now that the adrenaline has faded, every ache and pain is making itself known with a vengeance. *Totally fucking worth it.*

"He beat the hell outta Greer, man," Austin answers for me. "I was kinda pissed until he said it was because Greer hurt Denver. At first, I thought he was just being a jealous prick."

"I don't ever want to hear that bastard's name uttered in this apartment again," I finally interject. "Can't tell y'all what went down. Not my place. Just trust me when I say he deserves to rot in hell."

"I'm going to check on Denver," Maggie whispers.

"No, Maggie. Let me, OK? I don't think she'll want you to see her like that. She had a rough night."

She bites her lip and looks at Pete. He squeezes her

shoulder and nods. Maggie curls up next to him.

"I'm gonna wake her and get her fixed up and then you can see her, all right?"

"All right, Ransom," she concedes. "Make it quick though," she adds, as she blushes.

"Yes, ma'am," I say with a chuckle.

After I clean up in the bathroom, I head into my room and uncover her, leaning down and brushing a series of light kisses over her face and her hair. She's gonna be hurting. I slide one arm under her knees and the other under her shoulders and haul her to the bathroom. She starts murmuring something about time and tequila. It's freaking adorable.

"Denver," I call, setting her on her feet and propping her against me, as I reach in and get the water right.

"Hey, Ransom," she whispers, her voice sandpapery. "No yelling. You're right here," she reasons as she winds her arms around my neck. "You are really handsome, you know that? I like the way you make me feel inside."

My dick springs to attention. *Not now, fucker.* "Is that right?" I snap.

"Shh ... ugh, I think I'm still drunk," she grumbles.

I can't resist leaning in and planting a smacking kiss on her ear. "Ouch," she whispers again.

"That's what you get, getting tore up like that and all alone. That's not cool."

"I know. I needed to forget. Guess what?"

"Hmm?"

"I forgot," she mouths.

Chapter Thirty-four

Denver

UGH, IS THIS another version of the walk of shame? I wonder as I enter the living room after my shower. Austin, Pete, and Maggie sit lined up on the couch like a set of judges. I just want to get it over with, so I throw my hands up and declare, "Guilty. On all counts. No contest. I'm an idiot." I pause to focus on Pete. "I'm sorry for sneaking out, Pete. And for drinking all your liquor." He nods once.

My eyes shift to a wide-eyed Maggie. "I'm sorry for not talking to you, Maggie. We're gonna fix that."

I finally take in a smirking Austin. At least one person doesn't look scared out of his mind for me. "I'm sorry for kissing you, Austin." I hear an angry rumble from the kitchen and glance over to see Ransom glaring at Austin. "It's not his fault. He didn't do anything but try to reason with me. I was on a mission last night, and his neck got in the way of my lips." I don't know that helped. Ransom looks like he's ready to kill both of us now.

"Umm ... I'm gonna go now," Austin stutters and

scrambles from the couch. "Let y'all work this out. For the record, my neck *and* I are both innocent. Ransom, just remember who got her into bed last night … uh, not like that," he adds furiously as Ransom rounds the counter headed his way. "I put her in your bed," he throws out before he slams the door behind him.

Maggie and I both giggle at his theatrics. Wrong move. Ransom spins around and silences us both with a glare.

"Oh, Ransom, you're too serious. Nothing happened with him," I protest. It wasn't for lack of trying on my part though. God, I really am an idiot. If I'm going to slut it up, it obviously can't be around my new friends. Ransom walks past me, grabbing my hand as he does and pulling me behind him to the kitchen.

"Sit," he orders. I've missed bossy Ransom.

"Have you now?"

Shit. How does he do that? I say things I never intend to say to him and barely realize I'm saying them.

So I own it. "Yes," I confirm. I sit up straight as he slides some toast and coffee in front of me. I'm ravenous. I pull the toast apart and dip it in my coffee before bringing it to my mouth. I shove that piece in and dip another while I'm chewing. After I've swallowed a few pieces, I look up to catch a disgusted Ransom.

"What?" I mumble around another sodden piece.

"That's gross."

"Don't knock it till you try it."

"Yeah, no thanks," he says around the lid of his mug.

"What time is it?"

"Around ten," he tells me. About that time, Maggie

bounds in with a kiss and a hug.

"Pete and I are going to workout and leave you two to ... discuss. We'll talk when we get back, 'K?"

"Fine," I say, even though I really don't know what to tell her. Part of me wants to come clean about everything. *Everything.* I know she would understand and be supportive. The other part of me doesn't want to sully her with the ugliness. As soon as this throbbing in my temple goes away, I'll decide.

After a few minutes of complete silence, Ransom clears the dishes and leads me to the couch. He usually pulls me next to him and makes me watch one of his many DVDs. Today, he sits with a cushion between us and looks ready to lecture me.

I don't think I can take that, so I get a jump on him. "I'm really sorry I tried to seduce your cousin—"

"And Brent," he inserts.

"And Brent last night," I finish with a glare. We could have left him out of it since I didn't really do anything with him, but the intent was there, so I don't quibble. "I wish I could say I was drunk, but I wasn't, until later. I told you before that I use sex to forget and—"

"What were you trying to forget last night?"

My hand flutters around. "Oh, a multitude of things," I hedge as I run a hand through my hair. I make a makeshift ponytail with my hair and twist it up, wishing I'd taken the time to braid it. I let it down with a heavy thud while he just stares at me.

His sea-green eyes are soft and knowing, and the compulsion to lose myself in them overwhelms me. As always. "I read the note."

I nod, waiting for him to continue, and then it dawns on me. The. Note. I don't even remember what it said. He clears that up for me quickly.

"I wish you'd have told me it was him. I would have kicked his ass a lot sooner. I really would have liked to take him to the police station in pieces along with his stupid fucking confession, but I know that's not what you want and probably not what you need. I should've known it was him when you refused to tell me who hurt you, but I honestly didn't think he had it in him."

I swallow hard and glance down at my lap. I don't even know how to feel about him invading my privacy, but I imagine it wasn't that difficult since I passed out on his bed, his liquor all over me, and the note left out for anyone to see. And Greer didn't have it in him, not until I planted my diseased seed. I wonder how much he knows about me fucking Greer over. Will he hate me for that like I hate myself?

"The part that worries me more than anything else?" He hesitates. "Look here, Denver." I look up, waiting to see judgment. "You are blaming yourself for *his* actions. You said before you got what you deserved, and that's just not true. No matter what you did to him, you did *not* deserve that. Do you understand me?"

"Is he all right?"

Ransom's jaw clenches hard, and he bites out, "Yes. Probably needs a few stitches. He's lucky that's it."

I release a shaky breath. Greer deserved to have his ass kicked, but I still hate the fact that he's in pain because of me. I caused him enough of that to last a lifetime.

"Don't think I missed your evasion. You're getting reckless," he tells me. "I don't like it. Trying to seduce others for meaningless sex, going out alone, even if it's just with the rodeoers, bad shit can happen if you're not paying attention, as I know you are aware. Drinking, passing out." He pauses, his look foreboding. "You've got an itchy trigger finger, and it happens to be resting on the self-destruct button right now. I need you to step away from the fucking button, Denver."

It's funny how he says it, but I don't laugh because it's true. It's a pattern. After Blake tried to rape me, my mother and father refused to love me enough to help me, and Greer turned me down, I was ready to blast through life at full speed, taking everything and everyone in my wake. Greer finally offered himself up and ended up being my only casualty. I was working on forgiving myself for that because I know I didn't intend on hurting him and my head was, or is, so twisted.

He clears his throat, interrupting my reverie. I focus my attention back on him. "What does a horse that's gotten out of control need, Denver?"

My face reddens. He is *not* comparing me to a wild horse. He gives me a stilted grin, like he knows exactly where my thoughts have gone. I stir a little in my seat, not answering even though I know what he wants me to say.

"Say it," he orders, his grin widening. I pinch my lips together and some things start to fall into place where he's concerned. I think about the way he talks to me. The way people respect him. I picture the way he stared down on that girl the other night. *Oh my God.*

"A firm hand," I whisper. I sound turned on. I am turned on. My face is burning, as is my throat. Guzzling a gallon of water right now would not quench my thirst. This thirst is something else entirely.

"A firm hand," he confirms. "Discipline." Taking a deep breath, he sits up a little straighter, braces his elbows on his knees, and rests his chin against his folded hands. His pale green eyes sear me before his words do. "I like to be in control, Denver. And it's what you need—me to take control over you in a nice, safe way that makes you feel secure and treasured."

Yep, it's just what was running through my head.

He's not just bossy.

He is domineering

He is dominating.

"How many shades *are* you?" I find myself whispering.

His brow wrinkles in confusion. "What does that mean?"

As I recall my stolen moments with those books, my face reddens, and I bite my lip, succumbing to that action just like that female lead always does. How fitting. "I, uh, read some books this summer just before I came to college. They were my aunt's. Everyone was talking about them, so I thought I'd see what the fuss was all about," I rush out, like that explains everything.

"And?"

I straighten my spine and toss my hair over my shoulders like this is a conversation I'm prepared to undergo, like I do this on a routine basis. And I decide to fuck with him. "You're into BDSM," I say haughtily. If he knows the acronym, then I know there'll be no more dancing around the topic.

He throws his head back in laughter. "How do you even—?" He bridges his nose with his thumb and forefinger before running his hand over his buzzed hair. He tries again to ask me the question but ends up laughing again. I cross my arms and wait patiently.

Chapter Thirty-five

Ransom

I DON'T EVEN know what to say to that. Girls around here just don't know about this kind of stuff. It's like we're caught in a time warp. And if people do know about it, they damn sure don't discuss it openly. It's why I had to figure out everything about myself on the fucking Internet. I take a deep breath and shake my head before relaxing back onto the couch. I didn't want to have this conversation with her so soon, but I fear if I don't she'll do something she can't bounce back from. I knew this girl was going to give me a run for my money. I knew she'd challenge me in every conceivable way. But, of all the ways I imagined our conversation going, this version never crossed my mind.

"I'm sorry. Can you ask me the question again?" I ask with a straight face.

She squares her shoulders. "There was no question. I stated that you are into BDSM."

And so it begins. "You know what that means?"

"Yes, I had to Google a lot when I read those books," she punctuates that thought with a shiver. My curiosity is piqued, but we'll get to what about them made her shiver, later.

"What kind of books were they?" I ask, evading the question so that I can get more of a feel for what's running through her head.

"The romantically kinky kind," she murmurs, absently picking at the seam on the couch.

There are romance novels about BDSM? Well, that's handy. "Ah ... well, if it was in a romance novel, I'm sure some ... liberties were taken."

She grins, and her eyes find mine, shedding her moment of self-consciousness. "That may be, but they were enlightening ... and intriguing."

I wonder if she knows exactly how telling that comment is. I don't really know how much to tell her. Honestly, I don't know how much of it I'm into. But, I have a good idea what I want to start with. I decide to use the initials to determine what exactly she thinks she knows. "Well, I'm into the D for sure." Her eyes widen, and I'd bet money if I touched her, her pulse would be racing. "And the lighter side of the B."

She nods for a minute, taking that in. She doesn't disappoint. "So you want to tie me up and boss me around?"

"Something like that," I hedge. A pretty picture of her bare, tied, wanting and waiting, to my bed flashes before my eyes. I harden instantly.

"Would you want to ..." She struggles again, her face flushing pink, her nails biting into her palms, and I wonder where her thoughts are headed. I don't have to wonder long. Flipping her hair over her shoulder and steeling herself, she starts again, "Would you want to spank me?" she asks, her voice firm.

My eyes flare with surprise. Will she ever do the expected? "Do you want me to spank you?" I ask, feeling more turned on now than I've ever felt before in my life.

She licks her lips and runs her bright eyes over me, and I don't miss the little shifting movement she makes. "It depends on whether it's for pleasure or pain."

Holy shit! "Just because the one is there doesn't mean the other isn't, you know?" I tease.

She nods slowly. "Well, would you?" she prompts, undeterred.

My teeth run over my bottom lip as I pretend to consider it. She shifts again. I savor her squirming. I nod slowly before saying, "Yes."

I hear her breath catch and watch her hands tremble. "Why? Why do you want that?"

"It's what turns me on," I admit. "And before you get all judgmental on me, I know the thought of me telling you what to do and restraining you turns you on as well. It's written all over you this very second—your pulse is racing, your cheeks are flushed, your pupils are dilated—you're turned on." I hesitate, waiting to see if she'll protest or flee. Her eyes narrow slightly, but she doesn't call me fucking crazy and she doesn't head for the door.

I need her to know that I'm not a freak and that side of our relationship would not be common knowledge. "I'm trusting you with this information. Only two other people are privy to it. And I trust them with my life. You wouldn't have to worry about people gossiping about that on top of everything else. If anything, being with me would stop all that talk."

"So you want me to be your ..." She leaves that hanging in the air between us.

I want you to be my everything. I've wanted that from the get-go, but since she'd been violated, I was trying to give her time to heal. I know saying any of that will send her running, so I put the ball back in her court for now. "What do you want to be?"

She glances back down and studies her hands for a moment. "I don't think I'm ready for a relationship," she says, her tone regretful.

"You remember what I said about touching you while you were with other guys?" She nods. "If you agree to ... explore this with me, no other guys. I won't share you."

Her eyes find mine again, and she demands, "What about you?"

"What about me?"

Her mouth drops slightly before she snaps, "Every time I see you, you're with a different girl."

"Denver, I haven't been with anyone since we met at that very first party." She raises her eyebrows slowly. "Other than that lapse in judgment the other night," I concede. I'm still kicking my own ass for that one. "But I didn't have sex with that girl."

A hurt look washes over her features. "She was naked, Ransom."

"Was I?"

She bites her lip and shakes her head *no*.

"Like I said, I didn't have sex with her."

She accuses, "I've seen you—the different girls from the parties, the Baby Buckle Bunnies—"

"Baby Buckle Bunnies?" I chuckle.

She throws her head back and snickers. "It's what I call the groupies who follow the college circuit and not the pro. You know, 'cause they're Buckle Bunnies in training?"

I can't help but grin because that's exactly what they are, which is exactly why I'd never touch one, but she doesn't know about my rules ... yet. "It is very fitting. But just because you saw me talking with those girls doesn't mean I was with them. I'm not lying to you. And think about it, I have no reason to lie, even if I had been that was before you." I pause to bring this conversation back into focus. "If you do this with me, I'm yours. Only yours."

A look of disbelief mars her features. "Why me? I mean, we've only shared a couple of kisses—" I give her a look, and she blushes and adds, "—incredible, unforgettable kisses. But I heard you've never been with the same girl twice, so why are you willing to change that for me?"

That's a loaded question. I never thought I'd meet my equal this early in my life. Then, after I was already in deep, I found out about her reputation, and that sent me into a tailspin that had me pushing her away. Bottom line, none of that mattered. I still wanted her, still *want* her. *Why her? Because she's everything I need, and more than I ever hoped for.* But she can never be truly mine until she believes in herself. And I want to fix her. Not just for me, but also for her. It kills me to see her hurting. My eyes trail over her, sitting there brave and strong in so many ways, yet vulnerable in others.

"What we've shared has meant a lot more than a

couple of kisses, and you know it," I whisper before I clear my throat. Her nod is barely noticeable. "I see something in you, Denver. I want you to believe in yourself like I believe in you. And trust is what it boils down to—you trust no one, not even yourself, and I'm thinking not many people have given you a reason to do that. But I'm asking you to trust me so that I can show you how to trust yourself. Our 'arrangement' will make you stronger. And I want it to be just you and me."

Her eyes bulge. "You think I'm weak?"

Is that the only thread she finds offensive? "Hell, no. The exact opposite actually, or I wouldn't call you 'little fighter.' You have weaknesses, yes, but you're also one of the strongest people I've ever met." She quirks a brow at me, like I'm full of shit. "Remember your philosophy on winning over unworthy opponents?" She nods slowly, and I can see her gears turning. "Where's the fun in dominating a weak partner?" I'm so hard I could pound nails right now. I had no idea we'd end up talking this openly, but it's such a fucking turn on.

"So you want to break me because I would be a challenge."

I laugh lightly because ... well, yes and no. "I don't want to break you exactly. It's more than that. Yes, I'll be in control, but only so far as you'll let me. So, you'll be able to let go, knowing you're safe and protected, but you won't be blocking me out." I shrug. "Ultimately, you'll have all the control. And you'll learn to exercise control in your own life, even within your risks. It's all about striking a balance."

I wait to let her digest the simplest version of what

I'm proposing. She licks her lips again. She seems to relax a little and pulls her legs under her on the couch, draping an arm along the back. "I don't think I'm submissive, Ransom. I don't think I have a submissive bone in my body actually."

Mirroring her position, my fingertips graze hers. "Here's what I see. I see a young woman who has the weight of the world on her shoulders, with control of things she should've never had control over at such a young age. A woman who is clever, competitive, beautiful, talented … a woman who's lost control over her personal life and is about to piss away all the good she's got going for her," I hesitate before bringing up her "addiction," as she calls it. "You tell me you've been seeking to numb your pain with sex, and that's no way to live. It's killing you inside, Denver. I see that deadness working its way out, destroying all that good in its path. That's what I see.

"I also see a man who's been looking for a woman like you. I see a man who's already fallen for you in every conceivable way, who wants to give you what you need most in this world. Something you don't even realize you need …"

She swallows hard again. Her chest rises and falls with quick breaths. Her eyes glow with understanding and intrigue. I know she hears the truth in my words. Will she admit it aloud?

"What do I need, Ransom?" she asks finally.

Anticipation gets the better of me, and my grin's as naughty as they come. "An awakening."

Dear Reader,

I hope you enjoyed this wild, sometimes heart-wrenching, ride and you continue the journey with these characters and me.

What began as a standalone, in my head, morphed into more of a saga as I got to know these characters. As I began to explore what drove Greer, the more I realized how fascinating his and Denver's past was, and I had to show it to you rather than merely reference it. Once that unfolded, there was no way I could do Greer, Denver, and Ransom's complicated, intense future justice in the same book.

What does Greer have to say for himself? Is it over between them? Denver's forgiven him, but can we? How will Denver overcome her self-hatred and self-destructive compulsions? Will Denver say yes to Ransom? How on earth did this bull-riding badass become a "Baby Dom"? All these questions and more shall be in answered in Freed, coming April 2014. See, not a long wait at all.

Hearing from my readers, makes my day. And I have been known to gush over them from time to time. Message me at Lynetta Halat Author on Facebook or email at lynettahalat@gmail.com Wanna make me ridiculously happy? Pretty please, leave an honest, respectful review. Watch me get real fired up when you sign up for the mailing list at lynettahalat.com. I promise not to SPAM you, only new release information, free scenes, and interesting stuff like that.

Thank you for reading!

Love,
Lynetta

A Note from the Author

The date rape that occurs within this novel is obviously fictional, but date rape, as it is portrayed here, is not and happens much more than we realize. The research that Denver reads about are facts and statistics that I discovered about this topic while gathering information for my book. The way in which Denver is choosing to deal with this—silence and working it out on her own—may not be the most responsible way or the best course of action. Please see RAINN for help, support, and the facts.

About the Author

Since the dawn of time, Lynetta Halat has lived to read and has written innumerable stories and plays. A lover of good books, bad boys, and kickass heroines, she'd always dreamt of penning books that people could connect with and remember. She also has a secret penchant for wringing the emotions out of unsuspecting readers, and she collects reader's tears in much the same way that wine connoisseurs collect their favorite vintage.

Her first novel, *Every Rose*, was the perfect catalyst to launch her into the world of publishing, effectively burrowing her way into the hearts and minds of readers throughout the world. *Everything I've Never Had* was her follow-up adult romance novel. Now, she has penned *Used*, a New Adult Romance that she hopes sinks its teeth into you and doesn't let go.

Her love of the English language prompted her to pursue a Master's degree in English from Old Dominion University in Virginia, where she also minored in snark and interpretive dance. She lives somewhere along the Mississippi Gulf Coast with her adorable husband, two amazing sons, and two loveable dogs. When she's not writing riveting stories, she likes to focus on her macramé art and her scouring of eBay, where she buys locks of hair from her favorite rock stars, most especially Bret Michaels and Dave Grohl.

USED (UNLOVABLE, #1)

For more information about Lynetta and her books, visit:

FACEBOOK

https://www.facebook.com/LynettaHalatAuthor

WEBSITE

www.lynettahalat.com

GOODREADS

http://www.goodreads.com/author/show/6969980.Lynetta_Halat

TWITTER

https://twitter.com/LynettaHalat

Acknowledgements

To my family and my friends—thank you so very much for all of your love and support. Your support keeps me enthusiastic and your love keeps me writing.

To my photographer, Toski, and beautiful cover model, thank you for this incredible shot, and to Sommer, my cover designer, thank you for taking it and making it even more fabulous.

To my editor, Tracey, thank you for helping this baby shine for the world.

To all the book bloggers who believed in this book—I can never repay for you loving and promoting my book, my baby, but please know you have my undying gratitude. Thank you for making it your own.

To my awesome beta readers—Bobbie, Elle, Debi, Stephanie, Kelly, and Ashley—thank you so much for the invaluable feedback and falling in love with my story and my characters. More than anything, thank you for pushing me to be better and helping me grow as a writer.

To my fabulous author friends who keep me semi-sane, grounded, and laughing my butt off, thank you!

Without you, my readers, my book would just be a thing and not the living, breathing organism that you make it when you love, connect, remember, and share it. Thank you.

Read on! Write on! Love on!

CPSIA information can be obtained at www.ICGtesting.com
Printed in the USA
LVOW13s1016160514

386107LV00005B/59/P